MW01140364

The Hardest Ride

The Bean Recipe

by *Gordon L. Rottman*

Western Fictioneers Peacemaker Award
Best Western Novel 2014

Western Fictioneers Peacemaker Award Finalist
Best First Western Novel 2014

Western Writers of America Spur Award Finalist
Best Traditional Western Novel for 2013

Published By: The Hartwood Publishing Group, LLC,
400 Gilead Road, #1617, Huntersville, NC 28070
www.hartwoodpublishing.com

The Hardest Ride

Copyright © 2014 by Gordon L. Rottman
Digital Release: December 2013
Print Release: October 2014
Cover Artist: James Caldwell

Dedication

To my family on both sides of the border.

Acknowledgements

It is often said that writing is a lonely or one-person job. That's true to a point, but there are so many others who influence, inspire, and lend support.

First off, this book would not have been possible without CEO and Editor-in-Chief Georgia Woods, Executive Editor Lisa Dugan, cover artist James Caldwell, and the rest of the staff of Hartwood Publishing. Their help and innovative management created a great editorial environment. A big thanks goes to Jean Cooper for her excellent editing.

I am especially grateful to my wonderful critique group for their advice, support, and brutally honest and absolutely essential critiques: Stan Marshall, Linda Bromley, Heather Walters, Julie Herman, Malinda Childers, and Roxanne Carr. A special thanks goes to the Houston Young Adult Writers Group and the knowledge and expertise they all so willingly shared in support of each other.

A very special thanks goes to my cousin, Consuelo Garcia, for making certain the Spanish made sense. Of course my wife Enriqueta, all the kids, and our great family in Mexico were vital to this book's creation. I am most grateful to the many nieces who inspired me, especially: Christina, Cecilia, Elvia, Liliana, and Gabriel.

Last, but not least, I wish to thank the readers of this book and hope they look forward to further adventures on the Texas-Mexico border as much as I do.

Author Notes

A commentary on geographical directions:

When one speaks of the Texas-Mexico border or la Frontera and the Rio Grande or Rio Bravo—depending on which side of the border one resides—we tend to think of Mexico as "south of the border." In a broad sense, this is true; Mexico is indeed south of Texas and the United States. However, a look at a map of the south-central Texas border region shows the Rio Grande flows southeast from the upper end of the river's great loop, known as the Big Bend in West Texas, and snakes to the Gulf of Mexico. After the pursuit of El Xiuhcoatl (shee-oo-ko-ah-tl) and his banditos begins at the DeWitt Ranch ("the Dew") south of Del Rio, Texas, the Texans cross the Rio Grande traveling due west even though they are "south of the border." If they had kept heading west they would have reentered Texas in the Big Bend from the east.

Towns, ranches, and places—south Texas and northern Mexico, 1886

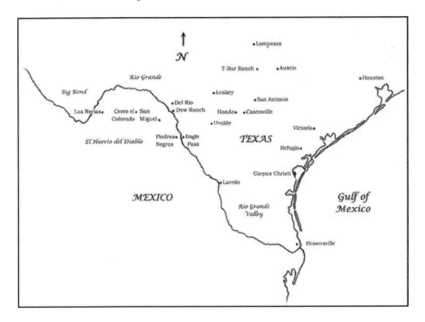

GORDON L. ROTTMAN

Chapter One

When I started working for Barnabas Scoggins at the Triple-Bar up in Burnet County, I thought I knew something about punching cattle. Heck, been doing it since I was thirteen. I'd had to do something to make a living since leaving home pronto was a good way of staying alive. Ma didn't much care for my "bastard ass." It was either me or her.

Then I met up with ol' Pancho Salazar, I didn't know so much about punching after all. It's no secret *vaqueros* know just about everything there is about cowboying. A lot of good ol' Texicans don't like to own up to that, but they know it sure as Texas Hill Country cattle tanks dry up in August.

When it came to roping, us Texicans only thought we could. Hell, those Mex 'queros could rope a full-run antelope underhanded from their horse, riding in the opposite direction and sitting the saddle backward.

Ol' Pancho was the *caporal* heading up the ranch's 'queros. That old man with his big droopy white mustachio had eyes that looked into far distances seeing things none of us could. He knew more of the ways of the *campero* and the balance of the world than any meager cowpoke.

I like how 'queros outfitted themselves with a bandana around their head to hold a sombrero on, short jacket, tight pants with a hundred buttons up the legs, and leather leggings, sheepskin chaps, gourd canteen, and always a big knife. Their hands are so tough they don't bother with gloves.

I got no idea why, but ol' Pancho took a liking to me. That

was strange because most them Mexes didn't much rub elbows with us gringos. There wasn't much tolerance between them and us Texicans. They worked with us fine, but we all knew they had about as much use for us as a dog does fleas. Their ways was just different. They didn't say much; even the one's what could talk American.

I'd been on the T-Bar only a week the first time Pancho talked at me. I'd shot at a water moccasin with my rifle. Killed it, but the slug bounced off a rock and took a chunk out of ol' Pancho's cantle, right behind his butt. Shooting his saddle set his horse to bucking and threw him, truly an embarrassing state for that old scallywag. I knew he was rankled when he pointed his Colt Navy conversion at me and said, "I gonna chute joo, *pendejo*." I truly feared he was, but instead he just made a long solemn speech in Spanish, ending it in American, "Joo ain't got nothing under joo hat but hair, gringo."

The second time he had words for me was weeks later when some of us were shooting tins and bottles. Something I'd got going because I believed in lots of practice throwing lead. Ol' Pancho looked at my Winchester rifle and Remington revolver, after asking if I were going to "chute" at him again, and said, "Joo like dee long-barrel guns."

"I do. The further off I can shoot them injuns, the better for me."

"That good, but I like to look them een dee eye when they die."

I knew he meant that.

Seeing both my guns were .44-40, he said, "That good joo guns chute same bullet."

"That's true," I agreed. It made things easier, two guns, one cartridge.

Pancho started telling a tale. "Me and Red, many year ago, *indios* come at us. Red make mistake, try to load his .45 Colt bullet into Winchester .44 like joos. He scared," Pancho laughed, but he paused like he was seeing that day in his head. "Eet go een, but stick, no work. Red throw that damn *carabina* down, so I peek eet up. Use *el cuchillo* to take out side-plate screw, take out bullet, and put plate on." He was going through the motions like he'd just done it.

I tried to see that in my head, him standing there all levelheaded and backing out a little screw with a jackknife with whooping injuns riding at him.

"I load with *correctas* bullets, keel *muchos indios.*"

Red, who'd taken two arrows and a bullet that day nine years ago, said, "That old turd shot down six of 'em redskins. Scalped ever'one of 'em. Ax him to show 'em to ya."

I did. Ol' Pancho had nineteen scalps.

When I hit a tin with my first rifle shot at a hundred paces, ol' Pancho took an interest in me. There was something else happened that I didn't pay no mind to, but Pancho took notice. One evening I found a calf what lost its mama. It was so weak I'd had to carry it back to the herd across Vaaler Creek. Never did find its mama, but found another cow that let it suckle.

"*Bueno, gringo,*" was all he said. But he winked, and that meant something. I guess most cowpokes woulda put the calf out of its wretchedness.

Pancho taught me how to break a bronco using patience and gentleness, not be a bronc fighter doing more harm than good. I learned how to make hackamores, to braid lariats from rawhide and mare's tail hair, shoe horses, to tie all sorts of knots—"Eef joo can't tie good knots, tie lotta knots"—how to rope from all angles, braided a *cuarta*—the horseman's short whip—and he helped me build my own double-rig Mex saddle with a gourd horn. He told me to carry a buckhorn-handle—for a better grip—six-inch hunting knife on my right hip. Showed me how to use it for a tool and for fighting. Made me pack my revolver on my left side, forward of the hip to draw easier when horsed.

That old man taught me to track. We spent a lot of time following deer trails and just about anything else on four legs, two legs too. He'd tell some of the Mex kids on the T-Bar to hightail it and give them a head start before I started tracking. He made me pay them a penny apiece. Heck, they'd of done it for free. It was a game to them. Them little scamps could surely lead me into some tough places to follow them.

There was something else he taught me, and I ain't even realize it back then. We'd be sitting at the fire, and he talked about hunts of animals and men and injuns. He'd say something like, "I keel and hurt many peoples, but I deed not like eet, except dee *indios*. There ees too much pain een dee world." He peered into the dancing fire like he was looking way back in time. "There ees too much pain, and a good man does not make more pain for peoples, unless they deserve eet. Do joo know what I mean, *Güero?*" He'd started calling me that. It means someone with light hair. Mine's kind of sandy.

"I don't rightly know. I guess you mean don't hurt no one you don't have to, or treat people right, like you'd wanna be."

"Joo not so dumb as joo act, *Güero.*"

"*Gracias*...I guess. Eh, I like your boots," feeling like I had to pay an accolade back.

"Can I trust joo, *Güero?* Can I take joo word for truth?"

"With you, *Tío*, you can bet on it." I'd started calling him *Tío*, means uncle in Mex.

"Not right answer."

"It's not?"

"Nope." After a long wait, "Any man should be able to trust joo word."

That was just like *Tío* Pancho, to tell it like it is. You can't get the water to clear up until you get the pigs out of the creek.

One time we were hunting whitetails on a ridgeline. "How do joo know to do dee right thing, *Güero*. Eet ees hard some time to see what ees right."

That was a tough one. "I guess I'd have to see how it'll shake out, go with my gut feeling." I looked at him, wondering if I got it right.

Tío Pancho looked thoughtful. "Almost right, *Güero*, almost." He didn't say nothing for the longest damn time. He could be madding like that.

"Almost right, *Güero*. Don't go by joo gut feeling. Go by joo *corazón*...heart."

"My heart?"

"You will know eef joo are dee man, I think."

That was the day I felt gooder about myself than I'd ever had. I hadn't been much raised to think that.

One day *Tío* Pancho told me about a bear cub what lost its mama to a hunter. "All 'lone, Cub wander the woods 'til Boar Bear find eet." He looked solemn. "Boar bears alway keel cubs, but this bear deed not. Eet teached Cub to hunt, find berries, to fish, how to hide from men."

Pancho crocked his leg around his saddle horn and lit up his pipe. "Boar Bear understand Cub was not of lesser value because eet small and helpless.

"One day Cub got loss from Boar Bear. Eet was afray, but eet hunt for food on own. A puma found Cub and follow eet. Cub saw Puma across da creek and deed like Boar Bear had teached eet. Cub stood and raised eets arms over head and try to roar. Eet only sound like leettle yelp. But Puma, she run off. Cub was proud for scaring off Puma, but he turn around and behind him was Boar Bear, standing there with his arms spread wide."

Ol' Pancho sat his horse for a long piece watching the dying sun pink the clouds. "Eet ees important to protect something what cannot protect eetself. Only real *hombre* can do that."

GORDON L. ROTTMAN

Chapter Two

Barnabas Scoggins sometimes doled out peculiar jobs. October was my turn to ride the fence line. Nothing curious about that, but he'd been arguing with ol' Cap Hooper of the Four Stakes about whose spread was bigger. It appeared the ancient deeds were of dubious repute with suspicions previous owners may have moved fences. I sided with my boss, it being the shrewd thing to do, and I sure didn't much trust that old conniver Hooper.

He was called "Cap" because he'd been a captain in somebody's army. Some said he'd been a sea captain, but I knew he didn't much like crossing rivers aboard his horse, and that didn't sound like something a sea captain would find objectionable. Since he never admitted what army he'd been in, I suspected he was on the side that wore federal blue in the War of Secession. The former Four Stakes owner, Isaac Scales, didn't come home from a visit to Virginia with the 5th Texas Infantry. Cap Hooper had showed up about a year after Appomattox with a deed and a closed mouth.

No matter. The two ranchers decided that measuring out their spreads' perimeters with a twenty-*vara* chain would take too long plus they knew us punches would take some shortcuts doing such a tiresome chore on foot. Instead, they'd each have one of their punches ride the fence line to count posts and be kept company by a punch from the other spread to keep things honest. I drew Coop Doolin from the Four Stakes with us both marking down posts. Another pair counted Four Stakes' posts. Whoever had the most posts obviously had the bigger spread. We were to make a tick mark in a tablet for each post, four marks and then a crossed one for the fifth. They didn't trust us to figure them up, and I sure didn't make the effort. I will say there were a lot of pages, and I wore that pencil down to a stub. Took two days.

Coop Dolin nor anyone else caught on that the fence dividing the two spreads, which had to be counted twice, had been set by Barnabas Scoggins, and maybe moved just a little, and the posts were about twelve feet apart as were all the Triple-Bar's fences. The Four Stakes' other fence lines' posts were set some fifteen, sixteen feet between them. I didn't say nothing to nobody, but after they summed up all those tick marks the Triple-Bar was declared way bigger. There were substantial bets involved, not only by the owners, but the hands too. I made six dollars off that.

The next month we were finishing up the fall roundup. In a couple of days we'd head them down to Austin Junction for loading on a train. That would only take a few days, and some of us punches would be laid off. I was hoping to stay on; I'd been kept on the last three years.

It was our last day before heading the herd to the Junction. We'd make a last sweep for stragglers. It'd been a lean year, and Barnabas Scoggins needed to round up every head we could. We'd be up at dawn, but maybe an hour before the sun peeked over the trees, there was a sudden ruckus at the kitchen. All the hands, excepting Smedley Eskrine, who had to be blasted out of his sack with dynamite, came scurrying out, guns waving all over. Lucky nobody got shot.

The cook was yelling, "Yit a yun, yit a yun, there's a yang of inyuns runnin' 'way!" Arnfried Bachmeier couldn't pronounce *g*. That kraut was all excited because he'd scart off a whole war party raiding the kitchen for groceries.

There ain't been many injuns seen for some time hereabouts. 'Course some folks were expecting an uprising because Geronimo had surrendered way over in Arizona a couple of months past.

With the sun up, I found tracks left by one pair of moccasins and a trail of airtights of white waxed beans and tinned cow juice lying in the weeds.

Barnabas Scoggins told me, "We can handle what's left to round up. Go git that renegade."

"Yes, sir." Bachmeier gave me some beefsteak sandwiches for dinner and a couple of airtights of beans. "Ifin ya stays out tonight." I wolfed down my bacon, biscuits, and grits and got my rifle.

After saddling Cracker, my big old dark bay, I set off following the tracks through the dewy weeds. He had a two-hour start on me. The trail led northwest into the Balcones Canyonlands, a place of dense oak, ash, and juniper crisscrossed by hills and gullies and open patches. I had to cut a fence and didn't know whose land I was on. I found an airtight of apple butter. That wouldn't do me much good if I stayed out tonight.

What was I to do when I caught the redskin? I was sure Barnabas Scoggins expected me to shoot him. He didn't cotton to thieving, and he sure as blue blazes didn't a give hoot for thieving, trespassing injuns. I knew he sure as heck didn't want me bringing him back. I don't know, maybe I could just scare him off. 'Course I had to consider the injun might try and bushwhack me. I kept my pistol in hand. Heck, in the Canyonlands he could be laying for me at tomahawk reach.

I had no regrets shooting an injun doing dire mischief, but this one had only made off with some airtights of grub. He ain't hurt no one, yet. Before long, the trail was harder to follow. There weren't any dew on the ground leaves under the trees. I'd crouch low, and the light slanting through the trees highlighted his tracks pressed into the matted leaves. On upslopes, I could make out foot scuffs, and one time, when I thought I'd lost him, I found some tiny mushrooms he'd brushed and spread their yellow dust. That's when I smelled oak smoke.

There was next to no wind, and I had to ride back and forth on a line until I could figure the direction it was coming from. Taking my rifle, I tied Cracker next to a big ol' double oak I hoped I could find again.

I saw no smoke, only the dim smell. The injun knew what he was doing, not that I'd expect an injun of not knowing. He was deep in trees and keeping the fire small, probably on low ground where most smoke would stay. He wasn't using any green, wet, rotten, or sappy wood. Hardwood smoked less than softwood.

I slipped through the brush quiet like a mouse. I checked the ground before each step. I stayed low, turned sideways to slip between saplings. Finally, I duck-walked to stay low enough to see under the limbs.

The wood fire smell was stronger. I heard a sound. A girl's voice. Dang! That's all I need, more injuns. A family maybe. Weren't no war party with a girl.

On hands and knees I creeped forward. Heard a man's voice—real quiet.

Peering under the sapling limbs, I made them out. Raising to my feet real slow like, I stood there, not moving, not making a sound.

After a spell, the buck slowly turned to me. My rifle was pointed between his eyes. Still sitting cross-legged he raised his hands. The girl turned and gave a little squeak. The buck shaked his head, telling her not to move. It was only the two of them. He was in a grubby shirt and a loincloth over greasy buckskin breeches. She was wearing a raggedy blue dress with almost white strips. The buck was maybe sixteen, seventeen, the plump-faced squaw even younger. They were sitting in front of a brush-limb lean-to with a few blankets and deerskins. A tin of sweet taters sat between them.

I jerked my rifle telling the buck to stand up and come with me. The squaw started wailing some chant. I motioned for her to stay put. The buck was plum scart. I took him back to Cracker. "You speak American?"

He just looked at me.

"*¿Usted habla Mexicano?*"

He nodded.

"Well, that don't help, because I don't." I fished the airtights of Boston baked beans out of my saddlebag and dropped them on the ground. Nodding at them, I said, "They're yours. Don't come back to *el rancho no más. ¿Comprende?*"

He nodded.

"Now *adios*, y'all."

He picked up the tins without taking his eyes off of me and backed into the saplings.

I looked at Cracker. "Don't you say a damn word about this."

When I rode in before dark, Barnabas Scoggins asked me, "Ya git him?"

"That buck was too far 'way when I sawed him. I give him a real scare," I swung my rifle up taking aim at a pretend injun. "He's

16

still hightailing it like a coyote with a lit tail."

"Good job," he said with a satisfied grin. In his view, we'd done our piece to protect the frontier citizenry from plundering savages.

Tío Pancho looked sharply at me. He saw right through me. He had no love for injuns, but he knew what I'd done. He nodded. There's times when a little clemency doesn't hurt.

— •●• —

Barnabas Scoggins poked at the coals in his stone fireplace. "You done real good by me these past three years."

Here it comes.

"But I gotta cut you loose, son. Gotta let jus' 'bout ever'one go. Time's real tough."

"Yes sir. I understand."

"I'm only keeping on four hands through the winter; the ones been here longest."

That meant *Tío* Pancho was staying on, Red too. Good. They'd be the last men Barnabas Scoggins would let go.

He was quiet for a spell poking around in the coals. "I done something to help you out. I got a pard down Laredo way. He owes me." He chuckled. "He's always saying we owe one another a lot, but seems he's forever paying me back more than I him. Anyways, I sent him a letter saying I got a good hand needing winter work." Taking a letter out of his jacket he said, "I got this a couple of days ago. He read it out instead of handing it to me for he knew I was a lot better reading trail sign than things on paper.

"*Mathew M. Picket, San Isidro Ranch, Laredo, Webb County, State of Texas, November 4th, 1886.*

"*I have in hand a letter of introduction on your behalf from one Barnabas Scoggins. I am long acquainted with Barnabas and have come to respect his character and opinion. He writes that you are well suited to cow punching and horse peeling and holds you up as being of high character. He also writes that you possess a skilled gun hand and an eye for tracking. I can report that I do have need for a man with such talents. Straightly put, we could use another gun. As of late, our herds have been plundered by thieving scoundrels. We reason that these rustlers are Mexicali desperados from across the Rio Grande. After last April's Election War in Laredo, there is no telling what will break loose hereabouts. If you want a job at the San Isidro and are able to meet me in Eagle Pass between November 20th and 26th, you can find me in residence at the Maverick Hotel. After I conclude my business there in the Pass, you are welcome to ride with me to the San Isidro in the comfort of my coach.*

"My best regards, Mathew M. Picket."

Barnabas Scoggins said he'd welcome me back in the spring unlessin' I found the San Isidro to be a good home.

Tío Pancho grabbed my shoulders, looked me in the eye and said they were getting a *vaquero primo*. I ain't never been glad-backed like that. It was hard leaving him behind.

I left after we'd driven the herd to Austin Junction. *Tío* Pancho told me to catch one of the half-wild burros to pack my gear. He said not to pick one with a bloated-looking belly and to stay away from ones looking like they were tippy-toeing because they had hoof frog infection.

Free-ranging burros ain't easy to rope, they being skittish. I ended up catching a one-eyed burro because it was easy to sneak up on his blind side.

Chapter Three

It was a long ride, about two hundred miles. I'd gone through San Marcos, New Braunfels—lotta square-heads there—then San Antonio. I'd stopped at a classy whorehouse on Matamoras Street—a gentleman's club they called it. It was too fancy for my blood and wallet. They even had a printed menu with things I ain't never heard of. One of them told what a painted lady would do to you with marbles in her mouth! I'd bought a too pricey drink and moved on, finding the White Horse Saloon a few streets back, what I think they call a disorderly house. A dollar for the comfort supplied by a fallen angel was more to my taste. Went through Castroville. That was some town, had a steam gristmill, cotton gin, brewery, and its own newspaper.

Uvalde was next. About a day out, I spied vultures drifting in circles. The wind was coming out of the northwest, and I pulled the collar up on my dark gray duck coat. The road was muddy, and the only fresh tracks were Mex sandals, four or five, yep, five sets heading south. I smelled them before I saw them. It's a sorta sweet smell, but not in a good way. There was the stink of blood, and shit too. It was making Burro nervous, but Cracker didn't pay no mind.

Through the brush, I could see something white on the ground. I knew what it was. There were four of them, a whole family, all laid out side by side. They were scalped, and their eyes poked out, and they were all stabbed up. Their throats were cut too, and they were full of bullet holes. The woman's tits were cut off, and all of them were butchered up between their naked legs. I guess they'd been violated in every way. They didn't look like people no more, just used to be.

There was blood, clothes rags, and stuff all over the stirred-up ground. Over to the side was where the deed had been done. They'd been dragged to where they were laid out neat, father, mother, a boy, I don't know, maybe ten or twelve years, and a little girl. I couldn't look no more, could barely tell they were Mexes. It was like something I wasn't meant to see, that nobody should see.

"Damn injuns." They go crazy sometimes for no good reason. I looked around and took out my rifle, laid it across my lap. They were killed a short time past. Doubtful any injuns were still around.

I made out moccasin tracks. They were all over. There were a few .50-70 Government cartridge cases and some old .40-50 Sharps too, even some little .32 Long Rifles and four 12-gauge shells. I picked up the empty shotshells. A gunsmith would buy them for reloading. Riding out a little ways, I made a circle and cut the injuns' trail. There were five, six of them heading southwest. They didn't stay to the road. Well, I wasn't going after them.

Poor Mexes almost never had guns. They were easy pickings when the Lipan Apache or Tuintsundé Mescalero or whoever took it in their head to get themselves some clothes and gear and have some fun with Mex women…and men. "Damn savages!" I shouted to no one.

The ground was as hard as rock and me with no shovel. The ground may have been rock-hard dirt, but there weren't any rocks to cover them with. I rode on south. I was thinking about them laid out neat. Injuns sure as hell ain't done it. Had to be that a Mex got away and come back, probably a kid. Imagine him having to see that and drag them over there. "Damn savages."

There wasn't any sandal prints on the road. Maybe he headed back north. I'd not of noticed that as the tracks I'd seen before getting here were of no import, and I hadn't studied them.

I'd gone a ways, maybe a mile, and I noticed sandal prints, an older kid's. He must of stayed to the brush before striking down the road. Poor kid. I picked up my pace, but I slowed for Burro's sake, and because it came to me that if I caught up with the kid, what was I going to do with him? I guess I'd put him on Burro and give him to the first Mexes I run across or drop him off in Uvalde.

It soon started raining. I hoped it would stop by night, its usual habit. A cold night was one thing; a cold-wet one was another. I'd no idea how far it was to Uvalde. I might be sleeping out. Burro made a complaining noise. "What you fussing at, Burro? If you weren't walking down this road you'd be standing around getting just as wet."

I tried not thinking much on what I'd seen back there and was hoping it wouldn't come up tonight.

Coming out a stand of blackjack oak, I spied a rider up ahead, a white man. We stopped a ways apart regarding one another. He looked tolerable, a lot older than me, a cowpuncher by his bearing and the look of his rig. "Howdy," I said. "Any troubles behind you?"

"Howdy, yourself. Nothin' troublin' back there. Hows' 'bout for you?"

"I runned across a Mex family, been butchered by injuns. The injuns headed off sou'west."

"That happens," he said with little concern. It was only Mexes after all.

We talked about how far back and how long.

He looked around. He had a pistol on his left side and big old horse pistol in a saddle holster. "That's been goin' on 'round here. Like the old days. Some Company D Rangers over at Brackettville catched a batch of injuns, shot 'em up and hunged a couple."

"Good thing, that."

"It is."

"I been watching these sandal tracks," pointing at them. "Looks like a Mex kid from that family. You run across him?"

"Nope. I ain't paid no notice. Ain't seen nobody since outside Uvalde. That where ya heading?"

"Yep. Any work thereabouts?"

He shrugged his narrow shoulders. "Maybe over west, but nothin' 'round there. I guess nothin' where ya come from?"

"Nothing."

"That be fine. I ain't lookin'. Headin' home for a spell."

"Where's home be?"

"Waco. Ain't been back to see the old woman for ten months." He chuckled. "I justa hopin' she ain't strayed off, and I'll havta round her up. But I'm expectin' havin' to do jus' that," he said with a long frown.

I tried to laugh, but it didn't come out. "About how far to Uvalde?"

"Ya'll make it by nightfall if ya press on."

"You have a good ride."

"You too." I could smell his tobacco and wet leather.

It was just another meeting of strangers on the trail, appreciated one day, forgotten the next.

Chapter Four

The rain had let up. I was minding the Mex sandal tracks close. I lost them sometimes where the rain washed them out, but I'd pick them up further down the road. I was watching them close, because if that punch ain't seen that Mex kid, it meant he'd hid when the punch passed. It weren't nothing to me, but it gave me something to think about instead of that sight back yonder. Just past a small wash the tracks went off the road to the right. A little further, they came back on the road. It'd been about an hour since I'd seen the old punch so the Mex kid wasn't far ahead.

Maybe he'd hear me coming and hide. That would be fine by me. I thought about singing and letting him know I was coming, but didn't have it in me. That sight back yonder, you know.

The tracks were clear since it stopped raining. Then they turned off the road to the right, just like before. He'd heard me. I untied Burro and snagged his lead rope around a bush. I don't know what set me to go after the kid. Seems something told me to. Maybe because it stuck in me what he must of gone through and could use a little help. Don't know why I gave a care. I dug my heels into Cracker's sides and trotted into the brush. His tracks headed to a stand of trees. I bent low looking under the limbs, and Cracker started. The kid busted out of the trees and into the weeds. Cracker was hard after him. To the horse, it was like cutting a calf, I guess. I let him have the reins, and he jigged and jagged through the brush after him. I almost stopped short when I saw..."That ain't no boy!"

A girl hightailed for some thick brush with a big bag slapping on her side. That gal could surely scamper, until losing her feet and hitting the ground face-first. She scrambled up when Cracker slid to a stop with mud a spraying and his haunches on the ground. I came off of the saddle, slipped in the mud, and slid right into her, knocking her down again. She turned over and sat up.

I got up on my knees. "Dang, girl! Look at me. I'm all covered with mud."

Even with the mud on her face I could see she was scart shitless and breathing hard. Her red eyes been crying. Grabbing her by the arm, I pulled her up. She tried to yank away, then kicked at me.

"Whoa, *niña*! I ain't going to hurt you." She kicked again, making a growling noise in her throat. "Dang it! *¡Alto!*" I pulled her over to Cracker with her tugging back like a roped calf. She even took a swing at me. Taking off the canteen, I handed it to her and said, "Clean off your face, *niña. Lavate.*"

She glared at me, more mad than scart now. She yanked the canteen away and splashed water on her face, never taking her eyes off me.

She was a little thing, not even five-foot high. She looked about like any other peon girl wearing a long-sleeve brown shirt, long, coming down over her hips, and a heavy black wool skirt and flannel petticoat. She had a waist-long brown cape with a square head hole. It was sewed up all fancy-like in red, orange, and tan thread. A brown wool shawl was wrapped over her head. Everything she wore was pretty grubby and smelled of wet wool. The bottom of that skirt and petticoat were all muddy. A big tow sack was slung over her shoulder with everything she owned, I guessed. Must of weighed as much as her.

She handed me the canteen and stepped back, still glaring at me. She looked to be an ornery little toughie.

Set in her oval face with high cheekbones were big brown eyes so dark they looked black being made more so by heavy black eyebrows. She had a wide straight nose and a small mouth, but her lips were full and dark. It didn't look like she'd ever smiled, not that I could blame her owing to recent events. I had no idea how old she was, not being around girls. Maybe twelve, maybe eighteen for all I knew.

She didn't look so scart now, but glared at me all mean like. I never paid no attention to Mex gals. I mean I'd seen some good-lookers, but they weren't my kind. They had their ways, and I had mine. I'd never paid much mind about them having their own troubles and the things they liked and didn't like. This little gal was kind of pretty, but had a flint-hard edge.

"Now what am I going to do with you?" It would be easy to just ride off. She wasn't my problem. All she had to do was keep walking, and she'd find her own kind somewhere.

She stood there waiting for me to make up my mind. She even looked like it was no matter to her for me to ride off. Heck, she was probably hoping that's what I'd do.

So that's what I did. I hung on the canteen and climbed onto Cracker. "Well, fine then. *Adiós, niña.*" Her expression didn't change. I trotted back to the road. As I rode, something was troubling me. "She ain't no concern of mine." Don't know if I really meant it.

Then I remembered what ol' Bill Tuckworthy once told me. "Ya don't see no lone Mex gals out 'cause ifin ol' Pedro finds one they're reckoned whores. They'll jus' have their way wit' 'em. Some good ol' boy Texicans'll do the same."

I thought about that little gal and what'd happened to her family and what could happen to her. "It ain't no matter to me," I remindered myself loudly.

I knew full well what'd happened to that Mex woman back there, and that little one too, maybe only four or five years old. Even trying not to think on it, it made me belly-sick. Picking up Burro, I turned south onto a long straight stretch. I looked back. Nothing. "There's right and wrong," I told Cracker. "Maybe I should take her along, but she'd only slow me down. She don't want nothing to do with me anyways. Hell, she's just a Mex. Got more Mexes 'round these parts than white men, chinks, niggers, and micks and injuns all together."

I moseyed on. "There's right and wrong," I reminded Cracker. I looked back again and saw her trudging down the road. Sure looked small out here. "Well, shit."

Cracker snorted.

I stopped, and she kept coming. Took a while, but she finally came up on me and just kept going right on past without even a

"*Buenos tardes.*" Didn't even look at me.

I kept going, staying even with her. "Would you like a ride?" I pointed back at Burro. "Ride, *niña, el burro?*" Burro blinked his one eye.

She kept going, paying me no mind.

I trotted ahead a little and dismounted. She tromped on by, and I caught hold of her tow sack's strap. She turned on me like a wildcat, threw up an arm, and twisted out of the strap smoother than a snake slipping into a gopher hole. The dang thing was heavy with blankets and a big crock pot.

Backing away a couple of steps, she stood there, all the less than five-foot of her, crossed her arms and glared at me. She stuck an arm out for the bag, but I held on to it. Stamping her foot, she jabbed a finger at me. That girl's surely mean-looking with little creases between her eyes when she's pissed. I smiled and slung the bag onto Burro. I patted Burro's rump. "*Ándale, niña.*"

She looked at me, staring into my face with her snapping black eyes. After a piece, it seemed like she'd decided something about me. She nodded sharp and stepped up to Burro. Glaring at me, she stooped over, locked her hands together, and stood back up.

"Oh, you expect me to give you a boost. Well, I guess you need help, you being so puny." Sincerely hoping some cowpoke didn't happen along, I bent over, locking my hands. I ain't never figured myself doing this for a Mex gal.

Sitting on Burro, she pulled a wicked-looking boning knife out of her sleeve and dropped it in her bag. *Well, crap. I'd best mind my manners.*

She nodded, and I took that as permission to mount and off we rode. For someone who don't say much, she surely says a lot.

Chapter Five

"What in the blue blazes am I doing?"

I keep looking back, and she always still there on Burro. Least she weren't talking none, not that I would of understood much. Least there wasn't any rain.

The sun dropped in the west, and I kept plodding along. The old punch said I'd get to Uvalde sometime around dark. Well, it was nearing dark, and I'd ain't seen no sign of nobody, much less a town. I'd crossed what I judged the Frio River.

I was ready to call it a day. What with the dark clouds, night would fall dark real quick. I was played out, and I was sure the girl was too. Burro gave a bouncy ride, I expect. That girl must be having some powerful troubling thoughts. Must be tough after what she saw. She'd moved them dead Mexes—her ma and pa, and little brother and sister. I couldn't even think about having to do that, especially a girl doing it, even if she's just a Mex.

I didn't need no town. Probably wouldn't be able to give the girl away at night no how. I headed for a grove of trees to hide in. The girl slid off Burro, so I could lead the animals into trees. She started fetching firewood, lots of it. I unloaded, hobbled the animals, and laid out my bedroll. Then she built a fire. Kind enough of her to pitch in. I figured I could share some grub with her, what there was of it. I was aiming to provision-up in Uvalde. It seemed strange, though, I'd never shared food with a Mex, excepting *Tío* Pancho.

27

The girl piled leaves and laid her blankets on them. She only had two blankets and a heavy serape. Taking the lid off her big pot, she started stirring it and sprinkling something in from little cloth bags. I took out my skillet and the square of bacon I had left. When she saw it, she was on her feet and motioned for me to give them over to her. She must be making some kind of stew and was willing to share. I could do that, I guess. Cutting the bacon up, she started frying it in the skillet, then dumped it in her pot, grease and all. I put on the graniteware coffeepot. When the fire burned down to orange coals, she spooned whatever was in the pot into my skillet. She kept stirring it with a big wooden spoon. It smelled good. I was getting real hungry and no longer distressing about breaking bread with a Mex.

I pulled out some hardtack squares and offered them to her, but she shook her head and took out some tortillas. They looked a lot better than tasteless hardtack jawbreakers. She laid them one at a time on a little frame of green sticks she'd fashioned and sprinkled water on them. They ended up soft and hot. With a sideways glance, she offered some.

"*Gracias, señorita.*"

She smiled back.

"*Mi nombre es Güero.*" I pointed to my hair. *She sure don't talk much.* "What's your *nombre?*"

Her smile changed to a sad look, and she pointed to her mouth, shaked her head, and pointed to her mouth again.

"You can't talk?" pointing at my mouth, then her.

She shaked her head again.

"That's a damn shame." I wondered how that came to be. Heck, she couldn't even tell me her name. A woman what can't talk, according to some fellas, was a first-rate deal, but it made me sad. Well, I bet she never got her mouth washed out with lye soap for saying dirty words. I surely had when I was little, sometimes for only speaking my mind.

I filled up my tin cup with coffee, and she had a little cup-size clay bowl. It was colder, and we put away a couple of cups. She did make a face when she tasted my coffee, but that ain't bother me none. I didn't much like it my ownself.

I hung one of my blankets over my shoulders. She wrapped her serape around hers.

My mouth was watering by the time the stew was ready. It smelled plum good, sharp and spicy. I handed my tin plate to her, and she filled it and her own bigger bowl.

In the firelight, it looked like frijole beans, but sure smelled different. She wolfed hers down with the wooden spoon.

I loaded up my spoon with the thick frijole beans. Here goes nothing, me eating with a Mex. Poking it into my mouth, my eyes musta popped open wide, for the girl laughed for the first time. Her laugh sounded kind of strange. I ain't *never* tasted nothing like those frijole beans. I shoveled in three more spoonfuls before I said, "*Niña*, what in dickens you put in these?"

She looked at me with a smug crooked smile from under her shawl. Fire flickered in her eyes like lightning. That shoulda told me something about her then.

Those frijole beans were spicy *and* sweet. I could taste the bacon and ham, but I'd no idea what all else was in it. There were all sorts of bits of something else, green and red stuff the best I could make out. She spooned the stew onto a tortilla and rolled it up, and ate it that way. I tried that too. She gave me a second plateful, but she didn't eat no more. Chow always tastes better when you're real hungry and even more gooder when the air's cold and the grub's hot. Those frijole beans would of tasted good no matter what. We had more coffee, and I rolled a cigarette. She watched that real close, how I did it.

I leaned back against my saddle and burped, causing her to laugh. Then she burped too, and we both laughed. Well, the sky hadn't fallen because I supped with a Mex gal.

"Your frijole beans, they're *mucho bueno, señorita*."

She gave me a little smile. Collecting up our eating gear, she poured in a little water and scrubbed them down with sand. She put the lid back on the bean pot with a wire bale clamp.

Cold as it was we collected up more wood. Then she crawled into her blankets. It was going to be *mucho* cold tonight, and she sure didn't have much of a bedroll. I had plenty so I got up and spread a wool blanket and my gum blanket over her. Her head came up real quick-like when I did that. She nodded and buried her head under the blankets.

"*Buenas noches, niña.*"

She answered with a grunt.

I sat there a spell, thinking about that girl's family lying back there for the coyotes, what she must be thinking. I thought about that old punch, him looking for his woman, and me finding this girl. I guessed she was tagging along with me for her protection. That's only natural, I don't blame her. Don't know why she trusts me, but I guess she does, some. I thought about what that thin boning knife might feel like slipped between my ribs. Yeap, I'm going to be the perfect gentleman.

Just what the hell am I going to do with her? I thought about those frijole beans. She didn't mind sharing her chuck, I guess because I added to the pot. Tossing a couple of long-burning logs on, I bundled up knowing sometime in the night I'd freeze out and have to chuck more wood on the fire.

I woke later. The fire was barely burning. I listened to a strange sound and tried to make it out. The girl was sobbing, a deep moan that kept on. The pain flooded around us both. I'd wanted to do that once, wish't I could, for I'd lost something too, a long time ago.

Chapter Six

It was a gray morning. I was shivering cold, but my need to pee drove me from under the blankets. The girl was blowing life back into the fire, and she was shaking more than me. After piling on wood, I loaded up the coffeepot. She opened the bean pot and spooned them into the skillet. I was surely looking forward to them frijole beans for breakfast.

"*Buenos días,*" I said, and she sorta smiled back. I could see in her eyes she'd had a rough night. I turned away when she frog-squatted in the weeds doing her business. She carried an armload of wood when she came back. I trotted around to warm up while she stirred them beans.

Dipping hardtack in my coffee, I jawed on that while she served out the frijole beans. They were as good as last night. She cleaned up our gear, and I loaded up. We were both feeling better, but she showed me the bean pot, and it was empty.

"*Alimentos. Uvalde. ¿Comprende?*" I'd get some grub in Uvalde.

She nodded with a little more of a smile.

I didn't say nothing about unloading her in town. How could I? No words for it. It would be for the best.

We were on the road and soon passing nesters' houses, and within an hour we were riding into Uvalde. Adobe and board buildings and tents lined the mud streets filled with cowboys, railroad workers, sheepherders, farmers, lint-backs, goatherders, and riffraff.

A lotta buildings had board fronts, but adobe backsides. Freight wagons and teamsters lined the main street. Uvalde sat midway on the San Antonio-Del Rio Road. I watched two of them riffraff stomping a Mex into the mud with a scart goat tied to his leg. Folks stopped and watched. The girl stayed real close to me *lavate* all wide-eyed.

Near one of the plazas was the Presbyterian meeting house. I headed over with the girl following, hoping she'd not figure out what I was up to. There were two men in suits out front, and I asked of the preacher.

The tall one said, "I'm Reverend Bridges of the First Presbyterian Church, and this is Reverend Johnson of the Baptist Church of Christ. They're using our meeting hall until they can raise their own building," he added.

The Baptist preacher asked, "Who is this girl and how old is she?" real uppity like before I could proper introduce myself.

"Well, that be my problem, Reverend. I don't know her name. You see, she can't talk." I tried to tell the tale, but they kept interrupting me and each other getting in a confab about "morality." They must not been in Texas too long. This morality business was something new that ain't taken hold in these parts.

Then the Presbyterian sin-buster started preaching about why I should get out of Uvalde post-haste. "At night this town is infested with sheepmen and cattlemen, who often come into town filled with whisky, and sometimes fight each other and even the sheriff if he comes out of his office. Drunkenness and faro gaming and cock-fighting are common sins as is the too reckless use of the six-shooter. The railroad workers are from the slums of New York, as wild and desperate a set of men as I have ever seen." He was looking a little wild-eyed by this time.

"Last Sunday a gang of roughs tried to stampede my congregation by firing a pistol inside the church, while drunken men tried to climb through the windows. Son, you should save yourself, rid yourself of this harlot, and leave this den of sin before you are tempted to partake." He sounded real sure of that.

I wasn't sure what a harlot was, but by the way he said it, I didn't like the girl being called such. "Yes, sir. That sounds like good advice to me. But my problem is I can't be dragging this Mex girl around Texas. I'm hoping one of your good churches could show pity and take her in."

That was met with a long silence and empty stares. Then one of them said, "Seeing she's a Mexican you might find the Catholic church more receptive," and then they real fast excused themselves for important business.

An American-speaking Mex pointed me to the Sacred Heart Catholic Church at another plaza. We tied up outside and walked into the cool, dimly lit church. I wasn't sure of what to do, but the girl quickly walked up the aisle, crossed herself, and got down on her knees. I stood in the aisle looking around. It was real quiet, kind of pleasing. There were pictures on the walls, of some half-naked fella toting a cross and candles burned on a corner table. Even though we'd come to another church I was hoping she still had no idea what my aim was.

A man in a long black coat, almost looked like a dress, came from a side room. "May I help you, my son?" He had a quiet face.

"Ah, yes, sir." I told him my name, and he said he was Padre Bernard. "I got this girl here who can't talk none, and her family was murdered by injuns."

"Let us speak elsewhere. Please come this way."

"Will she be fine leaving her here?"

"She'll be fine."

We went into a little room with a table and chairs. He offered me a glass of gin-clear water poured from a fancy glass jug. "Please tell me your story, son."

"Yes, sir. Yesterday I was riding along minding my own business, and I come across this Mex family all dead..."

I finished up telling him she was a hard worker, a prime frijole beans cook, and could do about anything needing done. He was quiet for a while and seemed to be thinking deep. Finally, he said, "Son, your act of kindness and the protection you've offered this girl is a pious act. You will be blessed."

I didn't know what that'd get me, but I guess it was supposed to be good.

He looked a little nervous. "Unfortunately, I am afraid we cannot take her in."

That was surely a letdown, but I didn't say nothing because the padre was being so understanding about it all. "I gotta ask, Padre, what am I supposed to do with her? Nobody wants her."

"You do have a problem my son, and I sympathize. Possibly, you can find a Mexican family willing to take her in." He paused and looked at me closely. "You need to make sure it's a good family, or it would be like putting her in slavery. I hope you simply don't abandon her on the road. That would be a terrible fate."

"I thought that's what you were supposed to be concerned about." I felt bad saying that. "Sorry, Padre."

He looked sad, but met my eyes. "I understand your feelings, but we simply do not have the facilities or funds to take in orphans. I have no staff, and it certainly wouldn't be proper for her to remain here with me." He looked a little embarrassed. "I hope you understand."

I was guessing maybe his wife wouldn't like it.

"I don't know what to do with her, Padre."

He stood, so I guess that meant I was going. "You are on your way to Eagle Pass, you say?"

"Yes, sir. I got a job lined up."

"There is a larger Catholic church there, and there are many Mexicans. Perhaps you'll have better fortune." He looked thoughtful. "Be warned my son, the Methodist circuit-riding minister described Eagle Pass as a Sodom-like city."

That could be good or bad, I thought.

We walked back into the chapel, and the girl was still kneeling and praying. I turned to the priest. "I wish I knew what to call her."

The priest was watching her. Holding his elbow in his hand and touching his fingers to his chin, he said, "There is the story of Martha and Mary in the Gospel of Luke, two sisters who offered hospitality to Jesus and His disciples. Mary listened to the Christ as He talked, but Martha was left with all the work. When she complained, Jesus told Martha not to worry about small things, but to concentrate on what was important. We think the girls may have been orphans." He looked at me and said, "Martha might be a good name to bestow on her. In Spanish, it is Marta. I'll pray for you and Marta on your journey."

That didn't mean much to me, but I thanked him anyway.

"And son..."

I turned, "Yes, sir."

"You're an admirable young man, as I said. You have undertaken a graced effort. I'm sure you will do what's right."

That didn't mean much either. "Yes, sir."

"Good things will come to you."

Sure, I bet. The padre walked over to the girl and spoke to her in whispers. Don't know what he was telling her, maybe what her new name was or giving her some kind of blessing. I went outside and was as much at a loss of what to do as before. I guess all I could do was take her along to Eagle Pass and hope for the best.

She came stomping out glaring at me, and I boosted her onto Burro, after making sure no one was looking. What's wrong now? "What if I call you Marta, that fine? *Tu nombre es Marta. ¿Está bien?*"

She arched an eyebrow, still frowning.

The priest said, "I told Marta her new name. She seems to approve." He nervously fingered the cross on his chest. "I also told her you were trying to find her a new home. *Vaya con Dios, hijo.*"

Oh, no. It was my turn to frown. That ain't going to help. No wonder she was giving me the mean glare. Her eyes were so big and dark.

"*Lo siento.*"

She turned her head away. Saying I was sorry wasn't good enough, I guess. "Fine then, Marta. Let's go get us some *alimentos* and leave this sinful town behind."

She kept glaring, making me feel unhappy about my ownself.

GORDON L. ROTTMAN

Chapter Seven

I found the Nueces General Store. *Bodeguita* was painted on the sign's bottom so Mexes knew what it was. It held the fresh and musty smells of a general store. I knew what vittles I needed to stock up, but Marta had her own idea for what would go into her bean pot. She stomped up to the counter all put out looking and ignoring me. The shopkeep was smiling, "*Buenos días, señorita.*"

Marta nodded and pointed at the shelf with sacks of pinto beans.

"She don't talk," I said.

"You must be blessed." The fella took down a five-pound sack. Marta slit the top with her boning knife, sniffing them. She pointed at airtights of tomatoes holding up three fingers. "She knows what she wants, doesn't she?"

"Yes, sir."

I walked around looking at things and came across a box of hand mirrors. I picked one up. Maybe this could be a gift to Marta and might make things right. I'd never given a gift to anyone. Made me feel queer.

Marta got a package of salt, some dried green things, salt pork, a lump of ham and another of white bacon—sow belly—a two-pound sack of rice, some onions, a bunch of jalapeños, and a sack of *harina*—tortilla flour. It surprised me that she got a small can of coal oil. I didn't know why, but I figured there was no point in arguing about it. I added a pound of Arbuckles' Ariosa coffee, soda crackers, a package of twelve boxes of matches for a dime, and Bull Durham cigarette makings—a five-cent sack would make thirty-three rollies. "The Cheapest Luxury In The World" the package said.

I paid for everything and didn't let Marta see the mirror. It thinned down my money stash.

The shopkeeper's wife said, "That's a good idea, son, buying her the mirror ifin y'all had a fallin' out."

"We ain't never had a falling in, ma'am," I said.

"It takes a while sometimes," she said with a smile.

I didn't say nothing to that. How'd she figure we were…whatever she was thinking?

We stopped at a livery yard, and I bought Cracker and Burro some oats. Marta was still ignoring me as hard as she could. I'd always heard women had that annoying knack. I knew horses and cattle inside out, but women? They were a mystery. The boys at the K. B. Webb Ranch had treated me to a whore when I came fifteen, but knowing painted cats ain't the same as knowing customary women…or Mex girls.

It came a downpour, a real frog-floater, and we waited it out under the livery yard's pole barn. When the rain finally let up, we were well into the day before we turned south on the muddy road to Eagle Pass.

We came across a couple of freight wagons at a flooded creek ford. I helped dig out one of the wagons and with getting them across the flood. Marta pitched in too. It was a couple of hours of hard work in calf-deep mud and listening to the teamsters grousing how the railroad was ruining their business. For all that muddy work, they gave us cold bean sandwiches for dinner.

Another rainstorm blew through. I put on my yellow slicker and tried to help Marta bundle up in the gum blanket, but she wasn't having none of that. She did fine on her ownself with her serape. We were pretty drenched and cold, so I stopped early, well off the road. A fire would help dry us out. The trouble was there wasn't any dry wood to be had. Marta collected up wood and piled it. I was thinking she's got some old Mex trick for drying it out. She doused it with coal oil, tossed on a match, and we had a blaze. "I'm glad somebody's thinking ahead."

We stood there drying out our clothes, and Marta was still acting like I was someplace else. I could tell she hadn't been too awed by the bean sandwich, so she started fixing supper. It wasn't frijole beans. She browned some rice in the skillet, melting in a chunk of white bacon. When it was sizzling, she threw in some cut-up ham and onion and chopped up jalapeños. She cut open one of the airtights of tomatoes, dumped them in, and covered the skillet.

I made the coffee and collected more wood as she stirred the tomato-rice. She spooned the meal into my plate and her bowl. I shared out the soda crackers and coffee.

It was a dang fine meal. Felt like I was eating alone, though.

After she cleaned our eating gear, and I tended the animals, I handed her the mirror. That got a little reaction, a quick glance, and a nod. She sat there looking into it for a piece, like she was staring at a stranger. It made me realize how much her life had changed in one day.

We bedded down on opposite sides of the fire. I heard her crying. Made me feel sorry for her. "*Niña, lo siento por tu familia.*" I told her I was sorry for her family. I don't know if I said it right. It was the longest thing I ever tried to say in Mex.

It came to me that I'd never much felt sorry for anyone like this.

GORDON L. ROTTMAN

Chapter Eight

The fire was out in the morning. The sun was well up and only seen through ragged cloud breaks. Marta was not to be seen either. On the pad of leaves where she'd slept, she'd left the wool blanket and gum blanket and the mirror. Struggling out of my bedroll, I checked the provisions bag and all the grub was there. Checking the animals, Burro was gone. Marta's sandal tracks led back to the road and turned north to Uvalde. Damn that girl! I was trying to make up to her. I got no idea why, since I was still conspiring to get rid of her. I couldn't blame her for taking off, but taking Burro wasn't right. "I'm going to wallop that Mex's butt until it's bloody raw. No, I ain't," I grumbled aloud. I'd had that done to me.

I turned left onto the muddy road for Uvalde. Freight wagons had already passed. I stopped and asked myself why was I following her now that I'd gotten my wish. She ain't my problem anymore. I'd follow a stray calf; it had a money worth. But this stray was a bother. Thinking like that made me feel bad. She's smart. She'd make it on her own…I hoped. Heck, I'd miss them frijole beans too.

I hoped. You don't just hope. If you're a man good for his word, a man that can be counted on, and a man who treats folks right, then you make things happen your way. At least give it your best. And she stole Burro, dammit! I dug my heels into Cracker's sides. "Let's go get her," I muttered. "I don't cotton to any burro rustling."

Something was nagging at me looking at the sandal tracks.

41

Why ain't she riding Burro? Well, I'd had to boost her up. Then why'd she steal Burro, but left the blankets I'd given her, and the mirror too. She didn't take any grub either. Damn Mex girl. Ain't making no sense.

A mile down the road the sandal tracks disappeared. I rode back and found a spot where there was a patch of little prints. Studying them, I figured she gotten on a freight wagon. The little rustler must have stringed Burro to the wagon.

I was back in Uvalde before noon. She could be anywhere. She could even have kept going through town on a freight wagon in any of three directions—east to Hondo and San Antonio, west to Del Rio, or north to Leakey. Why am I doing this? I asked myself again. I wanted Burro back, didn't care about her. But I kept thinking about someone having their way with her. She didn't deserve nothing like that, not after what all she'd been through. On the busy streets, there was no following Burro's tracks. I asked first at the livery yard and the general store. Every teamster I saw unloading or stopped at saloons for a dinner, I asked of her.

It turns out I didn't have to follow any tracks. Looking down a side street, I spied a rack-bed freight wagon with Burro tied to it, standing there, one eye blinking. Unstrapping my Remington I rode up and asked the teamster why he needed a burro to push his three-team wagon. He was straight away suspicious and stepped toward the wagon seat where I guessed he kept a scattergun.

"Hold there," I said putting my hand on my pistol grip.

He did.

"That burro come with a little Mex gal?"

"Yes, sir, it did."

"Whereabouts you drop her off?"

"Back yonder at Getty and Mesquite streets. She shore don't talk much."

That was near that Catholic church. She musta left Burro in payment. "She stole that burro. I'll be taking it with me."

"Now don't be so fast passin' judgment, mister. When I pick that little gal up, she was tryin' to chase that burro off. It was follerin' her."

"Why'd you give her a ride?" Myself being suspicious of his intentions.

He bristled, figuring I was thinking bad things of him. "She looked lost and in need of a lift. Jus' tryin' to be decent. How I know that y'all's burro?"

"He's blind in the right eye."

Leaning over, "He shorely is. He's all yours. I don't need no half-blind Mex donkey."

Stringing Burro to Cracker after moving over all the gear I'd piled on Cracker, I headed back to the church. I dismounted and tied Cracker to a hitching post. I don't know why I turned and looked across the plaza. I spied a tiny figure sitting cross-legged beside a saloon door. I walked across the muddy plaza leading the animals.

She held her eating bowl in her lap. A passing mechanic dropped in a coin. Two of those wretched New York railroad trash came out of the saloon door. They said something to each other, their heads together. One laughed and hocked a gob of chewing tobacco at her bowl. He missed, splattering it on her shawl. Marta didn't move, didn't look up. They laughed mean like and saw me coming.

"Here's a sporting cowboy. You want a piece of that chili-popper, fella?"

"This here greaser runt's free for the takin'," said the other with no room to talk, seeing his shirt and pants front were black with grease.

I clutched my revolver's grip and felt a pistol-whipping coming on. I kept a hold on my temper and paid them no mind. The two maggots smartly left without saying nothing more.

She was shivering. I knelt down and wiped the spit off with my bandana. "Disgusting damn Yankees." There were tears in those big dark eyes.

I don't know why, but I stood and reached out my hand. She glanced at me, seemed to sigh, reached for my hand, hesitated, and then took it. A chill shot though me, but it wasn't from her cold hand. I don't know what it was. Gripping me like she'd never let go, she held on tight until I wrapped her serape around her and lifted her onto Burro. I didn't care who saw it. She sat there sort of limp, looking all played out, just staring at the ground.

"Let's go to Eagle Pass. I'll get that job, and we'll see what'll happen."

Marta was still shaking with tears in her eyes and her lips quivering. Taking out a pair of wool socks, I worked them over her hands.

"We'll stop early today, build a big ol' fire, *fuego*"—I made hand signs—"and we'll have your frijole beans."

She gave a sorta smile and nodded. I stuck the hand mirror into her tow sack. I felt real queer and couldn't explain the feeling in my belly.

— •●• —

We rode past the campsite we'd bedded down in the night before. I saw more freight wagons. The few punches I came across, traveling in ones and twos, knew of no work. The coal mines on either side of the Rio Grande only hired Mexes at starvation wages. I was mighty glad I had that letter from Mr. Picket.

It was going to be a dang cold night, and by the feel in the air and smell, a wet one too. Marta built another coal oil-lit fire and started on her frijole beans. My mouth was already watering. She was slap-pressing tortillas.

I pitched up my bedroll's canvas cover and got everything under it, including my saddle. Marta piled her leaves and laid out her blankets. I took the gum blanket and my slicker and rigged the best fly tent I could for her.

Brewing the coffee, I gave Marta the sugar candy stick that came in the Arbuckles' sack. She didn't know quite what to make of it. I knew what to make of her frijole beans and tortillas. They were grand and different from before.

I bundled up for a cold wet night after tossing logs on. Marta sat under her fly staring at the fire and would look into her mirror too. No telling what she was thinking. Poor kid.

She sat with her knees up, arms crossed over them, and resting her chin. The fire danced in her eyes, but I think she was staring at me.

I don't know what she thought she was going to do there in Uvalde by begging. There'd been three pennies in her bowl, which she'd pressed into my hand. I couldn't figure it. I was trying to give her away so someone could take care of her. Instead, she'd rather be on her own with all the shame and danger. Or she's willing to stay with me. I got no idea why. Maybe she thought I'm taking good enough care of her. That's a laugh. Maybe because I didn't make her do anything she didn't want to. She pitched in doing what needed doing. It occurred to me that I was doing the same, pitching in for the good of us both. I don't know; I couldn't figure out what was going on.

It started drizzling and came down harder to douse the fire. I woke up to the sound of a hard wind. The rain had stopped, and it was colder. A lot colder. I could hear ice crackle on my canvas tarp.

I woke again with crackling ice and my blankets rustling, startling me for a second. Marta squirmed into my bedroll. I was lying on my left side, and she spooned up, her back to my chest. She shivered something terrible even though wrapped in her blankets and shawls. I didn't know what to make of it. This is the strangest thing that ever happened to me, a Mex gal crawling into my bedroll. Pretty amazing. She must trust me. Then I remembered that boning knife. Beforelong I felt warmer. Well, what the heck. I laid my arm over her shoulder. She tightened her fingers around my hand. Even with the socks, her fingers were freezing. She didn't cry any.

Morning and she was still there, lying against me, all warm and soft. She smelled of mesquite smoke and fiery spices. I ain't never shacked up with no Mex gal. Well, I reasoned, the earth ain't cracked open and the sky ain't felled.

I think she was already awake, because when I moved she scrambled out of the bedroll into the freezing air. She lit up the fire with coal oil and gave me a quick smile from over the blaze. We rushed around doing our chores of heating up frijole beans and coffee, feeding the animals, and packing the bedrolls while trying to act like...I don't know, like we ain't been cuddled up so close. It's like nothing curious had happened. I busied myself keeping my mind off of things. Cracker and Burro weren't too happy, them being cold too and ready to walk themselves warm.

We started south on the road crunching over the frozen mud and plodded on through the morning. It had warmed up some. I'd make Eagle Pass and a job in a few days.

I heard a whooping yell from the right, and I knew what made it. I waved at Marta to hang back, lashed Cracker's flank with my *cuarta*, and tore into the mesquite, dragging out my rifle.

Chapter Nine

I come out of the mesquite and saw the damndest thing. Two injuns was working over a cowboy lying in the mud. He was in a bad way seeing that one buck was holding his legs down and whooping up a storm as he knifed him in the ass. The other was scalping that fella. He was getting it from both ends, you might say. I levered a round into the Winchester and blew the back of the head off the injun doing the stabbing. The other buck jumped up holding the scalp and shook his bloody knife at me. Letting loose a whoop, he come running dead at me. It's embarrassing to tell this, but my shot plum missed him as Cracker stepped back when the hollering buck started for me. Instead of being fancy with a head shot, I shot him in the chest. But getting off Cracker, I found the buck was still breathing with blood bubbling out of his mouth and nose. I shot him through the heart. The other buck was lying on his back looking real sorry with his brains in the mud.

That poor fella on his face in the mud started moaning.

What am I going to do now? He was bleeding mighty powerfully, and I figured he'd not be with us much longer. He muttered something laying there in a big puddle of blood. I kneeled down and said, "How you doing, partner?" That's all I could think of. Seems kind of silly considering the state he was in.

He said, "I ain't figured to check out this way."

I surely felt for him. Rolling him over, I took his bandana and put it on his head after folding it. I'd never seen someone scalped and still living and bleeding. Hell of a thing.

If he didn't bleed out, I thought I could get him into town, and maybe he'd make it. I'd heard of an old boy that'd been scalped and lived to tell of it. His barber gave him half off haircuts, but still charged him full for a shave. "Hang on, partner. Maybe we can get you out of this." The cowboy wasn't much older than me.

"No, that sumbitch gave me the knife in the kidney." Blood was coming out of his mouth now, and then I saw blood under his backside. It was flowing like a redrock spring creek. His face was death white and his voice feeble.

That's when I hear a whoop and see a horse coming. I grabbed up my rifle. Of all things, here comes another buck. He had a shotgun and was bearing down on me fast, maybe seventy yards. I aimed real good, had the time to, and squeezed, and dammit if I didn't miss again. Two misses in one day! I aimed again, and the shotgun boomed. A swarm of hornets hit me stinging like the dickens and damn if I ain't missed again when I directly fired. I levered in a fresh round and brought her to my shoulder and saw I was aiming at an empty horse. I guessed I'd hit that buck after all. There he was on the ground. He sat up though. Damn! Maybe I needed more practice. He was up and coming at me with a tomahawk. I'm thinking there's only so many cartridges in the rifle, so I'd better start paying attention to what I'm doing. I put one in him as his horse ran past me. The buck dropped like a sack of wet flour. I hoped he was a deader. Then it occurred to me there might be more injuns. The buck laid there moaning and groaning. I'd gut shot him. Damn! I ain't wasting no more cartridges. He'd commence a squealing and screaming before long, but I wasn't hanging around to hear that.

I took a look around and didn't see any more marauding savages. I felt little burns all over my left arm and side. I pulled up my sleeve and there were polka dots of blood. I'd been hit with a birdshot from a long ways off. It stung, but that was all. I'll have to pick out the shot.

The buck in question was crying and wallowing around in the mud and cactus. It was high time to get out of there. I would have that scattergun. It was laying in the mud way behind him. I picked it up and broke it open. Both shells had been fired. I only remembered one shot. I looked at the buck, and it looked like I'd only got him with that gut shot. I be damned, the fool had fired both barrels and knocked his self off that horse. I would have that horse too.

Going back to Cracker, I got out my carton of cartridges and reloaded. Seven rounds were left in my rifle. That's when I wondered where Marta was. I turned to holler and there she was on the injun's pony with Burro in tow. "*¡Buena chica!*"—Good girl! She didn't smile, though, as she was looking over the carnage and the screaming injun. She looked plum good sitting that pony. That's when I realized it had a saddle, saddlebags, and bedroll. It was a little sorrel and must have belonged, I mean, belongs, to that cowboy.

I wondered what that girl's thinking about all this mess after what happened to her family. I wished she'd hadn't seen this. It dawned on me she had caught that excited sorrel all by her lonesome. I be damned. That's pretty good.

I went over to the fella, and he was a goner. Heck, I'd no idea what to do now. Like with the girl's family, there was no burying the fella. He'd have to stay. I didn't have any Bible words to say over him. So I simply said I hoped he'd make his way to a better place with sweet green grass and good water. He could sit in the shade watching his enemies ride past to hell. Marta slid off the sorrel, and I think she was saying something for him in her mind. She crossed herself a couple of times.

I went through that fella's pockets and only found a jackknife, cigarette makings, and some American coins—less than two dollars—and three Mex eight-reales coins worth a dollar each. No papers, no wallet, no name. I laid his bloody bandana over his face. His rig had a .44 Smith & Wesson Russian with only eighteen rounds counting the ones in the cylinder. Those injuns had got the drop on him good. His revolver hadn't been fired. His boots were fair, but he'd died in them, and I'd leave them be. I hated the thought of them going to waste anyway. I picked up the bucks' three knives and that tomahawk. Damn injuns. They ain't had a gun one among 'em. Must be reservation bucks on a fling. I spied an empty whisky bottle. Damn injuns. Marta picked up the fella's hat, stepped behind the horse, pulled her shawl down to her shoulders, and put the broad brimmed, low-crowned hat on.

We had to go. That buck's squealing was getting on my nerves, and it wasn't doing Marta no good either. There was a green canvas and russet leather shotgun case on the sorrel's saddle, and I wiped off the scattergun and stuck it in. I started to climb onto

Cracker, and Marta grabbed my arm. That was the first time she'd ever done anything like that.

"What?"

She had an angry look in her dark eyes from under that big…hat. She pointed at the screaming buck.

I looked at her. "*¿Qué?*"

She pointed again, jabbed her finger hard, and stamped her foot.

"You want me to finish him off?" I didn't think she'd care none about his sufferings. Heck, these injuns might be the ones kilt her family, except they didn't have any guns.

She jabbed her finger again, glaring mean at me.

"Well, fine then, dammit! He's going to croak anyways." I cocked the rifle. Dang woman, making me waste another cartridge. "These things don't grow on trees, you know!"

She pointed again, and I could almost hear her say, "Cowboy up and finish the chore!"

She didn't turn away when I shot him. We rode off. I was still riling against my marksmanship, "Eight cartridges, eight. Three injuns. Shoulda taken no more than four, five tops."

I was thinking about that fella with no name. Going like that, just being left to rot out in the prairie and making a meal for coyotes and buzzards. On days like this, nesters' soft town life seemed a mighty good idea. I looked back at Marta. At least, she wasn't scowling no more. She surely looked good on that sorrel.

Chapter Ten

We came upon a creek well before sunset. I woulda gone further, but that stream seemed mighty useful seeing I needed doctoring. I unsaddled the two horses and unburdened Burro, simply dumping everything into a pile under a willow. I was starting to hurt enough where it was making me irritable. Marta was kind of looking at me queer like, but she got her fire going. I hobbled the horses, and they kind of hung around each other introducing themselves and biting on one another, seeing who's boss. Cracker is. I laid my saddle blanket by the fire, sat cross-legged, and doffed my shirt and long johns top to feel the chill.

Marta got all wide-eyed, not because she ain't seen me out of my shirt, but because of all the little pellet holes in my arm and side and some smeared blood. She got the coffeepot water boiling directly, and I gave her that fella's jackknife.

After washing out my bandana and then pouring hot water on it, she washed me down. "Ouch, that stings." She popped me on the side of the head and gave me a hard look that said, "Tough it out." She held the blade in the fire, let it cool a spell, and commenced picking out the birdshot. That hurt more than the process of them getting put there. There were only a baker's dozen of the little pellets.

Marta gathered sage leaves while picking up more firewood. She ground up the leaves and stems in a tin cup and added a little water to make a paste. She dabbed that on my wounds.

"For a scamp of a *niña*, you sure know what to do. Like a doctor's nurse."

She shrugged her shoulders like she knew what I'd said.

While Marta cooked up supper, I went through that poor fella's gear. Most of it was a sorry lot. His saddle and bridle were long hard-rode. His saddle blanket was way too dirty for the horse's good, and he had the beginnings of back sores. Marta saw that and put some of that sage paste on them. He was fresh shod, though. She took time to wash the sorrel's saddle blanket. That would help its back. She seemed to know something about horses.

His saddlebags were lean pickings. They yielded two tins of Boston baked beans and a tin of peas, a pound can of corned beef, a jar of lick, a handful each of jerked beef and corn dodgers, coffee, salt, a wooden canteen with the cork stopper replaced by a corncob plug, skillet, eating gear, and so on. His bedroll was only four blankets, one threadbare. He had a gum blanket and a brown corduroy coat, a good heavy one, blanket-lined with a canvas collar.

In a paper packet was three 16-gauge shotshells; that's all he had. The shotgun was a very fine Parker Brothers double-hammer, which I reloaded. Its barrels were longer than my arm. I pocketed the spent shells. The Russian Smith was good too, but a little old. On his belt rig I found the letters "I.N."—or maybe the "I" was a "J". In script writing, they looked the same to me. There was nothing else naming him.

Looking at his guns and things like that corduroy coat, I'd say this was a once well-off cowboy who'd fallen on hard times. That Parker was at least a forty-dollar shotgun. I wondered if he'd worked around here or if he was heading to Eagle Pass like me. Or maybe going to Uvalde or San Antonio.

He had a lot of gear I could sell. I don't think he'd mind. He'd know a cowboy's lot is tough, and he'd of done the same his ownself.

Marta was making tortillas, and I was thinking all what I'd sell in Eagle Pass. Watching her press the dough balls flat and throwing them in the skillet, I realized that some of these things would be of use to her. I stood to make a lot of money, with any luck. That sorrel and saddle, for instance. Then I thought about how good she sat the horse, and she'd caught it her ownself. But, it would bring in a lot of money. Then I thought she never looked all that comfortable on

Burro. I liked the idea of keeping the horse, and Marta might like it too. It would surely look grand, me coming into town with my…with…with her sitting on a good horse. Not riding a burro or walking behind me like most Mexes do when hooked up with a *gringo*.

She could use a couple of wool blankets, and that gum blanket, and that corduroy coat too. I climbed up—it didn't hurt too bad—and picked up those things, choosing the best blankets. Folding them up, I laid them beside her, and the canteen too. "For you," I said spreading my hands toward the gear and then at her, "*Por usted.*"

She looked up at me and then at the things, and back at me, shaking her head, kind of confused.

I nodded and smiled and sat back down. I tossed that fella's jackknife onto the coat. Everyone needs a good knife, not that boning knife.

Her eyes were as big as the tortillas she was making. She dropped the knife in her tow sack and picked up the coat. The firelight showed tears in her big ol' eyes. I don't know what the big deal was. It was only some poor old drifter's gear he didn't need no more.

Supper was grand, her frijole beans. The way she nursed me, you'd have thought I'd been bad hurt. She even wanted to feed me, but I wasn't having none of that. Marta cleaned my arm and side up again before we turned in.

I had to lay on my right side because of the birdshot. Marta spooned against my back, her head against my shoulder. I could feel her tits pressing against me, and she put her arm over me. Strange this, I thought. We could hear coyotes yelping a long ways off. I guess talking about what they'd found, out there on the prairie. We slept warm that night and the next too.

Chapter Eleven

E agle Pass sorta sneaks up on you when riding over a low ridge. Going up that ridge, you're expecting more mesquite-covered prairie, but there's the town. You can't see the Rio Grande, it being down in a wide gorge.

Marta is sitting the sorrel about as tall in the saddle as she can, which isn't much. What a sight. A Mex girl on a shod horse with a saddle and shotgun, and all decked out in that big gray hat and coat. She drew rein beside me and took out that poor fella's cigarette makings, pulled the tobacco pouch string open with her teeth, rolled a cig, and handed it to me. I lit up, and she rolled another and hung it in her mouth with a look saying, "You gonna give me a light?" I lit her up and said, "If this don't beat all. I expect you'll be wanting that fella's revolver rig next."

She clicked her tongue and bumped Cracker's rump with her foot to get us moving toward town. Coming down off the ridge, we followed the railroad track in, and then took some dirt streets where there weren't any houses.

We crossed over the bridged ravine separating the town from Fort Duncan on its east side. I said howdy to the guard and told him I had some injun gear to sell. He called the corporal of the guard, and the corporal called the sergeant of the guard, and he called the first sergeant and a bunch of troopers collected. There wasn't much to do around there, I guess. I laid them three knives out and bidded them off. Marta squatted by the horses watching bored-like.

I sold the first two knives for a dollar and some change each. When I showed them the one that scalped a white man and still had blood on it, the bidding got lively.

"I got two Morgan dollars," shouted one big soldier straight off.

"I'll match that and ten cents," muttered the corporal of the guard.

"Two-twenty," and so it went.

Two injun scouts, black Seminoles, stood off to the side laughing at the goings-on. They had Comanche knives on their belts, and I can guess how they got hold of them—which ain't no easy thing to do. They might laugh, but I got three dollars and two bits for that killing knife.

I brought out the tomahawk. It was only an old trade hatchet that I'd tied on some buzzard feathers to fancy it up. Still it'd been used by an injun and he'd tried to kill a white man with it, me. "I took this off a buck that missed me by a hair's breadth before I shot him." I was kind of grateful Marta couldn't understand my tall tales. It'd be embarrassing to fib in front of her. I showed them my shirt's birdshot holes and pointed out the shotgun on the sorrel. Marta's eyes narrowed when I pointed at the scattergun. I guess she suspected I'd sell it.

The tomahawk brought almost as much as the scalping knife.

An officer came up. He had gold doodads on his shoulders, and everyone saluted. He asked me about how I got the injun gear, and I told him the story. He seemed miffed seeing he missed out on the bidding. That's when I brought out the Russian Smith.

The officer said straight off, "I'll give you fifteen US dollars for the whole rig."

I'd heard officers like the Russian S&W because it's fast reloading. I didn't think it'd be too smart to offer it to a higher bidder, him being an officer. Heck, those soldier boys only get thirteen dollars a month anyways.

"Seventeen," I said.

"Sixteen," he said.

"That sounds good to me, captain." I didn't know if he was a captain, but he didn't say nothing otherwise. We shook on it, and I'd made twenty-two dollars all told. With my own money and what I got off that poor fella, I had fifty-four dollars. I'd never seen that much money in my twenty-two years.

Marta was back on the sorrel before I got through.

The first sergeant said, "Your woman there. Queer she's carrying a shotgun."

"She ain't my woman." I didn't know what to call her. "It's my shotgun. She just carrying it."

Leaving Fort Duncan, we rode Garrison Street downhill to the river landing. That's when we started to draw notice, or Marta did with her riding that sorrel with a shotgun. I'd already decided to keep that shotgun for game hunting. I tried not to think about all what I could get for that sorrel and saddle. I'd made up my mind though to keep it, so long as she was tagging along. Most folks I saw were Mexes. Maybe I could unload the girl here, and then I'd be rich after selling the sorrel.

I didn't have much luck at the river landing. There were a couple of boats going back and forth; not too many folks about. I'd never seen a tramway before. It was this steel cable stretched all the way over the Rio Grande from the Texas shore up to the bluff on the Mex side. Up there sat Piedras Negras town. I wondered if I might unload the girl over there. That tramway was pretty neat; it was a big wooden box slung on the cable. A Mex, speaking good American and selling bent nails he'd hammered straight, told me they had oxen up there that pulled the box up and then let it slide back down slow. They put coal and goods, animals, and even people it in. Pretty amazing.

I stretched my lariat between two saplings and hung that poor fella's two old blankets on it along with his spare shirt and long johns and set out his other gear. Other folks were selling tools, empty jars and bottles, old clothes, sacks of charcoal, and other stuff. Mex hucksters hawked their goods. One said something to Marta, but she pointed to her mouth and shook her head. I got a silver dime for the old blanket and twenty cents for the other. His cooking gear and shaving gear didn't bring much more. I ended up selling his spare duds to a clothes dealer. He was going to only give me a dime, but Marta haggled and doubled it, purely with finger-jabbing, stamping her foot, shaking her head, and using her eyes. Pretty amazing. She gave the old shaving brush to a Mex kid.

Next stop was the gunsmith near the courthouse. Marta stayed out with the horses to watch the guns.

The shopkeep was a skinny dude in a leather apron. Could of taken a bath in a shotgun barrel. "Good day to you, friend," he greeted me.

"Howdy," I said. "It's been a good day so far, but I don't like them clouds."

"It does make for a dreary day. How can I help you?"

"I need a carton of 16-gauge. What's good for rabbits and such?"

"That would be Number 6 shot." said the shopkeep. "Good for squirrels and birds too. What kind of shotgun you got out there?" he asked looking through the window.

"Parker Brothers. You give me anything for these?" I set the six empty 12- and 16-gauge shells on the counter.

"Penny for two. You let your woman out there have a shotgun? Don't mean to pry, friend," he added quickly.

"She ain't my woman." What would I call her? A trail pal?

"She got her own shotgun?" He sounded troubled.

"She's just carrying it for me. Everybody here ask a lot of questions about other folk's business?"

He put on a shopkeep's smile. "I'm sorry, friend, not being nosey. We seldom see Mex girls toting shotguns. No offense intended."

"None taken. How about a carton of them Union Metallic .44-40 cartridges and a bottle of paraffin gun oil."

"Sure enough. Four-ounce or eight?" Holding up one of each.

"The little one. You got any buckshot for that 16-gauge?"

"Sure enough. Single ought or Number 1?"

"Do I have to buy a whole carton? I don't need no twenty-five shells."

"I'll sell them to you singly. Two for a nickel."

"Give me eight of the Number 1's, then. No, ten."

It all came to almost three dollars.

"Friend, can I give you a little friendly advice? I ain't trying to nose into your business"—he sounded a little antsy—"but it might be a good idea to carry that shotgun your ownself." He was trying to smile. "Folks in these parts arn't used to that."

"I'll think on it. What would a Russian Smith, a Number 3, be going for with a rig and all?"

"I'd give you twelve, thirteen dollars, depending on the condition. You got one to sell?"

"Not no more." I figured I'd made a good deal with that captain.

"You staying in town long, friend?"

"I guess folks *are* nosey round here."

"Don't mean nothing, friend. Only hoping you'll be back."

"I'll think on it."

I didn't hang the shotgun on my saddle until we were around the corner. Marta frowned when I moved it. I don't know why, seeing she didn't know squat about using it.

Most buildings in the town were adobe and some whitewashed. Some were brick. The streets were potholed and muddy, no board sidewalks. About the only trees were mesquite. I asked a scarce white man wearing bib overalls where the Maverick Hotel was. He weren't no cowboy.

He gave me directions, but said, "That your woman there?"

"Folks surely are nosey around here."

"I's just sayin' she's well mounted, friend."

"I surely got a lot of friends today." I thanked him anyways for the directions.

Marta stayed with the horses again at the hotel. It was big place, two floors. I walked right through the front door, and the fella behind the counter gave me a hard look over his spectacles. "Can I help you?" Something about the way he said it made me think he didn't much approve of a trail-muddy punch walking in like he belong there. The lobby smelled of cigars and brandy.

"I'm looking for Mr. Mathew Picket of the San Isidro Ranch."

Still looking over his spectacles, "Mr. Picket departed three days ago. Sorry." His "sorry" had a way of saying, "Skedaddle, drifter." "However…" He turned around and looked in a bunch of little boxes on the wall. "What's your name?"

I told him.

"He did leave this for you," he said and handed me a letter. It had my name on it and a date. I ain't never got a letter straight to me before.

Outside I stuck the letter in my vest. I guessed Mr. Picket had had to leave early, go back to the San Isidro, and this was directions. I was looking for a real home-cooked beefsteak supper, and I thought Marta might like that too. I sure wasn't going to buy it at the Maverick because of that uppity clerk. I asked a teamster on the street where a good place was to get a beefsteak supper.

"That would be the Fitch Hotel." He gave me directions to Commercial Street. He had no comment of Marta, but I figured him being a freight teamster gave him more sense than most hereabouts.

Anyways, a hotel might be a good place to find out where I could unload the girl. I was feeling a little bad thinking about unloading her, but I couldn't be dragging no girl all over Texas. It weren't no good for her.

Chapter Twelve

The two-floor Fitch Hotel faced the river looking into Old Mexico.

We rode around back into a muddy yard. I told the girl *quédate*—stay put—and went to the backdoor. Probably best not to barge in through the front with a Mex girl. Taking my hat off and stamping mud off my boots, I knocked on the solid door.

Presently a lady come to the door.

"May I help you, young man?"

At least she ain't called me "friend." She was older, lotta lines of gray in her black hair. She wore a real nice shiny green dress with white ruffles and puffy sleeves. Her eyes looked kindly.

"Ma'am, I'd like to buy a beefsteak supper, but I don't think you'd let my…" Dang. What do I call her? That was the third time I'd troubled over that. "If y'all don't want this lost Mex gal to eat inside we can eat out here. It's no matter."

The lady looked us over. "Son, that makes no difference. You're both welcome to eat in the dining room. Many of our clientele are Mexican ladies and gentlemen."

I didn't know what a clientele was, and I ain't never heard no Mex being called a lady or gentleman by a white lady. This town was proving strange.

Anyways, I said, "Thank you much, ma'am. Can I unsaddle and bring my guns inside?"

"Why surely. You are packing some iron, aren't you?" She'd noticed the rifle and shotgun.

"Yes, ma'am. We won't be no trouble."

"I should not expect so," she said. "You can stow your tack in the stable and water your horses and burro," pointing to a long shed. "And please do enter through the front door."

Once inside she led us down a hallway to washrooms. I guess we were kind of trail-rank.

Marta came out with her face all scrubbed, but that shawl still covered her head.

"I'll show you to your table," and we followed her across the big room.

That was surely a queer thing to say. All she'd had to do was point at the table. I could see where it was for my ownself.

"It's early, so you're the only diners."

Diners. I guessed that's someone who's eating dinner. What was someone eating supper? Suppers? I didn't want to think about what someone's called eating breakfast.

She brought us water in real glasses and filled them up again, and she said there was no charge when I asked. The floor was covered by a green and blue rug, and there was eating gear laid out on the table with big white folded bandanas.

"May I ask your name, young man? I like to know who my clientele are."

Now I knew what a clientele was—we were. "Bud, ma'am. Bud Eugen."

"I am pleased to meet you Mr. Eugen. I am Mrs. Moran."

"Thank you, ma'am, but shucks, ain't no need to call me mister."

"I'll call you Bud, then. Is that alright?" She had a pleasant smile.

"Surely, ma'am."

"And your young lady?"

Young lady? It was surely a strange town. "She's Marta. That's what I call her. I don't know her given name, seeing she can't talk."

The lady looked genuinely sad. "I thought she was unusually quiet." Facing Marta, "*¿Como estás, Marta? ¿Bien?*"

Marta nodded, smiling.

"Do have a pleasant dinner. *Buen provecho*."

Presently, a young Mex woman in a white dress and blue apron brought out two china plates with big beefsteaks, little taters with no skins, beans—but they weren't frijole beans—cooked collard greens, and another plate with big baking-soda biscuits, and a tub of butter. I ain't never seen a feed like that and felt kind of queer. Marta's eyes were looking at it all like a frog blinking in the rain.

We admired it all for a spell, and I picked up my knife and fork, "Let's tuck in." Marta had some trouble working the knife and fork, holding them like hammers, but the beefsteak was so tender you didn't need no knife. Anyways, I cut mine up in little pieces and swapped plates with Marta. They brought coffee and kept filling the fancy cups. There was sugar too, all you wanted. It tasted a lot better than my own brown gargle. Those cups, I was scart one of us would break one. I ain't never had beefsteak like that on the trail or in a bunkhouse.

I don't think Marta liked the biscuits much, being used to tortillas. They surely were good for me. She picked at the taters and greens, but she finally ate them all.

Then the lady brought us some hot apple pie. Marta played with it with her fork before tasting it. After she did, she looked at me all wide-eyed and ate that pie faster than I've ever seen a starved horse eat oats. It was kind of sweet for me so I gave most of mine to her. She chopped it up with her fork and gulped it down.

"Did you enjoy your meals?" asked the lady.

"Surely, ma'am. I ain't never had no feed like that."

"I am pleased you appreciated it."

"I don't know if I can afford all that."

"It is two dollars and fifty cents. Yolanda will take it."

"Each?"

She laughed, real nice like. "No, no. For both."

That was a relief. That was still a lot of money, but I'll never forget that meal. And there was another reason coming up for never forgetting that meal.

"Ma'am, could I ask you a favor?"

"Certainly, Bud," as she topped off our coffee.

I pulled the letter out. It embarrassed me, but the lady seemed like she'd not say anything unkindly. "Could you read this for me. My reading ain't so good."

She gave me a sad smile. "You should open it."

"I've never opened one."

"Simply tear the end off, close to the edge."

"Yes, ma'am." I slid out the paper and handed it to her.

Unfolding the paper, she cleared her throat:

"Mathew M. Picket, Maverick Hotel, Eagle Pass, Maverick County, State of Texas, November 22nd, 1886.

"Dear Mr. Eugen, I am a man who holds his words as a promise if I can. I know I offered you a job at the San Isidro, but it distresses me greatly to report we had ourselves a passel of bad luck here at the Isidro, and I fear I am not able to stand by that offer. The winter is harsh, and of late, Mexican scoundrels have rustled a goodly part of our stock, so we have no use for extra hands. If you need traveling provisions, stop at the ranch, and we will be happy to oblige.

"My regrets, Mathew M. Picket."

It was like I couldn't hear anything. I had a hollow feeling in my guts. Damn, if that don't tear it.

The crinkling noise of her folding the paper made me come back.

"I am sorry, Bud. That must be a terrible disappointment." She had a sad look. "I know Mr. Picket well. He has fallen into hard times. Many ranchers have."

"Yes, ma'am. It surely is." I tried to keep my voice even.

Marta looked at me sad, like she figured something was wrong.

"May I speak with you?" the lady asked. "In private."

"Yes, ma'am, but the girl here, she don't know any American."

"May I sit, Bud?"

"Surely, ma'am." It's her table, but I didn't say anything, it being a strange town.

"Could you tell me what your relationship is with your young lady?"

My young lady? "Surely, ma'am, but she ain't my woman or nothing. A week ago, I found this dead family, kilt by injuns, and I found Marta here just walking down the road..." I told her everything that happened since. She was a nice lady and easy to talk to.

When I was through, the lady sat there all quiet like. Marta had lost interest and was smoking a cig and looking out the window after eating a third piece of pie.

The lady startled me when she finally spoke. "I've been watching you and Marta. I know she's not your woman, although around these parts, she is of age." She smiled. I started to say it wasn't like that, but she went on. "I will tell you this, you have been taking good care of her and protecting her. You are a good man, Bud Eugen, a genuine Texican." She reached over and gave my hand a squeeze. "Let me ask you this. Do you like her?"

That was a surprise. I'd not thought of it like that. She turned to Marta, who stubbed out the butt and smiled at her. I guess I was quiet for a long spell, because the lady was looking at me steady. "Well, yes, ma'am, I guess I kinda like her. She's ain't much trouble." I was kind of fibbing there. "She don't eat much…'til now, and she's a prime cook."

She nodded her head, "Then I will tell you this, Bud Eugen, before you turn her over to some stranger, you need to think hard about it and ask yourself if whoever you are leaving her with will be good for her, that they will treat her right." She had a look as serious as a poker player with a winning hand. "There are some bad people out there. I do not need to tell you that."

"Yes, I mean, no, ma'am." I didn't know what else to say.

"There is one other thing, Bud, since we are speaking frankly."

"Yes, ma'am?"

"If you like her, Bud, and I know she likes you, why would you want to give her away?" She glared at me like a hawk. "You think on that, Bud."

"Yes, ma'am." She was making sense, but I'd have to really think on it.

"Well, while you think on it and maybe find someone who can take her in, if that is what you think is best, I could use a little help for a few days. There is a caretaker's room in the stable, and I will provide you meals, including this one, and board your horses too. Would you like that, Bud?"

"Surely, ma'am. We're most obliged to you." I didn't say nothing about hotel work being beneath a cowboy, but it would feed us.

The lady put a little smile on her lips. "Do you realize you just said 'we,' Bud?"

There were two cots in the caretaker's room, and Marta pulled them together because it was cold. Mrs. Moran gave us a big old quilt for the bed, and I laid my puma hide on the floor to stand on in the morning. It surely smelled like a stable, hadn't been mucked out proper.

"Do you realize you just said 'we,' Bud?" I didn't figure out what Mrs. Moran meant until that night, after we bedded down. But I had said "we." I guess that meant I was thinking of someone besides my own ornery self for once.

Chapter Thirteen

Mrs. Moran fed us fried eggs, ham, frijole beans—nothing like Marta's—grits, biscuits with pear preserves, and coffee. Seeing we were hired hands now, we ate in the kitchen, which was all right, because we didn't have to worry about fancy manners. Directly, after breakfast a coal wagon showed up, and I shoveled its load into a bin. The Mex teamster told me the coal came from Mexico and that Piedras Negras means black rocks, because of the coal mines. Marta helped Yolanda, a handsome, quiet girl, in the kitchen and with cleaning. They surely did a lot of cleaning in that hotel.

I mucked out the stables, cleaned stoves, shoveled coal, and cared for the hotel's wagon horses and the clientele's horses for the rest of the week and then some. They even gave me money tips for taking care of their horses.

The next day when I came back from buying a blue plaid flannel shirt to replace my holey one, Mrs. Moran had another sit-down with me. She told me Yolanda had been talking to Marta, asking yes and no questions, which took some time.

"She likes you, Bud."

"I don't rightly know why."

"You saved her life."

I shrugged. "Only trying to do right."

"Marta says you treat her right too. That you are a

gentleman."

I had to laugh. "No one ever called me that."

She laughed too, but said, "Do not undercut yourself." Then she said, "She is sixteen, having turned last month."

I nodded. "She tell her name?"

"That is hard to figure, Bud. Yolanda asked her a lot of names, but no luck. She is satisfied with Marta."

"I like it too."

"Marta likes the way you part your hair down the middle." That made me smile. Mrs. Moran got all solemn looking. "Bud, we know why Marta cannot talk."

I looked at her, "Yes ma'am?"

"Yolanda asked her questions, and Marta parted her hair on the left front. There is a scar there and a bit of dent in her scalp." She looked grave. "Yolanda worked out that she was kicked by a mule when she was about nine."

"So she's got brain damage?"

"It looks like it, but it only means she cannot talk. You know yourself she is as smart as you and I."

"Yeah. Smarter than me." So now I knew. It didn't make no matter. I just felt sorry for her, mule-kicked in the head, her whole family killed, no one wanting her. Life deals you a rotten hand sometimes.

"She cannot read or write."

"That just about makes two of us, ma'am."

"There is something else Yolanda told me, something you need to know."

I looked at her.

"She says Marta, well, her family, was what they call *nómadas*, wanderers. They have no home; they are people of the road. They work in fields and do odd jobs."

"Yes, ma'am?" I wasn't following her.

"Yolanda says she is not like most Mexican girls. She is more of a fighter, defiant, knows the rough ways of the road, and has to be clever to survive. She is more...earthy."

I chuckled. "I can see all that in her." I understood too because I'd been raised rough.

"Bud."

"Yes, ma'am?"

She fixed me with a stern gaze. "Marta is special. You could do worse in this life than take care of her."

With a comfortably snoring Marta snuggled up to me, I thought on what Mrs. Moran had said about me being a gentleman. A cowboy gets needful urges. I pondered on that. I'd taken her under my wing because I knew ruffians would take what they wanted from her. Well, I swore I'd not be that way. This little gal had been through hell, lost everything. I wasn't taking nothing else from her. It was the only decent thing to do. Besides, there was something else about her, something I couldn't quite figure.

One day Mrs. Moran said if I shot some quail and jackrabbits, she'd pay me. It was a nice change from mucking out the stable twice a day. When I saddled after breakfast, Marta was right there. She climbed up on a nail keg, hoisting her saddle onto the sorrel. I said, "You get back inside." I'd learned she could understand my meaning…when she saw fit. She crossed her arms and glared at me, tapping a sandal atop the keg. I could see there wasn't no point in arguing.

All we had to do was walk through the grass outside town and plenty of them old mule-ear jacks and quail were scart up. It was easy shooting. Marta was toting a feedsack, and it was full in no time. She pointed at the shotgun and thumped her chest.

"You wanna shoot this thing?" The girl was sure full of surprises. "Well, hell, why not? I gotta see this, you getting knocked on your scrawny butt."

Taking the gun, she arched an eyebrow like she was saying, "Watch this."

She loaded and cocked a hammer like she knew what she was doing, I guess from watching me. I'd noticed she'd watch real close when someone was doing something. She looked funny trying to heft that long-barreled cannon up.

"Well, fine. Now pull it hard into your shoulder 'cause it's going to kick like a mule." I shoved it hard into her showing what I meant. Then I thought that was ignorant to say since she don't know what I said, and she knew about a mule's kick.

She nodded and tramped forward a-hunting. I stayed right behind her not wanting her to swing that cannon around all a sudden.

A quail lit out fifty feet away, and she blew that bird clean out of the air before it cleared the sage tops. And she was still standing.

"Well, I be thumped."

She was mighty proud of what was left of that bird. She glanced at me out the corners of her eyes. She might as well have said, "Stuff that in your tobacco pouch."

Then I remembered the shot shells where her family been murdered. Her pa must of had a shotgun.

Coming back, I ran into a greasy-beard cowpuncher in front of the hotel and asked him if his outfit were hiring. He sounded funny because his lip was slit open up to his nose and never healed proper. "We ain't hirin' no hotel-chore boy nurse-maidin' a Mex."

Guess I'd not be working that spread. "Thank you, friend," I said.

On Friday, Mrs. Moran told me to put my spare duds on because Marta was going to wash clothes. On Saturday after the guests were done, Mrs. Moran said we could use the bath. I'd gone first, put on my clean duds, and was in the stable room repairing a hackamore. It was blowing cold-wind, and Marta came running in wearing one of those white Mex dresses with a towel wrapped around her head.

Sometime ago I was in a café in Beeville, and this lady had pictures on the wall of her ma and pa. They were black paper cutouts of their heads, what she called sil-lo-wets or something. Marta stepped through the door, and the sun hit highlighting her shape like one of those sil-lo-wets. She pulled that towel off, and thick black hair fell over her shoulders and back. I ain't even known she had that much hair, all wavy down to her hips. Damp-wet, it glistened like black oil. She saw me then. We sorta stared at each other for a spell—those eyes. Then she got all embarrassed looking and brought that towel up over her hair. I was up and out of there, embarrassed my ownself and feeling queer. Had to feed the horses anyways. Lodged in my head was that sight in the door and all her hair. Pretty amazing.

Chapter Fourteen

Being Saturday night and feeling peculiar, I moseyed down to the Blue Saloon, because I'd been told it was a bad place to go to. Something about Marta was troubling me. I'd think one thing and then something else. I was starting to like having her around, and that made no doggone sense.

There was a bunch of punchers and peelers at the bar—planks lying across whisky barrels—lanterns hung all around the walls. The dirt floor was covered with straw, and I asked the barkeep what for.

"It makes it easier to clean up with all the tobacco spit, puke, and blood," he said, wiping down glasses dipped in a scummy bucket. Top of the water had kind of rainbow colors in it.

I said, "That makes sense." Now that he'd mentioned it, the place smelled like all that.

I knew I dranked too much. I started with beer, but ended up on tequila. It was like belting down wet fire.

That greasy-beard, slit-lip punch from the other day asked what for I was letting a Mex gal tote a scattergun around. He talked big being backed by his pards. I recollect telling that bunch of boys this was the nosiest damn town I'd ever had the misfortune to pass through. They agreed that it was a good damn idea that I was passing through, and they hoped I'd continue my travels real soon.

The barkeep got me out of there without the help of Slit-Lip and his pards who were more than willing to toss me out. I went to the noisiest place I could hear, a Mex cantina down the muddy street.

Those Mex boys were real friendly and weren't nosey. We drank beer, drawing bottles floating in a cold-water barrel, and they were singing up a storm. This one *vato* was prime on a guitar. There was a couple of Mex whores flirting with them boys, and this one started hanging around me when I started buying rounds. It'd been a long time, and she was looking mighty good. She kept playing with my hair, standing behind me, wearing a red dress showing a nude shoulder.

Now I ain't never had no Mex whore, and I ain't proud to admit I'd gotten sorta curious. I felt real lonely, and I went with her to a tent outback. She hoisted up her dress, but I told her to take off everything. She shrugged her shoulders and peeled off and laid on the cot. It was cold, but I took no notice. Her skin was like coffee with a slug of milk, long black hair, eyes just as black, big dark nipples, and a patch of thick black hair. In my head, I could see Marta's sil-lo-wet standing in that door.

I gave her two eight-reales. I thought I'd made some good money of late, but she was probably rich at this rate. I was feeling pretty good and at the same time real down. It was all queer and confusing, and I don't think it was because of the booze. Those Mexes, some could speak American, were slapping me on the back and saying, "*Adiós, amigo*," as I headed out. It was sure cold. I walked straight back to the Blue Saloon. I've done dumber things, just don't recollect what.

I walked up behind Slit-Lip and them other punches hanging on the bar and bawled, "Y'all a bunch of damn nosey bastards and ain't got no call telling me what for about that girl carrying a twice-barrel shootgun.

Instead of being pummeled with fists, they all turned around and started shouting things like, "Greasy Mex lover," "Get your ass and your Mex whore outta town," and "Stick that dummy greaser bitch's scattergun up your ass, boy."

That's when I threw a beer bottle at Slit-Lip, who was wild-eyed drunk. That's when I got pummeled with fists. And dragged across the floor, thrown out the door, kicked about, and stomped into the mud and horse shit. I remember that mud was real cold. Slit-Lip pulled this foot-long skinning knife and came at me. I put my arms up, and he fell on me like a barrel of rancid salt beef. I don't recollect no more.

I woke up with someone banging on pots. There wasn't any straw on this dirt floor, but there was puke and blood, mostly mine I think. The banging was a fat turnkey with shaggy ginger-and-gray hair and tobacco-brown teeth a clanging on the cell bars with a ladle. He was saying, "Someone here to sees ya, dumbass."

"What happened?" I asked. My mouth tasted like a wormy cow had shit in it, and I felt like the rest of the herd had stampeded over me. I was real cold and shivering like a leaf.

"Ya real lucky, ya dumb sumbitch." The turnkey was standing there snarling down at me. "Deputy Wilcox conked that big punch on the head wit that grub-hoe handle he carries. Or you'd be in the Chinaman's parlor with him having to stuff your innards back in."

"Well, thank him for me when next you see him." I heard moaning in the next cell and there layed Slit-Lip among the contents of a kicked over chamber pot.

"Y'all dumb as a keg of lard," grumbled the turnkey, looking at me. "Anyways, someone here to sees ya."

And there stood Marta with a big frown. I all a sudden had this powerful guilt feeling in my innards, the ones the Chinaman should be stuffing back in.

The turnkey said, "Mrs. Moran brunged her down to give ya some blankets. It's powerful cold." He scowled at me again. "Ya oughta be 'shamed yourself making that fine lady havta come down to the hoosegow on a night like this."

Marta pushed two blankets through the bars and was worried looking. But she gave me a scowl and ran out. I guess she didn't approve of the state I'd gotten myself into.

"Tell Mrs. Moran I thanks her from the bottom of my heart." All that talking was hurting my head.

The turnkey only growled.

— •●• —

The turnkey banging on the bars woke me. "Mrs. Moran here to co'lect y'all."

The glaring morning sun slanting through the bared window made my head hurt more. I managed to make it to my feet once I'd crawled out of the cell.

"Y'all one damn lucky sumbitch, dumbass. That they brunged ya 'em blankets," he added.

I didn't say nothing. My teeth itched, and my tongue was asleep. The blankets were hanging over my shoulders. It was colder than a witch's tit on the Texas Panhandle.

"That punch what tried to knife ya, he froze death las' night. He ain't had no blankets. A powerful bad blue norther blowed in."

I was expecting an ass chewing, although I don't think a fine lady like Mrs. Moran would call it that. She was standing there wearing a long beaver-skin coat and a stone-cold look. Marta was there too wearing her corduroy coat and shawls, and her face matched Mrs. Moran's.

In a stern tone, Mrs. Moran said, "I expected better of you, Mr. Eugen. I trust you will work hard to redeem yourself." I only nodded, but that hurt. Her wagon was on the street, and I took the reins for the four blocks back to the hotel. She didn't say nothing more to me that day. Of course neither did Marta. It was the worst ass chewing I'd ever had.

Chapter Fifteen

On Monday, I bought a hair brush for Marta at the Watkins Store. She smiled a little, I guess forgiving me, sorta.

I told Mrs. Moran I didn't belong in a place like this. I'd just get in more trouble. I thanked her and said, "I need to be pushing on, find work with some outfit. I'll find someone to take in Marta before I leave."

"If you insist on going alone, Bud, you can leave Marta here."

"That'd be mighty kindly of you, ma'am, but shouldn't she be with her own kind?"

"Yolanda is here. Most everyone in this town are Mexicans."

"I'll ask around, ma'am. We'll see. Maybe I'll take you up on that offer."

"You do that." She didn't sound real happy with the idea of me unloading the girl. "Besides, where will you go? No one is hiring."

"I don't belong in no town, ma'am." But she was right. I I didn't have nowhere to go.

I talked to the customs agent, and he told me if I took the girl across the river, and I didn't find any place to leave her, she might not be allowed to come back. I asked at the St. Joseph's Academy on Church Street, a private school for girls. There were Mexes there, but since she couldn't talk, they didn't think it would work. Neither did I when they told me it was twenty dollars a month.

Tuesday, after chores, we rode down to Our Lady of Refuge Catholic Church. Marta figured out what was going on. Mrs. Moran had said, "I hope you know what you're doing, Bud. Remember what I told you about finding trustworthy folks." Before turning to go back inside she added, "You need to think on this some more."

That woman sure enough had a way of making a man feel loathsome. Well, hell, it's a church, right? What better folks to take care of a stray Mex gal? I had to admit to my ownself that I kind of liked her being around, but she was making me feel too queer. Now since this girl showed up, I didn't know how I felt. I had to be looking after her and not feeling right about…about how I was feeling.

When we rode up to the church, I looked at Marta, and she wasn't angry like before, she was plum scart. It was like she knew that this time I was giving her away for keeps. We got off our horses, and she ran up to me, grabbing my arms. Looking up at me with those big ol' eyes from under that hat, she was shaking her head. Her lips were in a tight line. I ain't never seen a dread like that in nobody's eyes. She was begging me with her eyes. I be damned if I got this big ol' lump in my gizzard. I ain't never felt like that before.

"I help joo, *señor*?" A voice behind me said.

I pulled my eyes away from Marta's. She was still gripping my arms, hard. I was looking at a Mex priest. He was wearing a brown robe thing, had a little fringe beard and looked friendly enough. "You got any need for a girl to do some work here, Padre?" I think I sounded real weak-kneed. "She's a hard worker and a real prime cook." I told him her family was all dead and how that came about.

"Joo may call me Brother Miguel," he said. "No, I afraid not. We have the girls and womens who work for us. I am sorry. Besides," he said, looking at Marta, "eet look like she no want to leave joo."

I figured that was his real reason for saying no. It was like a load was lifted off me. Something had been decided for me. I looked back to Marta's eyes. Tears ran down her face. That hurt me. I muttered to myself, "Don't do that, girl. I don't know what to do." I had to get us out of there. "Well, *gracias*, Brother Miguel. I was just seeing."

"*Vaya con Dios*," he said.

We rode back to the Fitch Hotel. I couldn't meet Marta's eyes. I knew I'd be hearing the after-claps of that little storm for some time. But, I'd hurt her, hurt her bad. I'd no idea how to take away that hurt.

— •●• —

The next morning I was lying on my cot with Marta pressed up against me and feeling her breathing and warmth. She was still cross with me, but she set that aside at night. She'd bed down still wearing her wool dress, but it weren't warm enough. She'd wrap her feet in one of her shawls. I thought she's not just some Mex gal. She's like anyone else. She's got her fears and hurts, and wants to see good things happen, not the life she's had.

I went back to the Watkins Store and bought two sets of long johns, small size, and three pairs of black wool socks. That made a dent in my funds, almost five dollars. I'd set them on her cot and that got me a big hug and a sweet smile for once. She wore the long johns to bed that night.

I guess we made a silly picture in the mornings. We'd run into the kitchen in our long johns, me wearing boots and she her sandals with our clothes in our arms. Yolanda would be laughing at us as we dressed as fast as we could by the stove. Something about her in them johns, but she kept all that hair hidden under a scarf. I'd fetch coal while Marta poured our coffee, and then helped with breakfast. It was pleasant times.

Chapter Sixteen

I kept asking around for any news of ranch work, but in winter, there wasn't nothing. I sure didn't want to ride the chuck line, drifting from ranch-to-ranch through the winter taking opportunity of ranchers' hospitality, especially in these hard times. Professional chuck-liners—tramp drifters—had a reputation I didn't want.

Marta had settled down after her scare of my trying to give her away, but she was forever going to the stable seeing if I was packing out. Marta still bundled up with me at night, and she'd hang onto my hand. I'd be splicing a rope or cleaning a gun and catch her gazing at me, like she was willing me to stay. Her full lips and intense dark eyes, they were something to behold.

I'd try and shake off those queer feelings. I didn't need to get myself tied down and besides, I still had my doubts about her. She was just a lost Mex kid.

One morning I was mucking out stalls, and Marta came tramping out wearing her coat and hat with thick socks under her sandals. An old pair of socks with finger holes covered her hands. She saddled the sorrel and mounted with the shotgun, shell pouch, and a feed sack. Without even a "by your leave" she rode out. Three hours later, she came back with a game bag sprouting rabbit ears and tail feathers, a big grin, and shivering cold. "That girl is something else," said Mrs. Moran. "Bud, if you do not see what I see…" She let it hang.

I'd about give up hope finding work and didn't much like being a charity case for Mrs. Moran. That night she called me into the hotel. Sitting in the parlor was a lean man with thick white hair and a big white mustache. He was wearing a prime suit and hard-worn cowboy boots. His sunbaked face held clear sharp eyes. In his fist was a fancy glass of whisky. It all branded him a rancher.

"Bud," said Mrs. Moran, "this is Mr. DeWitt."

The man rose. He was tall, and he looked straight in my eyes. "Clayton DeWitt, son, I own the Dew spread up Del Rio way." His handshake was a firm grip. I knew he meant whatever he said.

"Bud Eugen, sir. Pleased to meet you." I'd been taught to call important people sir or ma'am. I had mama's knots on my head to prove the learning.

"Clara tells me you're a tracker, a puncher, bring in full bags of game birds, and have had a ruckus with injuns with you coming out on top."

I was caught off guard with "Clara," then I realized he was speaking of Mrs. Moran. "Yes, sir. I am guilty."

He chortled deeply and looked like that was something he wasn't a stranger to. "How about you sitting yourself down, Bud Eugen. Clara, fetch this boy whatever he wants to drink."

"Coffee be fine, ma'am." I didn't need any whisky.

"Now tell me this story about you bushwhacking injuns." He offered me a cigar. I thanked him, but didn't take it. I'm happy I didn't after the production he made of cutting the ends off with a little snippy tool, rolling it around and so on before lighting it. I'd of looked the fool.

"Well, sir, I ain't exactly bushwhack them, but kinda stumbled on them having their way with a cowpoke..."

I told the story, and he asked me questions about tracking and hunting. It wasn't like what ranchers or foremen or *gerentes* mostly asked punches. He never took his eyes off of me except when he was laughing.

"What kind of guns you tote, Bud?"

"I got a Winchester '73 rifle and a Remington '75 revolver, both .44-40, and a Parker Brothers double 16-gauge."

"My, my," said Mr. DeWitt. "We got us a real gunfighter here, Clara."

I guess I turned red, for he laughed heartily.

"Clayton, you are embarrassing the young man."

Bending forward he slapped my knee. "That's all right, son. I can tell you're a man who takes his business seriously."

"Well, sir, guns is only part of making a living, but I ain't no gunfighter, just a punch."

"Clara, I like this boy. Son, how would you like to work for me?"

I wasn't expecting that so sudden, so I thought a spell. "If I can ask, sir, what would I be doing?" Going by what he'd been asking it didn't sound much like I'd be following the rear ends of cows.

"Smart question, son. Shows you're thinking." He got quiet for a moment. "The Dew is right on the Rio Grande, and of late, we've been having bandito troubles. They been coming across the river and rustling cattle, horses, and sheep. Who the hell troubles with rustling woolies?" He seemed exasperated. "Anyhow, these banditos are even coming over and pinching horses from my boys. They take the horse, saddle, and their guns. So far, nobody been killed, but I worry about that mightily."

He was looking at me, watching how I'd react, I guess. "What I need son, is somebody who knows how to use a gun, someone to monitor things. I need a tracker too, and with you, it looks like I get both."

"So I'd be doing both?"

"Yep. I've already got a couple of boys monitoring, and I hope to pick up another or two. But what I don't have is a decent tracker."

"You say tracking, sir. That sounds like maybe you wanna tail them into Mexico."

"Exactly, son." He stretched out his legs getting comfortable.

"Cross the river?"

"That a problem, son?" he asked gravely.

"Do you have any *vaqueros* what know the country over there?"

"Yes, I do. Damn fine hombres, too."

I didn't ask how good. I didn't suspect this cattleman hired half-assed hands. "Then it's not a problem, sir."

He nodded. "I'll start you at twenty dollars a month, meals, and everything your horse needs. If you work out it goes to twenty-five the following month. How's that sound?"

"That sounds mighty generous, sir." We stood and shook hands. I liked his grip, and I liked his eyes.

"In that case, Bud, you can call me Clay."

"Yes, sir, and you can call me Mr. Eugen."

"Ha, ha, Clara, I truly like this boy! I've got business here for a few days, Mr. Eugen. But I need to get you up to the Dew. Can you leave tomorrow? It's a two-day and an early morning's ride."

"Yes, sir." I was already having troublesome thoughts about what leaving meant.

"How about I stake you for the trip?"

"That's fine, sir. I'm all set."

He nodded. "Can I stake you for cartridges?" He laid a Gold Eagle on the side table. Ten dollars would buy a lot of cartridges. He didn't have to say they'd be needed. "You might want to pick them up today if you're leaving early in the morn."

I took the gold coin, and I was in.

"Will you sup with me? I'll fill you in on the Dew and the troubles." "Troubles" he called them. If only I'd known.

— •●• —

I walked to the gunshop. I had to think. Mrs. Moran said she'd take good care of Marta with me leaving. I knew that. But that wasn't good enough. Just leaving her here and riding off, it didn't seem right. Something was tugging at me about my proposed leaving.

"Good day to you, friend," said the gunsmith with a smile.

"Howdy." It wasn't no good day at all.

"How can I help you?"

I set a sack of empty shot shells and the Gold Eagle on the countertop. "Tell me when it's used up."

"Yes, sir." He saw I was in no mood for gabbing.

"Three cartons .44-40, a carton of 16-gauge Number 1 buck and—What was that I got last time? Number 6 shot?"

"Yes, sir."

"Two boxes Number 6, then. What I got left, enough for another carton of .44?"

He set two more fifty-round cartons on the counter. "Looks like you're going to be doing some serious hunting. That woman of yours still hunting?"

There's no secrets in this town. "She ain't my woman, and

yep, she likes to hunt." I couldn't help but brag on her. "Guests at the Fitch are getting filled up with rabbit and squirrel stew."

He gave me some coin change and said, "You come back, friend."

"I might."

— •●• —

Marta's cot setting next to mine was empty that night. She slept in the kitchen. It gave me a taste of how lonely and cold the trail would be.

Chapter Seventeen

I had a sunrise breakfast with Mr. DeWitt. He handed me directions and a pencil map to the Dew. "My foreman's Lemuel Cleland. I'll tell you only one thing about Lee, don't make him wait."

In the stable, I found all of Marta's gear, even her cot, was gone, I guess moved into Yolanda's room. I didn't see the girl nowhere. I had a real empty feeling, and I think Mr. DeWitt knew I was out of sorts. Mrs. Moran was godawful quiet, so quiet you wouldn't hear thunder.

I told her, "Ma'am, please ask Yolanda to tell Marta I'll be coming back when I get time off. It's only a two-day and a morning's ride."

"Why don't you tell her yourself?" She was looking at me real displeased like, her arms crossed.

"I can't talk Mex, ma'am."

"I think she will understand you, Bud."

The idea of having to do that about scart me to death. Mrs. Moran didn't push it, seeing how I was looking like I'd been run over by a mob of mustangs.

I saddled and loaded the horses and Burro. I was selling the sorrel at Juan's livery. The shotgun I hung on my saddle and that didn't make me feel no better. Felt like I was stealing the sorrel and scattergun from Marta.

From the backdoor Mrs. Moran shouted, "Please come

around front. I have dinner for you to take along."

I brought the horses around and found Mrs. Moran on the front porch…with Yolanda and Marta. The girl was wearing her riding getup, her shawls and coat and her big hat. Her tow sack, stuffed full of gear and the bean pot, and her bedroll and canteen were all sitting on the porch.

All bundled up and shapeless, she'd never looked prettier. Her eyes held something. It was hope. It came to me that above all things, she wanted to come with me.

I shook my head.

Her eyes melted onto a great sadness, and a lump stuck in my gullet of the likes I ain't never had. She had a pleading look, and it hurt me to no end. I didn't think I could make smart choices at that point.

Right then I didn't care what I sounded like or who was hearing it. "Marta, I can't do this. I can't take you." I had to stop and try to swallow. "Where I'm going ain't safe. There's bad people."

Yolanda was whispering to her. Marta's face fell into a look of everlasting sorrow. I only wanted to turn and gallop out of town beating Cracker as hard as I could with my *cuarta*. "Tell her I'll be back sometime." I don't know if they heard me. I sawed the horse around and trotted off to turn up Main Street. I was fighting not to look back.

At the livery, I untied the sorrel from my string. Juan checked its teeth. He'd already offered eight dollars for the saddle.

I heard a muddy splash behind me, and the livery man said, "Joo woman, she ees here, *Señor* Bud."

I tuned, and Marta was climbing to her feet in the gate, her chest was heaving from running. She's covered with mud and loaded with her bulging tow sack, bedroll, and saddlebags. I'd been wondering where them saddlebags were, they'd fetch a few dollars. Long black hair was falling out from under her hat. She was twisting a strand in her hand. Her face held a wild unsure look.

I ain't never had nobody chase after me just because they wanted to be with me.

I walked over and yanked the saddlebags from her. She started to tug them back, but let go, like she'd gave up. She staggered back against the fence. I tossed them behind the sorrel's cantle and lashed them on with the latigos. "Forget it, Juan, the sorrel ain't for sale."

"I give joo forty-five *americano* for dee *sorrelo*."

"He's been called for, *amigo*."

Marta's just about jumping up and down and tossed her bedroll and tow sack, with the bean pot, on Burro and started throwing diamond hitches. She hung her canteen on the sorrel and giving me a quick look, took the shotgun case off Cracker and hung it on her horse.

"Juan…"

"*¿Sí, Señor Bud?*" He scratched his shaggy head.

"I got no idea what the hell I'm doing." Marta was at the frosty water trough trying to wipe off mud.

Juan laughed. "Joo doing good thing, *señor.*"

"Yeah, you bet." I climbed on Cracker, and Marta followed me out the livery yard.

I looked back as we passed the railroad station and cotton presses. From under her hat brim all I could see of her face was a big shit-eating grin. Now what? I thought.

Chapter Eighteen

Just what the hell *am* I doing? It was about forty-five miles to the Dew, so I had a lot of time to think on it. The first thing that came to mind was what they were going to say when I showed up with a shotgun-toting Mex girl. She wasn't part of the deal. There ain't a lot of punchers or wranglers, trackers or monitors, or whatever the hell I was, have a girl following them around like a faithful dog. Hell, the hands'll be bedding in a bunkhouse. What am I supposed to do with her? The foreman might tell her to hit the trail and maybe send me packing after her. Then what? I'd be out of job and owing Mr. Clay DeWitt ten dollars.

"I'm in a fix," I said out loud. I looked back at Marta, and she was looking at me with sort of a smile and a frown at the same time. Maybe they'll let her stay because she can help with cooking, washing, and mucking out the house. She'd work for vittles and a place to bed down. And where would that be? Not in the bunkhouse with me. Why was I even pondering on that? Maybe this would be a way to put some distance between us. If they let her work, they'd give her a place to bed down.

There was something else. Before, she was tagging along. Now I was taking her with me, on purpose. Well, it wasn't like I'd put a brand on her or anything.

We took the road easy, it having been a couple of weeks since we done any real riding. Most of the time, I guess we were one to three miles from the Rio Grande. Never did see the river down in its gorge. The land was low rolling ridges covered with yucca, sagebrush, creosote, and cactus, but mostly mesquite. Seemed like there was a creek every five or seven miles, down in thirty-, fifty-foot deep gorges.

About noon, we stopped at a creek for dinner, after crossing it. I always cross before stopping, even if only to water. Mrs. Moran had given us cold fried chicken, jam jars of frijole beans, and biscuits left from breakfast. She'd given me a jar of lick too. Marta had taken a liking to molasses on biscuits…and toast, cornbread, crackers, tortillas, and just about anything else you set in front of her. We unsaddled to graze the horses. Marta laid a saddle blanket out and sat right beside me and patted me on the shoulder. She was grinning the whole time. At least someone was happy around these parts.

It was cool, but clear skies; that meant it'd be cold tonight. It was so quiet after that town. The horses were content and so was the girl. She may have been worrying me, but I had a job with good pay, a good boss. I only hoped I knew what I was getting into. Monitoring all alone with a band of banditos causing mischief sounded kind of one-sided.

After eating, we came up out of the gorge. The bluff was lower on this side and rounded a bend at the top, and this Mex stepped onto the trail. He a held a pistol with a bore as big as my thumb and aimed it between my eyes. He said something in Mex, but I knew exactly what he wanted. The hammer clicked back real loud, and I slid out of the saddle with my hands over my head. Damn, just when things were looking up. When my feet hit the ground, I heard a double click behind me. Without turning around I knew what was up. The Mex dropped his cannon and reached so high he was about standing on this toes.

I kicked his cannon away and stole a look back at Marta. The road agent's line of sight had been blocked by me on the horse, and she'd pulled out the shotgun sight unseen. When I got off Cracker, he found her pointing the shotgun at him. I looked around to see if there were more desperados and picked up the cannon. It was an old Remington Army .50-caliber rolling-block. I opened the single-shot pistol's breech, and it was empty.

He's surely scart with Marta holding that scattergun on him. Pulling my revolver, I thumbed back its hammer and poked the barrel between his eyes. He went as white as the peon duds he wore.

I dropped my arm and eased the hammer down holstering it. "Shit, some desperado you are, *mano*." I went to my saddlebags and took out the dinner leftovers—couple of biscuits and a chicken wing—and gave them to him.

"*¡Vamos, bandito!*" I chucked a rock as he took off running. That's when the shotgun went off making Cracker and me jump like toad frogs. The Mex went down head over heels and flopped on his back.

"Marta, no! For Christ's sake, you got no call for that!" Is she crazy? "What you done?"

She was laughing in a queer way. *She's gotta be loco.* I looked back at the blowed away Mex when she pointed, and he was a sittin' up slapping hands all over hisself. He was up and running even faster, after grabbing up the vittles.

"Girl, you're a treacherous wench. Don't ya ever do nothing like that again!" I tried to keep from laughing.

She grinned and reloaded. I guess in her way she'd told that ol' Pedro to mend his wicked ways. I shoved his old pistol in a saddlebag. It wouldn't bring much. Who'd want a single-shot pistol?

Marta wore a big grin now. I shook my head at her with just as big a grin. "You're some piece of work, *niña*."

I laid my rifle across my lap. That showdown had been a reminder that the borderlands were also the badlands. We needed to keep our eyes peeled.

— •●• —

There wasn't much traffic on the Eagle Pass-Del Rio Road—the daily stage and a few freight convoys, three or five wagons. They had a couple of shotgun guards. One even had an outrider who rode up and gave us a look over. There were few lone riders, just some drifting punches and a mule skinner. We exchanged road news, all the creeks being passable, no washouts, and had a laugh about our road agent. They all wanted to see that old pistol, but nobody was keen on buying it.

Since we were keeping the sorrel, I figured he needed naming. I thought about Rusty because of his color, but that wouldn't make no sense to Marta. I asked a teamster what Rusty was in Mex. He said *Rojizo* was a good name—Row-he-zo was the way he said it. It meant reddish. Marta nodded, liking it when he told her.

Dark comes early in the winter making for short riding days. I started looking for a place to make supper, a spot away from the road and from where we could see anyone coming. I rustled up wood as Marta built a kindling pile. She dumped an airtight of beans into the skillet and cut up jerky to cook in the bean juice making it soft. Soda crackers—with Marta pouring on the lick—topped the meal off, followed with a pot of coffee and smokes.

I watched her squatting in the dirt by the fire, a rollie hanging on her lip. She laid a finger against her nose and hocked out a gob of snot. Yeah, I don't know. Just another Mex.

Kicking the fire out, we picked our way in the dark over to a low ridge. No watchers would see where we camped. I hobbled the horses, and Marta laid out our bedrolls. No fire tonight. Marta sat for a spell and then patted me on the arm before lying down. We bundled up, and she was softly snoring in two minutes.

I watched the moon for a spell and wondered what was in store for us. Us. I'd better think on that.

Chapter Nineteen

We took it easy on the second day, and on the third morning, we crossed Pinto Creek, the ranch's southeast boundary. It was still a few miles to the ranch house. After crossing four closely spaced arroyos, we came to a wagon trail to the right climbing over a pretty barren ridge. As Mr. DeWitt had promised, there was a split post set in the ground with DeW branded on it. It was about a mile and half to the ranch house on the backside of the ridge. As we turned off the Eagle Pass-Del Rio Road, which split the 48,000-acre ranch, we put the Rio Grande behind us. Del Rio's only fifteen miles further on.

Topping the ridge, we spied the Dew. There weren't much to it from up here at half a mile. There were some whitewashed adobes and corrals nesting among mesquite trees. A windmill turned in the breeze, and a line of chimney smoke drifted to the southeast.

It didn't look like much, but it was how we'd be greeted that mattered.

There wasn't a soul in sight except some Mex kids making mud pies by a water trough. That was until someone behind me said, "Can I help ya, stranger?"

Sitting a horse was a rangy-looking punch with a carbine across his lap. He'd come out of a mesquite stand.

"Howdy," said I. "I'm looking for Mr. Cleland. Mr. DeWitt hired me on."

The rangy punch rode around us giving us the once-over

without saying nothing. Giving me a hard look. "Where'd this happen?"

"Eagle Pass. I met him at the Fitch Hotel. Hired me as a tracker."

"Tracker, uh?"

"You bet."

"Well, fine then."

He hauled up next to me, our horses facing opposite, and gave me his hand. "Musty Musson."

"Pleased to meet you. Bud Eugen."

"That all ya do, Bud, foller after folks?"

"Nope. Punch, break horses, wrangle, shovel shit, whatever needs doing. And something about being a monitor."

"A monitor, uh?" He was looking over my guns. "Well, I tells ya, there's a lot needs doin' here." He nodded toward Marta. "What's your woman do?"

"She ain't my woman. Whatever needs doing. She cooks, washes, mucks out houses, and eh…hunts." *It's sure starting to look like she's my woman, like it or not.*

"I bet, seein' that scattergun she's a totin'. Strange."

"She is sometimes."

"But she ain't your woman?"

"To tell the truth, I don't know what she is. What's your rifle there?"

He cradled a lever-action sorta like a Winchester, but not. He grinned, "My cannon," holding it up. "Whitney Kennedy .45-60."

"That *is* a cannon. Never seen one."

"Good for takin' down antelope and whatever else."

"Guess I need to sign in with the foreman."

"Lee ain't be back 'til they change out horses after noon. Let me shows y'all to the real boss 'round here. Go 'head and water and let your string loose in that *potrero* over yonder. I'll be back directly."

We hung our saddles, and Musty walked up with a tall Mex woman. "*Buenas días,*" she said. "I am Gabriella Guerrera." She rattled something off to Marta. Marta smiled, nodded, and looked at me.

"Bud Eugen, ma'am. This is Marta. I only call her that because I don't know her name or nothing much about her. You see, she'd been mule-kicked in the head when she was little and don't talk none. She's real smart, though," I added.

Gabriella looked like a no-nonsense lady, like the school teach I'd had for a short piece. She had a serious look, but when she smiled her face brightened up. Looking Marta over, Gabriella said something that made Marta grin. "I will talk to her inside." Looking me over, I could tell she was gauging me. "Musty says Clay hired you as a tracker." She spoke real good American.

"Yes, ma'am." I called her ma'am, not because Musty said she was the real boss, but because she acted like a real boss.

"The crew will be in at noon. You can see Lee, the foreman, then. In the meantime, care for your horses. I will take Marta to the house, and she can clean up."

"Yes, ma'am. She's a real good cook, washes, and mucks." I hesitated, but said it anyway. "She ain't my woman or nothing like that." I was hoping these folks wouldn't get all morality on me.

Gabriella smiled and said, "Very well, Bud." Turning to the girl, "*Marta, ven conmigo.*"

They walked off and I said to Musty. "She *is* the boss, ain't she?"

"Ya got that right. Gabi's a damn fine lady. Mr. DeWitt calls her his majordomo."

"What's that?"

"House boss. Lee Cleland may be the range boss, but he listens to her too."

"Mr. DeWitt said something about sheep. We don't gotta herd any woolies, I hope."

"Nope, they got Mexes does that."

I could see two yellow-haired girls on the front porch and a couple of Mex girls too. I looked Musty in the eye. "This a good outfit to work for?"

"It be good. Hard sometimes, but it be good."

I nodded. "You a monitor, bein' on guard and all?"

"Nope, only my day to keep an eye on things here. The monitors, they be down at the river. I expect you'll get to know that river, and the Sycamore, real good." Musty mounted and rode off with an, "*Adiós.*"

— •●• —

As promised, the crew came a roaring in at noon. There were nine of them, and they made a show of coming in. The yellow-haired and Mex girls were back on the porch with a couple of other Mex women, and Gabi and Marta—I wondered what they'd been "talking" about. There was a tall white woman too, and I guessed she was Mrs. DeWitt. Mex kids were running up to the corral as those hands runned their horses in, whooping and squalling and smacking their mounts with their hats.

Before the dust had settled, they were dragging saddles off and hanging them on the fence. The horses were at the water trough, and the boys headed to another one, splashing water on their faces and on each other. One ol' boy threw a hat of water on the back of another, and they started scuffling, but they were only horsing around. One of them boys was a Mex, and it seemed no matter to anyone.

They all headed to a pole barn near the big house, and there was a long table set there. Some Mex girls were standing behind big pots, and the crew lined up. Gabi waved at me to come over. She was talking to a barrel-chested, sorrel-haired man.

"Hi," he said. "Lee Cleland. Mr. DeWitt hired you?"

"Yes, sir. Bud Eugen."

"We'll have none of that, Bud. Call me Lee." His face was creased and leather-brown, hooded eyes with heavy eyebrows. His handshake was a firm jerk. I gave him a quick rundown on my hiring.

"Well, that's mighty fine. You'll give them boys out there now a break. Let's dig into the chuck, and we'll talk. Chuck was mashed frijole beans, tortillas, and goat stew with tomatoes.

I got introduced to all the crew. It would take me forever to remember all their names.

Dodger Lampe I liked the looks of. Little sinewy guy making jokes. "I just throwed a horseshoe in the coffee and it sank. The coffee ain't ready."

After dinner, I asked Lee about Marta. "I kinda picked her up a time back and ain't been able to shake her. She ain't my woman or nothing. She don't talk."

Lee stopped me holding up a scarred hand. "Gabi says she's right as a trivet. She helped out with this feed. Gabi'll put her to work for room and board, if you're good with that."

"That be fine by me." I'd ask Gabi where Marta would be bedding down. It would feel queer asking Lee.

"I'll be seeing you this evening," said Lee, scooping up beans in a folded tortilla. "We moved some cattle up to the Sycamore to water. They're there now. We gotta move them back to the southeast, or they'll just stay there. Those banditos been roaming that creek and making off with cattle, cutting through the V-Bar-M to the northwest."

"Word is a lotta ranches been losing head, hard winter."

"You heard right, Bud. We lost some, not only to banditos, but to the cold. We're keeping them in three herds and head them to behind sheltering ridges. You know how cattle are, not always so dumb. They head themselves there now." He was pulling his boot back on. "Damn corns. Clay had the fore-sense to stock up on hay and cow cake too."

Lee called a fella over with his left arm all taped and splinted with two boards. "Stone Eskin," the gangly punch mumbled.

"Tell Bud why you're nicknamed Stone." He was laughing.

"My given name's Graves."

"Graves Stone," cackled Lee. "Get it? Old Stone had a pony roll on him, so he's doing what he can here. Lucky he ain't got one of them Graves stones planted over his head." Lee rose to his feet with a groan. "He'll get you anything you're needing."

Every hand scraped his leftovers into the squirrel can, washed his dishes in a tub, and headed to the remuda corral.

"You can get settled in today," said Lee. "How about in the morning you be ready for a couple or three days out? I'll turn you over to Gent Podger, and he'll get you started monitoring."

"Sounds good, Lee."

The show at the corral was only starting. It was a Mex-style corral—a *potrero*, round in shape, pairs of cedar posts with cross-laid mesquite limbs stacked solid between them. The old limbs at the bottom rot sooner or later and as the fence shrinks in height, fresh limbs are stacked on top. A fence like that'll last forever.

The hands were in the big corral with the remuda. They were pointing and shouting as they roped their afternoon horses from the herd of spares. Some were getting in each other's way with all the lassoing going on. The boys worked in pairs after catching a horse. One would ear the horse to the ground and hold him there while the other saddled him, sat the saddle, nodded, and came up off the ground with the horse pitching. One humped up his back and started topping off something fierce, and everyone was a whooping and yelling. The Mex kids were on the mesquite fence yelling too. Everyone finally got their favorites saddled and settled down.

After the crew dashed off, I wandered around seeing the place's layout. The bunkhouse was a big adobe room with doors front and back and windows on both sides—with glass even. There were bunks with warbags under them or hanging on pegs and a coal stove, a table and not enough chairs. A couple of bedrolls were spread on the plank floor. There's always some hands preferring the floor. There weren't any spare bunks.

The washstand out back had a tin roof over it, tin sides on the north and west, wash pans, big round clay water pots, and mirrors. Nearby was a respec'ably clean two-hole shitter. I knew about cleaning shitters. When I was a young'un, one hog-scorching July, mama nailed me into one for two blessed days for doing a poor job cleaning it.

I could tell the Dew was bringing on extra hands, because there was a tent out back with four cots. Extra quilts were piled on those. I bet those ol' boys cold-footed it into the bunkhouse for the stove first thing.

The hay barn was open-front and beside it, a shed full of feedbags, salt blocks, cottonseed cake, and pails. I was thinking I could bed down there on some hay since there was no spare bunks. I'd have to ask the majordomo. The tack room was clean and organized, and there was a workshop next to it with a blacksmith set-up. The place had all the fixings of a good ranch.

Behind the big house was another long adobe house with six doors for the house-Mexes, probably Lee too. There were courtyard walls on both sides running from the big house to the back house with a gate in each. Some Mex kids were playing with wooden toy animals.

A Mex fella came past leading a bull. It was huge shiny black critter. The kids all ran over to pat its slab sides. It was as gentle as a milk cow.

Stone said it was Mr. DeWitt's prize bull, Quicksilver. He'd bought in St. Louis the past spring. It had cost a pretty penny, not only for the bull, but to railroad it to Del Rio. "He's got big plans for improvin' the stock."

Everything I'd seen and heard told me this was a serious ranch.

Well, I decided, I couldn't put it off, so I went to ask Gabi about bunking in the feed shed.

Chapter Twenty

I knocked on the kitchen door on a room sticking out the back of the big house. Marta was at the door smiling big and wearing a white shirt with the sleeves rolled up and drying her hands on a checkered apron. She waved me in, gripped my arm, and led me to the dining room door. The kitchen floor was ox blood-coated dirt, linseed-shiny and smooth. The rest of the house had varnished board floors.

Gabi came over with a smile. "Can I help you, Bud?"

"Ma'am, I don't mean to bother you none, but you know, Marta ain't my woman or nothing, but I was wondering where she might be staying."

She looked surprised. "I've been talking to Marta, asking questions. You two stay together?" She wasn't shy about asking it.

"Sorta, ma'am. She gets cold being a little thing. It's best if she stays with her own kind."

Gabi gave a little frown. Don't know why. I was just saying.

"Maybe I can stay in the feed shed for now, seeing there ain't no extra bunks."

"You can sleep there, but it has the scampering mices to keep you awake."

"I'll be fine, ma'am."

"Marta can stay with Carmela and Inés, the cooks."

"That'll be good, ma'am. I don't wanna be no trouble."

"Marta will be sad. I think she wants to stay with you."

I shook my head. "I don't think that'll be good for either of us."

She nodded, leaning against the door frame. "I will have Roberto make two more cots."

"I'm much obliged, ma'am. Don't mean to put no one to trouble. The hay's fine to sleep on."

"Roberto needs something to do," she said. "I will tell Marta." She frowned again.

I felt easier now. "I'm supposed to be a going down to the river in the morn for three days to guard. I guess I need to get some grub from you."

"Inés will get you food."

Inés wasn't much older than Marta. She was a pretty girl, not beautiful pretty, but pretty because she was always smiling; her eyes smiled too. It looked like her and Marta was buddying up. That was good. The two of them loaded me up with airtights of beans, peas, and peaches; jerked beef and venison, some bacon in wax paper, and hard biscuits and tortillas. Gabi said the monitors could ride to the house for one meal a day, whichever one we wanted.

— •●• —

After pitchforking sweet-smelling alfalfa hay into a corner of the feed shed, I set my bedroll and gear there. Roberto, who was forever humming, was banging and sawing away in the workshop. He said the cots would be finished tomorrow.

The crew rode in at dusk and weren't so much for putting on a show. They looked tuckered out. Lee and his number two, Lew Cassels, gave me a rundown on the crew. Lee had a good handle on things, and I could tell by the way the boys talked to him that he was respected and a straight dealer.

We had us a treat for supper—Marta's frijole beans. The boys couldn't stop praising them beans. "I ain't never had no frijole beans like 'em," announced Musty Musson. He was picking through them naming off what he found. "Tomater, onion, what's this, green pepper? All this ham hock and bacon, and some green stuff."

"That's jalapeño, Musty, ya idgit. Ya sounds like a damn Yankee."

Lew declared, "Its pepper hot and sweet at the same time."

I think Marta poured in a dollop of lick.

What with Carmela's biscuits and dried apricots and pears boiled syrupy, the crew was well satisfied.

Lee said, "I didn't ever think I'd see the day the hands didn't miss fried beefsteak for supper."

"Ya got yourself a hell of a cookin' woman, Bud," announced a fella whose name I ain't learned yet.

"She ain't my woman, but she can do a righteous job on frijole beans."

No one disputed either of what I said.

The boys had a fire going outside the bunkhouse, and they sat on buckets, nail kegs, and dry-goods crates, speaking of the day and asking about myself. They liked the injun shootout and road agent stories, especially about Marta touching off the scattergun to scare the piss out of the supposed desperado. Nobody said a word about Marta being my woman. I was thinking Gabi had said something to them. There's always some busybody what gotta speak his mind.

I didn't like much talking about myself. If it started sounding like you were blowing about yourself, you could lose your place at the fire.

Dodger Lampe, I found his given name was Tom, was telling stories. "I worked at this spread near Lampasas and that ol' man had some new-fangled modern ideers. Sometimes they even worked out. One of his ideers were to drive 'bout a thousand head of turtle up to K-City."

"Turtles, ya say?" asked Rick "Snorter" Cadwell, a big, slow-moving, but powerful East Texan.

"I ain't shittin' ya. Turtles. Said 'em damn Yankees likes 'em in a delicacy soup."

"Damn Yankees et some outlandish vittles. I heard tell they even et oysters," said Stone Eskin.

"What's oysters?" asked Jerry Twining.

"It's something lives in the water inside a seashell. Supposed to be nasty," declared Stone.

"Stick 'em oysters up your ass," grumbled Dodger. "Let me finish my story."

"Well, go on then and stop talking about what them damn Yankees eat," shouted Lee.

Dodger threw a cow chip at Lee. "Well then, y'all don't interrupt me no more." He took a deep breath. "Slowest damn drive I ever been on. We'd play three, four hands of stud, break a couple of mustangs and shoe 'em, and then catch up with the herd." He chunked a stick on the fire, building suspense. "One night, after we had the herd all settled in, the ol' man tolt us to go and turn all 'em turtles over on their backs."

"What in hellfire fer?"

"I tolt y'all, don't interrupt me. I'm losin' my place here." After a long pause, "Well, I ask him jus' that, why for we turnin' these turtles on their topsides? We goin' to havta do it all over in the mornin'.

"That ol' man looked at me like I'd plum lost my brains. 'Can't ya see a storm's a comin'. Y'all ever see a herd like this stampede?'"

"That ol' Dodger, he tells tales as tall as a southbound goose," Stone howled.

The fire died to coals, and we could see our breaths in the cold air. The hands wandered off. I was getting up to head for the shed when Marta walked up. She stood there glaring at me, her arms crossed. All I could say was, "*Lo siento.*" Sorry.

She turned and walked through the courtyard gate to the cook's house.

Chapter Twenty-One

Things never seem to go my way sometimes. When I woke up Marta was bundled beside me in the hay. Like a damn pup that won't go away even when you chuck rocks. Yeah, I hung on to a pup like that once.

She crawled out of her covers when I was pulling on my boots. She stood glaring at me like the night before, making me feel low. Snorting she headed for the kitchen and her chores. There are some people that are going to have their way no matter what.

Dodger said there was a lot of talk among the crew about her stomping out of my shed that morning. No one else said anything.

Lee and I rode northwest after a big breakfast. We were going to Sycamore Creek and follow it to the Rio Grande. The Sycamore was the northwest boundary of the Dew. The Vermejo-Maxwell Ranch, or V-Bar-M, was on the other side of the creek.

"The banditos like to come up-creek from the Rio, until we started to monitor it," Lee said.

"They still try and run up the creek?"

"Nope. They run through the V-Bar, crossing the creek at different places."

"What's the V-Bar crowd say about it?"

"Not much." Lee was squinting in that direction with a

frown. "They ain't much help. I think old man Maxwell's got an arrangement with them."

"Any particular place they cross the creek?"

"There's over a half-dozen crossing places, and we share nine mile of creek with the V-Bar." He spit into the mud. "That old man's a sumbitch. I don't trust him at all."

"How's Mr. DeWitt deal with him, if you don't mind my asking?"

"Clay tries to keep things cordial. We don't want no troubles with Maxwell. But he knows that sumbitch can't be trusted."

The Sycamore made a few big loops as it ran toward the Rio Grande. It was down in a gorge twenty to forty feet deep, higher on the V-Bar-M side than ours. The creek made a big loop to the north starting about two miles from the Rio, and the Rio itself made a big loop to the west, bending into Mexico. They called it the Sheep's Head owning to its shape.

"You'll be spending a lot of time hereabouts, Bud."

Even being winter, it was pretty country. What would be the top of the Sheep's Head was a big grove of blackjack oak, green year-round, like the wooly head of a sheep. The sheep's snout was separated from the face by a gentle twenty-foot bluff. The lower sandy ground beyond that bluff, in the Rio's loop curving into Mexico, was covered by carrizo cane.

The higher ground on the V-Bar-M side was bothering me. Anybody could come up unseen. If they were quiet, they could be on top of any monitor on the low side before he knew they were there.

As we followed the Sycamore, Lee showed me the crossing places. "They come down into the creek, and then follow it one way or the other, to come up someplace else."

He looked around with the eyes of a hawk, able to see anything out of the ordinary. I wanted to learn this place that well.

"I'm hoping to scare up Gent Podger. That polecat's most likely watching us right now." He chuckled.

"What do the rustlers usually do?"

"Them Mexes'll grab three or six head, or whatever they can get, and run them to the Rio. "Hell"—with a disgusted look—"they'll run them down the bluff and through the cane breaks on the flats below." His expression grew sour. "They don't give a good damn if they break the cattle's legs. They grab what they can and hightail it outta here."

"They make off with a lot? I was gonna work for an ol' boy down toward Laredo. He couldn't take me on because he'd lost so many head to Mex rustlers."

"It's only worrisome so far," Lee muttered, sweeping the tree line. "But the way they're picking away it'll start us hurting before long...bastards." We rode toward the woods. "We don't chase 'cross the Rio after them, because they have bushwhackers laying in wait. Last month we had a fella shot in the leg and his horse killed trying to do that. This is getting back like the old days," said Lee.

"How so?"

"J. King Fisher," he said in a less than amiable tone. "Ever hear of him?"

"Nope."

"King Fisher had a spread down near Eagle Pass, right on the Rio Grande too. Banditos were always coming across raping, looting, and rustling. Brigandage was rampant. King dressed real flamboyant, bright-colored shirts, sashes, carried a pair of nickel-plated pistols with ivory grips. His gang of vigilantes would chase after raiders, and they started doing their own raiding and rustling."

"So he was just like the Mexes."

"Right. He wasn't the only one. Other ranchers were doing the same thing. Had shootouts all the time with the Mexes and each other, whenever the urge struck them. There was a regular war going on. Texican or Mex, they were just a bunch a gangs. One time Fisher's gang argued about sharing the loot and he ended up shooting three of his own men."

We reached the Eagle Pass-Del Rio Road slashing through the ranch. "Clay's been wanting to fence both sides of the road. Passers-by sometimes ride off with a cow. Guess we'll put that up someday, when he gets the money."

Lee hooked a leg around his saddle horn and took out his makings. "Anyway, old King was no better than them Mex desperados. Worse, some said. Least he didn't raid other ranches on this side. There's were some done that." He handed me a rolled one and stated on his own. "It only got worse with reprisals. King was so brazen he thought he owned the county. He even set a sign that said, 'This is King Fisher's road. Take the other one.'

"Finally the Rangers had enough. You know how the Rangers

are. When enough's enough, they end it, usually shooting someone. Damn ranchers were causing more problems than the Mexes. The Mexes would slack off, but the ranchers kept going at them, and the reprisals would all start over."

I lit up Lee's cig, then mine. "Reprisals?"

"Getting back at you. Old Lender McNelly, heading the Ranger's Special Force, he was chasing the Mex banditos across the border. Never mind the governor telling him to stop. That was Captain McNelly, did what needed doing and to hell with the politicking niceties. One night he raided Fisher's ranch and arrested that scoundrel." With his face smiling, Lee said, "They came to a gentleman's agreement, not that I'd of called either of them gentlemen, that Fisher would retire from his lawless career."

"Did he?"

"Oh, yeah. In fact, he become the county sheriff up in Uvalde for a time."

"Where's he now?"

"He cashed out in a gunfight in the Turner Hall Opera House at San Antone two year ago." Lee yawned. "Hell, I wish we had the likes of Lender McNelly around here now. That was a man who'd charge hell with a bucket of water. He died of consumption some time back."

"Did you know him? McNelly?"

"Oh yeah. My cousin Enoch was one of his Rangers. Enoch Garret would be good to have here too, excepting he got shot in a Mex whorehouse, sixty-four years old." He laughed. "I should hope to go that way."

"I've heard that name. Something about a wolf?"

"Yeah, Enoch caught an ol' boy who'd been dry-gulching farmers. Tied him up to a tree and tied two wolf pups he'd found to him. The mama wolf wasn't too happy when she showed up."

Thinking about that made me shiver. "She kill him?"

"Nope, but he changed his ways. I guess because you can't hold a gun proper when you don't have all your fingers."

Not far from the road saw sometime brown and white in the mesquite. We rode over to find a fresh dead cow missing a hind-quarter.

Chapter Twenty-Two

"What a waste," I said looking at the dead three-legged cow.

"Been happening a lot of late. Hungry drifters shooting themselves a bigger than usual antelope, so to speak. We'll send a wagon out for it. We'll be eating on it for a few days." He stopped and said, "Take a look around, see what you think."

I circled the carcass. Lee hung back watching.

"There were two of them." Studying the prints around the cow, I saw where they mounted horses and headed toward the Rio. "Looks like they're going across the river, but they ain't Mexes."

"How come you say that?" I had Lee's interest.

"Mex boots have lower heels. That's easy to see in this mud, and their toes are rounder."

"Fine, you impressed me. Let's see where they crossed."

I knew he was curious about what else I could see on the ground.

We were almost three miles from the road and nearing the low bluff that dropped down to the river's loop, the sheep's snout. I smelled cooking beefsteak and wood smoke.

"Them boys must be hungry, but smart enough to back away from the road," said Lee.

"What you wanna do about it?"

"Put the fear of God in them." Nodding to our right toward the bluff head, "There's Gent."

I saw a rider looking at us and pointing with his rifle back down the bluff.

"We'll move in closer and go in on foot," said Lee, nudging his horse forward.

Gent met us in the brush at the bluff head. He nodded to me. That was all the introduction we had. He was concentrating on the job at hand.

At the bottom of the bluff were two punches roasting a haunch of beef over a fire. Their horses were hobbled nearby. I kind of felt sorry for them, two out of work and hungry cowboys. Leaving our horses, we worked our way down the gentle slope through the mesquite.

Thirty feet from them Lee said, "You boys got enough dinner for everybody?"

That kicked quite a reaction. They were both scrambling for guns, but when they saw three rifles leveled at them, they only reached for the sky. I didn't see any rifles, just their pistols.

"What in tarnation you boys up to?" shouted Lee. He lowered his carbine, Gent and I didn't. Lee walked toward them, took a knee. "Have a sit, boys, and lose them hoglegs."

The two of us moved around to the sides.

"How about you two throw a couple of ropes over a stout limb on that oak over yonder?"

I looked at Gent. He said, "Sure, boss."

Gent fetched the horses, and I stayed with Lee, but he was kneeling and keeping his carbine on them and I joined Gent when he came down.

"He serious about stringing them up?"

I musta had a silly look, for he laughed. "Nah, he's scarin' the horse piss outta 'em." Offering his hand, "Gent Ponder."

"Bud Eugen." I told him of my hiring as we threw over our lariats.

Gent told me of events along the Sycamore and about the bandits. The Mexes sounded better organized than I'd expected. We watched Lee making a lot of arm gestures and the two punches nodding their heads.

"Lee can pitch such a fit that he'll make a fistfight look like a prayer meetin'."

"What you think he's telling them?" I asked.

"Oh, how the hen laid the cackle-berry and that nothing's free 'cepting your mama's tit."

I mulled that over. My mama probably made me pay.

Lee waved us over. "This is Pete Weyland and Earnest Sessuns. I hired them, and they invited us to share their chuck."

I didn't know what to say. Gent said, "I guess we don't need 'em strings, then."

Lee and Gent rode the new hires in, leaving me to monitor. I didn't like the looks of Weyland. He seemed a hard character, eyes jerking about all the time and never looking you in the eye. Sessuns seemed fine, but was kind of unsure of himself, saying little. Both them been out of work for some time, broke as a piecrust. Sessuns' boot soles were so thin worn he'd be able to feel if a silver dime was heads or tails. They said they'd sold their carbines. They'd hooked up in Eagle Pass, so hadn't known each other long.

Gent came back out before sunset with a wagon, and we helped Roberto load up the cow. Gent filled me in more on what was going on. I moseyed around getting familiar with the Sheep's Head. I picked a place to roll out my bedroll near the first crossing over the Sycamore.

Gent had brought out some cold fried beefsteaks, but we fixed that with a little fire. He was going to stakeout another crossing.

That's some little gal you got there," he commented.

"She ain't my woman."

"Right. I heared y'all shack-up in the feed shed." He was smiling.

"It ain't like that." I was trying to keep from becoming annoyed.

"Right." He was still smiling and wisely dropped the subject.

We talked a spell. I was surprised to learn he'd been a deputy marshal in both Gonzales and Seguin.

"Why'd you quit law-manning?"

"Too many troublemakers. It's quieter out here, and the fellas ya work with are real...mostly," he added.

"Yeah, so here you are waiting to dry-gulch banditos."

He chuckled. "Yep, don't that beat all? At least I ain't gotta watch my own back like in a saloon."

Chapter Twenty-Three

I spent four days out on the Sheep's Head. I had to keep reminding myself that anything could happen at any time. The peaceful countryside was misleading.

On my second day out I was trotting along a mesquite line when I got a chilly feeling up my back. I was being followed. I edged into the brush where it was thinner, a natural drift for a wandering monitor. But I fish-hooked back, and bending low under the limbs, I worked my way back to my trail as quiet as a deer. The limbs blocked my view, so I dismounted and hung Cracker's reins over a limb. I left my rifle as the brush was thick. I worked my way to my backtrail. I'd take a couple of steps and listen. Every few steps I'd take a knee and scan beneath the brush, and listen. I finally heard it, the rustle of a horse passing slowly through brush. I unshucked my revolver, but didn't cock it for fear of being heard. A flash of white caught my eye and I saw the horse's legs, one with a white sock. Hunching down further I could see knee-high leather leggings, a vaquero's right leg.

The 'quero nudged his horse forward a few steps, and I used the slight noise as cover to move myself. He stopped. Must be listening for me. We were both still for a long spell. I was maybe twenty feet from him. His horse moved its feet, impatient, then nervously nickered ever so quietly. The 'quero whispered and lightly patted its neck. Cracker heard it and moved. The 'quero's right leg disappeared as he silently slid off his horse. I could barely make him out crouching and looking for movement in the direction of Cracker.

He made the mistake of not looking behind himself. That reminded me to check around myself. All was clear. He moved to his right, deeper into the mesquite toward Cracker, maybe forty feet away, but unseen.

I duck-walked beneath the mesquite and got behind his horse, unnoticed.

The horses nickered quietly at one another, like they knew something furtive was going on. The 'quero edged forward, ducking his head lower looking under the brush.

I holstered my revolver, run to his horse, and with my hands hitting its rump, vaulted into the saddle. The horse took a leap forward, and I drew my revolver. "Stand and show your hands!"

The *hombre*, with a look of grand surprise, left his revolver on the ground and rose with his arms spread.

Cocking my revolver, "What you doing here sneaking around."

He sorta smiled. "You Bud?" he asked just like I'd met him walking on the street. "Gent told me to be on lookout for you."

"And you're?"

"Héctor Vega."

I dismounted and called Cracker, who came trotting over.

"They call me Flaco. That mean Skinny." He was well set up, though, and had a couple or three years on me. Had heavy hair hanging down to his shoulders.

He looked skinny, in a hard, lean sort of way. He had a neatly trimmed mustache and goatee. He spoke good American, almost sounded like a Texican.

"Can I pick up my pistol? You got the drop on me good." He was smiling, but it looked to be painful.

I nodded, but didn't holster mine until he had his own tucked in.

I was going to have to work with him, so I said, "Sorry about sneaking up on you, but I'm only learning the place. Don't know who's who."

"That is good." Not that he really meant it. "You can no be too careful."

We shook hands regarding each other and mounted our rightful horses.

When I asked where he hailed from he said, "I do not know

if I was borned in Del Rio or Las Vacas on other side. They all argue about it in the family."

I thought that was funny. I might not be sure who my daddy was, but at least I know what country I was borned in.

"What brings you to monitoring?" I was curious on what cut him out special for the job.

He shook his head with a crooked grin. "I was bandito."

I guess I looked surprised for he was really laughing. "You're shitting me."

"I tell you true, for more than a year, *amigo*. Then the *Rurales* catch me."

"No kidding."

"You know they have the *ley fuga*."

"What's that?"

"*Ley fuga*, the Law of Flight. Caught bandito is give two choices, die between an adobe wall and a row of carbines, or he can go to run for it. If he dodges the bullets, he is let free. Most run, would not you? The *Rurales* claim shot trying to escape. That way, *Rurales* no have to bother transporting prisoners, no annoying trial, no monies to feed in the jail.

"You ran for it?"

"No, no. I thought I have to, but they tell me I must join them."

"Don't that beat all. Why?"

"As I stand before God, I do not know. Except maybe they need more of the men."

"I be damned."

"Probably. Some other *Rurales* were banditos too. I was in the *Rurales* almost two year."

"They let you quit?" I was trying to figure out how I'd gotten the drop on a *Rurale*. Hell, *Los Cuerpos Rurales* was almost like Texas Rangers.

"Oh, no. They never do that. I just leave one day. Ride to Del Rio." He pulled his coat open. "I still wear this." He was showing a red necktie.

"Well, I be dipped in horseshit."

He pulled out his revolver. It was a .44-30 Merwin Hulbert, issued to the *Rurales*. "We carry three of these. I sell other two."

"I ain't never seen one."

"The Merwin, it is good. It load *mucho* fast."

"Can you even get cartridges for it? That's only used by the Mexes, right."

"I get in Del Rio, but they cost too much."

He showed me a short-barrel .45 Smith & Wesson Schofield in a saddle holster hidden under a cowhide flap.

Flaco had a good eye for the land. We spent the day exploring the crossings on the Sycamore, even riding on the V-Bar-M side.

Before nightfall, we were down on the cane flats on the Rio Grande, the snout of the Sheep's Head. It wasn't long before a couple of 'queros rode out of the mesquite. The river's only about a hundred yards across. It wasn't too cold that day and instead of being wrapped in *serapes*, they wore their short tight jackets, thick brown trousers laced up the sides with high leather leggings, and big tan sombreros.

Them and Flaco were shouting back and forth, I guess talking about the weather. Then I heard my name.

"I introduce you," he said.

"Oh, good."

"They good. I know these *vatos*. They from *Rancho Mariposa*." Looking at my expression, he said, "They have troubles from banditos too. We tell each other what we know."

"What's Mary-posa mean?"

"Butterfly."

Who'd name a ranch after a butterfly? Mexes, I don't know about them sometimes.

They *buenas nochaed* each other, and Flaco and me rode back to the bluff to part and set our own camp sites.

"*Amigo*," he said quietly.

"Yep?"

"You know you no have to say anything about what happened today to Lee or any of the crew." He was gritting his teeth like he could bite through a rifle barrel.

I winked. "I don't know what you're talking about, partner."

The third day out I was riding along Quicksand Creek—that's what they call it, but no one knew of any quicksand—near where it ran into the Sycamore. I saw a rider some distance away on the other side of the Quicksand. I watched and realized it was Marta on Rojizo wearing her coat and hat. Marta had split her black wool dress up the front and back and sewed them together making it easier to sit a saddle. Presently, she dismounted, un-holstered her shotgun, and started walking through the low brush. I watched her for a spell, bagging half-a-dozen jackass rabbits and wasting only one shot. She'd pop a rabbit and run through the mesquites to fetch it. I could see I was going to have to buy some more birdshot when I got into Del Rio. Maybe Clay would stake me since she was hunting to feed the ranch. I liked to watch her, frisky as a filly on a spring day.

Mounting Rojizo, she surprised me by waving and lit out at a gallop up my ridge. She made a slow circle around me and held up a rabbit, nodding. Looks like we'd made up. At least, she wasn't glaring at me like that morning in the feed shed.

I collected sticks and cow paddies as Marta stripped off the rabbit skin and gutted it. Cutting a can of pork and beans open, I set it on the fire. She roasted the rabbit on a spit. Tearing off shreds of meat, we wrapped them in tortillas, ate the beans too with tortillas. That simplest of meals was tops.

Marta sat on a blanket and leaned against me. We put an arm around each other. The sun set in Mexico with pinks and blues and colors I couldn't name. After a spell, she turned around on her knees and looked into my eyes for the longest time. It made me feel queasy and warm and good about things.

She rode off to the ranch house to fix their supper.

It was a long four days and three nights. Lonely too, except when I went in for a meal. Marta ran out and give me a big ol' hug and a sweet smile. Kinda embarrassed me around the crew. The meal she'd always serve me herself, sometimes sneaking me a glass of buttermilk. The way she let me know she missed me was she'd wrap her arms around herself and give a shiver like she was cold.

She showed me the new-made cots in the feed shed. They were real nice with laced ropes to hold the straw-filled tick mattresses. There were even buckwheat husk-filled pillows. They were as close together as a cow and its newborn. That's the way it's going to be I suppose.

My first night back in I saw Marta carrying an oil lamp into the feed shed.

She was sitting on her cot kind of humming. I plopped on mine, and she turned and tugged my boots off. In my long johns I crawled under my blankets and quilts. Marta joined me and was lying facing me, her white teeth flashing a smile. She ain't never done that, laying facing me. Wrapping her arms around me, she gave me a big ol' hug and made this funny contented sound in her throat before turning over. She must be happy about something. Dang, I'd rather her be crying, because I didn't know what to do with her being so happy either.

— •●• —

Marta had made a good friend with Inés. They'd be washing clothes and splashing suds on one another and laughing like kids. Marta was strong willed, got her way when she set her mind to it, but she was still a kid.

I admitted missing that girl on those nights out, but I liked being out there too. No matter if it was cold and wet most of the time. Some days were warmer, nice days with cool evenings. I could sit in the saddle or on my bedroll and listen to the wind and the voices of the coyotes, all free of people bothering me. There were amazing sunrises and sunsets and that big ol' moon to watch. I'd see Marta's dark eyes in my head, always watching me. I was liking those eyes a lot.

Sometimes I'd see 'queros on the other side and they'd wave. I'd meet up with Gent or Flaco, and they were good company.

I'd get a night in at the ranch house once a week. One day when I came in Marta was in a foul mood. Wouldn't even look at me. That night she didn't come in the feed shed and her blankets were gone. I went to Gabi's room.

"I been looking for Marta, ma'am."

"Bud, she is staying with Carmela tonight," she said sadly.

That threw me. "What did I do?"

She gave me a tight smile. "Is not you. It is her time of the month."

I'd heard rumors of this sort of thing, never thought about it. Didn't never think Marta would do mysterious things.

"She'll be fine next time you come in."

"Nothing I did, ma'am?"

She laughed. "No, Bud."

Things changed one night, but I don't know how. Marta came in our room and turned the oil lamp low. With her back to me, she doffed her shirt and skirt down to her long johns. Turning, looking at me curious like, she dropped the scarf covering her hair. It fell in thick waves down to her behind. All that hair gave her a wild look. It was in her eyes too. It was like she'd showed me something inside her, something more than only letting her hair fall. She'd been shy to show her hair before. It was exciting for me, but she was just so innocent about it.

It reminded me of about the only friend I'd had as a kid, Billy Stummer, and reminded me of his kid sister. Marta reminded me of her, I couldn't even remember her name, Violet, Veronica, or something. She was familiar, a friend, someone who was always around, sometimes glad for it, sometimes an annoyance. Marta and I were just here, together. I didn't know what to make of it, other than having a comfortable feeling. That made me uncomfortable.

GORDON L. ROTTMAN

Chapter Twenty-Four

One of those days I was out, Mr. DeWitt returned from Eagle Pass. I came in that night. Most of the crew was sitting around a fire on a chilly evening telling tall tales and speaking of the day.

Mr. DeWitt came out to say howdy. He was accompanied by his wife, Iris, and their two girls. Mrs. DeWitt was a pretty woman, blond hair, green eyes. She was real friendly with the boys, greeting them all. The girls were Agnes and Doris, as blonde and pretty as their ma. Dodger Lampe said they were fourteen and sixteen. Agnes seemed a little shy, but Doris was talking to some of the boys about horses. "Good rider, that girl," said Musty from his log by the fire.

Mr. DeWitt came over and welcomed me to the Dew reminding me to, "Call me Clay. Mrs. Moran asked me to tell you and Marta hello. How's it going out there, Bud?"

"It's good, sir. I like Gent and Flaco, good men." I had to add, "I can't believe Flaco was a bandito and then a *Rurale*, and changed his ways.

Clay laughed. "Well, I don't know if he exactly gave up his bandito ways because of the *Rurales*, Bud. You look under the barrel of that short-barrel Schofield he carries; it says Wells Fargo and Company, Express. I don't think he found it or bought it."

Clay soon herded his family inside after giving their goodnights.

Dodger Lampe was sitting nearby. I was liking Dodger. He'd

been punching all his life. Started off as a wrangler like most young cowboys, not the favorite-most job.

"Problem were, I was jus' sooo damn good they kept me at wranglin' forever and a day," Dodger declared. "Thought I were gonna go past my prime chasin' after that remuda," he muttered while wittling himself a toothpick. "Finally tolt 'em I were goin' to pick a string of horses and run away to another ranch."

"What'd they say to that?"

"Said I couldn't do it 'cause that'd be horse-stealing, and without a wrangler to handle the remuda, they'd not be able to chase me." He shook his head, "Shit, with reasonin' like that I couldn't leave."

"Where was that?"

"Over at a little spread near Indianola on Matagorda Bay." Sticking the finished toothpick between his teeth, "I finally had it with wranglin', so one night I drove off the remuda and hid them on the other side of Powderhorn Lake."

"They didn't fire you?"

"How do ya think I come to be here?" He grinned. "I wonder how 'em folks fared over there. Indianola got blowed away in that hurricane a few months ago, for the second time."

Marta had come out and huddled up beside me in her serape. She was all comfortable after rolling us smokes. It was kind of embarrassing for me with all the boys there and me the only one with a woman, even if she weren't my woman, exactly.

It didn't seem anyone took any particular notice except for Pete Weyland, the cow-killer. He sat across the fire glaring at us for a spell. Earnest Sessuns said Weyland had been complaining about only getting half pay for the first month owning to the murder of that cow. Sessuns said that was pretty ungracious considering the alternative, and the month had been partly run through anyways. Sessuns was no longer partnered up with Weyland, him being too quarrelsome. "Damn fool'll stand downhill and piss uphill."

"And forget to wipe the mud offa his boots goin' in the bunkhouse," added Musty.

Dodger decided to poke a little fun at Weyland. "I were over at Refugio when this snake-oil peddler come through. He had this bottled wonder ar-tic-u-lation elixir that were to make animals talk. That flannel-mouth claimed ya could converse wit your livestock to find what were ailing them, what they liked to eat, and so on."

"Say it ain't so," said one of the boys. "I ain't never heard of nothin' like that."

"It's true," declared Dodger. "Ask ol' Weyland here. He were there runnin' a mob of cows through town."

Everyone turned to look at Weyland for confirmation, but he stared back like a double-blank domino.

"That peddler were harpin' 'bout his wondrous elixir sayin' horses have a better vocabulary than cows 'cause they's smarter."

Everyone nodded in agreement.

"Ol' Weyland was sittin' his horse, the same one he's still a ridin', and said all nervous like, 'See that brown heifer on the end? Don't believe a word she says, she's a liar!'"

Everyone busted up, except Weyland, who stammered, "That's a lie, I ain't never been to Refugio!" He sat there fuming.

The party was breaking up, and Marta lit her oil lamp with a stick from the burned down fire. Weyland walked up and glancing at the girl, "So seein' you're always sayin' she ain't your woman, then I guess the dummy's free for someone to cut-out." He had a nasty look in his eyes, made all the more so by the fire's glint.

Calling her dummy and cutting her out, that brought up my hackles real quick, but I paused before saying anything. I was in a sudden quandary. I was the one always saying she weren't my woman, but then when that polecat said she was free for the taking. He was right in a way. I had no real claim on her. Or did I? Anyways, I didn't think she was in any mood to be cut-out by some horny punch. Did I have a say? It came to me that I'd made myself responsible for her. Mrs. Moran had said I was her protector. Maybe she was my woman, even if we hadn't done nothing. That all was confusing and right then I didn't have time to think on it.

Raising to my feet, "You'll not be layin' a finger on that girl, Weyland. Don't even think about it."

"Who are ya to tell anybody anything? Ya ain't even a workin' punch, only ridin' 'round out there on a picnic while the rest of us cowboys do the real work." I was guessing he was still sore over my hand in catching him butchering that cow.

"Back off, Weyland," said Sessuns.

"Ya shut the hell up!" Weyland shouted.

Several of the other boys were muttering for him to settle

down. I glanced over at Marta. She knew something bad was brewing. My turning away was a mistake. Weyland grabbed a burning stob and underhanded it at me. I dodged, stepped back, and tripped over an evaporated milk crate to land on my ass.

Weyland came in low, slamming into me as I rose. We both went down, but I half rolled to the left and swung my elbow into his jaw. That dazed him enough for me to get to my feet. Everyone was shouting and yelling. As he came up, I kicked him in the face, staggering him to the left. He spit out a tooth, grabbed a burning log, and came at me. I dodged to the right, tripped him, and kicked him in the ribs. He rolled, letting go the log, and bounced to his feet before I could close in for another kick. I kicked anyways and missed. He grabbed my boot and shoved me backward. I went on my back, knocking the wind from me. He kicked my thigh, but his lunge forward made him lose his balance and go to his knees.

As I pushed myself off the ground with both arms, he swung a punch into the left side of my face and another into the right. That just about knocked me out, but I kicked out before he could swing again. I crab-crawled back and made it to my feet the same time he did and just in time for me to catch punch in the nose. Dang, that hurt! I blocked his follow-on and stepped back. I swung with my right with all I had, catching him in the side of the head. That hurt too. He was too hardheaded for it to do any harm. He kicked at me and danced right. I threw another right, and he blocked with an arm.

I swung again, but he ducked, grabbing for the still burning log. I dove at him while he was crouching and off balance. Catching him in the waist and my shoulder slamming into his belly, he hit the ground with a loud *woof*, and the log flew out of his hands. I pushed myself back and rose as he kicked weakly.

Both of us were gasping. The boys were yelling, and I heard someone shouting, "Enough of that!" My head was spinning. Weyland was on his feet, wavering, but he was lifting that damn burning log.

There was an orange flash and a shower of sparks, and Weyland hit the ground, his back ablaze with flames. I was pulling my jacket off, and others were already beating on him with coats and jackets, sparks leaping all over and Weyland screaming.

"Boys, that's enough!" Lee bellowed. "Keep this up and one of y'all'll get hurt."

I dropped to my knees feeling like I was going to pass out. Weyland was facedown in the dirt, his jacket smoldering with little sparks floating around. I looked up, and Marta was standing behind him, her chest heaving hard with a wild look in her fire-lit eyes.

"Shit fire, Bud!" brawled Stone. "What the hellfire ya bring amongst us? She's fightin' like a Kilkenny wildcat."

"She threw that oil lamp right into his back," said Jerry Twining. "At least ya two was fightin' a fair dust up 'fore she done that."

Lee was plainly pissed. "Weyland, get your ass in your tent, and you'd better be in your saddle in the morning."

"I ain't started nothin'..." he slurred.

Marta flipped her cig butt at him.

"My ass!" shouted Lee. "I saw the whole damn thing. You pull something like that again it's *adiós* for you. If someone gives you an ass whooping for it, I'll just stand and watch."

Weyland was up and pulling off his jacket. "Lookie what she done my jacket." Glaring at me, he shouted, "Ya owe me for it. She's your woman!"

"Shut up, Weyland," ordered Lee, "You're lucky it weren't you ugly face what got lit up."

"That Mex bitch ain't nothin' but trouble," complained Weyland.

I almost agreed with him on that, the trouble part, but... "Don't be calling her no..."

"No women or girls around here are going to be called that, Weyland," said Lee real low. "And none of them's getting cut-out either. And don't ever call her a dummy again. She's a damn sight smarter than you." He paused. "You'll get your ass torn up by that wildcat." Sweeping his eyes over us both. "No hard feeling," sweeping his eyes over us both.

Weyland stomped off, muttering.

I didn't say nothing either way.

"Ya had it comin'," Sessuns barked at Weyland.

Lee asked, "Think he'll be holding any hard feelings, Bud?"

"Likely."

"I expect so too. Go to bed."

"Yes, sir. I'll be back to patrolling before dawn."

"Good idea." He looked at the ground and shook his head.

"Don't worry about your woman none. She'll be fine. That's why she stays with Carmela and Inés when you're out."

"I'm sorry, Lee. I didn't expect her to be troublesome."

"Don't worry. I like her frijole beans as much as anybody, and I like that rabbit stew she hunts up, even if she don't ever pick out all the shot. You got something special there. Was I you, I'd take care of it."

"Yes, sir."

Marta stepped up to me and laid her hand on the side of my face barely touching it, worry in her eyes. She had a wet towel. I had a queer feeling. I thought I was the one protecting her. But it felt pretty good knowing someone was watching out for me.

That night Marta whispered, "Bud."

My eyes snapped open, but it was only a dream.

— •●• —

The next time I came in, I was sitting cross-legged on my cot in long johns and cleaning cartridges from my gun belt. They'd gotten wet a lot. It was just about bedtime. The sacks of molasses-oats gave the room a good smell. Marta came in and shucked her shawls, shirt, and skirt. Wearing long johns, she faced me, kneeling, with a big grin. I looked at her, still couldn't get used to all those waves of black hair. I didn't need to go out and see the sunset to see something as pretty as her. She had a mischievous look.

"¿Qué?" I asked.

Still grinning, she held up a rawhide string with big orange, brown, and blue beads like the land and the sky. They were about an inch apart and held in-place by knots. She put her hands around my neck and tied it on. Holding up her mirror, she showed me a white and a tan bead side by side. She fingered the white one and pointed at me and then the tan one pointing to herself. I did not know what to say. Nobody, no girl, had ever give me a single thing, at least not something as special as this. I put my hand over my heart, and then touched her lips. She threw her arms around me with a funny little laugh I'd never heard before, gave me a long hug, and squirmed into the blankets making her contented sound.

There was something then that I wanted to tell Marta. I'd always protect her. I'd always be there to look after her. But I didn't know how to say it.

I've never ever taken off that necklace.

GORDON L. ROTTMAN

Chapter Twenty-Five

I rolled out of the bedroll's warmth into the cold night air and pulled on my boots. What had I heard? Crouching, I listened. Nothing. I knew I'd heard something. Felt like something was coming at me. Was it only a dream? I heard Cracker move in the brush. "Was it you, boy?" I whispered. I had no idea what time it was, midnight? An hour before dawn? My head was filled with wet straw.

Two pops, then a whole bunch more. From the west. "Crap! We're being raided."

I searched for Cracker, dragging my saddle along. I listened for more shots. One, then another. I cinched the saddle, ran back to belt on my revolver and fetched the Winchester and canteen. Bounding onto Cracker, he snorted and didn't move. I slid off and undid his hobble while he nickered, "Shame on you." More pops, closer. I cracked the *cuarta*. "Go!" I yelled.

There was no mad dash forward, but a cautious trot. With the overcast, there was no telling the ground from the sky. More pops and pounding hooves. Cattle hooves. Then there were pops with flashes, and they were coming from my right. I turned that way. "What's coming at us, boy?"

Scattered steers ran past. More hooves came at me, and I could make out horses. More cattle. I think a mounted man went past, but I wasn't shooting. I didn't want to hit one of our own. An anxious feeling soured my belly.

A thought came into my muddled head. If I couldn't tell who that man was, they couldn't tell who I was. I sawed Cracker around and was behind two steers heading for the Rio. A Mex shouted to my right. I yelled "*¡Ándale!*" hoping I sounded like a Mex. There weren't no more shots. More steers surrounded me.

I was at a loss where I was. Then I found myself going down the buff and was among the cane on the Sheep Head's snout. I followed some steers as they naturally found their way to trails heading to the Rio. They were at a slow trot now. I listened for voices, and heard some real faint to the right. Coming into a little clearing with three clumps of cane, I knew where I was. Another trail ran in from the right, and one led out to the Rio. I stopped behind the clump to the far left figuring the voices I heard would come this way. Dismounting, I cocked the Winchester. I could shoot better from the ground. If things get bad, I'd be better off hightailing it into the ten-foot cane than tearing down one of the trails with them after me on horses. Dust and gun smoke filled the cold air.

I heard Mex voices and a laugh, then some shots further away. Flaco or Gent maybe.

A steer busting through the cane scart the shit out of me.

Cracker nickered quietly, and I hushed him.

Horses at a trot, two, three, were coming my way. I could see their shapes against the clearing's sandy floor. Aiming at a shape, I raised my muzzle to barely above the lead horse. Squeezing the trigger, I levered off five shots as fast as I could and don't recall the recoil. Each flash showed a different picture of Mexes and horses and steers. Pistol shots flashed, and I dodged into the cane doubled over, went right, came up and shot three more times, shooting low like ol' Pancho'd taught me, then went flat. Crashing into the cane, a Mex came at me on foot, pistols in both hands blazing away in all directions. Bullets were snapping past me though the cane. I couldn't bring the rifle around. I got the big Remington out and emptied it. He went down, but was up and horsed and gone. Near scart the pee out of me. There was Mex cussing—I don't know what they were saying, but I know cussing when I hear it. They emptied their pistols and beat it down the trail to the Rio still shouting.

I laid there for a spell, and then reloaded. I wanted to make sure no one was waiting for me to poke my head up like a turkey. Some steers rustled cane in the clearing. No more shooting.

Presently, I came out of the cane, listened, and called Cracker. He came over, his withers giving little shivers of excitement. He nickered and another horse answered. Two steers were standing there half asleep after all their excitement. Past them was a horse. I went to him and tripped over a body. Jumping back, I pointed my rifle. He didn't move. Crouching down I laid my hand on his chest. He was as dead as lead could make him. It took me some time to find his pistol, a Colt double-action Thunderer, .41-caliber. I tied his horse up and climbed on Cracker. I figured I'd wait a spell and listen for Flaco and Gent.

I sat there listening to the quiet after all the commotion. Damn, that was something. A fluttering feeling ran all through me. "Settle down," I told myself. In the east, the horizon had a pale yellow outline.

— •●• —

Gent showed up after dawn. We found Flaco on the other side of the Rio talking to three 'queros. Wadding back on his horse, he drove four steers with DeW brands. He said the *vaqueros* lost a few head too. It was hard to tell how many head they'd run off with all the other tracks about. Judging by the scattered tracks leading into the Rio, maybe twenty. I figured there'd been at least five banditos, four now.

We rode back to the dead Mex and his horse. The Mex looked like any 'quero, but had a big yellow neckerchief. My .44 slug had hit below his left collarbone and come out through his spine between the shoulders. He'd been well mounted, had an American-style saddle. He had a Remington rolling-block carbine, .43 Spanish.

Looking over the dead Mex, Flaco said, "He belong to *El Xiuhcoatl.*"—pronouncing it shee-oo-ko-ah-tl.

"That be the Fire Serpent," Gent muttered.

"Scary name."

"That's the ideer," said Gent.

"He bad, have big *cuadrilla*...gang," said Flaco. "He bad *hombre.*"

"How bad?"

Flaco looked around. Gent glanced at him. "One time he cut a *hombre's* balls off, stuck them in his mouth, and sew his lips shut with saddle thread."

"Why'd he do that for?"

"The *hombre*, he cheat playing *Siete Loco*…a card game."

That sounded mean enough to me.

Gent was looking over the horse. "Well shit, this is Jerry Twining's horse and rig. They took it from him a month ago."

"He'll be happy."

"How big's the gang?"

"Some say twenty, some say hundred."

We found blood down the trail.

"Look like you wing one, *amigo*," said Flaco.

"Damn," I said.

"What's wrong?" asked Gent.

"I'm out here again with a dead man and no shovel. I'm going have to start carrying one."

Flaco dismounted. "You want his boots?"

"Nope." I'd already gotten everything off of him worth anything. He only had four pesos.

After taking the boots and tying his lariat around the bandito's bare feet, Flaco dragged the body toward the Rio.

"Guess we don't need no shovel."

"Maybe he'll wave when he floats past Eagle Pass," said Gent. "Ya look down, Bud,"

"I ain't never killed no man."

"'Em injuns."

"Don't count." I was thinking of Marta's butchered family and that murdered cowboy.

Gent and Flaco stayed out, and I took the horse into the ranch. I turned it over to Fred Laffin, the kid wrangling the remuda. Said he was sixteen, but everybody knew he was barely fifteen, between hay and grass. When Jerry came in, he was happy to see his horse and saddle. Over dinner, I told Clay and Lee what all happened.

"You done good, son," said Clay nodding at me. "There wasn't much more you boys could've done. Maybe it'll give them pause before they come back."

Lee was shaking his head. "Or maybe they'll come back for revenge. That's the first time we killed one of *Xiuhcoatl's hombres*."

Lew Cassel, Lee's number two, spoke up. "I think it'll be a good ideer to post a sentry here at the house at night, two-hour watches. Maybe give another man to the monitors." Lew used to be a corporal, two hitches in the cavalry. "Least fer now."

Clay was looking round the place. "Who you want for monitoring, Mr. Eugen?"

I tried not to smile. He was showing some faith in me. "Dodger Lampe'll do fine."

"Well, cut him out and take him with you."

Before riding out Marta gave me a stack of tortillas wrapped in paper and a Mason's jar of tomato-rice for tonight's supper. Gave me a big ol' hug too, and a long worried look into my eyes. She gripped my arm, peered at me, and nodded. I knew she was saying in her head for me to be careful. Inés caught Marta's arm and whispered in her ear. Marta cut her eyes to me, and they were both laughing. I surely wish I knew what they was talking about.

I decided there was something I had to tell Marta. She didn't never have to worry about me trying to give her away again. I wanted her to stay with me, just as a buddy. She could have whatever I had. I don't expect that would ever be much, but we could make it, and she'd not have to worry about where she'd go.

Now I got to figure out how to tell her that.

Chapter Twenty-Six

Nothing dire happened for a spell. Gent got shot at from across the Rio once. Dodger and I both found hoof prints coming from the other side, but never saw anyone. Flaco made a lot of visits to his *amigos* across the river. The 'queros weren't being bothered none by the banditos. Maybe shooting that Mex done some good after all.

I always shaved when I came in. The next time in, Marta had an old rocking chair with the rockers knocked off in front of our feed shed. "*Afeitado y corte de pelo—shava & hairs cut*" was painted on a plank with boot polish.

She had a tray with a mug, brush, straight razor, and Cody Carpenter shaving soap, and a big mercurochrome bottle. Grinning, she patted the chair, had a towel hanging over her arm. She started stropping the razor on a harness strap real businesslike. I didn't know about this, what with the blue bottle of mercurochrome handy. Ain't never no one shave me excepting my ownself.

She arched an eyebrow firmly at me.

"Well fine," I said.

A bunch of the giggling Mex kids collected to watch the bloodletting.

I was a bit nervous, but she put me at ease real quick after soaping my whiskers with the lavender soap, and she started scraping real gentle like. I almost dozed off as she sorta hummed some tune—sounded like a cat growling low. She trimmed my hair too. Holding her hand mirror up, she'd changed the shape of my mustache some. I liked it. I liked her even more that day. Maybe I should be claiming her as my woman.

I found out that she'd started giving most of the boys their shaves, once a week for most. She got a nickel a shave, same for haircuts. She didn't charge me. Some of them boys needed to be thrown like a calf to take a haircut. Found out, too, Gabi was paying her a nickel for the rabbits and squirrels she shot. I knew one thing; she liked being on the Dew.

— •●• —

Three days before Christmas, Clay let half the crew go to Del Rio. The rest could go in for the New Year. Flaco, Musty, Dodger, Snorter Cadwell, and I went, planning for some high times. Clay had paid us a week early for the occasion. Problem was Weyland went with us. He was pissed having to drive the supply wagon. Made him feel less a cowboy. He tied his horse to the wagon and brought it along anyways. Lee came with us with a long list of supplies.

Our mob departed the Dew with a word from Mrs. DeWitt cautioning us to spare our mortal souls. "You boys remember it's the Christmas season, and for your own good, shun low women."

I felt bad about leaving Marta, but Gabi said she really didn't want to go. She took it that Marta didn't much like towns.

San Felipe Del Rio was sorta like Eagle Pass, but even though Del Rio means "on the river," it sat several miles from it. San Felipe Spring poured out of the ground with a creek running to the Rio Grande. Irrigation canals ran all over.

My first stop was the gunsmith, who also repaired timepieces according to the sign.

"Welcome," he said looking up from a pocket watch with its innards exposed.

"Howdy, I got some guns to sell." I laid the dead Mex's Remington rolling-block carbine, the Colt Thunderer, and the old rolling-block single-shot pistol on the counter along with a sack of spent 16-gauge shells. All the cartridges I had too for the Mex's guns, a lot, three bandoliers.

Looking them all over, peering down barrels, and cocking and snapping the Colt, he made offers. "'Fraid there's not much call for the Remington carbine, but I give you seven dollars if you toss in the ammunition."

I hadn't expected much. I nodded.

"Colt's good," he said rotating the cylinder. "They're twelve dollars new. I'll give you eight, nine if you throw in the ammunition and rig. Fancy rig, that."

I nodded.

Picking up the Remington single-shot he cocked the hammer and thumbed back the breechblock to glance down the bore. "A little pitting, been around a while. Hell, it's older than you." He looked up at me over his spectacles. "Be honest, I don't think I could sell this for a buck. Ain't no call for single-shot pistols."

I dropped it back in my flour sack.

As he counted out the spent shotshells I said, "Need two cartons of those, Number 6 shot. One more of Number 4." Clay said the heavier Number 4 would be good for geese and ducks, longer ranged too.

"Got any 16-gauge slugs?" They'd be good for deer in thick brush and for banditos too.

"Yes, sir. Carton or singles?"

"A dozen." The marble-sized lead balls killed game good, but weren't accurate over forty yards.

He counted out the spent shotshells, stacked the new cartons and figured what he owed me for the guns after deducting the shotshells. "Wait a minute," he said. He started rummaging through boxes and tins on a shelf and came up with a carton. "I recalled, I got eight rounds of .50-caliber for that old pistol. If nothing else maybe it'll help you sell it. They're on the house."

"Why, thank you," I said. "I can pay."

"Doing me a favor getting them outta here."

We got rooms at the San Felipe Hotel. Dodger and I doubled up. The other boys flipped nickels to see who doubled with Weyland. Snorter Cadwell lost.

Baths were in order, and the barber was complaining because none of the boys needed shaves or haircuts, excepting Weyland. Appeared he didn't trust Marta with her razor at his throat. Can't say I blamed him. They did some slicking up on their own, pasting their hair down with bear grease pomade and gussying up with Cuticura soap.

The crew had decided another heating stove for the bunkhouse would make winter more tolerable. Those staying back had pitched in. Those living in the tent pitched in too because they'd spent time in the bunkhouse including dressing. "Musty" Musson was in charge of the purchase, and he took a couple of hands with him to the Hansen General Store. They got a Merit Sunshine coal and wood stove for thirteen dollars. It took a bunch of us to load, it weighing over two-hundred pounds.

Lee studied the stove and said, "You bunch of knot heads; don't you think you might need some stovepipe?"

Musty stomped back in. "Ain't figured that into the money."

Wandering the streets, I found an outfitters store. I got Marta a blue flannel shirt, smallest they had. On a whim, I picked up a pair of black whipcord wool pants. Maybe she'd not like pants, and it might be considered strange by some, but dang, we still had a cold couple of months before us. At an emporium, I got her a proper hair brush. It was feeling like a real Christmas coming up.

The boys liked the Double Eagle Saloon, their regular hangout. Reasonably honest dealers they claimed at the poker, faro, Mexican Monte, and twenty-one table—no waxed cards. It was a fancy and clean dive and not too rowdy.

"That dive's as hot as a hookhouse on two-bit night," declared Musty.

"Two bits? Them days is gone," responded Dodger.

There was a shotgun-watcher sitting on a high chair at the end of the bar. We had to check our guns.

I wasn't much into gaming. Played twenty-one, lost three dollars. I felt better hanging onto my bucks. I'd never had so much money. Instead, I drank beer and watched the stage shows—singers, readers, a lady playing a mandolin, and some dancing girls—they coulda at least *tried* to make the same moves at the same time. One of them readers read from *Last of the Mohicans*. Told us about injuns bushwhacking soldiers and settlers. Everyone listened and got riled up. I watched the goings-on, gaming, arguments, and some almost fights.

I figured the fights were started by punchers driven nuts by a booze called Tanglefoot. Snorter claimed, "That coffin varnish's made from corn alcohol, sugar, turpentine, and chewin' tobacer."

The watcher in his high chair didn't put up with any fighting. He had a three-stage way of stopping fist swinging, kicking, and biting. First, he'd click the hammers back on his 10-gauge coach gun. If that didn't get the troublemakers' attention, he'd slide down and easygoing-like stroll up to the adversaries and stick the scattergun in the most troublesome's face. If they paid him no mind, he'd let the hammers down and beat them into the plank floor until they behaved or went away. He was a big fella. If that didn't work, I reckoned he'd take the next step and re-cock his double-barrel hand-cannon.

Dodger and Snorter and I were arguing which beer was better, Buck, Erlanger, or Alamo. Before, we'd been arguing about those new bottles compared to keg beer. We'd been trying them all. Musty wandered up with a lanky calico queen hanging on his arm. She looked a little frayed, but that could be said of most "low women."

"Ya buncha clods." Musty said stamping his boot. "They's all bottled by Lone Star up San Antone way."

I looked at the labels and it was so. "You right, partner."

"No matter," Musty declared. "They all first-rate. Them krauts knows how to make beer. There's more square-heads in San Antone than 'mericans and Mexes." The whore was tugging on his arm; time was money on her busy schedule. "Gotta go, fellas, my lover can't wait."

"Here's how!" Snorter bawled, hoisting his bottle in a toast.

"Put in a knock for me," shouted Dodger. Looking at me, "Ya gonna get some of that?"

I didn't say nothing. I'd been pondering that, me hooking up with a painted cat. Marta and me, I don't know what we were. We did things for each other, counted on each other. I wanted her to stay with me. But that was it.

Dodger said, "I likes 'em whores, can't help it. A public woman earnin' her livin' makin' a lotta boys happy is more better than a married lady set on ruinin' one man's life."

There's nothing wrong with a man needing a woman. Marta didn't have no claim on me like that. I still felt like hell even thinking about hitching up with a painted cat. That didn't mean I weren't any less horny.

"What the hell happened to ya?" said Dodger breaking my pondering thoughts.

We jumped to our feet. "Lordy Slick, ya tangle wit a puma?" shouted Dodger.

"Slick" Sealeger was standing over us kind of lopsided and all muddy, his face all woppy-jawed and his eyes sported shiners.

"Got mugged, boys. Sumbitches took all my money and my pappy's watch."

We took him up to his room and cleaned him up. We staked him some money. He told us about getting waylaid at the outhouse. One of the muggers had a deep gouge in the outside of his right boot heel. He noticed that while getting kicked. "Big feet. I ain't never seen anything that big that didn't breath on its own."

We spread the word among the boys, and they'd be on the lookout, for his fancy watch too. Dodger said, "I recomember that watch." We all did. A couple of the boys headed out to nose around.

Stepping out for some air I found Flaco moseying down the street, told him about the mugging. I noticed he wasn't wearing the red *Rurales* necktie. He said he was going down to *Cantina El Cielo*. "*Cielo* means heaven. Eet is quiet place, no fights... Well, not many. Good *cerveza*, clean *chiquitas*. Wanna go?"

Chapter Twenty-Seven

A few 'queros glared at me when we walked in. Flaco said something to an older fella with a short gray beard, hooded eyes, and a huge sombrero. That *vato* said something to another, and no one paid me further mind. Another fella sat on a stool in the corner playing a big guitar real quiet. Most of the 'queros were drinking beer or playing cards, *Pokar*, Flaco called it. "Not like American poker," he said.

Three *señoritas* came in, one thin, one chubby, and one in between. They started dancing, swirling their skirts with the guitar fella playing a real fast tune. They were something to watch. They showed a lot of leg, hiking up those gay-colored dresses. Never seen no white girl dance like that.

Flaco waved the girls over, and we bought them beers. He was telling them stories. I figured out he was telling about me, about shooting the bandito. They were big-eyed, peering at me in awe.

The thin one, her name was Elvia, talking through Flaco, said she liked my blue eyes. When she saw her first blue-eyed *americano* she thought they could see clearer than Mexes with dark eyes. We had a good laugh on that. We made up the girls some rollies.

Flaco had me tell them *chiquitas* about a time I hunted a puma. I'd told it to him and Gent one night out monitoring.

Elvia started talking, and Flaco told her story. "She was at her cousin's farm. He had strips of meat cooking on the fire, and he want her to taste it. She ask what it is, and he say puma, told her to eat it."

"Puma!" I said. "I ain't heard of no one ever eating puma."

Elvia laughed and said something else.

"She eat it, and it not bad. Her cousin say it not puma..."

"*¡Es gato!*" Elvia smiled with her wide mouth.

"Cat! *¿Comiste gato?* Well, I be dragged through a cactus patch."

"*¿Quieres ir a una sala?*" Elvia's eyes narrowed at me.

"She ask if you wanna go to room?"

I raised my eyebrows at Flaco.

"Just nod your head, *tonto*. She want to take you through *la puerta negra al cielo*."

I knew *tonto* meant fool; ol' Pancho had called me that enough. I didn't know the rest. "What?"

"The black gate to heaven. Or hell," he added.

Sometimes a man needs a woman's touch. I went with her. Flaco kept the other two for his ownself.

To make a short story shorter, nothing happened. It was kind of mortifying. It just didn't feel right. She looked real good when she shucked off that blue dress, big jugs and a hairy pussy, but... I don't know. I liked and wanted her, and then didn't want her. She didn't let it bother her none. I paid her anyways. I think she was telling me to come back sometime. I didn't wait on Flaco. I headed back to the Double Eagle trying to convince myself it wasn't because of Marta. I just wasn't in the mood no longer, too cold or too much beer maybe.

I heard a noise behind me and turned to find Weyland standing in the street. "Don't get enough of that Mex pussy back at the Dew?" He had a drunk, mean look.

What's blowing wind up his asshole? "Butt out, Weyland. None your business."

"I'm making it my business." His hand dangled by his gun butt. "Some of us don't cotton to Texicans takin' up with greasers."

I marched up to him, covering the half-dozen steps in two heartbeats. "Don't do nothing stupid, Weyland. You're too drunk." Not that I was all that steady my ownself.

He came back with a snappy, "Fuck you, Mex lover!"

"Let's not do this now, Weyland. We're too—" His roundhouse slammed into my left jaw staggering me back. His hand reached for his gun.

"Let's have none of that, boys." Standing on the sidewalk was

Lee, all duded up, even wearing a flowerbed vest. "Lose the guns, boys, then finish your business."

I dropped mine in the mud, and Weyland pulled his, and it went off with a near blinding bang, twice. I threw myself into him, catching him at waist level, and we hit the ground hard. Grabbing at his gun hand, I found he'd lost it. I jammed a knee into his belly, but he caught me with his own in my balls. I rolled clear of him, giving me seconds to deal with the pain. I whacked my elbow into the side of his head a bunch of times, despite the pain. Wished I'd had that Mex gal. Felt like I'd never partake of that sort of sport no more. He got his hands up to my throat choking me. I kept hammering with my elbow. He finally let go, and I could almost breathe. Now I rammed my knee into his belly, and he stopped struggling. I was glad for that because I was hurting something powerful.

"You boys finished?" said Lee, real easy like.

I tried to get up, but had to sit in the mud. Weyland stayed where he was kind of groaning.

"Get up, shithead." Lee held Weyland's gun around its cylinder.

I tried to push myself up. That hurt.

"Not you, dummy. Get up shithead," booting Weyland in the side. Lee ended up pulling Weyland up. I stayed sitting in the mud wondering if my balls were still in their customary place.

"We ain't having none of that." I'd never heard Lee so pissed. "Ain't no Dew hand pulling on another. I'll have you took up for intended murder."

"He's the troublemaker," muttered Weyland. "He pulled on me first."

"Bullshit, Bud didn't even touch his gun."

I thought Lee was ready to start whaling on him with the pistol. "You're fired. You've been paid off to the end of the month. I'll give you your gun back in the morning."

"That ain't fair! I—"

"Just get," said Lee in a voice that woulda scared me if he'd aimed it at me. "Don't say nothing you can't unsay."

Weyland wavered there a moment, and then turned away muttering to himself.

Lee pulled me up. "You able to walk, Bud?"

"Not real fast and don't ask me to sit no saddle."

He laughed. "You'll be fine by morning." Lee looked back over his shoulder. "He's nothing but trouble. I shouldna hired him. Meanness like him don't grow overnight. You seen Slick?"

"He's at the Double Eagle. Been mugged, boss."

"Got his watch, didn't they?"

I looked at him. "Yep. A couple hours ago."

"One of the whores told me there's an ol' boy at the Horseshoe Saloon flashing Slick's watch, that Dueber with a gold inlaid elk, silver case. She knows that watch."

"We going to get it back?"

"Some of us are. I don't think you're in fighting form."

Musty came out the Horseshoe Saloon. Snorter had taken over Musty's lover—next gentleman, same lady. "It's 'em all right. Saw that gouge on the one's boot heel. Damn big feets."

"What state they in?" said Lee.

"Oh, they full as blood ticks," reported Musty with a grin.

Slick yanked the strap off his Colt. "Let's go get 'em four-flushers."

"Pull in your horns," said Lee. "No sense giving that scattergun guard a reason to notch his stock. Need a plan. Wish Lew was here, he's good at planning."

Over the swinging doors Musty pointed out the three muggers.

"Well, hell," said Lee. "I know that old boy, Brownie Jaeger. Works on the Wormwood spread." He looked thoughtful. Turning to me, "You seen Flaco?"

"He's visiting heaven…or hell. Don't expect we be seeing him tonight."

"You up for this, Bud?"

"Yep. Just can't run very far."

"Fine then. No running necessary if this works. You'll be backup. Musty, get a wiggle-on and fetch that shoeshine boy over yonder."

— •●• —

"What'd ya tell that kid, boss?" asked Slick as the bootblack boy went through the Horseshoe's swinging doors.

"Gave him a penny to tell them old boys their foreman, Jim Corker, is in an altercation down at the Crystal Palace."

"He is?" said Musty.

"No, ya idget."

We were standing in an alley between the Horseshoe and a millinery shop. The Crystal was on the next corner down.

The shoeshine boy came out the swinging doors, nodded, and went to take up a front row seat.

Musty was standing at a hitching rail in front of the millinery. Them three muggers came out of the saloon doors bee-lining for the Crystal. Musty stepped into their path right after they passed our dark alley.

"Outta my way, cowboy," bawled Jaeger. He talked kind of funny not having no front teeth.

Musty stepped forward. "Friend of mine wanna talk wit' ya."

The three stopped, hands on their pistols. "What friend?" asked the brawny punch, confusion in his voice. A moment's hesitation, exactly what we wanted.

"That one," said Musty jerking his head to his left.

Slick was standing there, with Lee and Dodger on either side, their pistols leveled. The muggers' hands went up real fast, like to touch the moon. I was standing behind them ready to move to either side. I swear one them boys swallowed his chaw.

"Let's one at a time take your guns out real slow and drop them," ordered Lee.

"I'd like my timepiece back and my earnin's," said Slick. "Pronto."

Slick stepped up to Jaeger holding out his left hand while poking his Colt into the punch's belly.

"We was jus'—"

"You best keep your mouths shut and fork over the stolen goods," Lee said bluntly, taking a step closer. I'd been told Lee had a rep'tation among local punches as one to be taken serious.

Jaeger slapped the pocket watch into Slick's hand.

"Easy wit' that, it's a heirloom."

"How much money they take off you, Slick?"

Slick told Lee.

"I'm thorry, I thpent mos' of it," Jeager answered, looking as silly as an old maid what brung a funeral pie to a wedding reception.

"I'm sure y'all split it up," said Lee. "Give him all you got, Jaeger. Charlie and Patch, you boys make up the difference. Equally, we being all fair here."

"Yes, sir," they all mumbled.

They were real cooperative counting it out, like it was any old business deal. Five cocked pistols go a long ways making folks sensible.

"You got anything else to say, Slick?" asked Lee.

Slick whipped his Colt into the side of Jaeger's face, sending him staggering. He spit out one of his remaining teeth.

"That all?"

"That's all," said Slick.

"Our business here is finished, boys. There'll be no more words between us, understood? Or do we need to talk to the town marshal?"

"We all good here, thir," said Jaeger, rubbing his jaw.

"Good, so I don't need to be talking to Jim Corker neither?"

"No, thir."

"Say howdy to Jim for me."

"Yes, thir."

We watched them head back to the Horseshoe. "Forgive your enemies, but don't trust them," muttered Lee. After a piece being real quiet, Lee said, "You boys done good, sticking up for one another. That means something."

"Thanks, boys," muttered Slick. "I owes y'all."

"You bet," said Lee. "Now let's head back to the Double Eagle and spend Slick's new-found fortune."

Chapter Twenty-Eight

We were back at the Dew on Christmas Eve, bruised and tuckered out with a wagonload of supplies and saddlebags full of tall tales. I figured the number of foes faced in fights, the gallons of booze slugged down, the sum of gaming money won and lost, and the number of prairie doves laid, were at least doubled. Musty was so drunk he didn't know if he'd lost a horse or found a bridle. It all only made the hands staying behind more the ready for their next week's trip to Del Rio.

We even brought back a new hand Lee hired, Ewart Rosecrans. He didn't much like being called "Rosey," but it stuck. Lee knew him from the Thursday spread, a peeler with a rep'tation.

We all crowded into the big house's front room Christmas morning. Clay's girls had decorated a cedar tree with paper ring chains, little wooden toy animals, and popcorn strung on strings. They'd lit candles all about the room. The girls led us in a song called *Jingle Bells*. Doris DeWitt, the older of the two girls at sixteen, had a strong pure voice. Her two years younger sister, little Agnes, normally shy, wasn't shy about singing.

I'll tell you, us gravelly-voiced punches gave it our all, but it would of scart the one horse pulling that sleigh. Marta stood beside me laying her head against my arm. Clay gave each hand a leather pouch with a poke of Powhatan tobacco, cigarette papers, and a new-fangled Erie cap-lighter. Mrs. DeWitt and the girls gave everyone a pair of home-knit wool socks or a scarf. Marta got wool gloves and socks. Musty was right, this was a good outfit to work for.

We gave Mrs. DeWitt a silver serving spoon, both the girls little porcelain angels, and Clay an alligator travel bag; come all the way from Louisiana. This all only cost us hands four bits apiece, but the boss and his family surely appreciated it. We gave Gabi a mother-of-pearl hair comb. Back in a hallway I saw Gabi straighten Lee's necktie, and he gave her a little red paper package.

Lee said in his most grave voice, "Any y'all trying to be sentimental and give me something, you'll be finding yourself nighthawking for the next two weeks."

The next morning he found a German Solingen hunting knife on his doorstep at the back house. He couldn't pin it on anyone and couldn't set us all as nighthawks.

After a big breakfast with everyone sitting at the plank tables, I took Marta into our room. I gave her the packages with the blue flannel shirt, pants, and hairbrush. She threw her arms around me and cried up a storm for the longest. Dang girl, she choked me all up. Sniffing, she took off her split skirt and pulled on them whipcord pants, tucked them into her socks, and pulled her skirt back on.

Drying her eyes, she gave me a green paper package. Opening it, I found a pair of Mex nickel-plated spurs with twelve-point roundels. I later got out of Flaco that he'd picked them up after she drew a picture and gave him twenty nickels.

I ain't ever going to think about no painted cats no more. And, I'd been trying to give this girl away. That'll never happen again. My mama'd always called me a knucklehead fool. Guess she was right for once. I gotta get around to telling Marta she was staying with me for as long as she could tolerate.

That night, well, I felt those urges. I blamed it on that dang Mex prairie dove, bless her heart. Marta was snoring sound asleep. My arm was over her, and I kind of let my hand slip down over her tit. It was firm and round, and I fell to sleep. I drifted out of sleep sometime during the night and recognized Marta was awake too. I could tell by her breathing. Remembering where my hand was, I started to move it. I stopped. Didn't want her to think I'd done it on purpose. I lay still, trying to breathe like I was sleeping. After a spell, her hand touched mine and slowly eased it down until she stopped at her belly. Her other hand moved, and she slid my hand up under her long johns top. I'd never felt so comfortable and was soon sleeping again.

In the morning, we were still like that. She suddenly pulled my arm down and sat up. When I opened my eyes, she was smilin'. All of a sudden, she nuzzled her face into my neck, kissed me on the lips real fast, and was out of bed like a shot. I didn't know what to make of it, but it felt agreeable. I rode out to monitor that morning. It'd be three long days before I had another night in. Something to look forward to, coming home to see my woman.

Chapter Twenty-Nine

I rode in for supper the day after Christmas. I wanted to say good-bye to the boys heading for Del Rio in the morning. I gave Gent two dollars to pick up a Bedells' patent game and shell bag. It cost a bunch, but I wanted to give Marta something more. The boys bound for Del Rio sure had their tails up.

I staked out that night near Pinto Creek, the Dew's south boundary. Flaco was up near the Sheep's Head, and Dodger was someplace on the Sycamore. That morning Flaco had chased off a couple of Fire Serpents on the Sheep's Head snout.

I was staying up as long as I could last, keeping my eyes and ears open. Must have been near midnight, and I was taking it slow back to the campsite I'd picked. Two shots rang out to the north. I sawed Cracker around and jammed my spurs into him. Three measured shots. Flaco's in trouble! I lashed with my *cuarta*.

Shots started crackling like popcorn. I crashed through mesquite with branches snapping. I could hear the rumbling rush of cattle.

Guns were cracking. I could see the flashes. There were a lot of cattle in the run. I angled toward the Rio hoping to head them off. There was nothing I could do to turn them, but I meant to get a crack at the raiders. I reached the bluff leading down to the flats this side of the Rio and angled down it taking care. Do no good to take a spill now. The lead cattle were pouring down the bluff's slope.

Starlight let me see riders cresting the bluff against the sky. I pulled my Winchester, dismounted, and levered in a round. Cattle were coming over steady. I knew the herd they'd stampeded, at least three hundred head.

I saw a raider, but he was over the bluff's edge too fast and too far away. Then another came over, closer. I followed him down the bluff in my sights. My second shot unhorsed him into the stampede.

A couple of more banditos came over. I wasted some shots and then hit one. The herd was mostly past with a few lagging. I mounted and turned to follow, hoping I could take some shots as they crossed the river. Then I heard more shots, real far away to the northeast. On Cracker, I scrambled up the bluff. I could really hear the far shots now. They were carried by the wind from the ranch house. Marta!

I spurred and lashed Cracker for everything I had. By the time I reached the overlooking ridge top, there were no more shots. I could see a blazing fire among the ranch buildings. I made a dead dash for the house, apologizing to Cracker for the way I was treating him.

More gunfire sounded over toward the Sycamore behind me. I didn't turn back. I could only think of Marta.

Tearing in, I heard a lot of shouting. The hay shed and the tent behind the bunkhouse were burning. Everyone, even kids, was passing buckets and cans from a water trough to the shed. It looked hopeless as the dry hay had caught. The flames were throwing jumping shadows and light all about. They let the tent burn.

I ran to our feed shed. It was empty. Where is she? I ran to the fire.

Clay was directing the water-passers. I found Lee.

"What happened on your end?" he shouted.

I told him they'd run a big herd across the Rio. I'd not seen Flaco or Dodger. "I came straight here when I heard shooting. Have you seen Marta?"

"No, Bud. I ain't. Probably in the big house. We need to get everyone sorted out." Lee turned, "Clay. Clay! Give it up. We ain't saving it."

Clay was calling everyone off the fire. "Everyone to the house! ¡Todos a la casa!"

The burning hay shed lit up everyone in front of the big

house. Clay stood on the porch. "Lee, take a count, make sure all the hands are here." He told Roberto to count the Mex hands.

Snorter Cadwell had been shot in the calf coming out of the bunkhouse. A couple of Mex women were taking care of him.

There was a woman's cry inside, Mrs. DeWitt I thought. Clay turned real fast.

Gabi came out on the porch. There was blood on the sleeve of her white nightgown. "*Clay, por favor entren.*"

He rushed inside.

Everyone was there except Slick, Dodger, and Flaco. Those last two were still out and chasing banditos I hoped. Lee sent two Mex boys to look for Slick. He'd been out riding close-in sentry.

"What happened here?" I asked Musty.

"When the shootin' started over Sheep's Head way we horsed up and headed there. The herd was gone when we got there. We turned back when we heard 'em shootin' and whoopin' like injuns back here. By the time we got back they was gone."

Gabi came out of the house with a storm lantern. She was talking to Lee, and he didn't look good. He waved us all together. "Boys, Clay's girls are missing. Their room window's been busted out, and there's blood on the broken glass."

That sent a grumble through everyone.

Lee looked at me. "Bud, Marta and Inés are gone, too. Carmila's dead."

Everyone was turning and looking at me. I couldn't say nothing. Boys were muttering things like, "Sorry, Bud," slapping me on the shoulder. My chest was hollow.

I walked to our feed shed, sat on her cot, gripped her scarf I found on the bunk. Banditos had that little girl. I couldn't think straight. What would happen to her? She's tough, but they had her. It sickened me that I'd never told her I wanted her to stay for as long as she could bear me, that anything of mine was hers. I'd give my soul to the Devil just to see her eyes.

I came out knowing Clay and Lee needed me.

Two of the boys found Slick, shot dead on the ridge side. The Gomez boy, he'd been on house sentry. They found him behind the milk cow barn with his throat slit, his shotgun gone. One of the Mex kids, a six-year-old, was dead too, shot in the courtyard, probably running to the big house. Clay's prize bull, Quicksilver, was gone, the corral gate open. I went to Carmela and Inés's room where Marta had been. Carmela was lying in the door shot full of holes.

That tore it. I went back to our shed, grabbed up all my cartridges, stuffed them in saddlebags, and mounted.

"Where ya goin'?" It was Musty.

"I'm going after her."

"Now? By ya self?"

It was dumb, I know. She was in the hands of the worst kind of men. I knew what was going to happen to those girls. "I got no choice."

Musty grabbed my reins.

I jerked back on them. "Let go you sumbitch!"

"Ya can't do this, Bud! Not by ya self."

I came off the saddle and grabbed Musty's arm. He pushed back.

"What's going on here?" It was Lee.

"The fool's goin' after Marta by his lonesome," said Musty, yanking his arm away from me.

"That's crazy, Bud."

"I gotta do it, Lee. Get outta my way!"

"Get a grip. All you'll do is get yourself killed. That'll do Marta no good."

Musty led Cracker away. I didn't stop him. I pulled my hat off, ran my hand over my hair. I felt stupid, but I was scared for her, unreasonable scared.

Lee looked me in the eye. "Least you got some sense left. You know Clay's going, and he's counting on you. He's going after all those girls and taking all of us. Go pack your gear proper."

Some of the boys were finishing stomping out the fires. Others were collecting grub and packing bedrolls. The boys what lost their gear in the tent were throwing together bedrolls. There weren't no question of what we were doing next. Dodger and Flaco came in before dawn. They'd been drawn to the herd run across the Rio like I had. They'd gone all the way to the Rio, hadn't heard the gunfire from the house.

Lee called us all together. I found Musty and thanked him for keeping me from doing something dumb. He nodded.

Everybody wanted to know how Clay and the Missus were doing.

"Not good, boys." Lee looked around at us. "We worked out what happened, best we know. *Xiuhcoatl's* boys ran that herd we had near the Sheep's Head to draw away the monitors and us. They hit the house after we left. One group killed Juan Gomez, snuck into the courtyard behind the house, and busted through the girls' back window. Them the same ones what took Marta and Inés and shot down Carmela and the kid."

There was a lot of angry muttering. "Bastards." "Mother-fuckin' greasers."

"Another group took the bull, and then a third group came in shooting things up to cause confusion, started the fires throwing coal oil bottles. They brought up the rear covering the ones making off with the girls and the bull."

Lee glared at us. "Boys, they left a ransom letter." Everybody was listening. "They want five hundred dollars apiece for Clay's girls." He shaked his head.

"What about Marta and Inés," I asked.

"They didn't say nothing about ransom for them. They probably hadn't planned taking them. Just did."

I felt a rage building.

"The letter said they'd let Clay know where to leave the money later."

Clay came out on the porch. He didn't look good, but he was still acting the boss. He knew what he had to do. The boys were muttering their regrets and asking how the Missus was bearing up.

"Thanks boys. She'll make it, but she's taking it godawful hard." He looked around at us, and everyone was stone quiet. "Boys, I'm asking y'all a favor. No one has to go, and we'll hold no grudge if you want to sit this out. "I'm going after all those girls." He was looking at me. "Y'all know where we gotta go. I'm not hankering to pay those black-hearted bastards no ransom."

I looked around at the nodding heads, the hard looks.

"All I can promise you boys is tough times, no rest, and a hundred dollars bonus to each of you with me when we take the girls back."

Dodger looked me in the eye. "We'll get her back, Bud." He slapped me on the back.

Flaco came up. "We go to get her, *amigo*."

Damn straight, I'm bringing her home, and I got something

to tell her. I held a painful ache.

Chapter Thirty

The puny sun had barely crawled into the gray sky. *El Nortada*—the north wind—blasted across the ridge overlooking the ranch house, chilling us to the bone. There was grief in our hearts, fire in our bellies, and hate seeping all through us. Every man, woman, and child on the Dew stood before the four graves where our friends lay. Tim "Slick" Sealeger: they'd taken his pappy's elk pocket watch; Carmela Flores: a damn fine cook and Inés's mama; Juan Gomez: fifteen, just starting to turn the girls' eyes and so proud of being a guard; and Paco Suarez: just a little kid what got in the way.

Clay had his arm around Mrs. DeWitt as she sobbed quietly. There was dignity there even in her pain and fear. Gabi stood on the other side of her, arm around her too. Gabi's left arm was bandaged. She'd taken a graze. Gabi had squirrel-gunned a bandito out of his saddle.

The Mexes crossed themselves, some of the punches did too. Clayton DeWitt's unyielding voice defied the wind. "Our Father who art in heaven, hallowed be Thy name…"

Gent played the mouth organ and Rock Rockingham the violin. We sang "Will You Come to the Bower?" because we all knew its words like the Texas Army's fife corps at San Jacinto. It was the only piece they'd all known.

Will you come to the bower I have shaded for you?

Your bed shall be of roses, be spangled with dew.
Will you, will you come to the bower?
There under the bower on soft roses you'll lie.
With a blush on your cheek, but a smile in your eye.
Will you, will you smile my beloved?
But the roses we press shall not rival your lips.
Nor the dew be so sweet as the kisses we'll sip.
Will you kiss me my beloved?

We didn't stay up there long. We were leaving, crossing the Rio, going with *El Nortada* crossing our backs, heading west into Mexico.

How did I feel? I don't want to say. I don't like to speak of such vileness.

Chapter Thirty-One

Thirteen of us sat our horses in the blackjack oaks of the Sheep's Head top knot.

"Unlucky number," I muttered to Flaco.

"Not in Mexico."

"That's good seein' we're goin' there," said Dodger.

Grim resolve hung in the air. Maybe some of the boys were having misgivings, but they were all willing. Nobody in the crew was letting anyone down; especially they weren't letting down Clayton DeWitt. No cowboy worth his salt would let down a boss like him.

There was something else, unspoken. No one was letting down any of the girls, leaving them to an unspeakable fate. We all knew what was going to happen to them, they'd be violated—spoiled, ransom or not. And…this was hard to even think about, it had probably already happened to them. My chest felt empty thinking of Marta, any of them, going through that. My anger plotted out the sun.

"There a lucky number in Mexico?" asked Dodger.

"*Cuatro*—four."

"I'll havta think on that," said Dodger. "Gotta be something good 'bout four."

"*Caballo*—horse—have four legs."

"I reckon that'll do."

Clay, Lee, and Lew were off to the side in a powwow. Knowing Lew, the old horse-soldier, they were probably cooking up a plan. I don't know how Clay was handling it, what with his girls taken. It'd taken us a long time to get everything collected and ready. I saw him slapping his *cuarta* on his leg sometimes. I guess he knew we'd best have it all together before starting out.

Roberto and some of the Mex hands tossed bandito bodies from a wagon into the Rio. We were loaded down for a long trip. Every man had a rifle or carbine, many had two revolvers and all their ammo. I had my Winchester, Marta's shotgun—I'd brought all the buckshot and slugs, and my Remington revolver. I even stuck that old single-shot .50-caliber pistol and its eight rounds in a saddlebag. Only one other hand had a shotgun. Jerry Twining had a Greener 12-gauge coach gun.

We had bedrolls, rain slickers, two canteens or water bags, and all the chuck we could pack. There were four packhorses and we had eighteen horses in the remuda run by Earnest Sessuns. Lee had even brought a spare saddle, tack, and horseshoes, sacks of feed grain, a medical chest too.

I'd put Marta's scarf and gloves in my saddle bag. She'd need them. I lashed a shovel and pickax to a pack horse.

"What dat fer?" asked Jerry.

"I'm getting tired of not having a shovel when I need to bury someone."

"Oh, that's goin' to make everybody feel real good," said Dodger.

The only hands left at the ranch were Snorter Cadwell, shot in the calf, and Graves Stone Eskin with his broken wing. We left behind a hopping mad Fred Laffin, just a kid. He wanted to run the remuda. "That be my job, Boss."

Clay told him, "Son, you don't need to be part of what's going to happen over there."

He sent Roberto east to the neighboring Babcock Ranch with a note telling what happened and asking for two or three hands to help out at the Dew, keep an eye on things.

Clay sent Flaco and me out when it was light enough to follow the bull's tracks. We met up with the rest of the crew at Dry Well, a far-from-dry cattle tank, on the Eagle Pass-Del Rio Road. They'd followed the big herd. We made it sixteen, eighteen horses, the ones that had raided the ranch. There were maybe twenty head of cattle run with them making it hard to count horses.

The three bosses looked like they'd finished up their war planning. Lee waved us monitors to come over.

"Boss," I'd reported. "They crossed the Sycamore onto the V-Bar-M, then crossed the Rio a half-mile up. I think they want us to split up, some following the bull and the rest the big herd."

"They probably got bushwhackers coverin' both crossin's," said Lew.

"Why do you say they're expecting us to follow the bull?" asked Clay.

"'Cause that's where the girls are, I bet." I couldn't look at his eyes.

"Makes sense."

"I think the raiders with the girls and bull likely joined up with the others after they crossed the Rio," I finished.

"You boys think there's any bushwhackers still over there?" asked Lee nodding toward the Rio.

"Not no more," I said. "Probably think we ain't coming seeing it's near noon."

"That's good if they think that," said Clay.

"Still oughta cross further south," said Lew.

Clay looked at me, "What do you think?"

"Smart thinking. Then we'll swing north and cut the big herd trail and follow it to find where the other group joined up with them."

Clay nodded. "Lew wants to split us into two squads, one following further behind the other. In case we get bushwhacked, the other can circle around and hit them where they're not expecting. Calls it strategy."

Gent said, "Strategy? Sound like a good army word."

"Ready for your orders, sir," Lew said real army-like.

Clay arched an eyebrow. "Lee's taking the first squad and Lew the second. I'll be with Lee. Bud, you and Flaco's in first squad, Gent and Dodger with the second. The remuda'll follow the second squad."

Clay didn't sound real comfortable with them army words.

We crossed the Rio real careful like, our rifles out, with the second squad covering us.

Coming out of the cold water, we clattered across the gravel bar, up the sandy bank, and onto the stony ground, our passage unremarkable, unmarked, and unremembered as soon as the horses' hooves lifted off the ground. We were in Mexico.

The others came across with the remuda following.

Once on better ground, we turned north and came across the big herd's trail in half a mile. It followed an arroyo away from the Rio. We found about thirty head with Dew brands milling around. Didn't take us long to round them up. Two of the boys ran them back across and caught up with us an hour later.

Flaco rode ahead and to my left. I stayed on the right edge of the muddy trail looking to cut the trail of the group with the girls and the bull. The rest of the crew stayed back so not to mess up any sign. About two miles later I found it.

"They joined up here, Clay."

They had followed a cow trail down to the arroyo. Clay had a wicked grin. "Good going, Bud. Like you said."

I found their campsite to the right of the trail. They hadn't moved far after meeting up. We tried to count the flattened spots where they'd slept a few hours. It was hard to tell. Almost thirty, maybe. They'd made no fires. I tried not to think about what had happened here just hours before.

Clay reined up beside me. "You making it, Bud?"

"I'm making it, Boss."

"Don't lie to me, cause I know you're not doing do good." He looked around. "I'm not, that's for damn sure."

"Boss, I…" I didn't know what I was going to say, or if I even could.

"You don't need to say nothing, son. You and me both, we're going through the same hell." He looked me in the eye. "Harden your heart. We both have to."

Don't know if it was my heart, but there was something hard choking my throat.

On we went. It was near impossible to make out the bull tracks being trampled by all the steers and horses. Once in a while, I'd spot the bull's oversized tracks.

We'd gone maybe three miles. I was getting concerned. I'd not seen the bull's tracks for some time.

"Clay!" I rode back to him as he held up the squad.

It hurt to say this. "I don't like this, Clay. I don't see no sign of the bull. Ain't for near a mile."

He looked disappointed. "What do you want to do, Bud?" He was sure putting it on me.

"Backtrack. They could of split off to either side, but probably right because I ain't seen no bull hooves drift to the left. I'll take this side and Flaco the other."

It was made harder because both squads and the remuda had trampled over the trail we were backtracking.

Just over a mile back I found it. It jumped out at me. Don't know how I missed it; except I was so jack sure they'd stayed on this trail. They had turned up a rocky arroyo running down from higher ground. What gave it away was some mud tracked on the rocks. A ways up the arroyo was a washout and the bull's tracks, and some cow tracks were plain as day along with ten, twelve horses.

"What you thinking, Bud?" Clay was studying the ground ahead, thick with mesquite and scrub trees.

"I think the girls are with the bull."

"Why?"

"I don't think they're planning on improving their stock with the bull. Maybe they're holding it for ransom too."

"Yep, that was in the ransom letter too. Two-hundred dollars." He looked thoughtful. And?"

"They went to the trouble to join up with the big herd, follow along, and then split off to a hideout to wait and make the ransom deal. They want us to think they're still with the big herd."

"You sold me," muttered Clay looking at Lee. "He could sell broken eggs to a hen."

Lee nodded. "Told you he's smart."

"Well, let's see where they take us," said Clay. "Pass the word for everyone to keep real quiet. The second squad needs to stay way back."

Flaco rode up. "This'll take us to *la Hacienda del Rancho Mariposa*. Maybe three mile."

"You two ride ahead, real quiet like." It was late afternoon.

GORDON L. ROTTMAN

Chapter Thirty-Two

Flaco was in the lead. He'd been on *Rancho Mariposa*, but not this part. What little he knew was more than any of us, though. The arroyo led up to a road and curved away from it.

Flaco bent over in his saddle looking at the tracks. "They go left," he said sounding surprised.

"So?"

"The *primo hacienda* is right. I thought they take them there, a mile to the right."

We told Clay.

"I was hoping that old rake wasn't involved in this. Don Garza Alvarez, he's a good man."

"Where's this road lead?"

"His first son's *casa*—house," said Flaco.

Clay nodded like that was no surprise. "How far."

Flaco shrugged. "Don't know." He looked at me. "Come on. We sneak up there and come back." We took Dodger along.

The son's *hacienda* was only a quarter mile up the left road. The adobe house sat within a stand of scrub oak. There were eight horses in the corral and four mules. Of course, that didn't give you the number of men there, but it probably told there weren't no more than that. Ol' Pancho had taught me. Quicksilver stood in another mesquite corral contently chewing his cud. In a far pasture were about a dozen head of cattle, probably with Dew brands. No one could be seen, but the chimney was smoking. A farm wagon sat beside an outbuilding.

Then we barely heard a girl sobbing from inside. My guts clenched. I wanted to charge straight in there, now.

Flaco gripped my arm, shook his head. It steadied me.

"You hang here. Dodger, keep an eye on things. We'll head back and tell Clay."

We took off down the road. I *knew* Marta and the girls were in there. This would be over soon. I tried not to think about what might be happening in there. I ran harder.

I drew Clay a picture of the layout in the wet sand. We had a sit-down and talked about ways to do this. I chaffed at the bit, wanting to get going.

"The problem is they got the girls," Clay grumbled. "Whether we call them out or go busting in, they got the upper hand."

"Some of them bound to come outside," said Lee. "If nothing else to draw water, feed the horses, pay respects to the shitter. We could maybe grab a couple of them and swap them for the girls."

"Hell, those banditos jus' as soon let us shoot 'em ol' boys," said Lew. "They don't give a good damn. I don't see 'em givin' up the girls just 'cause we got a couple of their Pedros."

"That's true," said Clay. "You think the old man's son's in there?" looking at Flaco.

"Probably. He a crooked sumbitch."

"What if we go down and tell Don Garza about this? Bring him up to talk some sense into his boy."

"The banditos only take his son hostage too," said Flaco. "Tell the old man to give them money for him too. They don't care."

"We're in a fix, boys."

"Anything we can do to draw most of them out all together?" asked Lee.

"Start a fire," said Lew. Pointing at the picture in the sand. "In this shed."

Clay studied it for a piece. "Might work. Anybody think it might not?"

Heads shook. "Best hand we'll have I think," said Lee.

"I *will* have the girls out of there before dark. We surely don't need any gun play at night." He didn't need to say the reason.

We worked out who was going to do what. Lew picked places

for men to hide so they could cover all angles. All sides of every building were covered so no one could hide behind them once the shooting and running started. Gent would fire the shed. Clay was taking me, Flaco, and Jerry Twining with his coach gun, right through the front door.

Everyone was filled in on the plan, knew where they were supposed to go, and what they had to do.

"Know your targets, boys," said Clay. "No wild shooting. Don't forget the girls." He slit his eyes and said in a hard tone. "I don't expect any of those banditos to hear a night owl."

We all knew what he meant.

— •●• —

We were about thirty yards from the house behind a brush pile. I could see a couple of our boys in their places behind trees and brush. Couldn't see him, but Gent would be crawling up a ditch toward the shed. He had a can of coal oil, rags, and his new-fangled Erie cap-lighter.

Flaco had his two revolvers in his hands as did Clay with two Colts—one new, one good used. I had my Remington in one hand and my pick-ax in the other for busting doors. Jerry stuck two shotgun shells between his teeth for quick reloading. Besides his holstered revolver, he had another tucked in his belt.

"You boys be careful where you shoot." Clay didn't take his eyes off the house.

We all nodded.

I glared at the house. It had only a few curtained windows, one door in the front, one in the back. "Chico" Munoz, a crack shot, was covering the back, was told by Lew, "Shoot anyone coming out what ain't got *chichis*. A big water trough sat by the windmill. I knew a lot of rifles were pointing at it. We figured that's where most of the banditos would head when the fire started. Anybody at the trough couldn't see the house's front door. A couple of rifles covered the horse corral too. No one was getting away.

We'd seen only one man come out. He'd gone to the outhouse. He was toting his guns, but didn't even look around. We heard some laughing from inside a couple of times. That didn't feel good at all.

We needed to be watching the house, but our eyes kept

shifting to the shed, watching for smoke. Even when it caught, we knew it would take time for them to smell the smoke or hear it burning. In case they still didn't come out, Flaco was going to yell, "¡Fuego!"

A pebble rolled on the ground and we turned to look back. Musty was crouched low behind a cactus patch, waved, and started crawling toward us, fast.

Reaching us, he said, "There's four riders comin' up the road."

"Damn!" Clay jerked his head to the left, and the five of us scurried around the brush pile. We still couldn't be seen from the house. It was just in time.

Clay whispered, "I hope no one gets excited and starts shooting right now."

We heard a horse snort, could hear hooves, and made out their dark shapes through the tree limbs.

"You gotta to be shitting me," said Clay all wide-eyed like he recognized someone.

I heard a crackling sound and white smoke was pouring out the shed's door.

Chapter Thirty-Three

The house's door flew open and Mexes started running out shouting up a storm. The burning shed's smoke was blown by *El Nortada* straight to the house. Our boys' rifles started cracking.

Clay paid no mind to all that, but to the horses coming up the road. "Aim for the horses, I will have them bastards alive," whispered Clay as he rose up, Colts in both hands.

He wants who alive? I thought. Then, what about the girls? I wanted to charge the house.

There were two riders in the lead, side by side, and two following. The horses bolted with the first barrage as we opened up with all our pistols. The screaming horses bucked and rolled in the late afternoon shadows. I hate seeing horses shot, hate their screaming. It was bad for these. They ain't had no say on who's riding them.

"Take them alive," yelled Clay. Two of our boys were coming out of the trees, rifles leveled. One horse still kicked. I saw hands going up. Rifle shots rattled like hail on a tin roof back at the house. I turned and saw banditos going down all over and not even making it to the water trough. One turned back to the house and flopped into the mud, back-shot. There was a frantic American voice behind me, coming from the gunned down horses. "Don't shoot, don't shoot!"

Clay yelled for us to reload. I don't think no one got more than one gun reloaded, and we were heading for the front door ignoring the gunned down men behind us. Jerry was in front ready to blow the door's lock apart, but instead his shotgun blew a Mex back through the open door with a spray of blood and stuff. We were in a big room with a fireplace, all smoky and musty smelling, the odors of different food, different air, a different life. No one was there. I headed left through a curtained door into a bedroom shouting, "Marta!" The others were shouting for Agnes and Doris. I could hear the dread in Clay's voice. The two bedrooms on this side were empty. Three shots banged in another part of the house, and shots were still popping outside.

Going back into the big room, Clay came through a door on the other side. He had a pained expression and blood splattered on his legs.

"Nothing on this side, boss." I had a bad feeling.

"There's no one here, Bud. The girls aren't here."

I went through all the dark rooms myself, came across the bandito Clay had shot in a corner—two in the chest, one between the eyes.

"I was sure they were here, boss. I was sure." I raged at myself.

"Hold on, son. It's not your fault. We all thought that."

I went through the front door. I needed air. Leaning on the wall, everything was dark. *What am I going to do now?*

Clay came out the door reloading. "Come on, we don't have time for that." He's as tough as horseshoe iron. "We gotta get to the bottom of this."

Flaco came out dragging a crying Mex gal with him. "*¿Trajeron las chicas americanas aquí?*" he kept shouting.

She was yelling, "*¡Por la gracia de Dios! ¡No hubo chicas!*"

"She says no 'merican girls, *jefe*."

"How abouts Mex girls, Flaco?" I shouted.

"*¿Alguna chica mexicana?*"

"*¡No, no! ¡Por favor, protégeme!*" she begged.

Flaco looked at me and shook his head.

Smoke swirled around. There were several dead Mexes scattered across the ground and some not so dead. They were wearing yellow scarves. One was trying to get up, and Chico Munoz shot him in the head.

"Lew, save a couple of them," Clay shouted. "I wanna talk to them."

We had only one man took a bullet. "Rock" Rockingham got hit in the right foot, broke a lot of little bones. Gent was cutting a teeth-gritting Rock's boot off.

Clay headed for the shot-down horses. Musty and two others had their rifles on the riders sitting or lying on the ground. One looked real dead.

I shook my head. "What the hell!" I was looking at Pete Weyland tying a bandana around his bleeding leg.

"Weyland, you're like a bad penny, keep turning up," said Lee. "I hope you ain't looking to get your job back." Lee had an evil sneer.

Weyland didn't say nothing.

Clay stood over a big man on the ground, goatee and big lamb-chop sideburns. "What the hell's going on here, Maxwell?" Clay looked like he was about to bend his Colt's barrel. The look on his face was deadly. "Gentlemen, for those of you haven't had the pleasure, meet Mr. Theodore K. Maxwell of the V-Bar-M Ranch, my longtime *goood* neighbor." He didn't sound like he meant that last with any sincerity.

Standing over another man, Clay said, "Lay on your face, Mackley. You aren't shot." Turning to us, he said, "This is Tom Mackley, Maxwell's foreman."

Clay stepped over the dead man, pinned under his horse. He had two holes in his chest, and his right hand was half torn off. "Who's this?"

"Mario Garza. Don Garza's son," Flaco said flatly.

"Well, hell, the old man's going have a duck fit and a chicken spasm."

Clay turned on Maxwell. "What the hell are you doing here, Teddy?"

The chunky man looked up at him, plum scart white. "I was simply coming here to look over some stock, Clay. I don't know what's going on here. Why'd you start shooting at fellow Texans?" He was starting to sound indignant.

"So Mario Garza was only bringing you out to his spread to show some stock, and it just happens that *Xiuhcoatl's* boys brought my bull here. I guess it was only a neighborly stopover on their way to market."

"I didn't have anything to do with that, Clay."

Clay lashed his Colt across Maxwell's face knocking the old man onto his back. He grabbed him by the collar and dragged him up. "You son of a bitch! You had everything to do with this." Clay shoved him down to his knees and jammed his Colt's muzzle into Maxwell's left eye. "Start talking!" He hit him again. Clay's eyes held a fearfully wild look.

"Clay," said Lee softly.

Clay looked at him sharply.

"Don't kill him just yet, boss. I see what's going on here."

Clay nodded. "Tie their hands."

We cut latigos off the dead horses' saddles and tied their wrists with the leather straps.

Lee yanked Weyland to his feet.

"My leg!"

"You little piece o' shit. I fired you and you went to Maxwell, got hired on because he was planning to have Clay's bull stolen."

"I didn't have nothin' to do with this!"

"Bullshit!" Lee shouted. "Your new boss likes you so much he takes a new hire along on his business trips." He pistol-wacked Weyland on his shot leg.

"It's all come to me, Clay," said Lee. "I been trying to figure how the bandidos knew the Dew layout, about the outrider and the house sentry, where the girls' room was, and where the bull was. You sumbitch, you got Slick and Carmela and two kids killed!" Lee hit Weyland on the leg again, driving him to a knee.

"I wasn't there. I didn't kill 'em!" He gripped his leg. "Lord almighty, don't hit me again!"

"You might as well have pulled the trigger yourself, you cocksucker. And you shot at Bud in Del Rio, coulda killed him. Drawing on a Dew hand, that don't go! I shoulda stretched hemp on you the first time I had a chance!"

With Lee through, Clay turned on Maxwell. "This is all your doing, Teddy. You wanted that bull, cut a deal with *Xiuhcoatl* to steal the bull for you. Your *amigo* here"—pointing at Mario Garza's body still seeping blood—"was in on it too. They'd bring the bull here. You'd bring breeding cows over and take them back to your spread. Garza could breed the bull too for keeping it here. You thought I'd never look here."

"That's not the way it is…" Clay smacked him again.

"Bullshit!" shouted Clay. "What *Xiuhcoatl* got out of it was stealing my girls for ransom, and he grabbed a couple of our Mexican girls too." He was all loco-eyed. "I've always known you were a crooked son of a bitch, Teddy, but this is beyond anything one white man would do to another." He turned to Lee. "Pick a tree. Put three ropes over a limb."

Chapter Thirty-Four

Some of the boys fetched our horses from where we'd hid them, and Earnest Sessuns came in with the remuda. Lew sent men down the road in both directions so we'd not be surprised by anyone else.

Gent and Chico tossed ropes over limbs, two in one tree, one on another.

"Maxwell's going to need his own limb," said Gent without feeling.

Maxwell and the other two got all wide-eyed.

"I tolt ya not to do this," shouted the foreman at Maxwell. It was the only thing he said the whole time.

"You can't do this, Clay. I demand a fair trial. I'm a free white man."

"Fair like those kids got? Fair like what's happening to my daughters—?" He cut that off with a break in his voice. "I don't have time for you. You chose this path."

This was the sumbitch that put Marta in the cradle of hell. I wanted to gut-shoot him, right now.

Weyland started crying.

Maxwell shouted, "I'm a Texan and an American, dammit, and I demand a fair trial." He started to sound panicky and breathing hard.

"You just got one," barked Clay.

"You arrogant shitkicker," blared Maxwell. "I always said you

175

tried to rise above your station." His eyes were filled with hate now, not fear. "Now you go so far as to set yourself up as judge and jury."

"And executioner. We're in Mexico, you dumb son of a bitch. You know how it works here."

"I demand a fair tr—" Clay cut him off with a swipe of his Colt, sending teeth flying.

Looking around at us, he said, "Anybody think they need any more of a trial?"

"Not me, Clay." "Nope, boss." "*No, jefe.*" "Not no, boss, but hell no." Everyone looked stone cold.

"Anybody think they don't deserve what's coming to them?"

Same answers. Even the usually silent Chico said, "*Como dos y dos son cuatro.*"—As sure as two and two are four.

"Fetch three horses."

Maxwell looked scart now.

I took Cracker by the reins, but stopped. The bastards deserved what was coming, but I didn't want Cracker in on it. Damnest thing. There were plenty of other volunteers. Gent and Musty had a short stare-down on whose horse Maxwell was going to be hung from. Gent won the bragging rights.

It took three of us to get the bawling Weyland on a saddle. It didn't bother me none to put him there, after what he always said about Marta, and causing her kidnapping. I cinched the noose tight around his neck with him blubbering the whole time.

Tom Mackley, the foremen, got on quietly. He was shaking but he had grit.

It took four to get the fat Maxwell up, with him shouting obscenities to bring God's wrath on us all. I can't even repeat some of them.

The horses were all skittish. They sense things. Took a man or two to settle each of them down. Clay told Rosey to do Weyland, I guess because he didn't know him from before.

Clay didn't ask if they had any final words. He didn't say nothing.

Weyland was begging and crying something awful. "Please, I don't wanna die like this. I'm sorry, really sorry, and I won't never do any—" Clay nodded and Rosey jerked on the horse's reins. Weyland looked like he was running in the air, then kicked and jerked. The limb creaked, and he swung back and forth.

Dodger held Mackley's horse. The foreman looked straight ahead. I wondered what he was thinking, what he was seeing. Then he turned his head toward Maxwell and glared with pure hate. He only kicked a little.

Maxwell had his own tree. He yelled and bellowed. "You can't do this. You bastards will burn in hell for eternity!"

Clay said, "Then save us places at the head table," and nodded.

Gent tugged at his horse's reins, and Maxwell's screeches were cut off. The limb bent so that I thought it would break. He didn't kick none, looked like he was trying to reach for the mud. Guess it was his weight.

El Nortada rustled through the oaks. A horse nickered. The windmill made a thin whine pumping water, scarcely heard, water that gave life to the land. No one said nothing; no one moved. Under the clouded sky, among those shadowy trees and the gathering dusk, I guess we looked like dark angels watching over the earth's sinners hoping to change their ways.

"God forgive them," Clay said, barely heard.

"Amen," most everyone said. Some crossed themselves.

Still no one moved for long moments.

"Let's go get them girls," said Lee.

GORDON L. ROTTMAN

Chapter Thirty-Five

"We've got things to do," said Clay. We were outside the house. "Who's the girl? Mario Garza's woman?"

"*No, jefe*. She the cook," said Flaco. The girl was squatting under a tree crying her eyes out.

"Send her back to the big *hacienda* to tell Don Garza what happened here, least I can do. He's going to be as mad as a bottle of bees." He turned to Lee. "Where's those two live banditos?"

"One of them ain't a bandito, *jefe*. Works for Garza."

The peon shook so much he could barely talk. Guess he thought he'd be joining the three corpses twisting under the trees. He'd been grazed in the side and the leg, one lucky sumbitch. Flaco questioned him, but he hadn't seen any American or Mex girls. He had heard them say they had American girls. He had no idea where they were or where they were going.

Clay said, "Well, fine. Take down those three bastards and have this old boy take them in that wagon to Maxwell's place. Tell him they'll pay him there, and if I find out he didn't deliver them, I'll come back and cut off his balls and feed them to the pigs." He added under his breath, "If Maxwell's people don't shoot him for his trouble."

I thought that was mighty decent of Clay, letting this Mex go. I wanted to get along, but Clay wasn't done yet.

We turned to the bandito. Clay had a scary look in his eyes. This Mex was in bad shape; hit three times in the legs and one through the lung. Pink bubbles came out of his mouth, and his chest making sucking noises. He'd not be with us much longer. He still looked defiant and proud with his yellow scarf and silver coins sewed to his jacket. Behind us the shed kept burning.

Clay asked him a lot of questions. The bandito glared at him or looked off into the trees. "Where are they heading, how many men, what are their plans?" He got nothing out of that Mex. The only reaction from him was when Clay asked, "Did anything bad happen to the girls?" The Mex looked him dead in the eye and laughed real nasty, coughing up blood.

Clay, his face pale, looked at Lee and said, "Get me a couple of pieces of broken glass about the size of silver dollars." He jerked off the yellow scarf and pulled on his riding gloves.

"Hold him down."

Chico grabbed his head and Gent his arms. Flaco sat on his legs. Clay jammed the pieces of broken Mason's jar into the Mex's mouth bringing more blood.

After jerking the scarf tight around his mouth, without even a second's wait, Clay started lashing with his *cuarta* ripping gouges across his face. His screams were muffled by the bloody scarf.

"Clay!" shouted Lee. "You'll get nothing if you kill the sumbitch."

Clay stopped. He looked at Lee; his eyes had a crazed stare, and he was breathing hard. "Ask him the questions again," he ordered Flaco.

Flaco pulled off the scarf, and blood ran out followed by red spit and the pieces of glass. For all I could tell, the bandito was blind from the *cuarta* beating, his face covered with blood and torn shreds of meat.

He talked this time.

El Xiuhcoatl had eighteen men with him. Blood bubbled from his mouth. They were heading for his stronghold. When he hesitated, Clay whacked him again.

Flaco said, "He say *El Xiuhcoatl* return to his stronghold in little village called San Miguel. His people cannot endure his long absence."

"Yeah, I bet," said Clay.

The bandito said there was another place a lot further away they might go to, Las Norias. Flaco knew San Miguel and had heard of Las Norias, both to the west. The bandito said too that Maxwell was in on it all, for the bull. They were going to ransom the American girls. He said the Mex girls were being kept for cooking, washing, and fucking.

My guts rolled, and I eased out my Remington. I knew what I was going to do when Clay had no more use for the sumbitch.

I guess he knew he was already dead because he said, "*Todos chingaron a las chicas americana.*"—We all fucked the American girls.

I got some of his brains on me when Clay shot him.

Wiping the stuff off with leaves, I knew that had happened to Marta too. Little Marta, I could see her dark eyes and what she's going through. I walked around behind the house and puked up until I had nothing left.

I turned and Flaco was there. "We get her back, Bud."

I nodded, felt faint-headed, empty all through.

Clay looked as bad as I felt. "How far to this San Miguel?"

"*Seis leguas*, six leagues," said Chico.

"About sixteen miles," said Lee.

"And Las Norias?"

"Over thirty leagues," Flaco said as he cut the coins off the bandito's jacket.

"How far's that?"

Flaco's eyes squinted as he figured the sums. "Long ways."

"Well, we don't wanna go that far. Let's start moving before they decide to leave San Miguel."

"Dusk's comin' on," said Lee. "We ain't ate since breakfast and been up most of last night."

Clay knew Lee was right, no matter how much he wanted to get going.

"We need to get away from here. Don't need a pissed Don Garza showing up," said Clay. "We don't have time to kill him too." He looked around. "Get them three bastards down and toss them in the wagon. Then we'll go back to the big herd's trail and coil up for the night."

We collected up the guns and ammo and loaded them in feed sacks on a mule. Some of the boys picked up another pistol. I found a near new Smith & Wesson double-action. It was only a five-shot, the only good .44-40 I found in the lot. Three of the boys, Gent, Jerry, and the wounded Rock, were taking the bull, other cattle, horses, and guns back to the Dew. Gent and Jerry'd catch up with us tomorrow, following the herd's trail.

Dodger was holding something. "Boss, found this on that talkative bandito." It was Slick's elk watch. He kicked the body.

At the hanging trees, "Well, shit!" said Jerry Twining lowering a still limp Weyland to the ground.

Musty and Rosy were laughing at him. "Ya dummy, ain't ya never seen a hangin' before? Ya'd know to watch for steppin' on turds."

Two hours later, we bedded down in a hollow near where the mob we had just finished off had left the main gang.

No fires. A whisky bottle was passed around with jerky and hardtack. Lew set a guard, one-hour shifts. Lee figured *El Xiuhcoatl* had already reached San Miguel. Now that they were in the clear, forted up in their stronghold, maybe they'd send word to the Dew where the ransom meet up would be. I knew Clay wasn't thinking about forking over a ransom. He was thinking about getting the girls back and killing every one of the bastards.

I laid in my bedroll knowing Clay was going through twice the hell I was.

Chapter Thirty-Six

A misty gray dawn saw the start of our second day across the Rio. The sun was a pale white shape creeping over the trees. The crew were coughing and hocking snot. Cigarettes were being lit and someone said, "Pass that gut warmer bottle 'round."

"I'd give my eyeteeth for coffee, even bad coffee."

"That's what ya'd get if Bud makes it."

"Gib me a chaw off that plug tobaccer. What brand is it?"

"Even Change."

"Hardtack and jerky. That ain't goin' to give me no hard pecker."

"Ya don't need one today, 'specially if ya ridin' behind me."

"Ya got a whore stashed in the big ol' bedroll of yours, Musty? Y'all the last one crawlin' out."

"I shore as hell wouldn't tell ya if I did."

"Hell, y'all too tuckered out to use her ifin he did."

Musty gnawed on a cold strip of jerky. "I shorely could use some of Marta's frijole beans."

Me too, I thought.

"Y'all quit jawin' and put on leather," ordered Lew.

Even the horses were miserable. They didn't put up much fight when saddled, but they weren't partial to it either. I was giving Cracker a break. I was riding a slow, but sturdy dun, expecting a day of plodding along.

The first squad headed out with the second following, and

the fussy remuda was on their heels. The muddy trail wormed its way up a low ridge. It started to rain.

The herd's trail we'd been following was easy to stay on, but with the rain, I couldn't tell you a damn thing about it. Not only Clay, but all of us wanted to make good time. Rain, mud, and caution slowed us to a crawl. We took a short break for dinner. Musty got a fire going with coal oil under a fly tarp, and we had hot beans, bacon, tortillas, and coffee. We needed that boot in the butt.

"That'll put some lead in your pecker."

We were moving again in under an hour. I'd look back, and the ragged line of black and yellow slickers was strung out, heads down against the rain. Most of the boys were wearing Mex sheepskin chaps, real warm and they shed water. "This weather ain't fit for dogs or injuns."

We crossed arroyos running with hoof-deep water. Flaco said most of the year it's bone dry here. We'd not want for water.

— •●• —

Mid-afternoon Flaco came down the trail, crouching low, and signaled quiet. He pulled up beside me. "*Granja.*"—Farm.

Clay told us to scout it out and had everyone pull back and dismount in the thin mesquite.

Flaco and I looked the place over—an old adobe farmhouse, shed, outhouse, a couple of mesquite corrals with goats and a burro. Scrawny wet chickens pecked in the mud. An adobe pig pen sat off north of the house so it would be downwind in the summer. Flaco changed his slicker for a serape covering his pistols. Then he pulled out a yellow *Xiuhcoatl* scarf and tied it around his neck. He would bluff the farmer into thinking he was one of the gang what got left behind.

"I go to talk."

He banged on the door. A man talked to him and let him in.

It was almost quarter an hour before he came out. "Have some coffee, *amigo,*" handing me a steaming mug.

"Looks like you made an *amigo.*"

"*Sí.* Had to eat his frijoles. They shit. We go to talk to Clay."

Squatting beside Clay, "The man say *El Xiuhcoatl* come through yesterday, early afternoon. They have one hundred head of cattle, twenty men all together."

He looked down at the mud. "He say they have two *americano* girls, two Mexican girls. They are on own horses, hands tied." He paused. "*Jefe*, all the girls, they have bruises on the faces, black eyes."

Clay ground his gloved fist into his hand. I felt sick to my guts. Little innocent and happy Marta, soiled and beaten.

"Did the man mean exactly twenty or was that a thereabouts?" asked Clay.

"There 'bouts. That bandito yesterday, he say nineteen."

"Gives us a good idea what we're facing. Can you go back, ask him what the girls were wearing, maybe find out something more?"

"*Sí*. Have to give his coffee mug back."

We walked back to the house. Flaco told me to stay outside.

A horse snorted behind the house, Flaco threw his serape back and gripped his pistols. Two men in gray outfits and big sombreros with pistols hanging all over them stepped around the corner. They were as surprised to see an armed Mex and a *gringo* as we were to see two *Rurales*.

One of them yelled, bringing up a pistol, "*¡Alto! ¡Manos en la pared!*" Something about hands and a wall.

Flaco pulled both his pistols first. I got mine up after throwing the mug. All I remember is pointing and pulling the trigger, a lot of noise, and a lot of smoke. The two *Rurales* lay on their backs bleeding into the mud.

"Shit," was all I could say.

"You good?" asked Flaco, as calm as a pond in still air.

"Yep. You?"

"They shoot my serape."

We heard horse hooves pounding on the other side of the house.

"I think we need rifles," muttered Flaco.

"How about these." I grabbed one of the *Rurales'*, an old Spencer .56-50 single-shot. "Won't do." I threw it down.

Flaco said, "*¡Corre!*"

I figured straight off that meant, "Run!"

Chapter Thirty-Seven

A trumpet shrilled.

"What the hell's that?"

"*Embestida*—Charge," said Flaco.

I ran harder.

A dozen mounted *Rurales* came around both sides of the house with pistols firing. Mud sprayed all over.

The mesquite in front of us erupted with smoke. Looking back, I saw some *Rurales* knocked off their horses. They pulled up and scattered back. The blaze of fire meeting them took them by full surprise.

"What in hell's fire did you stir up?" shouted Clay.

"*¡Rurales!*" hollered Flaco.

"Shit fire. Let's let's get the hell outta here!"

"I thought it was *Xiuhcoatl* coming back," said Lee.

Bullets cracked through the mesquite from the right. Most of us got in a shallow rocky gully.

Let the bosses decide what to do, I thought. I only cracked off rounds at anything that moved. There wasn't time to be scared.

"How many ya think there are?" said Lew.

"Twenty, maybe more," said Flaco.

"We can't run," said Lew. "They'll gun us down in the open with that many rifles."

"They run us down, use pistols close," said Flaco.

Bullets came from the left.

Flaco looked around. "They...*desbordar el flanco*, go around..."

"Outflankin' us," said Lew. "They'll come around on both sides, surround us."

"*Sí, Rurales* always do that," agreed Flaco. "They have the numbers, more than us."

"Work our way deeper into the brush?" said Clay, looking over his shoulder as a barrage of shots sounded from the left.

Now I was thinking about finding time to get scared.

"No good, we make them come at us and concentrate our fire," Lew said, darting his eyes around.

"I can tell you got an idea, Lew. Tell me what you want to do."

"We go to that pig pen," pointing at the adobe-walled pen about twenty yards away.

"We'll get trapped in there," argued Lee.

"Hell, Lee, we're trapped right here. Over yonder we got good cover," said Lew. "We'll be concentrated, can mass our fire in any direction they come at us from."

Clay looked at Flaco. The fire increased. "*Rurales* like to ride down the enemy, get in among them and use pistols close-up. They cannot get in that pen with their horses, unless they jump the walls, and then they no got room to fight."

Clay glared at the low pen. "Let go the horses, most'll come back when it's over—if there's any of us left to come back to."

"We all go at once," said Lew. "If we go in groups, they'll concentrate their fire. If we all go as one there's too many targets."

"Pass the word, Lee. Everyone bring all their ammo and their canteens and water bags. We all go when I give the word. Start shooting and keep shooting on the run."

Horses were running back down the trail with a few whoops of encouragement from the boys. I told myself we'd surprise them with us going for the pig pen.

"Go!" shouted Clay.

Boys rose up and began firing in all directions. Dodger and I started running with Flaco behind us. I was shooting right, and Dodger left with our rifles. Flaco kept turning to the back blasting away with both his pistols. I saw somebody go down. The boys leapt over the four-foot wall. Mud splattered all around us, and bullets wanged off the walls.

"Holy shit!" shouted Gent.

"What the hell ya expect to find in a pig pen, ya idgit?"

"Get them porkers outta here," shouted Lee.

Musty held the gate open. As the half-dozen squealers ran out, a couple of them were hit. Bullets wacked into the walls and buzzed over us like hornets. There was a water trough and a feed trough half-buried in the mud and shit. We wrenched them out and slung them behind the gate to block bullets.

"Anybody hit, anybody not make it?" That from Clay.

"Bastards shot the top of my ear off," said Musty. Gent was tying a bandana around his head and over the right ear. Sure a lot of blood.

"I got creased across the back," said Rosy. "Hardly bleedin'."

"Sumbitches kilt my water bag." Sessuns was holding up the leather bag pissing two streams of water.

Lee said, "Chico went down."

We looked back and that *vaquero* was lying in the mud. His arm moved.

"Don't move, Chico," Lee shouted.

Flaco yelled at him in Mex.

Chico raised his head and that drew fire. Mud sprayed all around him. He jerked from hits. We all fired fast as we could, but ol' Chico was hit time after time until he stopped jerking.

Everyone cursed the Mex bastards and kept firing, but now they threw more lead at us. I wished for hell to descend on them because they were in my way of going to get Marta. It gradually died off as Clay and Lee told everyone to lay off and stay low.

We all sat in the slop, breathed hard, and reloaded. There were nine of us in that pig pen, maybe thirty-foot by twenty.

"Hell of a place to die," mumbled Musty.

"When you waller with pigs you're gonna get dirty." That from Dodger.

"This pen's too much like the damn Alamo," grumbled Gent.

"What you think they'll do now, Flaco?" asked Clay.

"Come at us on horses, all at once. They no wait long."

The *Rurales* opened up with a barrage, and the trumpet shrilled again.

"Sessuns, watch the back. Everyone on the wall!" shouted Clay.

Looked like twenty horses coming at us in a cloud of smoke. Bullets hit faster than ever. I fired until I'd emptied all fourteen rounds, picked up the Parker and let loose both barrels of buckshot. The gunfire was like nails driven into my ears. Horses rolled and plowed into the ground. I heard their screaming. One horse rolled on his rider. He didn't move no more. I saw one man get up and keep coming firing both his pistols, throw them to the ground, and pulled another, still banging away until he was hammered down with pieces of him flying off. Others were running off until back-shot. One climbed to his feet, had a leg knocked from under him and threw his hands up a'yelling something fierce, until his head turned into a pink and red mist.

The wind took the smoke away. Horses lay on the ground, dead, some kicking. Others limped around and others ran back with the retreating *Rurales*. There musta been ten, twelve *Rurales* on the ground.

I looked over the hellish mess before us, blood and guts of men and horses. I felt dirty. The scent of blood and shit and gunpowder, it turned my stomach. Dodger rose up and looked at me. I knew he felt the same. Without warning, a *Rurale* tried to stand with his hands up and Flaco shot him square through the heart. Some of the boys popped lead into the bodies, just to make sure.

Rosy was on his face in the mud with the top of his head blowed off. Lee lay on his side, his left arm bloody. A piece of bone stuck out.

Everyone reloaded, swilled water, and tried to ignore Rosy. Lew worked on Lee's arm. "It don't look good, hit below his elbow." Lee looked white.

"That broke them," said Clay. Looking at Flaco, "Now what?"

"They come at us on foot, one, two, maybe three sides." He peeked over the wall. "Soon."

But they didn't come. Instead, a *Rurale* crouching behind a rock waved a stick with a white rag on it. "They want to talk," said Flaco. "They do not do that too much. We be careful."

"Don't shoot," ordered Clay. Everyone pointed rifles at the flag.

"Keep watch to the sides and back," cautioned Flaco.

"Anyone got something white?" said Clay.

"My hat's white," said Sessuns. "Sorta."

He tossed it to Clay, who put it on a muddy stick.

"I go," said Flaco, "so we can talk."

"Just tell me what's being said. Be careful, *amigo.*"

A mounted *Rurale* came out of the mesquite and took the white flag. He wore two holstered pistols and crossed bandoliers as he cantered toward us. Flaco took the stick and hat and climbed over the wall. His pistols were under his serape. There was no way he could draw them fast if he had to.

The *Rurale* came on quick, I guess so he could get close to see into the pen and count noses. He sure paid more attention to us than he did to Flaco walking toward him.

That fella sure looked fancy. Lots of silver on his short gray jacket. Even the brim of his sombrero had silver lace, three silver bars on his shoulder straps, and he had a red necktie. He had big mustaches and a little chin beard. His eyes were hard as any *vaquero's.*

They started talking Mex, real fast. The *Rurales' jefe* was doing most of the talking and didn't sound real happy, sounded like he was demanding something.

Flaco turned a little, but could still keep an eye on the *Rurale.* "The *Capitán* say we fight good, we brave. We have shown honor, but it is over. He want the man that murder Mario Garza. We have five minutes to turn over the man, and then we can go in peace."

"Yeah, right," said Clay. "Don Garza sent them."

"What you say, *jefe?*"

In a real low voice Clay said, "Hell no." Clay didn't waste no time explaining his side of the story.

Before I could understand what was happening, Flaco dropped the hat and stick. Before the *Rurale* cleared leather, Flaco swung up Jerry's sawn-off 12-gauge from under his *serape.* He blowed off half the horse's and the captain's faces.

GORDON L. ROTTMAN

Chapter Thirty-Eight

Instead of a barrage of fire, there was stunned silence, for a short spell. Flaco didn't waste any time clearing the wall before the storm of bullets hit. It tapered off quick. To the right, we saw *Rurales* moving away through the mesquite, and we swung our fire at them.

Lew shouted something about them losing the initiative, whatever that is. He rallied his second squad, threw the troughs away from the gate, and charged though. They ran at a low crouch into the mesquite with the rest of us putting out a hot blaze.

I realized what this strategy deal was. We'd been on the defense, cut them down to size by making them come for us, took out their leader, and now we were going after them.

Suddenly, shots started blasting away from the left when *Rurales* started shooting back at someone.

"Who the hell's that?" shouted Dodger.

"Who cares," said Clay. "Let's go get them," and he went over the wall.

With rebel yells and Flaco's "*¡AHHH-haahaaa!*" we went over, following Clay, blazing away and running for the brush. Hardly nobody shot at us.

It was over in minutes. We heard a trumpet again, a different tune. "*Reunanse*—reassemble," said Flaco.

"What's that mean?" I asked.

"They're getting together to leave or to charge again," said

Musty.

"I hope they be leavin'. I've had enough of their noisy company."

Crashing out of brush to our left were Gent, Jerry, and a stranger rapid-firing their carbines. Just back from the Dew, they'd caught up with us at the best of times.

Before long, the boys were walking round finishing off horses and *Rurales*. Lew had his boys up at the house firing some farewell shots at the departing *Rurales*. One flipped over his horse's rump as he hightailed up the ridge.

Flaco limped around counting dead *Rurales*. He'd been grazed on the left calf. Jerry was nicked in the left arm. Neither was anything serious.

Flaco finally announced, "*Dieciocho*—eighteen." He had counted the two we'd first popped. "There was near thirty here, I think."

"We shore kicked their asses," shouted Dodger.

"We was only lucky," muttered Lew.

Sessuns held his recovered white hat. "Thanks, Flaco. Ya got my hat shot."

"Over here, boys." Clay stood in the pig pen.

Lee lay lifeless on the ground, his jaw hung off his face from another hit.

"He was trying to give us cover fire," said Clay. Clay didn't look so good.

Most of the boys gathered around, doffing their hats.

"Boys, there's not many men better than Lee Cleland." It looked like he wanted to say something else, but his eyes were blinking. "He knows we got us a job to do. Let's bury our dead and be on our way."

I thought about him becoming a friend and how good he treated me.

Several of us took turns digging Lee's, Rosy's, and Chico's graves on a little knoll. "Good thing ya'd brunged that pick and shovel," grumbled Dodger.

While we were doing that, the rest gathered up guns and bandoleers, some picking better pieces. Seems most everyone wanted one of the Merwin Hulberts. We'd dump the rest.

I'd of thought that Mex farmer would be happy with all the

loot we were leaving him, but he didn't want nothing to do with it. I guess because he didn't want to be found with it if the *Rurales* came back. Flaco finished talking to him. Flaco said, "He say all them girls were still wearing nightgowns, was wrapped in blankets. One was wearing long johns and a blue shirt."

That had to be Marta. They all had to be cold and wet…and scart out of their minds, and soiled. I lobbed rocks at a cactus. Flaco put a hand on my arm, shook his head.

Flaco said the farmer was none too happy he had all them dead *Rurales* and horses he'd have to bury or burn.

Little freckle-faced Fred Laffin came roaring in with most of the saddle horses, all the pack horses, and maybe half the remuda. The *Rurales'* dead horses gave up saddles for those needing them. The kid was grousing he'd wanted in on the action, until he saw what action looked like. He got kind of green-looking.

Clay looked put out he'd come instead of staying at the ranch. We all knew we needed every gun we could get, even if the kid was carrying a little .32-20 Winchester only good for shooting coyotes. It had a dent in the magazine tube so it just held six rounds instead of fifteen. Flaco found him a Mex Sharpes .50-70 and a Merwin Hulbert. That made the kid happy. "First guns I ever got that makes big holes." Clay gave him the wrangler's regular job tending the remuda.

I picked up a Merwin Hulbert. There was plenty ammunition in the bandolier, and I fitted its holster onto it, slung it over my shoulder, and let it hang on my right side.

The square-headed white-blond stranger with Gent and Jerry was Alois Makokicka. He had a guttural Czech accent and kept his shirt buttoned to the collar. Everybody knew him, called him "Snap." He used to work the Dew; Clay welcomed him with a back-slapping handshake.

Gent and Jerry had run across him on the Eagle Pass-Del Rio Road. He was working as a stocktender for the stage line and running some exchange teams down to a waystation. With the prospect for a hundred dollars and I guess loyalty too, he'd come back with Gent and Jerry. He'd paid Roberto to take the horses to the waystation.

"How come they call you Snap?" I asked.

"Oh, one day I snap my fingers at Lee to get his notice." He chuckled. "Lee say, 'If ya snap ya fingers at me again we'll be seein' if ya can snap them with ya fist shoved up ya ass'.'"

Dodger said Snap was a good man. That was good enough for me. He carried an ancient Old Yeller Henry Winchester and helped himself to a Merwin Hulbert.

Flaco showed the boys how to reload the Merwin Hulbert revolvers, fine pieces indeed. Had an odd but fast way of loading them.

Sessuns summed up what everyone was thinking about Flaco. "He's going to need two horses, one just to carry his balls, what with the way he walked out and blowed that *Rurales* chief 'way."

"Hope we don't run into 'em again," said Lew, frowning. "Shootin' him out from under a white flag of truce might not set too well with 'em." I guess Lew was used to the honor of soldiering.

"*El destino*. Fuck them," said Flaco. "They do the same to you."

We stood uneasily around the graves. Some sentries were set to be safe. Clay said his words. Some of us said something good about each of the men, especially about Lee. "As fine a man that ever stood in boot leather." Most said something about him being a fair boss or a good friend or there wasn't no better man to be in a pinch with. Musty mentioned Lee loaning him money to send to his sick mama and Lee wouldn't let him pay it back.

I could barely say anything, but managed, "I hope to meet him down that long trail someday."

We hated rushing it, but we had to get.

There wasn't much time. Clay paid the farmer to plant crosses, said we'd check them on the way back.

We readied to head out, but first Clay had something to say. "Boys, we've lost three friends. There's eleven of us now. Up to now we've been lucky." He glanced at the graves. He looked around at us, fixing each with a look in the eye. "We took them banditos and those traitors back at *Rancho Mariposa* with about even numbers. We beat three times our number of damn *Rurales*...*Rurales*, by God, right here." He looked at us, all proud. "But we got at least twenty *Xiuhcoatls*, maybe more ahead of us when we get to San Miguel. There ain't going to be any white flags there. If any of y'all want to head for home, I understand and no hard feelings."

It was drizzling and foggy. No one looked around, like they'd be embarrassed if anyone threw in his hat. Nobody moved, barely breathed for fear someone might question their manliness.

Clay looked a little emotional. He nodded. "Thanks boys."

We all murmured something.

He looked at us steady. "This is a hard biscuit to gnaw on, but anyone who's so irresponsible as to get himself killed doing this, your next of kin will get that hundred dollars."

Clay looked around at us all. "Okay then, I paid that farmer to burn us a big pot of beans. Let's get the horses watered. Fill all y'all's canteens and water bags, choke them beans down, and let's get this outfit on the trail."

Lew called out, "Ya boys what taken money from these here *Rurales*, y'all divvy it up fair." We all knew he was now the foreman. No one had a problem with that.

Musty boiled a big pot of iron-bottom coffee. Clay cautioned him not to put too much water in it, meaning, make it strong.

"Hell," said Dodger as he spooned down the sour-tasting watery beans. "I'm doin' this, so we can get Marta back and get some decent frijole beans." He winked at me.

That was as good as I felt all day, or for a long time to come.

Chapter Thirty-Nine

The rain was a heavy mist, enough to be annoying and make one's bones feel colder. The ground was rising gently. This is barren high-mountain desert, but a cold, wet one. We headed west.

"Ya know, if we keep goin' we'll strike Texas," said Musty. He's right; a big loop of the Rio turned into Texas, and we'd hit the Texas Big Bend a long ways across rough barren land.

Flaco called it the *Sierra Madre Oriental*—Mother Range of the East. He said this part is the *Sierra del Burro*—Burro Range—because burros were the biggest critters could stay alive out here. It's a good place for a fella to come to if he didn't want to be found. He could just as easily die out here too.

We rode through yucca, creosote, cactus, and mesquite, thick in some places, not so in others. Not a tree to be seen. There was lechuguilla too, called shin daggers because of being topped by sharp spines. The limestone soil sucked up the rain. It wasn't the kind of soil that left good tracking sign, but the trail left by the rustled herd was churned up good. Sometimes a bandito rider's trail was found to the outside, but most of the riders stayed in the herd's trail. It was impossible to guess their numbers.

I checked the tracks where they showed up better and finally found what I was looking for. A horse had a broken shoe. Most of the inside quarter's heel was broken off, almost two inches. It was my marker, an easy-to-find print to make sure we followed the right

199

tracks.

We rode on, our heads hunched down in our slickers, hats tied on with bandanas, and the horses bending their heads against the wind and rain. A ride like that set you thinking about what you'd seen and about what lay ahead. That ain't good. Mostly, I thought about Marta. I made myself stop, and next thing I knew, I was worrying about her again. When I did that, I tried not to think about what had happened to her, but about her, being with her, watching her. Watching her hunt, watching how she concentrated when she cooked, watching her brush all that hair. Heck, I surely missed that little gal. If…when I get her back, I'm going to… Well; I don't know what I'm going to do with her. I only wanted her back safe.

The ground leveled out, and I made myself check for sign. I was so foggy-headed it took some time for it to sink in that two pairs of horse tracks coming toward us. They were fresh and we sure hadn't met anyone. I halted everyone and pointed the tracks out to Clay. Flaco took a look at them too.

"I'm going to follow these and see where they pulled off the trail. They may have seen us."

"Hell, Bud," said Clay. "You could track a leaf blown across the ground."

Clay took the crew off the trail for a break, and Flaco followed me. On the lip of the level shelf, a couple of hundred yards back, we found where they'd stopped. From that point, they could have easily seen us over a mile away as we came up the slope.

"They know we come and how many we are," said Flaco.

The two lookouts had turned to the right and went back west through the brush. We followed. One had taken off at a gallop. The other had veered off to the northwest where the ground was higher. We headed back to the crew.

"Clay, they know we're coming and how many. One's most likely still watching us from up yonder. The other headed back to San Miguel to warn them I'd guess."

"Well, dammit all, I should have expected something like that." Clay really looked hangdog. "We're probably riding into a bushwhack."

"We could head out toward that ridge over yonder and come in a different way." Lew was pointing to a higher ridge to the south that bent around toward the northwest.

"They'd still see us coming," said Clay.

"Yeah," said Lew. "They'll know from which way we're comin' no matter where we head now." He frowned up at the high ground where the lookout was most likely watching us.

That gave me an idea. "There's something we can do."

"What's that, Bud?"

"Leave."

They looked at me like I'd grazed on loco weed.

Clay finally said, "*What?*"

"We leave. That lookout up there's watching us. He knows why we stopped, why Flaco and me rode back, and came here. He knows we know they've spotted us."

"So?"

"We call it quits and go home, or we make them think we did."

"But we don't go home, not really," said Clay, nodding.

"Yep."

"So we turn 'bout and head back like we chickened out?" said Lew.

"And then do what?" asked Clay.

"After dark, we switch back and come in another way, following that high ground to the north. Looks better than to the south."

"And they can't watch all the ways in, even if they think we may be tryin' to fool 'em," Lew said, studying the ground to the north.

"It'll be some tough riding over unknown ground all night," said Clay. "Then we hit them in the morning when they're eating beans."

Flaco hadn't said nothing, but he was thinking. "There a way we can fool them more."

We all looked at him.

"We do not attack in the morning," said Flaco. "We hole up in the hills. Much rough ground up there. Then we scout San Miguel in the day and attack them before dark, tomorrow night. I think they be ready for us in the morning, but we do not come. Maybe then they think we really did leave."

Clay and Lew looked at one another. "What you think, Lew?"

Lew nodded. "Scoutin' that place is real good ideer and

waitin' like that puts surprise on our side." He nodded again. "We can do this, Clay."

Clay looked at me and Flaco. I suspect he was thinking the same as me about leaving the girls in that hell hole another night.

I gripped Clay's shoulder. "This way gives us a better chance, better than if we go charging in there with them ready for us."

"Yeah. Yeah, you're right. Good going, boys. Let's leave this place.

— •●• —

It was a hard ride. Slow with stumbling horses. Gent even took a fall, and Snap too. The rain had let up and there were breaks in the clouds with the ghostly moon peeking at us sometimes. It was frosty cold. We could see our breath and the horses' too when the moon gave us weak light. We didn't really know where we were or exactly where San Miguel was. We'd got ourselves good and lost, which I guess is what we were trying to do.

Plodding along Flaco told us what little he knew of San Miguel. Maybe twenty houses, shacks really, people who wanted to be left alone, away from law and rules. There was a small *hacienda* with a wall around it on the west side of the place. That was *El Xiuhcoatl's fortaleza*—stronghold. He had some kind of arrangement with the *Rurales*. They left him alone. He did whatever he wished to do to the peons. It had been maybe three years ago that Flaco'd been there. He couldn't tell us much about the *hacienda* layout.

We headed back down the ridge, and right before dark we stopped and heated up cans of Boston baked beans, bacon, damp stale biscuits, and coffee too. Clay knew we'd need that to make it through this sleepless night.

Clay said it was midnight.

Lew picked us a campsite in a draw. He came up with another plan. He sent Musty and Jerry to build two fires a hundred feet apart on a ridge two miles behind us. They were to stoke them up and come back. The fires would burn out like campfires would. It might fool the banditos that a really big posse had been after them and was heading home.

With a sentry posted, we flopped in our bedrolls. The fire-starters straggled in way late. We didn't know where Fred and the remuda were and hoped he wouldn't go racing to the fires.

Clay woke me and Flaco at five. "Think you can find that place, San Miguel?" he whispered.

"*Sí*," was all Flaco said.

"I hope so. We'll be waiting here ready to go."

Chapter Forty

The sun was readying to come up. The smell of wind-drifting mesquite smoke led us to San Miguel two hours after we started.

There wasn't much to it. A muddy track with scattered adobes on both sides. Some houses were made of posts with mud-plastered mesquite limbs stacked between them like the corrals on the Dew. They had roofs made of layers of pointed yucca leaves and mud. Flaco called them *jacalitos*—shacks. A flooded arroyo ran along the north side of the village paralleling the track. There were pig and goat pens and free-ranging chickens. A few mules and burros stood sadly in *potreros*. The only movement was from animals and smoke trickling from chimneys or just a hole in the thatch roofs. It was boastful to call it a village, *pueblecito*—little village Flaco called it. The walled *hacienda* squatted at the far end, set further away from the village than Flaco remembered. Nothing fancy about it. The Dew cattle were scattered out beyond the *hacienda*. On a low hill sat the cemetery, looking livelier than the village.

Clay had given us a pair of little brass field glasses. Flaco showed me how to use them while we kneeled in the mesquite on an overlooking ridge. We counted only six horses in the *hacienda's* compound. That didn't look good.

"You think they left?" I said to Flaco, who was peering at the *pueblecito* with the glasses.

"Well, they ain't there."

"Smart ass, you know what I mean."

"Maybe they leave, but why? They want ransom monies, so why go away?" He was thinking again. "Maybe they out looking for us. Six horses—two guards, four girls stay here, maybe."

That made my peepers open. Is she in there? "Then what are we waiting for? Let's go get them."

Flaco was already sliding down the gulley.

We had to take a roundabout way. Flaco said if we went down the arroyo, someone coming out for water might see us, even if it was barely light enough to see. We crossed the ankle-deep arroyo behind the *hacienda* and holed up in some sage. The back wall was about fifty feet from the arroyo. The adobe wall was six feet high, and there was a narrow plank gate with a path leading to the arroyo and flat clothes-washing rocks. There were some loopholes cut in the wall.

The only thing we heard was a goat bleating from inside the wall. We took off our spurs and hats, checked our revolvers.

Flaco looked all around and said, "Wait here. I go first." He'd put on that yellow scarf.

Instead of sneaking up to the wall, he stood up and walked up there like he belonged. Made sense, he was a Mex after all. I could tell he was listening before he peeked over real fast like. He looked over again, taking his time, and ambled back.

He squatted down and drew in the wet dirt. "Here the house." It was one-story, had a door in the back, four windows, no glass. There was another smaller square house to the right, two mesquite-built sheds, and an outhouse.

"We go over wall, look in windows, come back. You go left, look in back and end windows. I go right and also look at little house. I take longer so you don't wait for me. Come back here."

I nodded. "If I hear shooting I'll come a running and…"

"If that happen, you run like hell, go back to Clay. Is more important you get word to Clay."

He was right, but I had a different idea. I wasn't running like hell if she was in there.

We walked to the wall and Flaco repeated the routine. Over we went. I looked back across the rocky arroyo. It was a long way to cover on the other side if we had to run for it.

Behind the house were loose chickens, a goat pen, and a burn pile with charred bloody rags and pig parts. I went to the first window to the left of the door. I feared at any second that door would fly open. I kept my pistol in hand. The room was dark and quiet, couldn't see a damn thing. Flaco looked in his first window and suddenly ducked down. He nodded at me, held up a finger, but shook his head. I took that to mean there was one man in the room, but no girls. He ducked under the window and headed for the next. I did the same.

As I eased up, I saw the light of a candle through the gauzy ragged curtain. A man sat on the edge of a bed against the wall. I eased down, waited and looked again. He stood wearing long johns and pulled on pants. In the bed was a girl, piled black hair. I ducked down again, my heart pounding. Was it Marta or maybe Inés? I really had to make myself look again, half fearing the man would be staring at me. He wasn't. He leaned over the bed and slapped the girl on the butt. She said something harsh and sat up with hair falling over her shoulders. The girl was naked. I couldn't help staring at her big jugs. It wasn't Marta or Inés—some girl older than them. Somebody'd had a warmer night than me. That made me miss Marta all the more.

I felt glad it wasn't Marta and disappointed at the same time. I kept looking at the girl. I ain't got time for this. The bandito said something else to her, and standing up she slapped at him, her jugs bouncing. He grabbed her arm, twisted it, and shoved her back on the bed.

I didn't need to see no more of that game. I went under the window and around the corner, after first taking a quick peek around. The first window on the end had a heavy curtain, and the room was black behind it. I listened, didn't hear anything. The next window was the same, but I heard a man coughing. I listened, but it sounded like a lone man and maybe hurt. I couldn't stand it in there any longer. I went round to the back and over the wall. I didn't see Flaco nowhere.

I waited a long time, but the place stayed quiet. I kept telling myself he was being extra special careful. Flaco came over the wall so sudden it made me jump.

"Come, we go."

We crossed the arroyo, almost forgetting our spurs and hats. I didn't like this because it didn't look like we were going to be rescuing any girls. Maybe he hadn't seen them either.

We went back to the mesquite we'd first spied from. Flaco

sat. "You see them? I didn't."

That was a letdown. "No, I didn't." Now what?

"I only see two men and a woman and little girl, cooking."

"I saw one man, heard another, and saw a girl, older, not one of ours."

He shook his head. "They no have a guard out. If girls there I think they have guard."

I wasn't feeling so good about this. "Now what?"

"We go back to horses. Then I go talk to them."

"You're going talk to them?"

"*Sí*, no problem."

"This I gotta see."

"You will. Wait here as safe as in your mama's arms."

That had never been a safe place for me, but I understood what he meant.

From out of his warbag tied behind his saddle Flaco pulled a gray *Rurales* jacket. Seeing my surprise, he said, "I take yesterday." He was thinking ahead again. "Hard to find one with no holes." He changed the yellow bandito scarf for his red *Rurales* necktie. "You wait here. If something bad happen, you ride back to Clay. Tell him *El Xiuhcoatl* leave with the girls. Maybe go to Las Norias, maybe someplace else."

I was feeling worse and worse.

Wearing the gray jacket and red necktie, he rode as plain as day through the village and right up to the stronghold gate. He hitched his horse and banged on the gate. That *hombre* has got some balls.

Watching with the glasses, I could see two men saddling horses. They turned real quick with one pointing a rifle. He stayed back as the other one looked over the wall. He was saying something to Flaco and then opened the gate.

Well, I be damned.

The bandito stood there talking to Flaco. It looked like he wanted Flaco to come inside the house, but he didn't—smart. Another man came out, and they all talked with some arm waving going on. Soon they shook hands all around, and Flaco and one man came out the gate talking some more. They shook hands again, and Flaco mounted. The banditos watched him ride off. I kept my rifle on them and would shoot if they raised a gun. It was way too far to reach them, but it'd make them duck and Flaco could run for it between the houses.

Flaco ambled on up the road. The men went back in. Nothing happened, that is until three *Rurales* rode past me. I didn't even hear them coming forty yards away. Rounding a rock outcropping Flaco rode right into them, and they had pistols pointed at him. There wasn't a thing I could do, not against three *Rurales* crowded around him.

He sat his horse with his hands up. Two *Rurales* dismounted and ordered him off. There was a lot of hot talk going on. One of them swung at him with a pistol, but he ducked it. That pissed the *Rurale* off, and he started pistol-whipping Flaco something serious, driving him to his knees. I got pissed with their kicking Flaco. The one doing the whipping shouted something, and the third man dismounted and took off his lariat.

What the hell? There ain't no trees for a hanging. The other man got his lariat too. The pistol-whipper—the leader I guess—had his gun shoved in Flaco's face and the other dropped a loop over him and cinched it under his arms. They knocked him over and started kicking him. Then they tied the other rope around his legs above his knees. They tied the ropes off to their saddle horns.

Oh shit! I shouldered my rifle. At least Flaco was on the ground, and the *Rurales* were standing giving me clear shots. One man remounted. I wanted to get closer to be sure, but there was no time, and they'd see me coming. Then something jumped into my head. When I shoot, the horses might bolt, even one of them and Flaco'd be torn in two or at least bad hurt. Shoot the horses first, bigger targets anyways. I took careful aim at the shoulder of the horse with the mounted man, just forward of his knee. I knew I'd have to shoot the other horse, and then still had three armed men to deal with. I didn't take time to think about what a long chance this was. Shoot the damn horses!

I fired.

The horse dropped its head and rolled over to the left onto its rider. The other horse humped its back, got white-eyed, and I got it in the shoulder. It dropped to its rump, tried to get up and slumped over toward me. The leader's horse took off. The dismounted leader turned toward me bringing up his pistol. I hit him in the arm, and he twisted sideways. Instead of giving him a second bullet I fired at the third man, who had both pistols out and according to the smoke, was firing at me. I hit him in the head, and he went over his horse. Another pistol went off, the man pinned under his horse. I shot the leader again, and he stepped back, tripping over Flaco and fell onto his back. The leader arched his belly up and kicked his legs, and the pinned fella fired again. I ran forward and as he tried to rise up on an elbow, I put two more in him. The second horse kicked some, and I shot it in the head.

"You good?" I shouted.

Flaco disgustedly tossed the chest rope off. I bent to help with the leg rope. "Go to look at the *hacienda*! What's happening there?" he told me.

Grabbing my rifle, I ran around the limestone outcropping and saw two banditos riding hell bent up the slope. One other was in the courtyard saddling. I didn't expect to hit nothing, but I fired the remaining six rifle shots, and it sure enough did the job because the two scurried into the mesquite pronto.

Flaco was up and running, holding a revolver in one hand and a knife in the other. Now I knew why the leader arched and kicked the way he done, a knife'll do that. Lashing and spurring our horses cruel mean, we crashed down through the mesquite. We didn't stop until we'd put a ridge between us and San Miguel. For all I knew, we'd next meet up with them boys from Del Rio what stole Slick's watch.

Chapter Forty-One

"Old friends of yours?" I asked.

"They know me from yesterday. They tell me no quarter for *despiadado*…cold-blooded killing their *Capitán*."

We rode in silence for a while. He was still shook and rubbing the knots on his head. Can't say I blamed him. After some time, he told me what he'd learned. It wasn't nothing good.

Flaco laid it out to everyone, except a couple of lookouts Lew had posted. In the meantime, Gent had been out scouting and ran across Fred and the remuda.

Flaco told them about us sneaking up on the *hacienda*—Clay wasn't happy the girls weren't there. I wolfed down the cold beans and bacon, and broke off pieces of hard crusty bannock they'd saved for us. Next, he talked about the run-in with the *Rurales*. They'd sure enough had remembered him in regards to the white flag. Then he told about riding back to the *hacienda*. He'd figured the *Rurales* were in cahoots with *El Xiuhcoatl*. He'd pretended he had a message for *El Xiuhcoatl* to see what he could find out. The banditos had no reason not to believe him. The ones left there were all wounded from the raid on the Dew. Three of them not too serious, but the other was bad enough to leave behind. The three were going to leave because of the Texican posse after them. The extra horses were either lame or wounded. *El Xiuhcoatl* had left with his sixteen men maybe a couple of hours before me and Flaco got there. They thought the *americanos* might come back with more men. They were heading to Las Norias.

"Well, hell, you never know what that bastard's thinking," grumbled Clay. "You get anything out of them about the girls."

"I say I heard they kidnap some girls. They say they take two American and two Mexican girls." Flaco looked at Clay. "I sorry boss, I thought best not to ask no more, or they get suspicious."

"I understand, *amigo*."

"They about five or six hours ahead of us."

It seemed to me like the closer we got the further away she was.

"Then we need to start moving."

"Mount up, boys," Lew ordered. "Dodger, bring up Fred."

Clay said to me, "I'm of mind to head to the *hacienda* and see what we can get out of the man they left behind, but we need to stay after them."

"No sense teasing something that ain't bothering ya none," said Musty.

Lew rode up. "What I'm worryin' 'bout is 'em figurin' out we're only eleven. They'll see us sooner or later."

"Any ideas?"

"Once we make contact…"

Clay glared at Lew.

"Once we catch up with 'em, we hang back, stay in eyeball contact with 'em with scouts.

"Bud, Flaco," said Clay.

"We're on it, boss."

"I'll spell you with Gent and Dodger."

— •●• —

We rode hard all day, changed horses in the early afternoon, and saw neither hide nor hair of the Fire Serpents. Only saw their tracks. There were over twenty horses—probably had some spares— and a couple of mules.

"You know anything about Las Norias?"

"It means waterwheel," said Flaco.

"Anything else?"

"Nope." After a few moments, he said, "This place we go, this land inside the big loop of the Rio Grande with Texas on three sides, it is called *El Huerto del Diablo*—the Devil's Orchard."

"I ain't seen a tree one."

"That's why they call it that; the Devil don't like trees. Empty land, good for nothing. Hotter 'n hell most of the year, excepting winter, it colder 'n hell. The *españoles*, they look for the cities of gold." He didn't have to say he thought they were fools.

"Any injuns out here?"

"No, they not stupid."

"But Mexes live out here?"

"Some stupid ones. They say white man can't live here."

"Best not say that to none of the boys."

"I don't."

Wish he hadn't told me.

— •●• —

It got colder, but the rain stopped. The sky became a giant gray blanket floating down trying to smother man and animal in the mud. We didn't belong here. The sun was just a myth. A glowing haze filled the air between the clouds and the earth. Couldn't see more than two hundred yards. The ground rose higher. The hard ground was covered with a gray paste. Dry, it would have been sand and limestone dust.

We gnawed jerky and corn dodgers for dinner without stopping. Lew tolerated a whisky bottle he carefully unwrapped from newspaper to be passed down the line, once.

Mid-afternoon. Dodger came in. "We spotted 'em. Two banditos bringin' up the rear. They were just ploddin' 'long. We saw those three from San Miguel join up with 'em."

"That gives them nineteen. They see you?" asked Clay, all anxious.

"Nope. We hung back. Gent's goin' to move up once in a while to check on 'em."

We were on their tail again. That perked me up.

"What now?" asked Lew.

"Depends," the boss said. "If they stop while it's still light enough to see where they bed down, we hit them at dusk. If not, if they keep moving 'til after dark and no fires, then it might be best to hit them at dawn."

"Or," said Lew. "We could get around the other side of 'em

during the night and let 'em ride into us in the mornin'.'"

Clay nodded. "Might be best. Something they'd not expect. We gotta see what they do, bed down or keep going. Dodger, ride back to Gent, pronto. Make damn sure they don't see you two."

— •●• —

The wind picked up. "It feel not as cold to you?" I asked Flaco.

"*Sí.* That wind come from southeast."

That's strange. The wind blew steady, not in gusts, and it got sorta warmer.

All a sudden the gray haze disappeared, and there were big ragged blue holes in the low clouds. Ahead of us and to the left, the tops of mountains could be seen. The clouds over us weren't moving, even with this wind streaming across the ground. Those mountains to the left, to the south, big soft white clouds were sitting atop them like the overflowing tops of cotton wagons. It was like they were resting atop the mountains with something pushing them over to fall down the sides. As the sky cleared more, far to the north the rolling clouds were black and charcoal gray reaching to heaven. Lightning flashed inside them. Looked like a war was going on.

"As God is my witness…" started Flaco.

"He ain't."

"God didn't finish this part of the world."

"Maybe he's finishing it now," I said.

He cut his eyes to me, gave me a tight grin.

We came up on Gent and Dodger.

Gent reported, "We had to pull back when it cleared up. They still ain't seen us far as we know."

"They shorely picked up their pace," said Dodger tying his hat on with a bandana, the brim bent over his ears.

Gent and Dodger stayed up ahead of us.

We were maybe an hour behind them, I thought. Maybe hit them tonight or in the morning. I kept thinking about Marta. Hitting them, that made me antsy. So many things could go wrong with all that lead flying.

"Glad we ain't up in them ol' mountains," said Sessuns with his reefer coat wrapped around him.

The mountains to the north were lost in the gathering

blackness. It looked like it was already night over there, but the true darkening night sky was in the east. The winds were gusting now and swirling hard around us. It's like the cold north wind coming out of the mountains is fighting the warmer wind out of the southeast as night came toward us. We could hear thunder now from the north.

Flaco shook his head. Clay and Lew had their heads together. "What you say, Flaco?" asked Clay riding up and looking to the north.

"We need to hunker down for a bad blow."

Dodger came hightailing back. "Gent wants to know what ya wanna do. It looks bad."

"We're going to stop up yonder," Clay said, pointing toward a low ridge. It looked like it'd give a little shelter from the strengthening north wind, now an endless roar.

"There's a big arroyo up 'head, couple hundred yards across. We cross it and that little ridge is just yonder," shouted Dodger.

"Let's get a move on, then," answered Clay.

Any more words spoken were only fighting the raw wind. You can't win that loud of an argument.

Flaco and I crossed the arroyo first to check out the other side where Gent waited. The low sandy and gravelly bank crumbled as the horses slid down, their forelegs out stiff and scooting on their haunches. The sides were only eight feet high. The bottom was flat, bare sand and gravel. The wind came down the arroyo from our right like an express train. It'd blow a dog off its chain. Lightning flashed, and thunder rumbled like long ways off cannons. I could feel the thunder. Then I could feel the ground shudder right through Cracker's legs. Cracker's ears laid back. I heard a low rumble. Flaco shouted, and I looked back and the other boys were too, and pointing to the right. At first, I didn't know what I was looking at. Then it made sense, a wave of water spanned the arroyo. It looked like the ground had lifted up with all the sand and gravel and rocks it was carrying, and up-rooted plants were coming with it. The wind made white caps on top of the water.

Cracker sawed himself around as the first sheet of sand-colored water swept around his hooves. Cracker didn't have to be urged none. We could feel and hear it rush past, getting deeper by the second. I'd seen Hill Country flashfloods coming down the narrow rocky riverbeds, but this was like the earth was slowly surging toward us. Then another sheet came through reaching Cracker's belly. He surged through the thick water, and his hooves were off the bottom. Times like this you let the horse do the thinking. He lunged forward, his ears down and eyes wide. In seconds, the sand-gray waters was brimming the top of the bank. The current pulled me off the saddle, and I clung to the saddle horn. Flaco hung on the bank edge trying to drag up his horse. Cracker pushed forward kicking hard, reached bottom and bounded up the bank as I fell off, but kept the reins. He dragged me out of the water, stopping when we were clear. Both of us were breathing hard. It'd been a near thing.

"It come out of the mountains," said Flaco, jerking his head to the north.

No one said nothing more. We watched for a piece. The horses just stood, the way they like to wait.

Clay was staring at the far bank with Gent over there by his lonesome. I looked over there too. We'd been so close, ready to end this. It was not enough man interfered, now God did too.

I never missed anyone so much.

Chapter Forty-Two

No fires were allowed that night. The rainstorm blasted through with lightning crashing like the gates of hell closing. I smelled brimstone. We hunkered down in the pounding rain, but it blew through in a couple of hours. I had to change into dry clothes.

It got cold enough for frost to crust on everything, and I mean everything—the plants, the ground, the horses, us. The sun was so pale that it might as well not have bothered to climb into the sky. Soon after it did, a drizzle started. The cold rose just above freezing. No fires in the morning either.

Nobody said much, not like other mornings. Only a lot of coughing and hacking, hocking snot, passing the bottle, and building smokes. Even the horses seemed out of sorts.

Musty staggered out of the mesquite looking kind of raw and folding up pages from the Montgomery Ward Wish Book. "My belly done shit so much I ain't gonna have to for the resta my life."

I checked the flooded arroyo before light and heard running water. Gent waved at me from the other side where'd he'd spent a lonely night.

By midmorning, the water went down to a foot and not too fast. We started across, but the bottom sand and gravel had turned to a deep muck. In places the horses struggled and snorted and bucked their way through. Some of the boys got cold wet feet going in over knee-deep having to lead and argue their horses across. Sessuns lost a boot, and it took Dodger's help to find it and pull it out of the gravelly muck.

"Hell without the heat," Dodger groused.

Once across we moved out. Clay had this idea *El Xiuhcoatl* might have been stopped by another flooded arroyo, but we only came across a few narrow shallow ones. No telling how far ahead of us they'd gotten.

By noon, cold, wet, and hungry, we were pretty miserable.

"Hell, we ain't even seen their shirttails," muttered Jerry.

"Swallow your grousing," I told him. "We'll see them any time now." I hoped.

The ground became more rock than sand and gravel, and it was hard to follow tracks. Usually some rocks get kicked out of the ground, and it's easy to spot the holes and dirty darker undersides of the rocks. The rain, though, filled up the holes and washed the turned rocks.

We came across a lame horse, worn out looking, left by the banditos. It had a Thursday Ranch brand, stolen no telling how long ago. I felt sorry for it.

We pushed hard, always the ground rising, the country turning more barren and rocky. By late afternoon, everyone was really down and cold and wet.

Musty said, "To think last August I was doin' a rain dance."

"Did it rain?"

"Nope. A successful rain dance is a matter of timin'."

The last hot meal we'd had was breakfast the day before. The four meals in the meantime were nothing but cold jerky, corn dodgers, hardtack, and sometimes canned beans. I can tell you, hardtack's hard enough without it being frozen. The horses ate no better. There was next to nothing to graze on.

I rode back to report to Clay we hadn't seen nothing. Lew said, "We need to hang on the feed bag, boss. The boys and animals are gettin' grouchy. Need some hot chuck."

Clay looked around gauging the foggy mist. "Make it so. Small fires making little smoke. The wind's to the north so they'll not smell it."

We cooked up beans, rice-tomatoes, bacon, and lots of coffee. The bottle went around, two or three times. Some splashed a whisky shot in their coffee. I wolfed my share and hustled back to

Flaco to relieve him to go chow down.

Musty stirred a thick, gray and lumpy looking concoction in his own pot. It smelled like life was something it had long forgotten.

"What you cooking up?" I asked.

"It's my particular grease gravy stew. Its real good ifin y'all's real hungry," Musty said.

"What makes it gooder?"

Lew said, "'Cause it's good ifin y'all's starvin' to death and ain't got no sense of smell."

I went back to the low rise I'd left Flaco and didn't find him. His red necktie hung on a tall yucca stalk telling me he'd gone ahead. I took the necktie and followed his tracks. Cresting another low rise, I saw his horse at the bottom of a higher ridge.

Lying beside Flaco, we looked across a broad pan, flat ground stretching for maybe three, four miles. I couldn't make out the ground clearly owing to the low ground-hugging fog, but we could see through clear air a high escarpment cut with huge ravines.

"That the *Estacado Múzquiz*, hundred *vara* high."

"How high's that in feet?"

"I don't know, over three hundred foot maybe. You see that dark place down the side of the *estacado*?" He'd handed me the field glasses.

"Got it."

He stuck his arm out with his hand pointing up, palm outward. "Three finger's width to the left."

I did the same and peered through the glasses. There was an angled line of black dots on the escarpment. I had to watch close to make out they were moving.

"Almost thirty horses. Some without riders, packs and spares."

A queer feeling ran through me. I looked at each little dot. I knew one of them was Marta. It was hard to breath. "Head back and tell Clay. They're saving you chow. Don't eat whatever Musty's having."

— •●• —

The crew sat their horses at the bottom of our ridge. Clay came up to our ridge and watched the last of the dots crest the distant escarpment. "Soon as they're over we're going." Endless higher ridge crests lay beyond the escarpment.

"Maybe it better we wait," said Flaco. "Wait 'til night."

"Hell, then they'll get further ahead, and we might lose their trail up that slope," said Clay.

"They might leave a lookout to watch behind them and stay until full night."

Lew lay there too. "Not so, boss, about losin' the trail at night. Look here. See that big rock outcroppin' to the right of where they climbed the escarpment?"

"Yep?" He said it so it sounded like, "So what?"

"After dark we aim to the right of the outcroppin'. Don't make no difference where we strike the escarpment. Then we turn left and keep goin' 'til we come across the outcroppin'. Can't miss it, must be hundred feet tall. We look for the trail right past that."

"You think you can find that trail in the dark, on such rocky ground, Bud?"

"Sure thing, boss. We can even use torches below the escarpment."

Clay nodded. "I like Lew's idea yesterday about riding through the night and getting ahead of them. Letting them ride into us in the morning."

"That might be hard to do," cautioned Lew. "In all those ridges and ravines up there it might not be possible to figure out which way they goin'. That's if we can even find a way through to get 'head of 'em and not get good and lost."

"Good point," agreed Clay. "Let's grain the horses and take a rest until dark."

As the pale sun set below the mountains, it got colder, but at least the drizzle stopped. We could see our breaths.

A half hour after dark we set out across the pan, probably bearing further to the right than we needed. Took us over an hour to reach the escarpment, another half to come across the outcropping, longer than we'd figured because the ground below the ridge was so broken and rocky. We made four torches from empty feed sacks soaked with coal oil. It took another half hour to find the trail. Didn't see a track one, but I finally found some horse shit and corn husk tamale wrappings.

It was hard to keep to the trail heading up the ridge, but we managed. Once up at the top we realized we weren't getting ahead of nobody. We didn't have to ride far to realize that in this maze of ridges, fingers, gullies and ravines, we'd get nowhere in the night but good and lost.

A glum Clay called a halt, and we bedded down to pass another cold wet night. The earlier hot meal, as much as it had perked up everyone, didn't help much now. Fred brought up the remuda, said that worn out Thursday Ranch horse tried to herd with the remuda, but couldn't keep up. We had changed out horses before heading up the escarpment. Fred would keep the remuda at the bottom until it was light enough to haze them up.

That long miserable day and night had been hard on everyone in different ways.

Jerry made noises, "We're goin' nowhere 'cept deeper into a cold hell."

"We're chasin' ghosts. Those girls are already dead," said Sessuns.

"Ya don't know that," said Dodger before I said anything.

"They're as good as dead or might as well be. Be better off dead seein' how they been soiled," Jerry said.

"Ya two best keep that crap to your own selves. Don't use your kindlin' up talkin' 'bout it," Dodger said.

It wasn't often I'd seen him with a look like that.

"No one's showing second thoughts, are you, boys?" I said, getting a mite heated.

"Accept my apologies, Bud. I don't mean nothing, neither does Sessuns. We only be spitting in the wind."

"Watch which way you spit, then."

They shut up. I hoped it would keep.

I held Marta's brown scarf tight.

— •●• —

The trail wasn't too hard to find in the weak dawn light. Flaco and I started out with me in the lead on a stocky dun I figured would do well in rough country. He was a sandy yellow, a good color for blending into the rocks and fog. The dun wasn't too agreeable with being saddled. Dodger had helped, biting that sumbitch on the ear until he gave in.

The trail led through a wide draw, its rocky sides about as tall as the two-story Fitch Hotel. Didn't look like we'd be in danger of losing them. There were scuff marks aplenty.

The dun's head exploded in a spray of blood, brains, and skull fragments. He fell out from under me as limp as a blob of fat. The buffalo rifle's crack echoed down the draw. My leg was pinned.

Chapter Forty-Three

The second buffalo-getter bullet hit two feet from me, blowing mud and gravel all over. I could tell another rifle firing from up in the rocks weren't no buffalo cannon, but a Winchester popping as fast as some bandito could lever it. The third buffalo bullet hit the horse making it jolt. Behind me rifles were going off steady. With the shooters so close, I played dead.

Then it was over with, excepting our boys were still popping rounds, just to make sure. Flaco went tearing by—didn't even look at me—followed by Gent. Dodger, Musty, and Snap came a running. "Ya good, Bud?" from Dodger.

"Get me out from under this damn horse. It's killing my leg."

It took some shoving and grunting to get me out. There were rifle shots from up ahead, but they died out quick.

"How you doing, Bud?" Clay was there.

"I'm making it, boss," stretching my smushed leg. "Anybody hit?"

"Nope, not a one. We were lucky." He paused. "Except they know for sure we're after them now."

"Rear guard," said Lew. "Even ifin they didn't 'spect we was followin', this was a good choke point to leave a rear guard jus' to make shore."

"Maybe they still think we outnumber them."

"They might try something like this 'gain," Lew said, as much to himself as us.

"Got one of them," said Flaco riding up. He held a Spencer .56-50. "The other got away. Gent, be on lookout."

"Damn. Sooner or later they're going to figure out we're only eleven," said Clay. "Then they'll bushwhack us, as sure as tonight's going to be colder than a whore's heart."

All whores weren't cold-hearted, I thought, but there weren't no point in arguing that right now.

"Unless we made it look like we gone away again," I said.

Clay looked thoughtful. "I can see that, but we don't know where they're going, don't know the country."

Lew piped in. "Right, we could go up some canyon or draw, and it ends up leadin' us off in 'nother direction or into a box canyon. We could lose 'em and not find 'em again."

Flaco was climbing off his horse. "Anyone want this thing?" he asked.

"That ol' Spencer's older than my pappy," said Jerry.

Flaco wacked it into a rock, breaking the stock, then chucked it into a gully. "I do not know the land here, *mal país*—bad country, where we are, but I have been to the north of here. It is better land, not so many gullies, ridges, and ravines. I do not think it is too far, but we have to cross rough land to get there."

"But we'd still havta find 'em, and we don't know where they're goin', don't know where this Las Norias is," reasoned Lew.

"Is there a road leading to Las Norias we can find?" asked Clay.

"I do not know of a road. There are mule trails, but they look like the many cow trails here. There is an old *volcán* up there, north, *Cerro el Colorado*. Bad ground, but not like here. I do not know how far, but Las Norias is straight west from the *Cerro*," Flaco paused. "If we go up there to where we can see the *Cerro*, then we know...the way to go."

"Get our bearin's," said Lew.

"*Sí*. Then we can go to cut their trail."

"Anyone got a better idea?" asked Clay.

He was answered only by shaking heads.

Flaco went on. "Maybe we can get ahead of them. They have more peoples. They travel over bad ground and have to leave men behind to watch for us. We can go faster."

"They'll not see us after them and think we've left, again, I hope," said Clay. "*If* they buy it again."

"They might," said Lew. "Even if they don't, they won't know where we're at and can't ambush us. Just like last time."

"One thing bothering me," said Clay with his eyes squinted. "They want to ransom the girls. I don't know what they're thinking, running like this. How they going to work the ransom?"

"Maybe they'll send a man back to deal with us," said Lew.

"Under a dead white flag," laughed Dodger.

Clay looked like he was going to say something he didn't want to talk about. "Boys, I got the ransom money on me. I said I wasn't going to pay them, but I gotta be real about this. To get the girls back I'll pay it." He got all hard-eyed. "Then we'll kill them."

That gave me a bad feeling and set me to worrying. It must of shown.

Clay looked me dead in the eye. "You boys leave me with Bud here."

They went off to check their rigs.

"Bud, I want you to know I got some extra money so we can buy back Marta and Inés…if we can."

"Boss, I can't…"

"Let me have my say, Bud," he said firmly. "I don't think they mean to ransom those two girls. They only grabbed them because they were there. They take strong young girls for work slaves." He shook his head. "They do that."

He didn't have to say what else they did with them.

"If we get the chance, Bud, I'll buy them back too, but it may not work. I want you to know that, son."

I kept trying to look tough, didn't do too good a job of it.

"Hang in there. I'm relying on you to find them all. We'll do whatever it takes to get them back."

I could barely mumble, "Thanks for laying it on me straight, boss. I'll do my best."

"I know you will, son." Louder, he said, "Let's mount up. Flaco, take us to *Cerro el Colorado*."

— •●• —

It took us all day, but in the late afternoon we came up out of an arroyo and there, straight to the north through the mist, was *Cerro el Colorado*. Flaco said that means "colored hill." The dome-shaped mass of rock came up about six-hundred feet above the surrounding ground. The flatland around it wasn't near as bad as what we'd come through before.

We turned northwest and found some easy-going ground, for a while. By nightfall, it wasn't so good. It was all low rolling hills, ridges and knobs, twenty to eighty feet high. It made for slow going, hard on the horses. Least there wasn't much growing to get in the way.

We found a good place to camp and had a much-needed hot meal. We grained the horses. Fred said we were good on grain for now.

All that time, that night too, I tried not to think about what was happening, had happened, to Marta, to all of them. But I did anyways.

Chapter Forty-Four

We had a pretty good breakfast after a night cold enough to freeze the nuts off a bull. We passed around cans of peaches after beans, bacon, and grits. That was a perk-up. Lots of coffee too and a whisky bottle. We knew this was going to be another hard day, and its end could be about anything you could think of.

The ride that day made my head numb. Just plodding along, up and down, nothing much to see, fighting not to think about what might have been, what could happen. I tried to think of the good things about Marta. It only made me think of what's been happening to her. I tried to think about other things, anything, about the spreads I've worked, men I've known, whores I've been with, even thought about when I was a kid. That wasn't no good, better think about something else.

Around noon, Musty said, "By my reckonin' its New Year's Day."

No one made anything of it, except for Jerry. "Hope it's better an' the last."

We rode, we walked, up and down. Flaco and me swapped lead with Dodger and Gent. Always looking for sign, a fresh trail left by a line of horses. We found some counterfeit trails. One looked new, but it was only the false likeness caused by the rain. Another was fresh, but it was only eight horses and bore northwest. There were burro tracks, antelope, maverick cow, even some stray horse prints.

When I cut the trail, it took me a piece to even see it for what it was. I dropped off the horse and checked it out close. It was over twenty horses, closer to thirty. Some of them were spares walking off from the main herd. There were two unshod mules. I found prints of the horse with the broken shoe. It was them for sure.

The find perked everyone up, especially Clay.

Me and Flaco got fresh horses and took off. It was really Gent and Dodger's turn to lead, but Clay asked if we could do it. He knew I'd push myself harder, had a reason to.

As we pushed on, I started to see how fresh the trail was on the flats. On the sloped ground water ran over the tracks making them murkier. On the lee side of a hill was a really big pile of horse shit. Most turds I'd found were soaking wet.

Kneeling, I dug into the pile and crumbled a turd in my hand. I turned to Flaco, "It's still warm."

He grinned. Me too. So did Clay.

We changed horses again. I dug in my heels, "Let's go get her, Cracker."

Me and Flaco left everyone behind.

An hour later, we were bellied on a ridge. Flaco handed me the field glasses. He didn't say nothing, didn't need to.

The mist had cleared and low sun ahead of us showed under the clouds casting a wet yellow light on everything. A quarter-mile away banditos were wandering around collecting firewood, what there was of it. The horses were on two picket lines. When we'd found them they were watering in a thin stream. There was a knot of people to one side, mostly sitting. I set my elbows solid and adjusted the focus as best I could.

There was Marta. My throat about lumped up. So small, on one knee breaking sticks. She had a red-brown blanket over her shoulders. Her long black hair was tied in a ponytail. She stood, and I saw she was only wearing her black socks and filthy gray long johns. Damn, she must be freezing. Six days of this and all else what had happened to her. I ground my teeth. I stared a long time. Something about her didn't look right. Like she could hardly stand. She looked out of kilter. The other girls didn't look any better. They were all wearing only dirty nightgowns, brown or gray blankets, and had rags wrapped around their feet. The two blonde girls' hair were matted and tangled. Wearing as little as they were and all wet and worn out, they must be shaking cold all the time.

Agnes, Clay's youngest, didn't look like she could stand up, just sat there staring off into the big nowhere. Doris tried to stay close to her, but one of the banditos set her to picking up firewood. Inés was setting rocks in a cook-fire circle. She crawled around on her hands and knees, too weak to stand and stoop.

My eyes kept going back to Marta. Flaco didn't say nothing. He was letting me take all the time I needed. This was the first time I'd seen her since she'd been taken. Six days. It seemed like a year since I'd seen her. Watching that little girl was tearing my heart to pieces. I had to get her out of there, protect her, the others too.

A bandito swaggered up to Doris, knocked the few sticks out of her hands and slapped her to her knees. He dragged her to her feet throwing the blanket off, punched her in the belly. *Why'd he do that?* He pulled Doris' nightgown over her head and arms to keep her from fighting, shoved her onto the blanket, and took her right there. The other scum didn't give the rutting animal a second look, it was so ordinary. The girls looked away with Agnes balling up with the blanket over her head with hands to ears. I dropped the glasses, fought to keep from puking and fought to keep from picking up my rifle and charging in there. Flaco gripped my shoulder.

It was over in short minutes. Doris only laid there. Pulling the blanket over her was the only sign of her moving for a long time. The animal walked away like he'd done nothing more than had taken a crap.

I made myself look the banditos over. There were nineteen. In all, there were twenty-six horses and two pack mules. That gave them only three spares. Best I could see every man had a rifle. Couldn't tell much about pistols seeing most were wearing serapes or ponchos.

There was one fella, not a very big *hombre*, who looked to be in charge, giving a lot of orders, shouting with arm waving and finger pointing. I don't know, I guess I'd had it in my mind that *El Xiuhcoatl*, the dangerous evil bandito chief, would be a big fella. Watching them long enough there was another *hombre* who looked to be a boss too, a little taller fella, wore a fawn-colored sombrero with a tall pointed crown with a yellow ribbon around it.

I finally gave the glasses back to Flaco and told him who I thought the two honchos were. He watched and finally said, "I think you right. That one with the yellow and red poncho is *El Xiuhcoatl*. The other one, with the red and orange poncho, is his brother."

"What's he called?"

"I don't know. May be *serpiente de un ojo*—one-eyed snake."

"Anyone know their real names?"

"Yes, but it's not me."

"Big help you are."

"I knew a cousin of his. Maybe she know."

We watched a while longer trying to decide if this was where they were holing up for the night. There was still three hours of daylight. Awfully early to be stopping. We could see they were tuckered out. Maybe they were stopping early because they needed to rest, or they might only be stopping to eat and then move to a more hidden night camp. Flaco pointed out they were collecting a big pile of wood, more than needed for only a supper fire. Looked like they'd be bedding down here.

Gent and Dodger pulled up below the ridge. Flaco stayed behind the brush we were hiding in, and I went down and told them what was going on, how many and all that.

Flaco came scampering down the ridge. "Six are leaving. They go west."

"That pulls a spoke outta the wheel," I said.

"Maybe go to Las Norias. They not scouts. I don't think scouts would go ahead or go that way first to circle around later and scout behind them," said Flaco.

To Gent and Dodger I said, "You two stay here, keep an eye on them. Just don't let them see you." I felt bad telling them that, they knew better. It was just that we were so close now that I was scart something would go bad wrong.

— •●• —

"Anybody got any ideas what those six are up to?" asked Clay.

I hadn't told him what'd happened to Doris. It wouldn't serve no good.

"I think they go ahead to Las Norias, but I don't know why," offered Flaco.

"One thing I can tell ya," said Lew. "They don't think no one's after them splittin' up like that. And they got no outriders patrollin'."

"I don't know," said Clay. "Maybe they know we're following, and they're going to bring back more men. Either way, we need to decide what to do."

"If theys want reinforcements 'cause they suspec' we after 'em, they'd only send one or two men," said Lew.

Clay said, "That's true, but they're leaving late in the day. Why?" He looked at Flaco.

"I don't know," Flaco said. "Sending off six men, they got to be doing something."

"Who knows what they're thinkin'." said Lew.

Clay looked back at Flaco. "I know you don't know any more about the lay of the land here than we do, but do you think we can sneak by those camped up ahead and catch up with those six?"

"What for, boss?" from Lew.

"Bushwhack them bastards, cut them down in size. Then deal with the others back here."

"If we do that we won't havta fight 'em later," nodded Lew.

"They got almost an hour head start on us," reminded Flaco.

"You think we can do it, not all of us, just five go after them?"

"We can try," I said wanting to get this going. "But, we gotta leave right now." Inside I didn't like the idea of distancing myself from Marta, but if we cut out those six, it'd be better in the long run.

"No," said Lew.

We all looked at him.

"We do like we talked 'bout before, we all go, exceptin' two who keep watch on the main body. Those two would keep the remuda with 'em. We put down the six, and that gets us ahead of the main body. They'd never knowed it until they ride into our ambush."

"Explain," said Clay.

"If that detachment"—Lew was using army words again—"is headin' for Las Norias, then that should be the direct route. Makes sense the main body'll go that way too." Lew summed it up. "So we take out the six and set an ambush for the rest. If the main body bypasses us, we cut their trail and hit 'em from behind 'fore they make Las Norias."

Clay nodded and wacked his leg with his *cuarta*, "Let's go."

We worked fast changing out horses. Fred would hold the remuda here along with the pack horses. The kid groused about being left behind again. Musty took off to tell Gent and Dodger the plan. He'd catch up with us. They were to shadow the main body.

We moved out circling north and lit out after passing a good distance from the encamped main body—encamped, that was a Lew-word too. Flaco was in the lead, and after an hour and a half, we cut the detachment's trail. They were maybe two and a half hours ahead. The question was, would they bed down or ride all night? If they kept on, we'd probably not catch them before they made Las Norias. We moved fast. It was hard on man and horse. Everyone—maybe not the horses—knew that this would help bring this to a sooner ending.

We were on their trail for three hours. The sun had dropped in the west, the direction we were heading. Flaco was in the lead when he trotted back and halted us.

"I see a fire ahead."

Chapter Forty-Five

I hoped for everything that no one breathed too hard. We were that close to the campfire. All eight of us lay there, each with a pistol in hand, excepting Jerry with his coach gun. Lew'd had us take off our hats, gun belts, spurs, and slickers too; they were noisy. We'd taken everything out of our pockets. He'd even had us jump up and down to see if we jingled.

The banditos all sat round their fire eating something that smelled good and hot. They talked a little. They didn't even have a sentry out. The plan was to get in as close as we could, stand or kneel to get the best shot, and open up on them when Lew fired. Six of us had a bandito assigned we were to shoot at until he stopped moving. The men on either end of our line, Sessuns and Snap, were to shoot anyone making a break for it.

Everybody knew that sitting around a fire you can't see squat behind you. If you looked back you're night-blind, only seeing black even with a man right behind you. If a bandito got away into the dark, we'd be night-blind too because of their fire. We'd moved in on hands and knees from the southeast since their horses were on the northwest. That put us downwind.

It would start any second. I knew Lew wouldn't wait long to lessen the chance of being caught. I kept telling myself we had them cold. There wasn't much chance of any of us being hit, I hoped. The Dew had already lost eight good souls. A lot of other men had died too. I'd not been counting.

One of the Mexes stood and my breath caught in my throat. He walked to his bedroll and crawled in. Some of the banditos laughed at him. Maybe he had a bellyache.

Shadows of Dew men rose out of the ground. I heard single-action hammers click and banditos were turning. All the guns went off at once. A couple of Mexes made it to their feet before getting blowed over. Everybody emptied their gun like Lew told us. The bandito in his bedroll didn't even start to sit up.

My bandito went down with the second shot. I wanted to believe he was the one I saw take Doris. His legs kicked until I fired all six shots.

It was over as fast as snapping fingers.

"Everybody good?" shouted Clay. The echoes still cracked, and then it was silent except for the wind and questioning nickering and huffing of horses. Everyone answered up.

"Somebody roll that Mex offa the fire 'fore he starts baking," said Lew. He checked each to make sure they were dead.

Nobody was skittish about dead Mexes. They were used to that now. Ol' Pancho had warned me about this, when man-hunting. "When a man goes after another man, his soul ees strips away; eet makes him something he's not."

Some of the boys helped themselves to Mex grub and coffee. Others gathered up the guns and ammo. We'd dump them later.

"What 'bout the horses?" asked Musty.

Everyone went quiet.

Sessuns said, "Oh, shit."

Snap said, "*Hovno*," which I took as the same thing in Czech.

We couldn't let them go. They'd head to Las Norias, or worse, back to the main body behind us. We couldn't keep them tied up someplace and for sure not here near the trail to Las Norias. That's when we realized the trail the six banditos had left would end here. That would give us away when the main body came through.

"Fine, maybe we ain't gotta shoot 'em horses," said Lew.

I think everyone breathed easier.

"I'll take 'em on ahead leavin' a trail 'til I find a good ambush spot. The rest of ya circle 'round to the north so your tracks can't be seen. The banditos will follow my trail right into us." The firelight showed he was smiling.

It was going to be another long cold night in the saddle.

Lew set us picking up empty cartridges and kicking dirt over the blood puddles. Lew even had us walk around tracking over the bodies' drag marks. We loaded them deaders on their horses. That was a tough chore, the horses not liking the blood. The campsite was off the trail a ways so we hoped the rest of them wouldn't come through here and see anything to put them on guard. We'd have to dump the bodies further away. There wasn't a real good bushwhack place on the back trail. We'd have to find something up ahead. The dark made it harder.

"This is gettin' complicated," said Lew.

Lew led the string of banditos' horses on west leaving the trail for the banditos to follow. We skirted a couple of miles to the north. The guns we dumped in a gully.

— •●• —

Two hours later, we spotted Lew way off on a low ridge lighting pieces of newspaper a whisky bottle had been wrapped in and dropping them to the ground.

Two low fingers split out from the front of the ridge. "Like a whore's spread legs," said Musty. Lew's trail led right up between those desiring legs to crest the higher ridge and headed on west. On the larger finger on the north side of the trail was a lot of brush and rocks, good cover.

Lew said, "If we put three men up on the higher ridge top they can fire right down the trail between the fingers, right into the column of banditos. That's called enfiladin' fire."

We all nodded like we knew what he was talking about.

"We position everyone else on that north finger and hit them with flankin' fire, from the side."

We all nodded.

"Kinda like catchin' them in a crossfire, then?" said Musty.

"Jus' like," said Lew.

"Then why the hell didn't ya jus' say so," said Musty, all flustered. That broke everyone out laughing, even Clay and me.

Lew ignored it and kept real serious like. He said the south finger was lower, but had a lot of rocks on its sides and top. "We don't want any of them making it to that south finger. That'll give them cover. If they do, the men up on the top of the ridge need to rush over to that side of the trail so they can fire down the length of that finger…"

"So we enfil-ladle 'em," said Musty.

"I see you're finally understandin' tactics."

Behind the ridge, we took all the horses up a draw to the north and picketed them. Sessuns and Snap led the banditos' horses further west, the bodies dropped in a heap, and the horses picketed. Those two came back and joined up with Lew on the ridge crest. He took that position since he knew all about enfilading and stuff. The other five of us spread out on the north finger. Flaco and I were on the east end of the finger's shoulder. Clay and Musty were a lariat's length to our right, then Jerry. I had my rifle, shotgun, and two revolvers laid out. Flaco had his carbine and four Merwin Hulberts. We laid on our gum blankets and pulled blankets over us. It was cold and no one slept much, just dozed on and off. We all had a canteen and jerky and corn dodgers because it would be some hours into the morning before we expected them to show.

Before getting into position, Clay told us all to be certain of our targets, not to shoot wild as the four girls were among the banditos. I told them the girls were all in blankets, and none had hats and that *El Xiuhcoatl* was wearing a yellow and red poncho and his brother a red and orange one.

We dozed in fits and shook awake frozen. As the sun tried to brighten the sky through the heavy clouds, it started to drizzle. The gum blankets didn't help much. It was a damn long morning.

With the weak light, the side of the lower finger facing us was in shadow. As the sun got higher, we could see how rocky and thick the brush was over there. It came down almost to the trail.

"We're going to have to do some fast shooting to keep them from getting in there and holing up like foxes," muttered Clay.

Flaco nodded while gnawing on a strip of jerky.

Instead of hoping to put off what was coming, all I could think was, *Let's get this done and over.* I hoped the banditos were as cold as us and were making good time for Las Norias. I aimed to shoot those bastards down, save the girls, make a fire from their rifle stocks and saddle frames if we had to, eat something hot, and go home to the Dew.

Having a lot of time, I thought about that. Save Marta and go home to the Dew. That was always on my mind, but I'd not thought about all what that meant. I knew it wouldn't be the same with the friends we'd lost. But the idea of just taking Marta back there. I liked that a whole bunch.

I heard a low whistle and recognized it as Lew's from atop the ridge. I nudged Flaco awake. Clay whispered, "Heads up, boys. We're going to feed them the coals of hell."

I was about to get my wish for the good or the bad of it.

Chapter Forty-Six

Hunkered down in the brush I couldn't see them coming until they were in my line of fire. We'd taken our hats off to hide better. I thumbed back the Winchester's hammer, held the sights on the lead bandito, and fought the overpowering urge to squeeze off the fourteen rounds in the magazine and one in the chamber. At this range, I could put out fifteen aimed shots in twenty seconds. I had to wait.

Lew would fire the first shot when he thought as many of the banditos as possible were in the line of fire. Three of them passed, and then *El Xiuhcoatl* riding proud, even though worn down. His stallion was well turned out in rich accoutrements. Anger grabbed me, and I had to fight it. It took everything I had to ease my finger off the trigger. *El Xiuhcoatl* had a nose like a chisel, and his eyes were flashing all over the place. I breathed hard, fighting this fear that something would tip them off, sour this bushwhack before most of them rode into it.

Right behind *El Xiuhcoatl* was Doris. This was as close as we'd been to any of the girls, only thirty yards. She was filthy, her blanket and what I could see of her nightgown too were dirty; her hair a tangled gummy mess, and her face bruised. Even with the movement of the horse, I could tell she was shivering. She looked back, I guessed checking on little sister, Agnes. I hoped Clay wouldn't do anything rash when he saw her.

A bandito followed Doris with Agnes behind him. Lordy, she

looked terrible slumped in the saddle barely staying on. As white as a sheet and covered with bruises, hair so messed up it looked like a yellow bush full of windblown leaves and twigs. Puke was splattered on the front of her blanket. Stay steady, Clay, I willed.

Another bandito passed, a real young fella, didn't look like he belonged. Then I saw Marta in a red-brown blanket. I wanted to shoot the nearest bandito. Again, I had to move my finger off the trigger. She had bruises, black eyes, split lips, and was as grubby as the others. Whatever happened, she hadn't made it easy for those bastards. She sat straight in the saddle, and her eyes were darting side to side, alert. That little girl—no, she ain't, she's a woman—sensed something. My heart ached as she moved out of sight. Stay steady, I told myself. My hands were shaking.

Inés came next, looking beat up too. She had a bandana around her head, and as she passed, I could see its backside was bloody. More banditos followed, and I picked out *El Xiuhcoatl's* brother, round face, shrewd eye, but not looking around. I say "eye," because he had a patch over his right. He was wearing that tall-topped fawn-colored sombrero. The rest of the banditos followed with the spares and pack mules.

I remembered what we'd talked about, where they were going and why, what their plan might be to get the ransom, and how they'd exchange the girls. It came to my mind like a kick in the head that maybe they weren't meaning to give the girls back. Taking them to this faraway place, why go to that trouble? Why go to…

The shot sounded like a thunder clap, and all hell exploded before me.

That shot touched off my trigger finger, taking the bandito following Agnes out of his saddle. I got another, but the horses were bucking, rearing, and running every which way. Shots were going off like firecrackers on the Fourth. Kneeling in the brush, I couldn't take a clear shot at the bounding horses. Horses were going down along with Mexes and both were screaming. Shots were coming back at us, but Mexes on rearing horses and those running for the rocks on foot were only throwing lead into the sky. Raising out of the brush, I could see better. Horses and men were down, others of both were running. Lead wanged off the rocks. The screaming horses and men, it was like a lunacy asylum. I wanted to find Marta in the melee, but I knew I had to keep gunning those bastards down to save her. In the back of my mind, I feared all the flying lead was doing the girls harm.

I took down one Mex's horse, and he rolled away pulling his rifle free. He went to a knee and was taking steady aimed shots with a Winchester, and I was doing the same back at him. His forward leg crumbled, but he fell on his side and kept firing, aiming at me it seemed. He rolled behind the dead horse, fired twice, jerked his saddlebags off, and made a staggering run for the rocks. My shots kicked up mud on his heels, but he made it. He had guts.

Two banditos ran on foot using the spares and mules for cover. Somebody hit one Mex, but the other made it to the rocks.

I turned right, and Marta's horse was down, and a bandito had her. She was whaling on him something furious, but he had her in a headlock and was dragging her into the boulders while still shooting. He threw her down behind a rock and swung a punch into her. I aimed, but her arms were still flailing. I couldn't get a clear shot. He commenced to kick her, and I had my chance, but his head turned into a spray of blood before I fired. Marta was up, but fell and I didn't see her get up. That young Mex was right behind her shooting pistols in both hands. He ducked behind her rock.

Another Mex in the rocks darted further in, staggered, crashed into a boulder, and crumpled to the ground. There was gun smoke at the top of the ridge. Lew had moved his boys to the other side of the trail and was firing down the length of the south finger, enfilading, I guess. The Mexes got hit from their front and left.

Clay shouted, "Shoot the horses!"

Except for answering muzzle smoke and bodies, there weren't no Mexes to be seen, but there were horses running all over. I knew what Clay wanted. Kill the horses so the banditos couldn't get away. The fire picked up, and when the Mexes realized what we were doing, they started shooting back double-quick. I set down my rifle and came up with the shotgun to hit a mule and spent the other barrel as a Mex popped up to shoot. Rock fragments hit him in the face.

A bandito wearing a blue Mex cavalry kepi ran out of the rocks, leapt on a horse, and started firing a pistol from low in the saddle. In desperation, he tried to run two more horses down the trail to safety. He passed one, caught the reins while the other's hind legs collapsed from under it, hit by Flaco. A slug caught the Mex in the shoulder, and he lost his pistol. He kept going until his mount went down, shot or stumbled, and he went headfirst into a boulder. Sounded like a melon popping.

I loaded slugs into the shotgun and fired at smoke puffs. Further up the draw, hot firing was still going on. I looked that way, and a Mex was dragging Doris from her fallen, but still kicking horse. The Mex screamed, "*¡Dejen de disparar! ¡La voy a matar!*" He had a pistol to her head. She'd lost her blanket.

"Hold your fire, boys," shouted Clay.

I could hear Lew further up bellowing the same.

"*¡La voy a matar!*"

"What's he saying?"

"Stop shooting. I'll kill her," said Flaco.

The man—I realized he was *Xiuhcoatl*—had his arm tight around Doris' neck. He was dragging her back to the boulders.

"*Deja que las chicas se vayan y dejamos que te vayas.*"—Let the girls go, and we will let you leave—shouted Flaco.

"*¡Voy a hacer lo que yo quiera!*" *Xiuhcoatl* yelled.

"I will do whatever I want," repeated Flaco.

The bandito chief tore open Doris' nightgown, pushed her to the ground, and bending over her ripped the dirty bedclothes completely off. He roughly pulled the naked girl up with his left arm around her neck, gripped one tit, and shoved his gun between her legs. He dragged her backward through the mud and into the boulders.

Clay must be going crazy.

The shooting stopped. Flaco and I jammed cartridges into our rifles. He watched the other side while I reloaded the shotgun. I did the same for him while he reloaded his revolvers. A couple shots banged to finish off wounded horses.

I breathed hard, my hands shaking. I watched the other side close, hoping to see a bandito's head, but hoping more to see Marta.

Clay shouted, "We got them cornered, boys, but be careful. It's like cornering a bull."

It was a mess in the draw. I counted fourteen dead horses and mules. No live ones were to be seen excepting a few standing out on the flats below the ridge. They were too far off to shoot at. I could see seven dead Mexes, and I'd seen two hit inside the rocks. There might be some more deaders in the rocks.

Clay crawled down to us. "What's your count?"

I told him.

"I think eleven. They got some wounded too," he said. "Got them cut down to our size." He sounded in good spirits in spite of Doris' humiliation and the iffyness of what could happen.

"We get anybody hurt?"

Clay's spirits didn't sound so good when he said, "Snap's dead and Jerry caught some rock splinters in the face, but he's good. I sent him up to the ridge top with Lew and Sessuns to cover the finger. There's only us three and Musty here."

"What's next?" I asked.

"Lew's got the finger's back slope covered. They're pinned, and they've got no horses to get away."

"They can get away in the night, even on foot," said Flaco.

"But they'd not get too far in the dark, and we'd ride them down after sunup," said Clay.

"Boss!" It was Musty up above us. "Riders comin' up."

GORDON L. ROTTMAN

Chapter Forty-Seven

The first thing that jumped into my mind was more *Rurales*, them seeming to turn up at the wrongdist of times. Before I could crawl back to a safe spot to look east, the Mexes fired. I could see Gent and Dodger lopping into some boulders. Further off was Fred loose-herding the *remuda*, and they soon disappeared behind a fold.

The Mexes had to be nervous now. They were down to maybe nine, and some were surely wounded. They could only guess at our numbers, but they knew three more had turned up. They knew they were boxed in, and it was a long time until dark. But, they had the girls. The girls.

Some of the boys flustered with the standoff, popped rounds into the boulders, including Musty's Kennedy rifle sounding like a cannon.

Xiuhcoatl yelled again.

"He say to stop, boss, or he shoot a girl," Flaco shouted.

Clay hollered to stop firing. I could see a lot of pain in his eyes.

Musty shouted, "I musta fired forty-eleven shots and only hit one of 'em turds. Might as well put a stamp on 'em bullets and mail 'em."

To my left I could see Gent and Dodger working their way like desert scorpions in this direction going from rock-to-rock.

"We got them boxed in, boss, but if we're still here at dark,

245

they'll make a break," I told Clay.

"They got no horses."

"They can find some at daylight maybe. They're scattered all about. There's even some holed up over yonder."

"Yeah." Clay rubbed his chin. "We need to deal with them, now." He gripped Flaco's arm. "You speak for me."

"*Sí, jefe.*"

"I'll give them the ransom money. They turn all four girls loose, and we let them leave free and clear. That'll be the end of it, we won't chase them."

"Some of the boys may not like that, boss," I said. "We lost pards, they'll still wanna get some licks in."

"Some of them Pedros in those rocks probably thinking the same. We need to let it go, and watch so they don't pull a fast one. I don't trust them no more than a rattler in my bedroll."

"So how much moneys you got to barter, *jefe?*"

"We ain't bartering. I got sixteen hundred dollars. Tell them it's all I got."

I had to muse over that, sixteen hundred dollars American. That's a hella lotta *dinero*. I'd never ever thought about holding that much money.

Clay suddenly shouted, "Doris, Agnes, you all right?"

"Daddy!" That from Doris, real weak. We heard nothing more.

Clay's face grayed, and he stared off into no place. It made me want to shout Marta's name, but she couldn't answer anyway.

Flaco moved behind a boulder and started shouting Clay's offer.

There was a long quiet. Then a hoarse voice shouted back, "*Voy a cortarle los chichis si disparan de nuevo.*"

"I think that *El Xiuhcoatl.* He say if we shoot any more, he will cut off her *tetas*...breasts."

"Oh shit," said Clay. He shouted for everyone not to fire no matter what.

Then Flaco and *Xiuhcoatl* started shouting back and forth for a piece. Gent and Dodger moved in toward the east end of the finger. We'd soon have them boxed in good. Then little Fred scurried across carrying two rifles and a water bag. Shit, I wish he'd stay out of it.

Flaco slid down behind his boulder. "*Jefe*, he say he want to see the moneys first. He want you to come out and him too. You show him the moneys, then maybe he let the girls go." Flaco gave a half smile. "He say he want to meet you and look into you eyes. He say he want to shake hand of man that not give up."

"I don't want to shake his damn hand."

"Best you do, *jefe*."

Clay looked at Flaco for a long spell. "Yeah, well, fine."

"He say you good papa, coming after you girls like that."

"I don't need no compliments from that bastard."

"I know, but that mean he respect you. That better for you."

"Fine. I think he's a gentleman and true hero."

"*Mi jefe dice que yo se…*"

"Shut up, Flaco, I didn't mean for you to tell that viper that. Tell him I'm coming out with a white flag. Him too. And tell him I don't want another finger laid on them girls, none of them, or I'll drag his naked ass through every cactus between here and Texas." He laid his Colts on a rock.

"You be damn careful, boss," I said.

"Hell, going down there un-gunned, there ain't much I can do to be careful."

"Just shake his hand, *jefe*. You don't gotta like it."

"I brought this from my war bag. Thought we might need it." Clay tied a white handkerchief to a stick. He pulled a leather pouch in his coat pocket and started down the side of the finger to the trail.

El Xiuhcoatl showed himself holding a stick with part of a nightgown on it.

Musty shouted, "Hey, Flaco. Don't shoot him jus' 'cause he got a white flag."

I could barely believe this was about over. Yep, it was still dangerous after we got the girls back—can't trust them snakes over there. But I'd have little Marta back. My hands shook, and it weren't from the cold. I could see those smiling black eyes in my head, like they were real.

El Xiuhcoatl had shed his serape and jacket and was wearing a red shirt, yellow scarf, and side-laced brown pants. He wore a small black sombrero with gold and silver coins sewn around the low flat crown. His two holsters were empty, but he still had his crossed bandoliers. He may have been small, but his big sideburns and mustaches with thick black eyebrows made him look meaner than a caged horny bobcat.

Another man stood not far away. It was his brother with a carbine cradled in his arms. He was dressed about the same, except he had a yellow shirt with red stitching on his pockets, gold Mex Army shoulder straps, and his high-topped fawn sombrero. His one eye was sweeping our side of the rocks.

Clay and *Xiuhcoatl* worked their way down through the rocks, cactus, and yucca, glancing down quick for their footing and then back at the other. They didn't want to shift eyes off their enemy.

El Xiuhcoatl's brother shouted something, and he answered back and shouted himself.

Flaco said, "*Jefe*, he say to tell those men better stop sneaking up over to our left."

"Tell them to hold up."

I shouted at Clay and Dodger. They disappeared into the boulders. Fred too.

Reaching the bottom of the draw, Clay and the bandit chief stood across the trail regarding one another. There were a whole bunch of rifles on them from both sides. I thought I was surely glad not to be in their boots. One of them sneeze, and they'd both be full of holes.

El Xiuhcoatl nodded and stepped onto the muddy trail. Clay opened the pouch and took out the stack of money and fanned it, showing it was for real. He pulled out a bill and handed it to *El Xiuhcoatl*. The bandito chief took it and kissed it, shoved it into a shirt pocket.

He stood there looking into Clay's face, and Clay was looking into his. Then without a word or sign they took a step forward and shaked hands. Just one short pump, then stepped back. After a few moments, they worked their way backward to their rocks, both of them almost stumbling. Seeing this was silly and wasn't working, they turned and made their way back.

When *El Xiuhcoatl* went into the boulders, his brother dropped out of sight too.

Clay was back in the rocks. Down near the end of their finger, I saw a Mex wearing a black sombrero with silver coins on the crown rise up, level a Sharps, fire, and disappear. Two-hundred yards away, Fred was standing straight like a beanpole. Looked like he'd been sneaking in closer. He crumpled to the ground.

Clay was yelling, "Hold your fire! Nobody shoot!"

El Xiuhcoatl was shouting too. He didn't want this to fall apart either. He wanted to get the money and get out of this fix.

Dammit, Fred was barely fifteen. Damn kid, wanting in on the action. For a flash, I wondered who his ma and pa were.

Clay dropped down behind our rock. "That's an evil son of a bitch. I saw immorality in his eyes. Now what?"

Flaco started shouting again, but it was a spell before the bandito chief answered back.

"He say no one else better move. He say for you to come back down with money, and he give you the girls. He want me too. He want to talk more."

"Fine," said Clay. He almost sounded chipper. "Leave your pistols. How do you carry all those damn things?"

"It is an easy weight, *jefe*."

The two of them set out. Flaco carried the flag.

They stood on opposite sides of the trail, barely more than a rifle's length apart. *El Xiuhcoatl* looked Flaco up and down. They were talking. I heard Clay say, "No," real loud. Then he wacked his fist on his thigh. There was some finger pointing going on and a lot of words, but they were keeping it down, like they didn't want things to go sour. Clay looked at the ground, shaking his head. More words. Clay looked back up and tossed the money pouch to *El Xiuhcoatl*.

The bandito chief looked inside, turned, and said something. He brother rose up holding little Agnes by the arm. She wore a muddy blanket. He gave her a shove forward, but *El Xiuhcoatl* shouted, and there was no more shoving.

Clay was rock steady, didn't twitch an eyelash. Agnes stumbled toward him like she had no idea where she's going. Even standing before her daddy, she didn't show anything, just stood there so limp I couldn't see how she stayed on her feet. Clay took her hand and with Flaco's help guided her to stand behind her pa. There were more words spoken, and then *El Xiuhcoatl* turned again and said something.

Another bandito rose up and had Doris by the arm. The torn nightgown hung on her, and she was covered by a blanket. When she saw her daddy, she started pulling toward him with the bandito holding her back. Clay said something, and she settled down coming forward, never taking her eyes off her daddy. When she reached him, she threw herself at him, making him stagger. He had both arms around her, and talking into her ear. She finally let go and took Agnes in her arms, then led her up through the rocks. I stood and motioned her toward me. I wondered how Marta was going to behave when she came back.

The two girls stumbled behind the boulder and plopped down hard like they had no strength left. They leaned against each other. I thought I was ripe, but they stunk to high heaven. Agnes kept her eyes closed, like she didn't want to see nothing and didn't want anyone to see her. Doris' eyes were wide trying to take in everything since she was among friends now. I gave them each an open canteen. Doris drank deep swallows, gulping fast. I had to slow her down. Agnes only looked at hers, holding it in both hands like she didn't know what it was. She tipped it over and let water gurgle out. Doris stopped her and held it to Agnes' lips, and she swallowed a little. They didn't say nothing. Agnes didn't look like she could if she wanted to.

"We'll get you girls warmed up as soon as we can build a fire, get some hot grub into you too."

Doris gave me a pain-filled smile and started crying real soft like.

I carefully touched her shoulder. "Everthing's going to be better."

Marta'll be coming up! I poked my head up, and all I saw were Clay and Flaco climbing through the rocks. There was no one on the trail and not a person to be seen on the other side.

Chapter Forty-Eight

Clay's arms were around his girls with Doris hugging him and crying. Agnes was as limp as a rag doll. I looked at Flaco, and he had a solemn look, shook his head, picked up his guns and took up a shooting position a good piece away.

"Give me a minute, Bud." Clay talked to his girls. I heard him tell Doris he had to finish this up, that he'd be back directly. He took a knee beside me.

"I'll give it to you straight." He gripped my arm. "He's not letting Marta and Inés go."

"But he said he was giving us all the girls for the money."

"Yeah, that's what that black-hearted liar said. He changed his mind."

I started to raise, a hand on my pistol butt. "He can't do that. He said…"

"Bud, don't do nothing rash. Sit down," he ordered. "Yeah, the son of a bitch said that, but I don't think he meant it from the git go. He's hanging on to them for insurance, to make sure we don't keep after him."

"Hell, don't he know by keeping them we'll stay after him anyways?"

Clay stared at me.

"We're going after them, boss, ain't we?"

He looked away from me. It was the first time I'd even seen Clay DeWitt unable to look a man, any man, in the eye.

"No, Bud, we're not."

I guess I opened my mouth, but I couldn't say nothing.

"*Xiuhcoatl* said he might let them go later."

"I don't believe that, do you?" I'm bristling mad.

"No, I don't. I got to get these girls home to their mama. Look at them. They've been…well, they've been used badly, been through pure hell. They don't have anything left inside them. They can't keep going. I can't send somebody back with them, couldn't spare them if we were to keep after them sons of bitches. I need to be with them until I can put them in their mama's arms."

"Then I'm going after them."

"And get Marta and Inés killed? Is it worth that, Bud? You think about that. I gotta do something here." He stood.

"Everyone listen up," shouted Clay for all to hear. "We got my girls back. They're hanging onto Marta and Inés, to make sure we don't chase after them. Said they might let them go later if we don't follow. They're coming out now to collect horses. We're going to make up what they need by giving them horses from the remuda. They'll be getting saddles from the dead horses. Everybody understand that?"

Everyone answered back. They didn't sound none too happy.

"There'll be no gun play. No accidents."

He told Flaco to tell the banditos where we'd taken the horses of the six banditos we'd killed. There was some shouting back and forth. They seemed real pissed realizing we'd dry-gulched their amigos. After a short spell, a bandito came out of the rocks looking around like he was expecting to get shot full of holes. There were rifles a plenty on him, including mine.

Once he wasn't gunned down in a hail of lead, others crawled out of the rocks. Three went out to catch horses idling on the flats, and others started collecting saddles, bedrolls, and so on from the deaders. I watched for Marta.

There was a lot going on, and I don't remember it all. Gent had to cut horses out of the remuda and bring them up. One Mex rode out for the six bushwacked banditos' staked horses. The others saddled and loaded up after taking everything they wanted from their dead. They even got two horses for their dead pack mules' loads. I can't blame Clay for doing all that, but at the moment I didn't much like him. My brain rolled around, not able to hold onto any thought.

Clay idled up to me and offered a rollie. I know he's trying to ease things up. I started to shake my head denying the cig. I didn't. I couldn't. *Clay's doing what he thinks best.* And I'm thinking I'm going to do what's best. I'm plum loco for even thinking about chasing after murderous banditos for a Mex gal who can't even talk. Then I remembered those frijole beans, her easy way of shaving me, her warmth at night, those eyes, and her smile, when she was moved to.

Gent and Dodger brought in Fred, shot dead-center through the breast bone. His face still wore a startled expression, like his last thought was, "This ain't a game after all."

The banditos dragged out Marta and Inés, both of them fighting like hellions. Marta especially. She was looking all about, like she's expecting me to come busting down there to save her. I want her to see me, to know that I'm there, but I didn't have the guts to stand in the open to let her see me doing nothing, *nothing* to help her. I don't want to speak of what I thought of myself right then.

Somehow, they got Marta and Inés on horses, lashing their ankles to the stirrups. We could see that Inés had been grazed on her right arm. They all rode over the ridge leaving their dead behind. They'd been upbraided real bad by half their number of gringos, in their own territory. We were all thinking they just might want to get even.

We only watched from the ridge crest. They rode on west; not a one of them looked back, excepting Marta. I watched until they disappeared into the gray mist.

We buried Snap and Fred on top of the ridge, hoping they could see Texas from there. We left the fucking dead Mexes to rot with their horses.

— •●• —

The boys scrounged up pants and shirts and other clothes for Doris and Agnes. Doris was coming out of it, but didn't say much. Agnes was still inside herself, deep someplace. We'd moved away from the battlefield and its smells. A fire was going for hot grub and coffee and to warm the girls. Sessuns picked rock chips out of Jerry's face. Some of the boys kidded him about it improving his looks.

It's time to go, to go home. Clay wanted to put some distance behind us and get into some rough ground to set a no-fires camp for the night. He didn't want us to be found.

Everyone was loaded.

Clay walked up to me. We looked one another in the eye. "You're going after her." It wasn't a question.

"Yes, sir."

"Got everything you need?"

"I got a couple of Mex saddles, some of the Mex grub and grain, some clothes for when I get the girls. I only need two horses."

Without turning around Clay said, "Sessuns, cut out the two best horses you got. You boys saddle them for Bud."

As we saddled, Dodger came up. "Bud," he looked anxious. "Bud, I wanna help ya, but, hell, I'm jus' plum tuckered out; we all are."

"You don't need to say nothing more." To the whole crew I said, "I ain't asking none of y'all to go. You'd be a dumb ass if you did. This has cost us ten lives. I sure as hell ain't holding it against y'all, and I don't think none the less of you. Y'all proved what you're made of. I'm crazy to go, but go I must."

Every one of the crew came up and shook my hand and wished me luck and a safe return, looking me in the eye. That helped.

Lew handed me half a bottle of Ashton Rye whisky. "Might do ya good when the goin' gets tough. I hope your cards run hot, Bud."

Musty gave me a bandana wrapped up. "It's some of Mrs. DeWitt's fruitcake." He's all embarrassed looking. "For the girls when ya get 'em back."

A little thing like that, it means something. I thanked him from the bottom of my heart.

Clay came last. "I wouldn't have been able to get my girls back without you, Bud. You make it back to the Dew, you hear? We'll be waiting for you, you and those girls. You got a home to come back to." We shook. He clasped his hand on my shoulder, then walked away.

I warmed myself over the dying fire. Didn't turn to watch them leave. I should of let Marta see me, so she'd know I was still alive. For all she knew I was dead. Maybe it was better this way, so she'll not expect rescue, because I didn't know if I could pull it off. Likely not.

Is this the right choice? I had a powerful feeling of being alone.

The fire burned down and wasn't giving up no warmth as my

excuse to stay longer. I wanted to get on their trail and find their night camp.

I don't know a bee from a bull's hoof how I'm going to do this. One against eight. If they got to Las Norias there'd most likely be more. I kicked a rock as far as I could. I gotta be nuts.

"If you want to catch up with them, we better get going, *amigo.*"

Flaco sat his horse with revolvers hanging all over them both. Two against eight.

GORDON L. ROTTMAN

Chapter Forty-Nine

"You ain't going to ask me if I know what I'm doing?"

Flaco shook his head. "*No, amigo.*"

"Good, because I ain't got no idea."

"That make six of us," said the *pistolero.*

"Six?"

"The four horses got no idea either."

We got on their trail. The horse with the broken shoe I guess was laying back on that dark and bloody ground. Too bad. I kind of missed him.

We didn't find their night camp. They weren't taking any chances. No fires. They were the hunted now, even if it was only the two of us, and they didn't know we were coming.

It was our eighth day out. We had cold vittles after a cold night, no better than a dog's breakfast. It began to drizzle. There wasn't much said by either of us. We spoke when there was something important to say.

Flaco did ask me, "What is you real name?"

I frowned at him. He arched his eyes.

I guessed he had as much right to know as anyone. "Athel. Don't say nothing to nobody."

We were able to take up the trail, even with the rain. Found their empty campsite too.

The country had turned into a maze of ravines, gorges, and box canyons. A man could get good lost out here, but the trail we were following looked like it knew where it was heading. They didn't blunder up any dead ends. The trail, running down a narrow ravine, looked more traveled too, even if rainwashed. Maybe we were getting close to Las Norias. I hoped not. I didn't want them to reach it before we did, whatever we were going to do.

Before noon the rain stopped. We'd be able to get a better idea of how fresh the tracks were. They'd been moving slow, but in the early afternoon they'd picked up their pace. The toes of the hooves were dug in a little deeper, and the distance between prints was a little further. It was like they were expecting to reach someplace soon. Las Norias? Maybe they needed water and there was some ahead. No water-running arroyos here except a muddy trickle down gullies. Maybe they only wanted to get a move on and get out of this weather. Sounded like a good idea to me.

We stopped in a wind-sheltered ravine for jerky and corn dodgers. We both shivered in the cold-wet, and the wind picked up. Sometimes we were out of it, but when the winding ravine made a turn, the north wind rushed down it like a river of air either chilling our backs or hitting our faces. The horses weren't happy either.

The ravine's steep sides were twenty, thirty feet high. Sometimes it was as wide as the trail, a few feet, and other times it was as wide as it was deep and ever wider. Rocks, scrub brush, and cactus.

They weren't far ahead, we agreed. Horse turds were fresh enough. They had slowed and then sped up again.

Late afternoon we were taking it slow, walking the horses some. It wouldn't do to run up on the banditos in this skinny ravine. We were hoping for it to open soon out into hilly ground. We wanted to be able to see them in the distance and hopefully find their night camp.

We didn't have any idea what we were going to do. We talked about stealing into the camp in the middle of the night, hopefully find the girls, and sneak them out without a fuss. That was hoping for a whole heap of luck. We'd have to "*ir al tanteo*," Flaco said, something like "take it to trial." Sort of like saying "play it by ear."

The shot was like a lightning crack down the ravine. The

horses reared, and we sawed them around colliding into the spares. It was an irrational run back down the ravine, a long straight stretch with leather cracking and hooves sounding like thunder. Mud sprayed behind us. Shots snapped one after the other with rock chips flying off the stony sidewalls. Looking back, Flaco was firing blindly behind him. The bullets kept coming no matter how far and how fast we rode. The run seemed to have no end. It was a continuous rattle of hooves on stone, bullets wanging, and horses gasping hard. I hugged Cracker's neck hanging on hard and kept low.

The shots stopped, but their echoes followed. Turning to look back, I saw three empty horses.

I reined Cracker to a sliding stop with the other horses piling into us. There was blood on Flaco's mount's neck. I tied the reins off on a mesquite and lopped down the ravine to the bend that put us out the line of fire.

I peeked down the ravine and lying on his side was Flaco, twenty yards away. I called his name a couple of times, but with the growing puddle of dark blood on the stones and the queer twist in his body, I knew he was done. Watching close, I stared at him for minutes hoping to see the slightest twitch. Nothing.

The despair chomped down on me. I'd lost my *amigo*, my pard, and my chances for saving the girls were cut in half. I stayed there a long time thinking on Flaco. It was a blur of thoughts. I kept an eye peeled down the ravine hoping the bastards that shot him would come down for the loot. I waited a long time, thinking. I reminded myself that I'd been willing to go it alone before this. I was still willing.

It was high time to pull out of there, but I didn't want to ride into those bastards' sights. It was the same deal when they almost got me that morning we came up the escarpment and they shot that dun from under me. Two men, one with a buffalo rifle, the other with a lever-action. It might be the same two men. Well, one of them, because Flaco had killed one the other day. I doubted they had earlier spotted me and Flaco. They musta left a rear guard just to be safe. Eight against one.

They may have left, they may still be there. I was going after them. Not seeing me come back right away, they may have thought I'd hightailed it. Something else, they only saw the two of us, but they might think there were more behind us.

Going right down the ravine into a Sharps' muzzle wasn't much of a notion. I looked up the ravine's side.

Further back up the ravine I found a chimney on the left side, sort of a vertical funnel to the top, over thirty feet up. I cut a piece of cord and tied it to my rifle so I'd have free hands. Leaving my hat and spurs with the horses, I tied them off loose so they could break away if I didn't come back. I didn't much like that climb, kept slipping on the wet rock. It helped me keep my mind off things, off Marta and Flaco, even as I was doing it for them. Scraped up my hands and elbows. Banged my left knee good.

Reaching the top, I peeked over and checked out the plateau top. Keeping low and moving from bush to bush to rock, I was guessing how far it was to the shooters' spot, if they were still there. I wanted them to be. The further I went, the slower I moved and quieter too. The long straight stretch we'd run up was easy to make out, and I figured they'd be where it turned into a bend. I didn't really realize how long that stretch was until I followed it up there.

I passed by the first bend, and then angled to the edge of the ravine. I listened. There was only the wind, and I realized how cold I'd gotten. A horse whinnied. It was further down the ravine. I turned to head that way, and then thought they'd picket their horses further up the ravine and they'd be back to my right. Maybe I could shoot the horses, and that'd put them on foot. But then they'd know I was here. Surprising them by putting slugs through them would be more better. Plus, I didn't have to shoot no horses.

I crept along the edge, staying back enough so I'd not be seen or knock any rocks over the side. I'd move a few steps and listen. Nothing. They were sure quiet.

I took a quick look over the side to get the lay of the ravine. I had to take a second look. They were thinking, that was for sure. Piled in the ravine was brush, deadwood, and broken mesquite limbs. That'll have stopped us if we'd charged on through. I moved a little further and peeked again. Nothing. The third time I looked over I saw a man, the one with the Winchester. I listened, then looked again. It was the bandito wearing the black sombrero with silver coins on the crown, the one that killed Fred. I'd have no regrets about what was coming. Looking again, I saw there was a Sharps lying beside him. I was sure slow today. There weren't two of them, only this one. No wonder I ain't heard no talking.

I looked again, and he was getting up, picking up the Sharps. I ducked back. I heard the crunch of gravel, and he was walking back to his horse. He'd given up on waiting. I took off moving as fast as I could and still keep quiet. Then I heard him pulling down brush from the barricade.

I got in a good spot where I could see the horse and thought about letting him get on it to give me a clear shot. But I thought if I missed, he'd have a better chance of getting away mounted. I didn't hear any more brush busting and listened, hoping the horse would greet the Mex.

He did. I looked over and the horse was looking up dead straight at me. The Mex looked up as I raised up and we fired our Winchesters at the same time. Rock spray hit me in the face, but I'd had an edge on him. I was expecting him, he was surprised by me. He got off a shot, but I got off four as fast I could work the lever. I heard the horse scream. Damn tarnation!

I rolled away trying to wipe rock dust from my face. Wished I'd brung a canteen up with me.

Now I was afraid to poke my head over the edge. He'd be waiting for that. I moved down a little further and took a quick look at the horse. He was still standing, but was twitching and nodding his head. I didn't like this. I ain't got no choice but to shoot the horse. I moved again—ol' Pancho taught me never to pop up for a look-see in the same place twice. I shot the horse twice and heard it kicking gravel. This was followed by a whole bunch of cussing. Didn't know all the words, but I got the idea.

Now came the hard part, rooting that desperado out. I couldn't pass until he was dead. Sure, at night he would probably make a getaway. Don't know how far he'd get on foot, even if he got his canteen, but I wasn't letting Flaco's and Fred's killer get away, no way. There were only so many places I could shoot from, and I was stuck on this side of the ravine.

Moving a little, I popped up and fired just to worry him. Didn't see him. I reloaded from my pistol belt. My fear was that he'd take off down the ravine zigging and zagging and using the turns for cover. Then he'd be ahead of me and probably waiting to bushwhack me for a horse. I shoulda brought the shotgun, had a better chance of stopping him at a run.

I thought I was in a good place if he made a run for it. Now to spook him out. I threw some rocks down, but that didn't flush out nothing. A bundle of burning brush would be nice, but it was too wet, not much dead brush, or living, for that matter. I'd have to go away from the ravine to collect it. Sure is hard doing this alone. That made me think about Marta. No time for that.

I sent some bigger rocks bouncing down the side. He moved. Musta been close. *I have an idea where he is now.* I dropped two big rocks, and he jumped out from under an overhang and fired three pistol shots with two twanging off the rock wall. That gave me an idea. I set a canteen-sized rock teetering on the edge and moved back to where I could see more of the ravine's bottom.

Taking careful aim, I shot the rock, sending it over the edge. He stepped out and shot at where he thought I was. I put a slug right through him, and he crumpled. Heck, that weren't so hard.

Chapter Fifty

I didn't have that shovel I'd brought, but I had rocks. I buried Flaco to the side of the ravine under sandstone. His guns I buried with him, but I kept his short-barrel Schofield saddle gun, stuck it in a coat pocket. His carbine in its scabbard had been hit in the receiver and cracked. Buried it with him too, but took the ammo. There was a *monillo*—Mexican buckeye—by his head. It would do for a marker. In the spring, it would show purple flowers. I stood there a few minutes. Just me and the horses, their heads hanging. It seemed like a rotten way to go after all the things he'd done, some good, some bad. I knew he was a good man at heart, and that's what counted. A question hung up in my head, "Why did you stay with me? You didn't have to come. I didn't expect it, didn't ask it." I wondered what I'd of done if we'd switched places. I hoped I would of gone with him.

He'd said something about relatives in Del Rio. No telling how many Vegas there were, but I'd ask around if anyone knew of Héctor "Flaco" Vega who'd been a *Rurale*. I wished him peace on his journey.

Damn if I didn't feel about as lonely as a preacher on payday weekend. The low dark clouds, drizzle, and the windy cold didn't help. It was right then that I walked over to Cracker, mounted, and turned his head to the Dew. "I can't do this anymore," I said loudly with a little echo down the ravine. "It's too damn much dying. Everyone in on this is going to die. I ain't changing anything if I keep going or I ride back to the Dew. Only when and how they're going to die is all I'd change." I cursed Maxwell, I cursed Weyland, I cursed *El Xiuhcoatl* and his cutthroats, I cursed the *Rurales*, and I cursed God. Lastly, I cursed myself for even caring.

Cracker snorted.

"Shut up," I said. I gave him his head, and he turned west toward the low sun and Marta.

There was blood beside the dead horse, but no Mex. "Damn! Shoulda shot him again after he was down." Just more dying, I thought.

His canteen and saddlebags were gone. I busted the stock off the Sharps and smashed the breech block against a boulder.

Tying Flaco's lariat to the hackamore of one of the spare horses, I ran it through the second one's hackamore and Flaco's, then tied it to Cracker's saddle horn. On foot, I'd haze them ahead of me hoping they wouldn't get away. They'd give me some moving cover.

I started the string off and soon came across more blood and a black sombrero. I picked it up to cut off the coins later. He didn't do like I'd hoped, start shooting from ahead as the mob herded down the ravine.

Instead, he was hiding in a niche in the right side wall. He announced himself by shooting under Cracker, and he got me. Cracker started bucking something furious. I hung onto his stirrup, and he dragged me down the ravine. I dropped my rifle and was trying to get my revolver out while stumbling and dragging. Expecting him to come after me, I rolled onto the ground and started shooting, but he wasn't coming out.

Scrambling behind too small a rock for cover, I whistled at Cracker. Bless his heart. He dragged that string to a halt and was looking back at me. He was out of the line of fire, but I was afraid that anymore shooting might set them off again.

I was past the bandito. I could keep going, but I sure didn't like the idea of having him behind me, even if he was on foot. I had to come back this way, too.

He didn't have much better cover than me, so I pulled out my Merwin Hulbert and fired all six rounds as fast as I could, dropped it, and came out from behind my rock with my Remington ready. He was doing the same, and all I saw was muzzle flashes so close I felt the blasts, felt a burn on my calf. I like to piss my pants.

He was lying on the gravel at my feet. We were that close. The smell of black powder swirled about. I knew I was hit, in the belly. I dropped to my knees and started barfing up breakfast. I fell back against the wall, heard Cracker snort.

It was a sharp gut-wrenching pain, right in the center of my belly. I didn't want to look, but I did. It wasn't right. There wasn't no blood. I felt around. "Well, I be damned. I ain't shot." I was so wrought up that the pain in my guts was only nerves. I started breathing again, laughing too. Climbing to my feet, I drank from the Mex's canteen washing the nasty taste out of my mouth. I rolled the Mex over, dead as year-old jerky. He'd been pistol hit in the belly and chest. The first rifle shot had bit him in the right side. One against seven.

Finding some *carne seca*—sorta like beef jerky—and stale tortillas in his saddlebag, I put the jerky in my own bag and fed the leather-stiff tortillas to the horses. I was laughing out loud, not believing I thought I'd been gut shot. I was thanking my lucky star for that one. Building a smoke, I sat puffing it. The graze on the inside of my right calf hurt a little. I washed it best I could. I tossed his two revolvers up onto the ravine top. Doubt anyone'd ever find them there. I left him lying in the middle of the trail. I took his Winchester, the gun that kilt Flaco, and its two cartons of ammo. It was a '73 like mine, but .38-40. Since there was only one of me, it might come in handy.

Rearranging the string of horses, I mounted Cracker and headed down the ravine. The whole time I was telling him how damn lucky I was. I hoped that luck would hold out. It perked me up anyways, and I kept thinking, *Marta, I'm coming for you. Hang on, girl.*

After a piece, I came to a place where they'd taken a rest. Trotting down the ravine on the wet ground, I spied a piece of blue cloth. It was the torn cuff of Marta's blue flannel shirt, had dried blood smears on it. I hoped it was only from wiping her bloody nose and not something worse. Dismounting and picking it up, it came to me that she still had faith in me coming for her. Was she letting me know she's expecting me? I felt like I was holding a piece of her. After holding it for a time, I stuck it in my shirt pocket over my heart.

Re-mounting, I spurred Cracker down the ravine.

I had to catch up with the banditos and fast. I had to end this. My best bet was to find their camp, and that meant catching up with them before dark. Night wasn't all that far off.

The ravine grew shallower and broader until it opened out into a wide valley. After sweeping the rocky valley with the field glasses, I moved on. There was nothing to be seen. The mist and bands of fog didn't let me see far details, and it was darkening in the east. The clouds were low. Night would soon fall. I had about as much chance of finding their camp or even catching up with them as I did having one of Mrs. Moran's beefsteak suppers tonight.

I didn't pay attention to the odd rock up ahead, but as I got closer, I realized its color wasn't right. In the poor light, I couldn't make it out proper. Through the field glasses I made out a *grullo*, a gray horse, laying on its side, no saddle. There was something behind it. I rode closer, slowly. Behind the stiff-legged horse was a reddish-brown blanket. I stopped. I couldn't make myself move forward. After a spell of just sitting and staring, I slid off and eased forward, circling around the horse. *This don't seem real, what I'm looking at. It's like a screaming puma will jump out at me. There's black hair hanging out of the blanket.* I sat staring for a long time.

Kneeling beside the lumpy bundle, I opened it with dread. I was and I'm staring at little Inés' battered face.

Muddled thoughts run though my head. I'm glad it's not Marta, but they'd killed Inés, a sweet, kind girl...why? Why do that? Do they know I'm following, is this a warning? That didn't make sense. Did the shot-dead horse have something to do with it? It had been shot through the chest.

I opened the muddy blanket further. Her face is black-and-blue bruised, swollen. I hardly recognized her with lifeless half-closed eyes, her lips swelled up and peeled back baring her teeth. There's sticky blood in her hair and purple choke marks. She could have been choked or beaten to death. Why? *Is it my fault?* My gut churned.

I carried her stiff body a ways from the trail and stacked rocks over her. I thought about her laughing, and her and Marta splashing suds. Nobody passing by would care, but I scratched "Inez" on a flat sandstone. I hoped she joined up with her mama.

As the sun edged down to the western hills, I swore over Inés' grave I was going to get Marta out of this, and if there's any way, I'd kill every one of them black-hearted bastards.

There's a low place in the far line of hills, outlined by the weak sun. The trail headed for that pass as straight as the Dew's north drift fence. I could keep going after nightfall, for a spell anyway. With the rolling ground, it's hard to tell how far that pass was. It might be three miles; it might be nine.

It was more like nine. The temperature fell with the darkness. I could see the horses' breath. Finding a wet arroyo, I watered them. They were played out. There was little for them to nibble along the trail. I was played out too, and my calf throbbed from the stirrup strap rubbing it.

The clip-clop of Cracker's hooves on hard scrabble made a hollow sound in my head. It's all I heard. It's pure dark when I realized I was going uphill. Cracker blew out a breath. We crested the pass.

Two orange dots flickered ahead in the darkness.

Chapter Fifty-One

It took over an hour to close in on the camp. They were on the side of an east-west running ridge spoiling the north wind. I was close enough to tell when someone walked past a fire.

I sat shivering for a long spell figuring out what to do. There's only so much one lone fella can do against seven. Two might be able to do more, with one distracting them, getting some to chase after him or something. That would only put the others on their toes, so maybe that wasn't so grand after all. I figured they didn't know they were being followed. They'd not have fires going if they did. Hopefully, they weren't expecting one lone dumbass punch to take them on. I felt as lonesome as a hunted coyote.

Of course, their bushwhacker ain't come back yet. It took this long for me to catch up with them so maybe they're not expecting him tonight or the fires were for him to find them. If I was going to do something, I'd better do it tonight. They had to be getting close to Las Norias. Sure seemed like we'd come a long ways. Thought they'd be there by now. I couldn't leave Marta with them any longer, after what happened to Inés. Her beaten face floated in front of me as I sat shivering.

I could only come up with one thing. I'd picket the horses far enough away they'd not be heard. I'd move in closer and wait until three, four o'clock, the hours of the dead. I'd have to guess, no other way to tell time. Those banditos were as played out, cold, and hungry as me. Some were wounded. They might have a sentry. If they didn't think anybody was after them, he'd be likely to doze off like any nighthawk.

The fires would most likely burn down. It would be pitch-black. I'd have to move like a mouse, or a scorpion hunting at night. How would I be able to find Marta's bedroll in the dark? I thought about that a spell, and then it came to me. They all had sombreros. Marta didn't. Then a sickening thought came to me. What if she was in a bedroll with someone? Well, I had a knife for that.

I even thought about creeping around slitting throats. I'd heard stories of injuns doing that. Had to be bullshit. A man dying that way, there'd be a bunch of trashing around to wake everybody.

I could easily be caught creeping around in there. A hundred things could go wrong. I had my three pistols. If it came to that, I wouldn't likely be coming out. Snap out of it. I didn't need to be thinking like that.

I moved the horses to an arroyo two hundred yards downwind. There was a curve in the arroyo with piled up rocks and gravel on the outside rim. There was trickling water for the horses. Before leaving them, I ate what I could while they grained. The supply was getting low. I was too nervous to eat much cold, dry grub. I checked all their halters, cinched their saddles, and made sure all the gear was tied on good. I took off my spurs. The last thing I did was hang Marta's shotgun on the horse she'd be—I'd hoped—she'd be riding. The pouch of shotshells was hanging where she could get to them. The canteens and water bags were full.

I was hoping that if I got Marta out, the banditos would just up and go home. Ol' Pancho taught me not to hope for the best. I rode Cracker a few hundred yards down the winding arroyo to a narrow spot. Tying two lariats together, I strung them tight knee-high and tied them off to stout mesquites. I hung my bandana on the rope so our horses would see it.

Back at the horses, I checked my revolvers and taking a canteen and the Mex's Winchester, I moved slowly toward the bandito camp. There was a rocky outcropping a hundred yards shy of the camp. That's where I'd wait, and I'd leave a canteen, the Mex's Winchester, and the two cartons of ammo. If we had to run for it, I'd leave it all there. My Winchester was still on Cracker.

I found a comfortable rock behind a mesquite and settled in for a long wait. I didn't take a blanket. I was counting on the cold to wake me if…when…I dosed off.

One fire was out and the other dying. I didn't see any shadows moving around. I waited. It was cold, the air still and misty. I was scared. I tried not to think. I was kidding myself I could pull this off. I thought a lot about Marta. It seemed so long ago since I'd seen her, touched her.

I'd doze off and jerk awake, then think about all kinds of things, thoughts that come to no good. One time I told myself to just get up and ride away. I even stood. But I couldn't do that, not after all the dying it took to get me this close to her. This was the right thing to do even if it meant our end.

It was clear there'd be more dying before this was over. And for what? It was all greed. It all started with Maxwell wanting a stupid bull that weren't his. Then he got *El Xiuhcoatl* into it, a rustler, kidnapper, murderer, and raper. I couldn't even count up how many had died because of all this. So many that didn't have to die. Ten Dew people now. Even those *Rurales*, they thought they were doing the right thing, doing their job. They'd been lied to and a bunch of them died for it. All this killing's gnawing at my guts. How many more have to die just so things can be set right? How many do I got a right to kill only so I can stay alive? No, I'm of no matter. How many do I have a right to kill to keep Marta alive? All of them.

— •●• —

I came awake shivering and just about couldn't stop. It was blacker than a coal mine at midnight on a moonless night. I was wet with dew, and it was foggy. The wind had picked up blowing hard enough to shake the bushes. That's good, it covered sounds. Today. Today I get Marta back! Nerves shot through me like Musty's coffee.

It must be three or four. There was no hint of a fire in the direction of the camp. It was so black that I wasn't sure where the camp was. I was downwind, and I listened hard. Not a sound except the wind gusting through the mesquite. I waited a few minutes to clear cobwebs out of my head. I took off my hat so I could move quick. After checking my pistols and knife, I shook myself, making sure I didn't rattle.

Unstrapping both pistols, I started forward. Flaco's Schofield was in my coat pocket. Ol' Pancho had told me that when stalking, start off as quiet as when you were just about on top of them. I felt with my toe with each step. Then set my heel down soft like. The wet meant no dry leaves and twigs or rolling pebbles. With each step, I listened, then took another. A sound. I stopped. I heard it again. I eased into a crouch, listening. There it was again, but this time the wind eased. I almost laughed to myself. Some *vato* was snoring. Good.

There was more snoring, one *vato* was really loud, a couple others weren't so loud or were only wheezing. I could even hear some regular breathing. I remembered Marta's sometimes little snore. Maybe I'd hear her. There weren't even embers in the used up fires.

I stayed in a crouch for a long spell. I looked and listened for any sign of a lookout. I fought between holding myself there and moving on. I had to be sure there wasn't a lookout. Being spotted among the sleeping banditos would be like sticking your hand into a rattlesnake den. The longer I waited, though, meant someone might wake up to take a piss.

I thought I'd been moving real slow, but now there's snoring right and left of me. I barely breathed, but my heart hammered so loud I'd wake the dead. I had to make myself stop shivering.

Now I was close enough to barely make out the darker shapes of bedrolls. I heard a horse snort. That was something I could have done if Flaco'd been here. I'd have sneaked in, found Marta, and if I'd been found out, he'd have stampeded the horses. No sense thinking on that now.

Something came out of the past. Ol' Pancho had told me, "Eef joo walk een dee camp of dee enemy, walk like joo belong there, not sneaking 'round." I did that; I walked upright, but still careful like.

There was a low snore right beside me. I crouched and made out a big sombrero. It looked like only one was in the bedroll. I moved on. The smoky smell told me one of the fire pits was near. Right past it was another bedroll. I had to get real close to hear the breathing and see the sombrero. Moving to the right, I found another bedroll and sombrero. I was confused and scart too. Moving around aimlessly in the camp, I couldn't tell which way to go. I was fearing I'd be wandering in here checking the same bedrolls over and over. I looked over another snoring bed, sounded like a wood rasp on a dry corncob. Nothing. The next was one I'd already checked. This was not good. I couldn't keep wandering around in a rattlesnake den without stepping on one. I remembered getting ant-bit a bunch because I was aggravating a red ant bed. My mama told me that if I played in pig shit I'd get some on me. She said that as she whaled the tar out of me with a trace chain strap. Why was I thinking of that crap now?

I've gotta get this moving along. I knelt beside another lumpy bedroll. It had a light-colored sombrero with a real tall crown, a yellow ribbon. I know this sombrero. It's *El Xiuhcoatl's* brother.

There was only the sound of the wind; there was no change in anything, but the feeling wrapped around me that someone or something was behind me. At the same time, I realized the bedroll was empty. The fear I'd been had ripped through me. There was a low cough. I just about pissed myself.

A hoarse voice whispered, "*¿Qué?*"—What?—something something. The brother.

As quiet as I could I said, "*Miada.*"—piss, hoping I sounded like a Mex. If I stood, he'd see I wasn't one of his.

Shit, I'm gonna be had. Do something, dummy. Now!

I could smell his breath as he leaned curiously toward me. My knife was in my hand. I rose slow, then twisted into him, clapped my gloved hand over his mouth, and shoved my knife hard against his throat. He went stiff, stopped breathing even. He knew he was about one second from getting a here-to-here throat smile. I didn't do anything for some seconds, only listened for anyone moving, getting curious.

Nothing. I tugged on him, and he knew exactly what I wanted. He stepped back keeping his hands to his sides. I kept pressing the six-inch blade against his throat, drawing some blood. We walked out backward so he'd be off balance. I wondered when he would start breathing. We were clear of the camp and faded back into the night quiet of the *campero*. I could smell him—stale sweat, wood smoke, and bean farts, feel his neck whiskers against my hand and could feel him swallow. I wanted to ask him where the girl was— *¿Dónde niña?*—but knew if I moved my hand he'd yell out.

I got him to the outcropping with no trouble, except he was barefoot, making it no fun for him. Hell, I ain't got a thing to tie him up with. I shoved his face into the mud, cut the strap off the canteen and tied his hands behind his back. I stuffed his scarf in his mouth, after letting him spit out some mud and slapping some cooperation into him, and tied my bandana around his mouth. I felt around. He wasn't carrying iron. Picking up the carbine and canteen we were moving again, back to the horses. It was surely hard on his feet—tough shit. One against six since I had him.

On the way back I worked out what I was going to do with this worthless puddle of pig shit. He might not be so worthless after all.

I led the string of horses back up to the outcropping while dragging the brother along. I tied his ankles with a cord and hog-tied him off to his wrists. Keeping quiet, I kicked him in the ribs a few times...well, a bunch of times.

I went back to my rock and took up my waiting position. While chewing on jerky, I figured they'd probably not find him missing until they were all up and it was light enough to see. Maybe at first they'd think he's out taking a shit. When they started calling for him, I had something to say to them. I was figuring I could get the idea of what I wanted across to them without knowing much Mex. Then I knew my troubles would really start.

Chapter Fifty-Two

The sky lightened in the east, and I made out the lay of the ground between me and the camp. The first sign of life was one of the fires flaring up. I could see their picketed horses and moving shapes, and I heard voices.

There was more moving around and as it got lighter, I looked them over with the field glasses. I saw her—Marta! Standing beside the fire wrapped in a gray blanket, she just stared into the flames. My heart pounded. Don't know how I missed her in my search.

Someone whistled, real shrill, followed by, "*¡Federico! ¡Ándale!*"

"*¿Usted nombre es Federico?*" I kicked him.

His one eye was wide, and he nodded rapidly. He was wearing his yellow shirt with a short green jacket.

"Well, I tell you what, Federico. I hope to hell you feel like going along with me on this deal, or you'll be seeing *el diablo* today. *¿Usted comprendes, pendejo?*"

He nodded. He got the gist.

"I hope so, 'cause I ain't got no temper for bullshit today." I sniffed the air. "You smell that? *Café.* Smell *bien*, don't it? I tell you what, if you don't cause no *revuelta* you'll be having a cup of that *café* soon enough." I looked down at him. "You'd like that, wouldn't you?"

He nodded real hard, blinking his one eye.

"Yeah, me too, but I don't know when I'm gonna have time to boil up a pot. Long time, I suspect."

There was another whistle, and someone shouted for Federico, probably telling him to break it off and get his butt up there. I figured they'd be looking for him soon so I might as well get ready. Can't put this off. I was shaking, either from the cold or from expectation. I checked the horses and cinched them. They knew something was going on. I had my rifle and the Mex's carbine laid out along with the shotgun loaded with slugs. I even set out that old Remington single-shot in its flour sack, just in case.

I heard "*Federico*" shouted again. One last thing I had to do before introducing myself. This piece of shit laying here had probably done Marta and the other girls. I stood and pissed on his face, to let him know his worth…and because I just didn't like him.

I drank some water, slipped the straps off my revolvers, and dragged the still sputtering Federico to his cut-up feet. I had to take this head-on. I was trembling scart, but I knew I couldn't show it. There was one person I was doing this for, and she looked awful lonesome standing there. I took one last look at her through the glasses. "Here we go, Federico. *Ándale.*"

Take it head-on. "Hey, y'all!" I shouted at the top of my lungs. "Look what I got here, you bunch of pepper bellies." I shoved Federico in front of me. "Get up you sumbitch!"

It was awful quiet in the camp. I put the glasses to my eyes, and Marta had the biggest grin I ever seen. "Fine, we're doing this."

Setting the glasses down, I stuck my Remington into Federico's ear. "Let's make a deal here. Any y'all *habla americano?*"

I could tell it was *El Xiuhcoatl* in his red shirt that grabbed Marta and held a pistol to her head. That weren't no surprise.

Someone hidden shouted, "Joo let him go or *El Xiuhcoatl* chute *la niña.*" I knew it was a bluff.

"No one's shooting anyone. No one else has to get killed, *muerto*. You give me *la niña*, and I give you back your brother…*hermano.*" That let them know I knew his worth to them.

There was a long quiet spell. I knew they were talking. I raised my revolver and cracked off a shot. The horses and Federico jumped. "Hey! I ain't got all damn day here! *¡Muy pronto!*" That oughta get them moving. I shoved Federico down and reloaded.

"Joo come out. Bring…*bandera blanca*. We talk."

I had to chew on that. Oh, a white flag.

"Yeah, I come out and y'all shoot me *muerto*. That ain't

happening. Let's trade and we'll all go to the *hacienda*." I'll stick it to them. "What do you want? To keep *la niña* or get your *hermano* back in *una* piece?"

It was another quiet spell. I figured they were talking about waiting me out or sneaking around behind me, but it wasn't worth it. They could say they'd hurt Marta, but then I could do the same to Federico. If I needed to, I'd remind them he couldn't spare an eye. The only smart thing to do was for them to make the trade.

"This your woman, the one with no name?"

"Yeah. *Sí, mi mujer.*" There, I'd said it. She's my woman. "I want her back. Now!"

"*Gringo*, joo one *vaquero duro.*" That meant tough cowboy. It almost sounded like he said it with respect. "We trade joo dee *niña.*" It seemed like they knew it was only me alone.

"Start walking her across and I'll start Federico." They might be surprised I knew his name. "*No fuego.* If I hear a shot or see any funny business, Federico's *muerto.*" I shoved Federico to the ground and cut the ties on his ankles and wrists. I thought about telling them to send Marta over with a cup of coffee, but they probably weren't that hospitable today.

El Xiuhcoatl hisself brought Marta out. He was the only one showing hisself. He said something to her, gave her a shove, and she started walking. They'd taken her blanket so she was only wearing that blue shirt, filthy long johns, and mud-caked socks. She didn't look back.

I pulled Federico up and set him off stumbling along barefooted. His footprints were bloody. I thought, *it's back to one against seven.*

These scoundrels are mean enough and stupid enough to start shooting just as Marta makes it here. They could drop her, maybe, and Federico could duck for cover in the rough ground. I'd be ready for that.

Marta was moving faster than the hobbling Federico so she'd be closer to here than only halfway when they passed. She saw that, I think, and started moving faster. *El Xiuhcoatl* saw it too and yelled something, I guess telling her to slow down. Being Marta, she paid him no mind.

As she got closer, I saw how bad she looks. It cut into me like barbed wire. But never mind, because I can see a glow on her face no matter how battered it is.

I kept my rifle on Federico as he closed on Marta. "*No fuego*," I shouted again. "Don't try pulling something *estúpido, pendejo*." She was eyeing him too.

And the stupid sumbitch did. As they passed, even though Marta kept clear of him, he leaped at her. She was quicker, dodged to the side. My shot hit him in the leg, more by luck than anything. Marta dropped flat and the Mexes started shooting up a storm. At a hundred yards they were throwing bullets all over, so I stood ground and emptied my rifle as fast as I could; picked up the Mex's carbine and emptied it. That was about twenty-five rounds in about thirty-five seconds.

I grabbed the single-shot pistol in its bag and threw it as hard as I could, "*¡La pistola, Marta!*" She scrambled a few yards to it and rolled behind a rock. She'd never fired it, but I judged she'd figure it out. I couldn't see Federico as I reloaded my rifle. I emptied it again as gravel spurted up around me. They were getting closer with their shots. As I reloaded, Federico came to his feet and headed for Marta. I guess he figured to get that pistol and use her for a shield. Before I could do anything Marta rolled onto her side, pointed that hand-cannon, and almost lost it to the recoil. Padding blew out the back of Federico's green jacket. He stumbled back, falling in a heap.

An unholy wail rose from the camp sending a chill up my back. It was followed by babbled shouting. The shots died off so I reloaded the Mex's carbine.

A sudden barrage of bullets fell on my outcropping, and dirt and gravel kicked up all over. They were firing all at once and emptied at about the same time, creating a lull.

"Marta, run! *¡Ándale!*"

I rose up and levered through my fourteen shots, snatched up the carbine, and let go with it as Marta leapt up. She fired a pistol shot over her shoulder for good measure and scrambled on hands and knees toward me. I was thinking it was now six to one since Federico had a bunghole though his chest—he ain't even twitched. Marta dove over the rocks, saw the shotgun, grabbed it up, and let loose one barrel then the other. Make that six to two, I thought.

I was reloading and was knocked off my heels. Marta threw her arms around me and was smacking kisses all over my grubby face. She was laughing this weird hoarse laugh, kind of scary.

"Whoa, girl! We got work to do here." I was trying to keep from laughing. She kept at it until I pushed her away. She was still laughing, but she took up the shotgun and reloaded.

I fired three quick shots and then turned to look at Marta. *Marta, here she is, here with me.* After nine days and nights of hell, I had her. I wrapped my arms around her as tight as I could. She's here, she's safe. I couldn't even hear the shots from the camp, didn't care. "I ain't ever letting you go, girl."

We had to get out of there, and we had a long ways to go.

GORDON L. ROTTMAN

Chapter Fifty-Three

"We gotta get, girl, *pronto.*"

She nodded, still smiling. Even with her smile, she looked bad beat-in. Her face was all bruised and puffy, her right eye half swollen shut, both eyes blacked, lips swelled and split, and a cut under her left eye. Even with all that, her smile and her eyes, it was my Marta. I brushed matted hair off her forehead. I wanted to tell her everything was going to be fine, but that was about as uncertain as which eye a buzzard would first pluck from a corpse.

We had to get. The outcropping would give us some cover when we started down the arroyo. By the time we'd be in their line of fire, we'd be two hundred yards from the camp. Not much chance of them hitting us partly hidden in an arroyo at full run. The main thing was to put as much distance behind us as we could. With Federico ventilated to death, there was no question what *El Xiuhcoatl* was going to do.

I pointed at the horses, "*Di adios.*"—Say good-bye.

Marta grabbed her shotgun and pistol and scrambled onto her horse. I started shooting, and she was off at a dead gallop, hugging the horse's neck with both spares following.

I was right behind her. I could hear bullets snapping over. I felt pure joy; I felt untouchable. I was scart.

They'd have to saddle, and they'd need to take up their bedrolls and gear. They couldn't afford to be without it. Every minute we could gain was gold. It might take us three, four days to reach the Rio. My feeling of joy ran off like water on a hillside. How much could we push ourselves and the horses? We were near rope's end.

I had to get ahead of Marta because of the trip-rope across the arroyo. Holding up my hand to stop her, she saw it, and her horses jumped it without slowing. I hung off the saddle and grabbed my bandana and sped off trying to catch up with that girl.

I looked back to see two riders round the bend. One of them was *El Xiuhcoatl*. I hadn't figured on that, some of them taking straight off and leaving the others to gather gear. I pulled the rifle and fired off three shots to distract them from the rope. It worked. *El Xiuhcoatl's* horse went down hard with him rolling like a tumbleweed. The other went straight over the horse's head, landing like a feed sack falling off a runaway wagon. *If he ain't broke his neck, I ain't got a saddle-sore ass.* I spurred Cracker. Marta hadn't waited; she's just a blue dot.

— •●• —

I was heading for Flaco's ravine where we'd been bushwhacked. I know one thing I wasn't doing. I weren't pulling no bushwhack stunt. But I was hoping they'd be fearing that and slow down. What else? If I'd had another lariat I'd put up another trip-rope. Didn't have one, though. We could throw back together that Mex brushwood barricade. That would buy us a few minutes, and every minute counted. Then I remembered. There was a lariat on that bushwhacker's dead horse. It was going to be a long day, but if we could stay ahead of them until dark, half the fight was won. It was going to be a hard-riding nine, ten hours.

We smelled the dead horse and Mex way before we got there. Some vultures flapped up. The birds and coyotes had had a feast. Marta climbed off her horse, pulled off the Mex's boots, and pulled them on after stuffing rags in the toes. She spit on the Mex.

I got the lariat off the bloated horse, and we threw every limb and piece of wood onto the brush barricade. Further down the ravine I sent Marta on, and I tied the lariat around a rock and angled it up, tying it to a gnarled pinyon growing on a sidewall ledge. It might be harder to see it angled like that.

I thought Marta would be way ahead, but I came up on her

standing over Flaco's grave. I told her who it was. She looked bitter sad and crossed herself, I guess saying some words in her head.

Out of the ravine and finally stopping, I got Marta into a too big pair of jeans, another shirt—brown, blanket-lined tan duck coat, and a serape. She tied my bandana over her head. Taking out the scarf I'd found on her cot, I wrapped it around her neck and pulled her wool gloves on. She nodded recognizing them. I rolled us smokes, lit hers up, and she puffed on it closing her eyes. We rode hard through the afternoon, but the horses were slowing.

I could smell the coming storm. The rain would wipe out our tracks, but I worried about being cut off by flooded arroyos. It darkened; clouds boiled in from the north. The wind was steady hard and colder, singing bitter notes through the mesquite. I knew we were beat down, needed food and rest. I kept looking for a good camp, a place out of the wind and no worries of flooding. I found some places, but I kept pushing on, fearing just beyond us would be a wide arroyo that would trap us.

Finally, we had to stop. Thin sheets of rain washed across the land, and I knew the big storm was coming from the steady lightning flashes closing in. We crossed a wide arroyo, and hoping there wasn't another right beyond, picked a camp. The dim glow of the sun squatted on the far hills behind us. I was hoping the storm would pass before dawn, and we'd be on our way before light, even if we had to walk the horses.

Marta fell more than slid off her horse. She stood swaying with an empty look, staring off into nothing. I didn't catch her in time when she crumpled into the mud. I got her perched on a rock, and she started chewing the Mex jerky and drinking water. We needed hot food, but it was not to be. After hobbling the four horses, hoping they'd find something to eat, I laid out the bedroll and pitched the gum blankets anchoring them with rocks. As much as we needed food, we ate little. I kept watching Marta. She'd start smiling for no reason, then go all sad. She'd look at me sad-eyed, and then look away. Sometimes she'd start shaking her head for a long spell. I was worrying how balanced she was.

She commenced to shivering, and I got her into the bedroll. Marta was on her side, looking into my eyes, not pulling her gaze away. I tried to smile, touched her gummy and greasy hair. Her pretty face was plum beat up. I pulled out the bottle of Ashton Rye and tipped it to wet my bandana. "This is going to burn, Marta, *caliente*."

She nodded, tightening her lips.

Putting my arm round her, I set her up and dabbed at the cuts on her lips and under her eye and chin, gentle as I could.

"I know it stings, girl. *Usted valiente*."—You're brave. She flinched, but toughed it out. It hurt me too. I took a belt of the firewater, and Marta did too, with a shiver.

Fishing out my necklace, the one with beads for me and her, she kissed it before taking my hand and holding it to her cheek. Marta nestled up, and we wrapped our arms around each other. Her shivering went away. She gave that strange hoarse laugh again, pressing her face into my shoulder. I held her as tight as I could.

Marta started humming some little song, and then quieted down. I could feel our heartbeats, slow and steady. In the near darkness, I pushed her away a little and looked into her dark eyes. They were full of tears. "I know it was bad for you, Marta. Badder than anything I could ever think of. You ain't gotta worry. That don't make no matter to me. I want you with me." I wished I knew the right Mex words.

She shook her head and pushed me onto my back. I thought she was playing, but her face was queer and hard-looking. So fast that I didn't know what was happening, she was straddling me on her knees. She slapped me hard across the face, then again. A chill shot though me followed by sheer disgust as she started dry-humping me making the most sickening grunting noises. She kept at it, shaking her head wild-like from side to side. I couldn't do anything to stop her. My stomach turned, and she slapped me again. Rolling off, she tried to crawl out. I grabbed onto her pulling her to me. "*Marta, stay!* ¡*Quédate!*" She strangled out a hysterical cry, struggled, but I'd not let her go. I saw it all then. She'd showed me a hint of what'd happened, what she felt, how she'd been used, and shamed. It was the only way she could tell me. She gasped hard, pushing away. I couldn't breathe my throat was so choked.

"You ain't going nowhere. You're staying right here with me. ¡*Quédate con mi!*" I begged. She stopped struggling. I held her tighter and felt every one of her shaking sobs shudder through me. She squirmed closer. She nodded into my shoulder and after a spell, she was softly wheezing.

I laid awake for a while, but we finally slept long and warm.

Chapter Fifty-Four

We tromped and stumbled afoot over the mud-sticky ground, picking our way across the rocks and cactus. The rain had stopped; the wind turned. I'd no idea the time. There was no sign of sunlight in the eastern sky, the way we were heading. Some arroyos held water, but not deep or fast-moving enough to be a problem. The horses hadn't much to eat. I was saving what grain was left for tomorrow.

We started riding when it got lighter. We ate what might be called breakfast in the saddle.

"I could sure use some *café*, how 'bout you?"

She nodded with one eye wide and wishful, the other swollen mostly shut.

"Maybe we can brew some *café* later."

She nodded, licked her swollen lips. I had to get used to her again seeming to know what I was saying.

We plodded along. I musta looked back every two minutes. I tried to keep from crossing ridge crests, but we had to sometimes so we wouldn't be winding like a snake and burning up time and strength. Every time we topped one of the low, barren ridges, I scanned the land behind us with the glasses. All morning and into the afternoon, the land behind was as empty of men on horses as it was in front. Had we lost them; had they quit? I wasn't expecting that no

285

more than a dust storm.

Late afternoon, we had to eat something hot. It had warmed up, so to speak—we couldn't see our breath—and the drizzle had stopped. The clouds were higher. We stopped beside a wet arroyo. Marta gathered firewood, and I broke out the cooking gear after unsaddling. The horses had had them on too long. There wasn't much to burn. I doused a little coal oil on the twigs and lit them up. Marta dumped a tin of beans into a pot, another of tomatoes, one more of peas, and set it on the fire. Next, she chopped up jerky and stirred it in. I've had queerer mixes on the trail. While it was cooking up, we got the coffee going and shared a can of peaches. When the pot of stuff was bubbling, she dumped some into two of the tins for herself, gave me the pot, and we commenced to spoon it down. The coffee was chewy with grounds and gritty water, but it was hot. That mess of grub and coffee got us warm, sorta.

I was saddling back up when I noticed Marta by the flowing water taking off her duck coat. When I turned again she was shucking her shirts and then, of all things, her long johns top—I swear to God, right before me. I almost tripped over my feet. She knelt beside the water and started cleaning up using my bandana. She was a mess. There were bruises on her arms and sides and some on her back. That hurt me, in a different way, as much as it hurt her. I stood gawking at her sil-lo-wet until she turned around. I was rooted there staring at her big ol' eyes, and everything else. Marta looked back like she ain't got a thing to hide after what she showed me last night in the bedroll.

She's beautiful.

Marta pulled on the brown shirt and gave her filthy long johns top a quick splash and scrub, then tied it dripping to her saddle with latigos.

We'd been here too long. I trotted to the ridge crest behind us for a look-see. Two banditos were two hundred yards away, coming hard at us. I looked back and the damp wood fire was smoking more than I'd realized. Ducking, I raced down the slope loud-whispering to Marta, "*¡Dos bandidos, ándale!*"

She started to mount and I said, "*No caballos,*" and waved her to follow me. She grabbed her shotgun and shell bag running in a low crouch. I couldn't get over her running around in only two pairs of socks, but I knew her feet were as tough as boot soles.

We scrambled into a brushy draw on the ridge side. I had sort of an idea. Working our way up the draw, I could hear their hoofbeats. We took it slow so the bushes wouldn't wave around. Halfway up I motioned for Marta to stay where she was, to watch below, and cover my back. Below the ridge crest, only about thirty feet higher than where our horses stood, was a line of brush. I went on hands and knees until I overlooked the fire.

One bandito was still mounted, looking around with his carbine in hand. The other was on the ground at our horses. He was holding a carbine too. I had a clear shot at the mounted bandito, and I took it, putting a .44 slug through both lungs. He hit the ground spewing blood and kicking. His horse took off like a birdshot-stung coyote. I raised the rifle at the second man, but he was behind our four tied horses, which were stirring after the gunshot. His horse just stood there waiting for whatever happened next, the way horses do.

I yelled, "Come on out and I won't shoot you. *Mi no fuego.*" If he understood and stepped out, I'd shoot him anyway. The other *vato* was still kicking, but not much. The man behind the horses either didn't understand or figured what would happen. He had five horses around him, and no matter where I moved he'd be hidden. I couldn't come down the bare ridge side in the open. Going back to the draw would give him a chance to tear out of there taking our horses with him. So here we were, in a Mexican standoff.

In the end he made it easy. He came dashing out of the mob of horses levering shots up the ridge and vaulted over his horse's rump, dropping his carbine. It was the too young *bandidito* I'd seen riding in front of Marta. He was so fast I didn't get a shot off until he was in the saddle. I cracked off five rapid shots, staggering the horse, but missed the *bandidito*. He galloped down the arroyo with water spraying until there was a loud double boom, and he parted company with the horse. He smacked into the water, and the horse smartly kept going.

The kid was trying to sit up. I noticed he had a bandage on his leg, I guess from the ambush. Marta stomped out of the brushy draw snapping shut the scattergun with a purpose. He drew a pistol, but didn't raise it, let it drop. Instead, he reached out a hand to her. They stared at each other a short spell—making me wonder. He actually smiled. She blew him back into the water, turning it rusty-colored.

All I said was, "*¡Ándale!*"

We both chugged down coffee straight from the pot. She took the coffeepot and cooking pot dipping them in the stream, threw the water on the fire, unluckily making it steam, and shoved them in their bag. I grabbed the banditos' guns, sticking them wherever I could to dump later. The lung-shot bandito had stopped kicking. Marta spit on him as she rode past. She stared again at the dead *bandidito* and turned away. She didn't spit on him.

Before mounting, I searched the other's saddlebags and found sacks of beans, tortillas, Mex jerky, and a sack of *maíz*! We sorely needed that grain corn. Taking the saddle and hackamore off the Mex's horse, I let it loose. It weren't no better off than ours, maybe worse, and it was just another grain-eater. He'd make it on his own. I felt sorry for the one that ran off still saddled and carrying a bullet and buckshot.

After a couple of miles, we stopped to dump the guns and sort our gear. Marta got her clothes back on, excepting the still-wet long johns top. She'd been shivering something bad wearing only that brown shirt. Graining the horses and feeding them the tortillas perked them up.

That sight of Marta at the stream still hung in my head. It'd perked me up too. Pretty amazing.

It got colder and the wind picked up. The north was dark a couple of hours before sunset. The stampeding clouds said another storm was coming in. I'd wanted to ride for as long as we could in the dark. It wasn't to be.

We rode hard, and right before dark, we came up a ridge side. There was *Cerro el Colorado*, its blunt top covered in gray and black clouds and lightning looking like the Devil's Throne.

I don't know if the sun set first or if the storm blacked it out. We rode until we couldn't see. It was hard to lay out the bedroll and rock-anchor the tarp and gum blankets. The horses were pretty miserable tied to their picket line. They stood there, their rumps to the blasting wind and heads hung, condemned to a long cold, wet night. We weren't much better off.

It began to sleet.

Chapter Fifty-Five

The last thing I wanted to do was crawl out of that bedroll away from Marta's soft warmth, but I had to pee like a banshee. I wiggled out, and Marta jerked awake with a whimper, throwing her arm up to protect herself. I squeezed her hand, kissed her forehead, and she settled down giving me half a smile and a hug.

The sleet blew parallel to the ground picking up wet, stinging sand. The sky was white. I guessed it was what a cowboy from Montana had called a white wind. The horses' manes and tails were clotted with sandy ice. Cracker grunted painfully and crapped.

"I know what you mean, partner."

Marta crawled out with a blanket and slicker over her shoulders. She looked like a rained-on lost puppy. She huddled in a lump while I saddled and packed the bedroll. Sneezing, she blew her nose on her sleeve.

It was after sunup, but I wouldn't have bet on it. We started off walking, keeping the horses to windward. The idea of getting up on a saddle with the wind-driven sleet like nails was too grim. We crunched over patches of frost clinging to struggling grass. It was too hard going so we climbed onto saddles anyway. It was pretty bad. I sucked it up, kept telling myself that it couldn't last forever. It felt like it would anyway.

We stopped to switch off horses and one was bad lame. I took off its saddle and hackamore and left it. I felt bad doing that, but I couldn't shoot it. I stayed on Cracker, and we kept on.

We were beyond *Cerro el Colorado*, a faint shape in the white sleet. Fat wet snowflakes were falling. Something didn't seem right. I looked back and Marta was fifty yards behind me with the spare. She sat there like a lump on a log.

I rode back. "Marta," I shouted against the wind.

She didn't move. With my second shout, she looked up. It was like she was staring right through me and saw nothing. I got off Cracker and lifted her down. She was limp, spent, had nothing left. I wasn't far from it my ownself.

"We have to keep moving." I gripped Marta's shoulders. "There ain't no way outta this. We can't bundle up in the bedroll, lay out here in the middle of nowhere with us and the horses getting weaker." There's no place to go, no place to hide.

She nodded understanding.

I got Marta up behind me and covered her up better. "You hang onto me, never let go." She cinched onto me, and that was better for both of us. I could feel her head against my back and her arms around me. Time, place, it all ran together. We couldn't stop. We'd die. Our only chance was to ride out of this freezing hell. I didn't know if it was light or dark, morning or nightfall. We rode through the never-ending howling sleet.

I heard a voice say, "I can't do this." I turned around, and there was nobody there, excepting Marta hanging on, limp. "I can't do this no more." It was me talking. When I gathered it was my ownself, it wasn't so spooky, so I kept talking. "I ain't never going to be warm no more, ain't never going to be dry, ain't never going to eat again." That bullet graze on my leg hurt too.

Marta wrapped her arms around me tighter, like she knew something was wrong. I shouldn't be talking that way. I started shivering more. "I can't do this no more, Marta."

She slid her arms up on my shoulders and pulled me around. Her eyes were half swelled shut with icy tears. Snot was running from our noses, and she grabbed my head and kissed me on the mouth like never before. Her lips were cold and swollen, but I felt warmth. Twisting in the saddle, I wrapped tight around her, and we held one another. I've never felt like that before, but I can't tell you what I was really feeling. After a spell, she let go and gave me a little shove, telling me to keep going, that we couldn't ever stop.

I put the horse forward.

— •●• —

Hours later, we were on a low ridge. What light there was, was dying. The sleet and snow had stopped. It was only freezing rain now. The wind had let up to just a tree-shaking blast. I was looking at adobes, a mud road; smoke was drifting from chimneys.

I was looking at San Miguel. Not a person to be seen.

Marta was barely hanging on now. We rode in, passing the *hacienda.* Two horses and a mule stood behind the wall looking awful sad. Probably belonged to wounded banditos left behind. I didn't care.

Marta stared at the compound fearfully, making me wonder what had happened there. I dashed that thought.

I stopped at a *jacalito* near the far end, a simple shack without windows, smoke coming out of the hole in the roof. I don't know why I picked that one.

I tied the three miserable horses on the lee side of the shack. Marta couldn't stand. Carrying her like a sack of wet feed, I kicked on the little door made from a wagon tailgate.

"*¿Quíen es?*" asked a nervous voice.

"*Por favor, amigo…*"—Please, friend—was all I could think to say.

The door cracked open, and an old muzzle-loading shotgun glared at me. I moved the bandana from Marta's swollen face.

"*Pasenle,*" said a round-faced, shaggy-haired man. His droopy eyes were topped by equally shaggy eyebrows.

The door opened, and I stooped in. It was smoky with the prairie-fire smell of cow chips and burnt frijole beans. It was barely warm, but a hell of a lot better than the other side of the door. The man and a woman were bundled in serapes and looked nervous. He kept that old shotgun close. The woman sat on the floor on blankets with two little kids hiding behind her, their big eyes staring at the queer strangers. The woman looked older than she probably was.

The two of us slumped on the dirt floor beside the fireplace. The man said something to Marta, but she only looked at him. Water dripped from the ceiling. The woman threw on some cow chips and whispered to the man. He sat on the floor cross-legged and nodded, "*Mi casa es su casa. Usted y su esposa están invitados a quedarse.*"

My house is your house—the traditional invitation. I think he said me and my wife could stay. No point in arguing about relationships.

The woman took a pot from the edge of the fire and ladled frijole beans into a couple of gourd bowls, stuck in wooden spoons, and passed them to me. There were bits of goat in it. I had to spoon-feed Marta.

The man messed with a blackened coffee boiler and put it on the fire. On a flat stone on the fire's edge the woman warmed corn tortillas. The beans were tasteless and so were the tortillas, but no matter; they were hot. I'll say one thing; this ain't where Marta learned to make frijole beans. The man finally poured coffee into gourd cups. That perked us up more than anything, and Marta started eating on her own.

Pulling my makings out, I rolled cigs and gave the first to the man. He watched us with droopy eyes. The woman didn't want a smoke. I lit up Marta's, then my own. The man seemed to surely like his. I brought the saddles in, and the man gave our horses a little hay and he helped me water them.

Marta leaned against me and was snoring in no time. I drank another gourd of coffee and tried to stay awake, not being sure it was safe. I wondered about that *bandidito* kid. It was like something had passed between them. It didn't matter; she'd shot him like any other bandito—she hadn't spit on him. The only sounds were the wind, the rain beating on the shack, and the fire's crackling pops.

— •●• —

I came to with the dawn. There was no wind or rain, only the crackling fire. It was like nobody had moved. The man and woman were sitting in the same places, and the two kids were still behind their mama peeking out with dirty faces. Marta and I went out, pissed, and then grained the horses. There was one more feed left.

Breakfast was the same as last night's supper. We smoked again, and I handed the man three rollies. I said, *"Muchas gracias,"* and handed him all the pesos I'd cut off the bandito's sombrero.

His eyes got big as he said, *"De nada."*

I put my finger to my lips and shook my head. I hoped he understood not to say nothing about us if someone came asking questions.

He nodded and winked.

I didn't trust him one damn bit. We took the out-trail pronto, heading east. On the ridge beside the road were three water-sogged graves. I told Marta they were *Rurales* me and Flaco had killed.

Turning back to San Miguel with the field glasses, I saw our host trotting up the road toward the *hacienda*. Didn't know he could move that fast. Marta didn't need the glasses to see the treachery. She bristled up like a javelina boar, jammed her heels into the horse's sides, and tore down the ridge. She stood in the stirrups, her elbows jutting, and her head down.

"Oh shit." I took off after her. I'd rather have run for it, the twenty miles to the Rio Grande. "Lordy, that girl can ride!"

We charged through the village leaving roster tails of flying mud and run a couple of peons off the road. Sliding to a stop at the *hacienda* wall, we found our host jabbering to two banditos, cornshuck rollies hanging off their lips. One wore a sling and stood with a crutch and a bloody bandage above his knee. All three looked up, stunned. The other bandito was hatless with a head bandage and brought his pistol up, but I already had my Remington in hand. I fired four times hitting him and his unsaddled horse. The bandito with the sling dropped the crutch and got off a shot before being blown smack into the wall by Marta's shotgun. Sliding down the wall, he left a smear of red. The peon host stood with his droopy eyes wide open. He slowly reached for the low clouds. The shot horse slung his head around and kicked a hind leg. The screeching mule ran in circles around the courtyard trying to find a way out. Marta clicked back the second hammer and aimed at the peon. He pissed his pants. In my head, I saw those two pairs of wide eyes looking out from behind their mama.

"*¡Marta, alto!*"

She looked at me with more annoyance than a question.

"*No, Marta. Los dos niños.*"

She stared a spell, and her eyes softened. She understood what I was thinking, those two little kids and their mama. Shoot their papa and they were just about doomed to death. She too understood that little things needed to be protected.

There'd been enough dying. This was *El Xiuhcoatl's* stronghold. The peons here had been cowed by the banditos, used by them. They owned this poor man and everyone here. Out of fear, he had no choice. I couldn't see killing him because of something he had no say in. He was trapped here at the mercy of a bunch of murdering bastards. Anyways, he hadn't ratted on us during the night. He'd given us a chance to get away.

"*Los banditos muertos.*"—The banditos dead.—I said, sweeping my arm wide, meaning all were dead, well, almost all.

He looked at me big-eyed, and then looked at Marta. She gave an evil grin and nodded.

I got off Cracker, reloaded, went through the gate, and opened the *hacienda* door. That gal with the big jugs I'd seen the other day stood inside real fearful-looking. She ducked into a room. I made arm motions for our host to go in. It's his; it's all theirs. He peeked through the door, but jumped so high his head hit the top of the frame when I finished off the wounded horse.

Marta pointed with her shotgun.

"*¿Qué?*" I asked.

She wanted the bandito's sombrero. I handed it to her, and she set the big straw-woven hat on her head.

We trotted out and back up the ridge. Looking back, I saw peons swarming in and out of the *hacienda* carrying all manner of things. Marta grimly smiled.

— •●• —

I stopped after we'd put two ridges between us and San Miguel. Marta looked at me funny, like she was thinking, "Why stop now?"

Sliding off Cracker I could barely move my right arm. Blood leaked from my coat sleeve. "Dammit to hell, got nicked on the leg, got a sore ass, a head cold, and now this."

I sat against a rock, and Marta gently took off my coat and with my hunting knife cut my shirt and long john sleeves open. It was a bullet graze halfway up my forearm, but it had cut down to the bone. It was bleeding a lot and getting all over me. She took the rag she'd washed with, poured water on it, and cleaned the wound. Next, she cut off my long john's sleeve at the elbow and slit it full length. After wrapping a thick wool sock around my arm, she tied the sleeve over it real tight. It hurt, but the bleeding stopped.

I drank some water, got my coat on with Marta's help and

said, "*Ándale.*"

I felt kind of faint-headed and a little belly-sick, but we mounted and were off with our one spare tied to Marta's horse. She rode alongside keeping an eye on me.

GORDON L. ROTTMAN

Chapter Fifty-Six

I didn't want to stop for nothing. Maybe eighteen miles to the Rio. Another five to the ranch house. We could do it in a day, even in our beat down condition. It was early, and we could ride at night if we had to, *if* we could keep going. I was hurting; Marta was weakening. She had her spurts, pushed herself, but she couldn't keep it up after all what she'd been through. I don't know what kept her going. I ain't never seen a woman like her. I didn't know what was keeping me going. One time I slowed to a stop. She was beside me, her big ol' eyes looking at me from under her sombrero. She touched my arm, and her eyes said, "You gotta do it, for us."

Marta demanded we stop at noon. Not for her, but for me. She made me lay on a blanket, and she built a little fire, put on the coffeepot of water. After peeling bark off a scrawny willow and throwing it in the pot, she cleaned both my bullet grazes. We ate warmed jerky and the last of the corn dodgers. The willowbark tea was bitter even with the sugar she put in, but it eased the pain a little. I wanted to get going even though I still felt faint-headed.

After telling myself for the twentieth time that *El Xiuhcoatl* probably called it quits after that storm and not finding our trail, I again said, "Don't count on it." I didn't see him giving up after seeing his brother shot dead by Marta's hand. Could be he quit, but he reminded me of a puma. He knew where we were headed. Even if we swung north or south to cross the Rio, he could be sitting on the Dew waiting for us, like a puma waylaying a goat. He could have gotten ahead of us if he'd gotten that notion early on. Give up looking for us and head straight for the Dew. Maybe we should head north to Del Rio, but that would add a day. We didn't have it in us. I wondered if Clay still had monitors out or if we'd have to make a dead run for the house. I knew one thing: we weren't safe until we reached that house…home. The closer we got to home the more dangerous it was.

No rain, the wind only a little gusty and the clouds were higher, with breaks in places. We saw a pale flicker of the sun at times. We took turns riding the spare, changing every hour. I hoped to have our horses rested, if you could call it that, when we got to the Rio.

I worried more about Marta. She seemed good most of the time, but when she dismounted, she had a tough time tottering around. I knew she was putting on a brave show when I caught her hanging onto a stirrup strap and her head drooping. She raised her head slow and saw me watching her. She popped her head up and gave me a smile with a rollie hanging on her lip. Pulling herself up onto the saddle, she finished off the rollie and flipped the butt at me with a tight grin as if sayin, "Let's get going."

The closer we got to the Rio the more cover we had with the thickening mesquite. I tried to keep to low ground. Late afternoon, I figured we were on *Rancho Mariposa* land. That set me to thinking there might be another trouble to face. Ol' Don Garza might be none too hospitable to any Dew hands found on his land owing to us gunning down his son.

There was a low, barren ridge off to our left, to the north. If I had my bearings straight, on the other side of that ridge was the trail we'd followed our stolen herd. Not far beyond that was Don Garza's son's house where we'd strung up them bastards that started this whole mess. I admit it now gave me a cold contentment they'd met their maker that way. Their dying was a damn sight easier than what we'd been through.

Marta was behind me with Cracker stringed to her horse. I rode the spare. I looked back, and she was peering real intent off to the left. I looked that way, and there was a rider on the ridge going in the opposite direction. A *Rancho Mariposa vaquero*? I watched him as he slowed down and even at that distance, I could tell he was watching us. Any ranch hand would be checking out strangers crossing their land. But of all the times Flaco and me visited with *Rancho Mariposa vaqueros* at the Rio, they were always in twos and threes.

He stopped and hoisted his sombrero, waved it. I turned to tell Marta not to wave, but she'd already flourished her sombrero, and her long hair blew in the wind. The next thing I knew, he fired his rifle into the air. I could tell he was shooting, and then the three shots' sound reached us. He'd signaled.

"*¡Ándale!*" I yelled and spurred the horse. Marta was already about to pass me.

The bandito was coming down the ridge side, and it looked like he aimed to get ahead of us. I'd no idea where or how far away his *amigos* were, but I figured they weren't far. There were only a couple of places near here that we could ford the Rio, maybe. With all the rain, we might have to swim the horses. I didn't know either where those fords were to where we were now. The banditos likely knew where. Maybe the best bet was to head straight for the river and swim it, if it wasn't too fast, which it could be.

The bandito coming off the ridge disappeared into the mesquite. We could run into him at any time. I didn't want him to see us because he'd fire more signal shots.

I looked back at Marta. She was plain scart. I winked at her trying to perk up her spirits. Her shotgun was in her lap. I brought my Remington out. We slowed down in the thickening mesquite. I stayed bent over trying to look under limbs. We moved forward slow, listening. Marta was to my right and a little behind. I looked back at her, and Cracker tossed his head.

I don't know if I heard or felt the rifle shot first. It slammed me forward into the horse's withers, and I fell to the left, hitting the ground. The horse jerked forward, taking me with it. He couldn't run the brush was so thick. Hitting the ground knocked the wind out of me so hard the bullet hit didn't mean nothing. My boot hung in the left stirrup, and the horse shoved through the thick mesquite dragging me over rocks. The shotgun made a double boom causing my horse to go faster or try to. I'd lost the Remington, but I pulled the Merwin Hulbert from its right side holster, almost lost it when I bounced, and fired into the horse's belly four times. He crashed to the right with his falling yanking me into his underside. A hind hoof clipped my jaw and right shoulder. That's when the hit in my left shoulder felt like a branding iron was jammed onto me. I couldn't even yell—I tried. All I could do was gasp. My head swam, and I puked all over myself. The dry heaves wrenched my guts out, each one feeling like a mule kicking me in the belly and shoulder. I dropped the pistol, tried again to scream. The only thing that came out was, "Marta!"

She was there, her lips a tight grim line, her eyes dark and wide open. All I could do was gasp. Lines of dirt on her face made her look older and grimmer. I only wanted to lay there, never move. Marta shoved the Remington and Merwin Hulbert back in my holsters. After twisting my boot out of the stirrup, she grabbed my right hand with both hers and tugged, trying to get me to my feet.

I pulled back, "No!"

She weren't having none of that. She slapped both hands together and stamped her foot. Her eyes said, "Get off your ass!" She grabbed my hand again, holding tight, around the wrist. Bracing her left foot against the horse's stifle, she leaned forward and threw herself back, giving it everything to drag me up. I was up on my knees, pain shooting through me like a hot poker was twisted into me. She got up under my right arm and heaved me to my feet. I gave about as loud a groan as I could.

Cracker was directly behind me. She couldn't have gotten me much further on her own. Marta shoved me up against Cracker's nearside. I got my right arm up hanging onto the saddle horn. She helped lift my left boot into the stirrup. I stood upright pulling myself up and got my right leg over. After putting the reins in my hand, Marta mounted her horse and moved up beside me. Using my knife, she cut away my coat and then the shirt. Ripping it open—that really hurt—she wadded up the bandana and a rag. I could tell where I was hit now. It went through the muscle atop my shoulder leading up to my neck. Felt like my collarbone was broke. Felt like the Dew brand was burned into my shoulder. Unbuttoning one of my coat buttons, she stuck my left hand into the opening to hold it up like a sling. I saw the dead bandito laying in the mesquite. Double loads of buckshot at thirty feet surely make a mess.

We set off with her leading, shotgun pointing ahead. Every step Cracker took was a burning jolt. We came out of the thick mesquite and onto sorta open ground sloping downward. That slope was covered with scattered yucca, sagebrush, creosote, and rocks.

The Rio was rolling past only a third of a mile away. It surely looked grand. I knew we weren't home free even if we got to the other side. That's when I thought of the others, the banditos behind us and coming this way hard. They'd have heard the shots and knew which way to head.

Marta gave the horses their head, and they loped for the river. She was taking it as fast as she thought I could take. Truth was, I couldn't take it at any pace. We'd closed short of half the distance when I heard, "¡AHHH-haahaaa!" My blood chilled, and Marta looked back, her face pure terror. I lashed with my reins in fury no matter the gouging pain ripping through me.

Marta's horse crashed into Cracker, about taking me out of the saddle. She slammed into me, bounced off, and went ass-over-tea-kettle onto the ground, her shotgun and sombrero flying ahead. Cracker reared, snorted, crumpled into the ground, and I rolled off to the right. The pain was like being dropped into a hog-scalding vat. I kind of remember hearing shots. Marta was on her hands and knees looking at the Rio. It might as well been on the moon. I dragged out my rifle and three banditos barreled straight at us.

Chapter Fifty-Seven

Marta scrambled for the shotgun and came up gripping it. She smiled at me, grim, defiant. She knew what was coming. She ran toward me. Blood ran down her left hand. Was she hit? I got up using my rifle, but I couldn't lift it to my shoulder. I dropped it and drew my Remington. I pressed my left arm to my chest trying to ease the numbing pain. Marta was right beside me. She didn't even reach chest high.

I'd figured on two. No telling where they'd picked up the third *hombre*. They came at us at full gallop like an arrowhead with *El Xiuhcoatl* in his fire-red shirt at the point. My hand shook, and I turned sideways to make a smaller target. I locked my eye on his horse's pounding chest, stretched my arm full length, and felt the recoil. The bandito *jefe* went straight over the horse's head when it plowed into the ground, tearing through yucca spikes. *Xiuhcoatl* slid across the rocks face-first. The man to the right was coming on with his pistol arm stretched forward, and it spewed smoke. I fired twice, and his horse took one through the neck and throwed the bandito off. Marta let go one barrel and then the other, and I fired, both of us aiming at the third Mex. His horse reared, running into a wall of buckshot and rolled hard to the ground. I shot at the man twice, hitting him once when he tried to get up. Marta reloaded and staggered into my side with the sound of a pistol shot. She dropped to her knees.

Lord, please don't take her from me, my mind screamed.

303

All I can do is fight back.

I dropped my empty Remington and pulled the Merwin Hulbert. Marta jerked again, slumped to the ground, and my heart shrieked. I shot the second Mex twice as he got to a knee and aimed at me. He fell backward, kicking.

El Xiuhcoatl rose off the ground. *He'll never stop!* His torn knees were bloody. There was blood on his face. With the red shirt, he looked like the Devil rearing from Hell. I aimed real careful, lining up the rear sight notch with the front sight blade on the Devil's face. I let out my shaking breath and squeezed the trigger. The hammer clicked. I knew what the Devil's grin looked like, and I'd take it to my grave. I clicked the pistol a second time and dropped it.

He lowered his pistol, dripping blood and vileness. He lunged toward us, glaring at Marta slumped against my leg. The Devil aimed his big Army Colt .44 at her. He wanted to take her away from me like his brother and everything else had been taken from him. I pulled Flaco's short-barrel Schofield out of my coat pocket, jerked the trigger six times, and fell onto the rocks on my side. *El Xiuhcoatl* staggered and crumpled to his knees and dropped his Colt, his Devil's mask replaced by a clown's painted face of surprise. But he still lived.

Marta was on her knees hanging onto me. The girl pushed herself up with the shotgun, sagged against me gripping my arm, and rose again with some huge effort. Marta staggered toward the Devil, swaying like a storm-blown sapling. She went through the steps of reloading, with great care, without haste. I couldn't see her face. I didn't want to. Standing before the Devil-once-was, she lifted the double barrels, lifted them like they were the heaviest weight in the world. She pressed the muzzles between his eyes. His eyes, not an inkling of a soul. He gripped the barrels in his bloody fists, like he'd chosen her to end his nightmare. She squeezed both triggers, and the top half of his head disappeared in a spew of blood and glistening fragments.

I died and finally felt safe.

Chapter Fifty-Eight

When I came back to life, I was blind. I was numb, until I made the slightest move and Hell's fire poured through me, the Devil's fire. I figured then I was still alive. That didn't seem to be that good of a deal right then. I laid there awhile, more or less warm. Trying to look around, I couldn't see a dang thing. All I could feel was pain, my whole left side, and I felt like I wanted to puke up, and faint-headed too with a fever. And weak, no strength to lift a finger.

I listened. I was outside; thought at first I was in a bed in a dark room, but I was in a bedroll, mine by the smell of it. It was sticky wet on the left side, and I knew it was blood.

I listened. Only the wind. I could tell I was among thick mesquite by the sound of the breeze. It smelled like any other time out on the range, but I could make out the smell of a fire and of water, the Rio, I guess. There was no light from a fire, only the smell. I said, "Hello," then called for Marta, not too loud. Nothing.

I drifted in and out of sleep, dreams of dying horses, the red Devil dancing in Hell's flames, Marta holding a blood-dripping skull. One time I woke and knew Cracker was gone. I'd had him over six years. I'd never known anyone that long. Marta and Cracker gone. I felt empty.

— •●• —

The dawn was lead gray and misty. More dark than light. I felt no different, the pain, weakness, the need to puke. I tried to touch my shoulder. It hurt a lot. It still bled. The wet sky lightened in the east. I could make out things close by. A burned-out fire and a coffeepot, a plate beside the bedroll, cold beans and jerky. I tried to chew on a piece of the meat, but it gagged me. There was an ice-cold cup of coffee covered by a tortilla. I couldn't deal with it either. Too bad she didn't leave her frijole beans, but she didn't have the makings. But she was back…and still with us I hoped. A canteen was laying there and I sipped some.

Nearby was a big pile of something. Before long, I could see it was saddles, horse jewelry, bedrolls, and saddlebags. I could smell death, the stench of blood and shit. As the gray-blue sky lightened I made out the lumps of men and horses.

I knew Marta had gone for help, or had she? Maybe she was laying someplace nearby, all bled out. I remembered her being shot and falling. Where was she hit, how bad? Did she even make it across the Rio? Was her corpse floating down the river? Was she laying out there on the other side too weak to move or worse?

— •●• —

"Bud."

My eyes came open, barely.

"You going to lay there all day, son?" I was looking at Clay DeWitt's anxious face.

"Damn, boy, ya'd best get y'all's butt up," said Dodger. "Its way past sunup, and Lew's goin' dock your pay."

I couldn't say nothing. My mouth and throat were sand dry.

Clay held a canteen to my mouth, and I drank it down. Its coldness felt good, like it was dousing my fever.

"Let us turn him over and look at his shoulder." It was Gabi.

It hurt a lot, them turning me. I smelled mercurochrome, then felt burning and more pain.

"I'll put a bandage on that," said Gabi.

That weren't no fun either.

I was on my back again. "Bud, we're going to get some laudanum in you. It'll make it easier for the ride home."

Home. I remembered that was a good thing. "Can't ride," I

whispered hoarsely.

"Ya can ride in a wagon, idgit," said Dodger.

There was something nagging at me that I wanted to ask. I remembered. "Marta. Where's Marta?"

"She's waiting for you, son. She came crawling up to the front door at two o'clock this morning. About kicked that door in. A dreadful sight to see, but one that gave our hearts joy."

"She was shot—how bad?"

"She's good, Bud," said Gabi with a smile.

"She got hit in the right side, busted a rib. Took nicks in the arm and a leg," said Clay. "She waded the Rio and lost her boots. Her feet, knees, and hands are all torn up walking and crawling all that way—five miles. She'll be as right as rain."

"Me and her don't need no more damn rain," I croaked.

"I bet you don't, son. Y'all had enough." He laughed. "Hell, that little gal even handed over the ransom money I'd paid them bastards. Plus over two thousand more she found on *Xiuhcoatl*. That two thousand goes to both of you, by the way," he grinned. "Bud, you got yourself one hell of a woman there."

I thought what I used to answer to that, but I said, "You're right. I do have one hell of a woman."

They sorted me out in the bedroll. I saw Gent and Musty on horses with rifles at the ready.

"Gotta ask you, Bud. There any banditos still hereabouts?"

"They're dead, all of them."

"You mean all of them?"

"All of them."

"Well, I be damned. Gabi couldn't work that out trying to talk to Marta. All of them."

"Marta killed half of them. Killed *El Xiuhcoatl* her ownself."

"Well, I be damned," muttered Clay, looking around at the corpses.

"*Xiuhcoatl* be the one missing his crown."

"I'm going have to make sure I don't ever cross that girl."

"Inés and Flaco's dead," I said.

"Yeah, we got that from Marta," he said sadly.

"The girls, the Misses, they good?"

"They're having rough times, Bud, but they'll pull through."

Clay, Dodger, Roberto, and a young fella I'd never seen, lifted my bedroll on the count of three. They hoisted me into the back of a wagon. It hurt. It hurt when they slid me across the bed planks. It hurt until I opened my eyes and saw Marta laying there swathed in blankets.

The young fella clicked his tongue to start the wagon team.

Clay grinned like a coyote. "Hang on, you two."

Marta's lips curved into a smile, her eyes glowing like nothing I'd ever seen. Those eyes said we're going home.

EL FINAL

The Bean Recipe

It was a cold wet December afternoon in Morelos, Coahuila, fifty kilometers from Piedras Negras and Eagle Pass, Texas. I love Morelos, and when I was introduced to it almost thirty years ago, I discovered a genuine ranch town with the mores and values of the 1880s.

It's a place of paradox—a hot, dusty, cold, wet place far from anywhere of consequence, yet the most essential place of all. It's ranching country, making it an unforgiving place where mistakes can be fatal, but it can offer beauty and delight in exchange for only some sweat and just a little blood. It's give and take…you give a great deal and take away little, in the material sense. But you can take away so much more, if you persevere and aren't too greedy. What comes back can be sweet, or at least bittersweet. It's a hard land and life. But even with the incursions of modern materialism, the nightmare of the drug war, and pervasive government corruption, a strong sense of tradition prevails. *Vaqueros* here are still respected, for they own horses, and they honor tradition.

We rushed from our pickup into my wife's cousin's little tortilla factory, *La Herradura*—The Horseshoe. It was a little four-room adobe house containing a very welcome warmth. The kitchen's where the flour tortilla dough is mixed, and the former living room houses the tortilla machine. This wondrous device cuts the stream of thick dough into lumps that are automatically pressed into perfectly round shapes and fed into the baker on endlessly rotating trays. The baked tortillas were laid on table-tennis ball-sized tables of chicken wire to cool. The smell was mouth-watering, especially since our last meal was a five thirty a.m. breakfast before heading out to the family ranch to start the roundup.

But on the kitchen stove was something that smelled even better. There was a big iron pot filled with frijoles. Now these weren't just any old beans bubbling in a pot, they were Licha's *frijoles charros*—ranch beans. They emitted a sweet spicy smell competing with the baking tortillas. We were chilly, hungry, and enlivened by the day's work and fun. Filling bowls and passing them out only increased our anticipation. The beans were filled with cubed ham, chorizo, tomatoes, green peppers, sweet onion, jalapeño, cilantro, and more. There was a stone bowl of sour cream, and we filled big mugs with steaming hot cocoa boiled with bhut jolokia peppers, vanilla, cinnamon, and a dash of ancho chile powder to give it a spicy kick. I smeared fresh butter on a piping hot tortilla, folded it, and dug into the beans. In this simple old adobe house with an entrepreneurial tortilla bakery crowded with family on a blustery day, I had one of the best meals I'd ever eaten.

With the door banging open, in tramped four teenage girls clad in jeans, denim jackets, Stetsons, and boots. Our nieces, *vaqueras* all. They'd been on the range since before dawn cutting out cattle, hazing them to the corrals, and helping out with branding. They're thirteen to fifteen years old and competent, trustworthy, and hardworking. They're tops in school, and at the weekend dances they're satin-dressed heartbreakers. Watching them wolf down *frijoles charros*, popping one another on the shoulder, and spraying others with shaken Cokes, I saw their fiery spirit. With those girls' no-nonsense smiles and flashing dark eyes, their liveliness, all the experiences I'd had working with *vaqueros*, and the atmosphere of this town, I had an idea for a story.

2 lbs dried pinto beans
1/2-lb pork belly or 2 or 3 smoked ham hocks
1/2-lb ham—diced
1/2-cup chorizo (Mexican sausage)—casing removed and crumbled
6 slices fried bacon—chopped or crumbled
5 roma tomatoes or 3 large slicing tomatoes—chopped

1 medium onion—chopped (delete or less if desired)
1/2-cup cilantro—finely chopped
4 cloves garlic—whole
6 jalapeño peppers—finely sliced (serrano peppers optional—
hotter)
2 tablespoons cornstarch
1 small green pepper—chopped (optional)
1 tomatillo (Mexican husk tomato)—chopped (optional)
Salt to taste (not much)

And some folks are happy with a can of generic brand pork 'n' beans, especially sad when you consider that back in Bud's time, canned pork and beans were actually chock full of pork, not today's single half-inch cube.

About the Author

Gordon Rottman lives outside of Houston, Texas, served in the Army for twenty-six years in a number of "exciting" units, and wrote war games for Green Berets for eleven years. He's written over 120 military history books, but his interests have turned to adventurous young adult novels—influenced by a bunch of audacious kids, Westerns owing to his experiences on his wife's family's ranch in Mexico, and historical fiction focusing on how people really lived and thought—history does not need to be boring.

THE HARTWOOD PUBLISHING GROUP

"Stories that echo in your heart long after the book is closed."

Hartwood Publishing thrives on introducing you to new authors and great stories. If you enjoyed this book, please spread the word.

41618607R00176

Made in the USA
San Bernardino, CA
16 November 2016